THE SUNDAY SERVICE

OTHER BOOKS BY HUGH MCMANNERS

MILITARY BOOKS

Falklands Commando
The Scars of War
Commando: Winning the Green Beret
Top Guns
Forgotten Voices of the Falklands War
Gulf War One: Real Voices from the Front Line

OUTDOOR SURVIVAL BOOKS

Crowning the Dragon: Travels in the Chinese Karakoram
The Commando Survival Manual
The Complete Wilderness Training Book
The Outdoor Adventure Handbook

THE SUNDAY SERVICE

HUGH MCMANNERS

NIGHTSTRIKE

First published in 2023 by Nightstrike Publishing Ltd,
62 New Walk, Leicester LE1 6TF

A catalogue record for this book is available
from the British Library.

ISBN 978-0-9928154-5-5

Typesetting by Ten Thousand | Editing + Book Design
www.tenthousand.co.uk

For Megan McManners

HISTORICAL NOTE
(UP UNTIL 1980)

THE NORTHERN IRELAND TROUBLES

The Northern Ireland Troubles lasted thirty years, from 1969 until 1998, and killed 3,532 people. Some 48,000 were injured and countless further lives destroyed in what must surely come to be understood as a civil war.

Most of the people involved were dedicated, loyal to their cause, and determined. Everybody was affected. It was also, as with most conflicts, utilised to the advantage of politicians, criminals, and members of the various security force agencies.

And over those thirty years, vast amounts of UK taxpayers' money flowed into Northern Ireland. Compensation, rebuilding, buying and selling information, and protection money were just some of the income streams that would dry up once peace was declared – another obstacle; along with the implacable hatred between the Loyalist Protestant community and the Republican Catholic minority.

THE EMERGENCE OF PIRA

The Irish Republican Army (IRA) had been the official army of the Irish Republic from 1919 to 1921 in the Irish War of Independence against Britain. But it then turned against the newly formed free Irish state to fight and lose a very bitter civil war.

The IRA was then declared illegal, with many of its Volunteers interned without trial by the Republic of Ireland. Thereafter it continued to resist British rule in the North.

In 1969, the police could no longer control sectarian rioting, and the British Army was called in, initially to protect the Republicans from Loyalist violence. The Dublin-based IRA didn't feel able to protect Catholics in the North, so in an acrimonious split in December 1969, the Provisionals (PIRA) were formed, recruiting in the North. PIRA declared war against the British Army, rapidly becoming the world's most experienced and feared terrorist organisation. Their objective was to force out the British by making the North ungovernable.

Over the thirty years of the Troubles, PIRA caused an estimated 1,800 deaths, 60% of the total lives lost: of which 705 were soldiers, 301 police officers, and more than 600 civilians. 292 PIRA Volunteers were killed. By comparison, Protestant Loyalist paramilitaries killed some 30%, the police and Army 10%.

DISCRIMINATION, RIOTS AND THE BRITISH ARMY

Northern Ireland is part of the United Kingdom; the six Irish counties that opted not to join the 26 counties of the Irish Free State when it was formed in 1921.

The first prime minister of Northern Ireland, James Craig, said that in the same way as the Free State described itself as Catholic, the North was "a Protestant state for a Protestant People".

For over fifty years, within this Protestant state, the North's Catholic minority suffered discrimination: they were restricted politically by extensive gerrymandering to ensure Protestant majorities in elections, denied jobs, and given sub-standard council housing.

In the late 1960s, inspired by the movement against racial segregation and discrimination in the southern USA, the Northern Ireland Civil Rights Association (NICRA) organised peaceful protest marches. These were aggressively opposed by Loyalist Protestants.

The Royal Ulster Constabulary (RUC) – the Northern Ireland police – was perceived by Catholics as a Loyalist Protestant force. In 1968 during a march in Londonderry, the police were filmed beating Catholic protesters. This was televised across the world, and led to violent counter-reactions. The RUC was unable to control the ensuing civil disorder. And so in the summer of 1969, the British Army was sent in to prevent civil war.

SOME KEY EVENTS IN THE NORTHERN IRELAND TROUBLES PRECEDING THE EVENTS IN THIS BOOK

1969 Loyalist attacks on NICRA marches led to riots in Derry, the British Army was deployed, and PIRA split from the IRA to fight them.

1971 The Westminster Government imposed internment without trial. Considered to have been the bloodiest year of the Troubles.

1972 PIRA bombings began in Aldershot, the British Embassy in Dublin was burned down, and the British Army shot twenty-six Republican men during the Derry "Bloody Sunday" march, killing fourteen of them and injuring twelve.

1973 PIRA began bombing the mainland: London, Manchester and Birmingham (twenty-four bombs in that year).

1974 August: the Protestant UVF set bombs in Dublin without giving warnings, killing twenty-six and injuring 300.

1974 November: PIRA retaliated with pub bombings in Birmingham, killing twenty-one civilians and injuring 182 after failing to give actionable telephone warnings. Outcry from PIRA supporters led to it postponing its mainland bombing campaign, refusing to admit responsibility.

1979 August: INLA killed Lord Mountbatten and three others; PIRA killed eighteen soldiers at Narrow Water Castle – also known as the Warren Point bombings.

SOME KEY EVENTS IN THE CAMPAIGN AGAINST PIRA (UP UNTIL 1980)

1971	Internment, with systematised intelligence gathering and interrogation.
1972	The Army's undercover Military Reaction Force (MRF) betrayed to PIRA, then attacked, to be disbanded, replaced by the Special Reconnaissance Unit (SRU), or "Det".
1976	The SAS were officially deployed to Northern Ireland.
1974–79	The RUC and Labour government worked to establish the primacy of the RUC police over the British Army.

ANNIVERSARIES IN 2023

- 54th anniversary of the deployment of the British Army to Belfast (August 1969).
- 42nd anniversary of PIRA's Armalite/Ballot-Box Strategy (strategy change May 1981).
- 25th anniversary of the Good Friday Agreement (signed on 10 April 1998).

CHAPTER 1

The whole thing had kicked off early the previous Sunday morning, with an anonymous telephone tip-off to the Det's weekend-duty chief inspector. The call came in on his direct line: "I got an address you's gonna want to know about. Better write it down."

"How d'you get this number?"

"Sharpen up, chief inspector."

The caller's accent was Belfast. But unusually, there was no trace of the tight-throated tension that usually characterised these calls.

The chief inspector started the tape machine.

"You'll know of Aodhán Ó Súilleabháin and Cormac Ó Ceallaigh…?"

The Irish names were pronounced carefully and correctly.

"How d'you get this number?" he repeated.

"You're sounding like the tape recorder, chief inspector."

The caller sounded amused.

The chief inspector was listening carefully for background noise. But there wasn't even the slight resonant reverberation you'd get from the glass in a public phone box.

"Those two names are familiar," he replied, adopting a more conversational tone. "Aiden O'Sullivan and Cormac Kelly are both of interest to us…"

"Thanks for the translation," said the voice. "So did you want to know where in West Belfast they're meeting?"

The chief inspector asked the caller to repeat the address several times. And then the spelling of the names of the two men. The duty line engineer would be trying to do a pathway trace.

The caller hadn't sounded at all bothered by the chief inspector's less-than-subtle time-wasting:

"Ask as many questions as you like, chief inspector. But that address was the one thing I'm actually going to tell you."

If this was to prove a genuine call, the tape transcript was far more important than whatever might come from the line trace. Senior people would need scapegoats for whatever came to pass. Provided the dialogue showed him trying to keep this guy talking, he'd be one of the heroes.

The caller ended it: "OK, that's enough. I'll leave you to work out the rest."

The line had gone dead.

The superintendent had been mysteriously "away" for the weekend – almost certainly with a new "other" woman. His last instruction on the Friday night had been "Don't phone me unless we're talking World War Three".

The duty chief inspector couldn't analyse the accuracy of the tip-off. But the location of a meeting of senior IRA staff officers demanded his attention; and as would have been obvious to the anonymous informer, required him to respond.

Every tip-off, especially the anonymous sort, could be anything: from the truth to a set-up, or just one of many false alarms. Without the superintendent to carry the can, the safe option was for the duty chief inspector to be seen to take action, but without disrupting ongoing operations; specifically, to order the insertion of an observation team. Their orders would be vague enough to ensure they didn't actually do anything themselves, but would show he'd addressed the situation. In fact, he could probably get away with just ordering them to get ready.

The location was West Belfast – Provisional IRA heartland, so some kind of a set-up had to be taken very seriously – an obvious deduction. But the duty chief inspector decided that the possibility of the tip-off being genuine could be judged to outweigh other considerations, including potential danger to the operators. The latter wasn't in any case his concern, as he summoned the SAS operations room sergeant major.

The Det (short for 'detachment') or to use its proper name, the Special Reconnaissance Unit, included a 20-strong SAS Troop. But all members of the Troop were out on a long-term ambush, a tip-off that a PIRA arms cache was to be moved; and the other Army people – 14 Intelligence Company – were "otherwise engaged". So the duty chief inspector covered his arse by ordering the SAS ops room sergeant major to tell his headquarters over in Hereford that they were to cover the deficit. By lunchtime, Hereford had agreed to fly over an officer plus two, with a fourth from the Northern Ireland SAS Troop to be extracted temporarily from their ongoing operation.

The crashed-out SAS reinforcements arrived that night from Hereford via Aldergrove airport. They were lugging heavy black equipment bags and expecting immediate action. But with less than twelve hours before his weekend shift ended, the duty chief inspector ignored them. Their actual deployment could wait another couple of hours until Monday morning, when the superintendent could make the critical decisions.

Making soldiers rush only to wait, or keeping them in the dark, wasn't something the Det's police commanders worried about, even though it made the Det seriously dysfunctional. Its discredited predecessor, the MRF – or Military Reaction Force – had been run solely by the Army for two years without police oversight. Soldiers had shot and ambushed PIRA members, imitating terrorist tactics, even using PIRA weapons to shoot Loyalist paramilitaries. Their intelligence gathering had gone as far as operating a discount mobile laundry service that analysed clothes from Republican households, testing for explosives, blood and firearms residue; and a "massage parlour" on the Antrim Road.

So now, although all that had been stopped and police primacy over the Army re-established as firm policy, there remained the problem of the British government in Westminster still thinking it was in charge. Which meant MI5 being over here in force, plus 11,000 soldiers.

Here in the Det, with MI5 vying for control, Special Branch was determined and unyielding. The duty chief inspector couldn't care less about inconveniencing soldiers, or however they might think of him. The people of Ulster deserved the rule of law, not MI5 spies and SAS assault teams.

SUNDAY 30 NOVEMBER 1980

Exactly one week later, four SAS men were on their fourth day of freezing slowly to death in a derelict roof space, watching the buildings opposite. It was nine o'clock, Captain Peter Straker looking down through a gap of broken tiles at a row of shops; at the flat above the shuttered betting shop.

On the other side of the road, at the far end where it curved round to the left, only the corner shop selling everything from newspapers to coal and tobacco had customers. It was open all hours, whereas the betting shop, butcher and bakery were padlocked and dark, and the television, radio and vacuum-cleaner repairer looked permanently closed. Behind the dirty window of the women's hairdresser, a single lightbulb burned with pointless persistence.

Straker was five foot eleven, slightly built and athletic – 165 pounds, with straggling dark brown hair and a short beard. In normal life he had blue eyes, but right now they were red-rimmed and bloodshot. His job was leading a four-man SAS reconnaissance team in IRA-controlled West Belfast.

Straker's face was concealed by a black balaclava, skin underneath smeared with drying, cracked camouflage cream, and a thick woolly hat. His dark grey overcoat was over-sized to accommodate four layers of mountain clothing, and he wore black civvie walking boots. However, being unable to move in this roof space, the warm air between the layers of his cold-weather gear had long gone cold.

All four of them were in hypothermia survival mode, the body conserving core heat in the abdomen and head by restricting blood flow to the limbs to keep the brain working. Several layers of wool neck-warmer and the balaclava shielded this flow from the insidious cold. But Straker's arms and legs were numb. With random heat-generating bouts of shivering, he was cold to the very bone.

Straker's four-man team had been in position since the early hours of Wednesday morning: three and a half days, one hundred hours of watching – two hours on, two hours sleeping. This might sound like a lot of sleeping, but wasn't how these things worked.

Their situation in this roof space was complicated, and Straker was still considering the implications. He'd been crash-moved across from Hereford just six days ago, leaving his Pagoda Team job, because, as the blank-faced MI5 "Det" coordinator at Aldergrove had told him, "all your people are otherwise engaged".

The briefing had been terse and bad-tempered. The Special

Branch chief inspector handed out orders and refused to answer questions, while everybody else kept quiet.

Straker had already done four tours over here, including one year in the Det as part of the in-theatre SAS Troop, so he'd seen this kind of thing before, but he couldn't accept it. Special Branch and MI5 played politics in warm offices, while the SAS and Army Intelligence people did the dangerous stuff out on the ground.

The vagueness of the chief inspector's briefing had been deliberate. The police were in charge, information their treasure, which they hoarded like paranoid dragons. Straker was deliberately being kept in the dark.

This wasn't the way to do business, but he'd deal with it. Even though he didn't know the SAS watchkeepers or their ops room sergeant major, he did know that they'd respect his authority as the "man on the ground". His radio comms connected directly to the SAS cell in the Det operations room. They'd only pass on the statutory SITREPs – the 24-hour situation reports, which were based on what the SAS watchkeeper decided to write in the radio log. Like everyone else, the SAS played their own passive version of the information game: delaying, withholding detail and so on.

Right now, on Sunday morning, freezing up in this roof space, there was boredom and uncertainty. Straker had been here many times before. As ever they were mushrooms – the universal soldiers' complaint at being "kept in the dark and fed on shit", while all the time trying to work out what they weren't being told.

Logic and sense of humour were the only push-backs, but the anxiety was insidious, made worse by cold and inactivity. He was also restless – absolutely the worst way to feel, as these surveillance operations were open-ended. But there was also fear; this wasn't just a policing surveillance operation, looking for criminals. Straker regarded the Provisional IRA – PIRA – as a formidable enemy. Any of the men or women they were watching down on the bleak, grim street below could be soldiers in what for them was a war. If detected up here, Straker knew they'd be lucky to get out alive.

Whereas the British government depicted PIRA as common criminals, denying them prisoner-of-war status in jail, prompting protests and now a hunger strike – making this a war without rules. With no Geneva Conventions, if captured, Straker's team faced torture, then eventually the mercy of a bullet in the back of the head. Straker had helped recover the body of an undercover soldier from one PIRA kidnap, so he knew exactly what to expect. If this operation was compromised, Straker would fight his way out, bringing his team or their bodies out with him.

So now, wide awake in his two-hour sleep period, Straker was working at reassuring himself. He made lists, ticking things off inside his head. They were observing all approaches to the building – tick; with no movement or lights – tick; no smoking – tick; no cooking, talking or radio noise – tick. The surveillance lenses were set well back from the holes in the roof through which they were observing, lessening the likelihood of tell-tale glinting if the sun shone – tick. He listed the indicators by which he'd declare them compromised – his most critical decision. Each of his team knew precisely their actions if he were to declare that decision.

Straker's other calming litany was their pre-determined IAs – the immediate actions they hoped would never be required if they were shot at by a sniper or drive-by, them taking casualties, and the unlikely possibility of an actual assault on their position. The details were what kept people alive, about which Straker was ruthlessly pedantic.

Lying beside him, swapping the two-hour observation stags, was Sergeant Major Ian Jackson. Straker only knew him from brief conversations at Hereford social events, the hanging around waiting to be told what to do, and then the rushed two hours they'd spent planning this operation.

Jacko was using the viewfinder of their camera's 75-200mm telephoto lens as a telescope, logging people on the street and creating narratives for what they were doing, in order to identify the locals. The anomalies, who didn't fit into the normal life of this area, were the potentially dangerous people – the unknown players. If Jacko was lucky enough to recognise any actual "players", he'd photograph them along with the people they were with, for handing over to the ops room Intelligence Corps sergeant on return to base.

The other two guys, Sergeant Graham Halliwell AKA "the Farmer", and Trooper "Hooves" Rendall, were lying behind them facing backwards, and probably wouldn't see anybody at all for however long they remained there. Watching the rear and side of their building was deadly boring but vital.

Straker rolled onto one hip, then with great care unscrewed the plastic cap of his two-litre pee bottle, waiting until he was quite certain everything was lined up before relaxing. He never drank much on these ops, but stress made him want to urinate, and pee-bottle overflow was a disaster. He was thinking about whether he could swap Hooves and the Farmer round without missing anything or making unnecessary noise.

"This is a fucking waste of time," muttered Jacko.

"I dunno about that," replied Straker. "What else is there to do on a Sunday morning? In any case, matey's still in there. That broken-up flat can't be his home, so he's definitely waiting for something."

"God knows what he's doing," agreed Jacko, "but I really can't see a risk-averse bunch of IRA quartermasters coming up from Tipperary for a meeting with Belfast Brigade staff officers in that shitty little flat."

"Neither can I. But the RUC do..."

"Only enough to order us to freeze off *our* bollocks, not theirs."

Fair comment, thought Straker. But he didn't say it. Just being here was dangerous – anything could happen, and returning to base with nothing having happened would be a good outcome.

"Do those guys ever come north?" added Jacko.

"No," admitted Straker. "Why would they?"

PIRA's first-line weapon caches were located in the border hinterlands, with the rest of their arms stores way down south.

"But this is definitely about *something*..." he added.

"I'm not so sure."

"You heard the chief inspector," replied Straker. "But they weren't going to tell *me*."

"I can't see him having sleepless nights," muttered Jacko.

The police briefing had been stressful. They hadn't liked Straker asking questions about the tip-off. But as Special Branch called the shots, they'd not given him any answers.

"They were maintaining security," said Straker, trying to be diplomatic. "Not telling us anything, and leaving telling us the bare minimum until as late as possible."

"That whole kick, bollock and scramble routine is unnecessary," grunted Jacko. "But it's not just mistrust – they resent us being over here, which is why they tell us fuck-all."

"I know," said Straker wearily. "But I'm not sure I blame them."

"I got taken off a long ambush in Omagh for this crock of shit," replied Jacko angrily. "Two weeks on a weapons cache the RUC said was about to be moved. Which is far more likely than this…"

Straker and his team had flown in directly from Hereford, whereas Sergeant Major Jackson was based in Northern Ireland, at the end of his one-year tour with the 20-strong SAS Troop permanently stationed over here.

"…and a much better way to finish off a tour," he added.

"I hear you," whispered Straker. "I've done five of those troop ambush gigs. It either happens or it doesn't. Whereas in here, *anything* could happen."

"Including nothing," muttered Jacko.

Straker had done a 12-month SAS tour, and three half-year emergency deployments with his parent unit 2 Para before that. He knew Jacko was right.

"Agreed," he said. "But while we're up here, the 'nothing' possibility is not what I'm worrying about."

Straker wriggled backwards away from the observation slot, then stood up slowly to walk along the plywood doors they'd laid across the rafters to make their observation platform. He knelt beside where Sergeant Halliwell was on stag. A huge bear of a man with a strong Somerset accent, hence being known throughout the regiment as "the Farmer", he was staring through a Swiftscope.

"Hey, boss," he whispered. "I keep hoping this bird I saw yesterday in number twenty-seven is going to get her kit off for me."

"This is how we win the war," whispered Straker. "Make sure you log it."

Trooper Gary Rendall stirred inside a green sleeping bag, his nose and eyes emerging from the hood. An Army cross-country champion, he was from the Household Cavalry, so he'd been nicknamed "Hooves".

"Anything happening out front, boss?" he whispered.

"Just another Tequila Sunrise," said Straker.

"Starin' slowly 'cross the sky," came Hooves' reply. They'd done this before.

"Our man's still holed up in the flat. Are you guys OK back there? I was thinking about rotating you to the front."

"No, boss, we're fine," interrupted the Farmer. "You got to stay up front; and I don't think Sergeant Major Jackson's gonna appreciate a spell back here just to give the two of us a change of scene."

Straker nodded. The Farmer was also being diplomatic. He, the Farmer and Hooves were the newbies – reinforcements from the Hereford-based Special Projects team, flown in four days ago after the RUC tip-off.

"I don't blame him," said Straker. "I'd have wanted to finish off my tour with the guys I knew."

They were in a square, brick-built, factory warehouse, and the roof space was dark except where the early morning light shone through holes where tiles had slipped. Three days ago, in the early hours, they'd been dropped off at the lorry entrance from the side door of a coasting Transit van, their gear in black canvas holdalls. Wearing long, thick overcoats, they resembled tramps using it as a doss house.

The streets and surrounding shops had been deserted, so Straker didn't think they'd been seen. Even so, he'd kept the team on full alert until midday the next day, only then going into the two-hour watch-sleep routine. They were ready to get out at a moment's notice.

Right from the start of this Straker had felt uneasy; at the bad-tempered Special Branch briefing, and now with an unsubstantiated feeling that something bad was going to happen. Being a high-threat situation, sleep was a problem – until exhaustion hit. The two-hour timeslots were OK for staying awake, but not for sleeping, and snoring got you elbowed awake. But now, even after three nights, Straker had still not settled into the mind-numbing acceptance necessary for long-term, open-ended surveillance.

In addition, his mind was playing tricks, which worried him as he didn't need distractions. In the two-hour breaks he wasn't sleeping, his brain kept generating a strangely vivid dream where he was looking through the rear sight of an MP5 in the split-second pause for target recognition. He'd align the fore sight, take up trigger pressure, then squeeze off the shot – actions he'd perfected over many hundreds of hours on ranges, in killing houses, and out on operations. The dream ran as a loop, showing him the faces of terrorists he'd memorised from operations-room photos, interspersed with the faces of his friends.

But the dream had turned him into a powerless spectator, watching with unbearable desperation as somebody else took the shots, at friend and foe alike. He'd wake to the sound of the shot, hyped up as if for real-world action.

He'd rationalised this as a fight-or-flight mechanism – the brain getting him ready for action. But making it more disturbing was that it was less a dream and more a playback of previous experiences in the killing-house training process. They used live ammunition, bursting into rooms to shoot straw dummies of terrorists placed beside living hostages played by their colleagues. In the dream he was making the same high-stress ID decisions, then squeezing the trigger.

Straker felt Jacko suddenly go tense.

He lifted himself back into full consciousness, automatically glancing at his wristwatch: two minutes after nine o'clock in the morning. He was cold and stiff, stretching uncomfortably to look down at the street below.

A pregnant woman with blonde hair pushing a pram had stopped for a moment beside the entrance to their building's small front yard. He watched her light a cigarette.

"*Over here, pregnant women with prams usually also have toddlers...*"

This thought came to him in a soft County Waterford accent, and was not his own. And because he knew what this was and what it meant, Straker's consequent shiver was nothing to do with the cold, but a painful twisting sensation inside himself.

Jacko pointed, but not at the woman. He was looking across the road where their subject was standing out on the pavement smoking a cigarette. He'd come down the staircase from the flat opposite, through the front door in-between the shop fronts.

"*What's happening here? Don't be telling me there's a smoking ban in PIRA safe houses...?*"

The voice came again to Straker, calm and with humour.

The man flicked the cigarette butt onto the road, then turned back into the dark corridor and the narrow stairs that led up to where he'd been staying these last two days. A ceiling light came on behind lace curtains.

"*It's the stress, y'know,*" declared the voice. "*Makes the smoking contagious...*"

The voice was something – or someone – to which Straker had learned to listen: the remembered lessons of his first platoon sergeant, 'Tiger' Phelan, his mentor from the early years of his time in the Parachute Regiment. The voice came when he needed it, speaking softly inside his head, especially when he was tired. He'd learned to talk with it, coming to joint decisions with it, as they'd once done together in real life.

But there was no comfort in this. The 'Tiger', as he'd been known in 2 Para, came only in times of danger.

Sergeant Tadhg Phelan had been born and raised down south in the Republic and was sympathetic to the plight of the people up here. He'd taught Straker that sympathy gave you a way of knowing what people were thinking and what they might do, closely related to empathy, from which came life-saving insights. However, right in this instant, Straker was finding Tiger's sympathy a distraction he wished he could switch off.

Straker liked the Northern Irish, but not in their tribal groups, when desperation made them dangerous. This made him sad for them, as the streets and housing estates for which they fought were so miserable and run-down, and they had nowhere else to go. But in being sympathetic, he'd also learned not to underestimate them.

In 2nd Lieutenant Straker's lonely first few months as a Parachute Regiment officer, learning the job on the streets of Belfast, Tiger Phelan had seemed exactly like one of the men he'd come to know as a schoolboy in Ardglenna, a village in County Tyrone – and reminded him specifically of his godfather's gamekeeper, Ian O'Neill. Sergeant Phelan had been a country boy brought up on a small dairy farm, by a labourer father. Their close relationship had given Straker a comforting connection back to the Ardglenna people; a mutual understanding that had got them both through a very violent year.

Movement drew Straker's attention back to the vandalised bus shelter immediately opposite, as a young man wearing a black pork-pie hat lit a cigarette and checked his wristwatch. Straker switched to the upstairs windows, and movement behind its grimy lace curtains as the other man re-entered the flat.

A Belfast Citybus pulled in front of the shelter, stopped, but then drove away almost immediately, revealing pork-pie hat still standing there with the cigarette.

"*Did you see anyone get off? If that guy was waiting for the bus, he should have got on. Does that mean the buses are non-smoking, or that there's another bus route using that stop?*"

Tiger had always asked questions. As now, Straker rarely knew the answers; as then, this made him annoyed with himself. Hijackings made the buses unreliable, so people mostly used the semi-legal black taxis, but he should have known about the bus routes.

When you get really tired, you tell yourself what to do, one thing at a time. He decided to shift his view to the left side of their observation slot to check again on the pregnant woman. But before he looked, he thought about her, that the headscarf and cheap raincoat made her look like a thousand other hard-pressed Northern Irish mothers. He then decided that was somehow significant. But while he'd been thinking about the bus, she'd moved on:

"*Wherever she's gone, it's not fair. Who deserves to live like this?*"

The vagary of this comment further annoyed Straker, but he'd been here many times before with these inner dialogues. In life, Tiger's wisdom had been Delphic; to the newly minted Straker, obscure, as if from some higher world. When he'd asked for specific advice, Tiger's answers had never been what he'd needed or wanted; which as it was now, had annoyed him.

But being annoyed meant you were paying attention. Which meant there was something important about this pregnant woman. So Straker tried to remember exactly what he'd seen.

"*Over here nobody's allowed to opt out*," interrupted Tiger.

Not even a pregnant mother, thought Straker.

"*No opt-outs*," insisted Tiger. "*You're either for us or against us.*"

This distracted Straker into remembering the chief inspector's hostile reaction to his questions during the briefing for this op. Asking questions meant you had doubts and were mistrustful when what the police required was your whole-hearted cooperation.

"*Either for us or against us...*"

Straker now stopped himself from slipping into a loop of reliving the replies he wished he'd made to the chief inspector. Tiredness required ruthless control.

He focussed back on the pregnant woman, trying to utilise his sympathy for her to gain insight, only to be sucked into the far worse distraction of her tragedy: motherhood and violence; her babies born into poverty, condemned to failure, the miracle of new life crushed by the complexity of worthless politics, the Catholic Madonna aloof, impassive with love, both small and huge at the same time.

Dear God, he thought, as this swirl of distraction expanded. So, once more, he shut it down.

Their subject appeared again on the pavement, this time pulling the flat's front door shut behind him.

Straker snapped back into the moment. Their subject walked past the bus shelter and into the corner shop.

"This is One-Zero," transmitted Straker. "Target has left the premises. Wait out."

They both watched the door of the corner shop. Up in the flat, the light remained on.

"*If he was sensible, he wouldn't come back... I wouldn't...*"

Sympathy again. But this time also a warning.

"Are you guys ready to move?" asked Jacko with uncanny timing.

Straker nodded. They always were. It was SOP – standard operating procedure.

This was Jacko's way of telling Straker what to do next. His "Are you ready to move you guys" question was partly diplomatic, but also emphasised Jacko's personal independence from this rushed and, as he thought, pointless operation. The subject leaving could mean anything, and from their point of view it made their presence less justifiable.

Straker twisted round to look behind him, then started clenching and relaxing some feeling back into his toes, fingers and legs, ready to crawl backwards to the ladder, and thought about what they'd need to do to get out of here.

But nothing further happened.

"This is One-Zero," said Straker after twenty minutes. "Matey went into the corner shop but hasn't come out. The flat is unoccupied."

Then forty minutes later: "One-Zero, matey's gone, flat's empty. What's the score?"

Straker was hoping to be ordered to withdraw, although not with any sort of expectation. He'd done this too many times to make that mistake – and Straker didn't have any tangible reasons for terminating the operation himself.

CHAPTER 2

Máire Carragher's clothes stank of tobacco smoke, which she hated. After returning to the house, she'd cleaned her teeth twice and was now changing, putting the jeans and anorak into supermarket carrier bags, hoping the smell could be sealed inside.

She'd stopped smoking herself on realising she was pregnant. Then, as part of the strange changes that accompanied this mystery, she found that even just the smell of cigarettes made her feel sick – similar to morning sickness, though it didn't last as long. She decided that as she wasn't eating coal – yet – and her husband Séan didn't smoke, it wasn't much of an imposition.

But she wasn't going to repeat the "Belfast smoking mum" of this morning, and was now debating the rest of her wardrobe. Another drab headscarf – vital to cover up her obvious blonde hair, a jacket rather than the long raincoat, and this time a short skirt, which was almost always the right sort of distraction. Most men would remember only your legs, and they'd all pause long enough to give you the advantage.

Máire was keeping her mind busy with details, trying not to think of her husband. Falling pregnant had been unexpected, and in most ways of looking at it, seriously inconvenient. But she'd welcomed it as a sign that God approved of her decision to pursue Carragher. He was a man like any other; she loved him and wanted to bear his children.

Although they were not currently the sort of parents a parish priest might wish for, she was most definitely pregnant. The Church would baptise their baby, so her parents would have to attend. And thereafter, one could only live in hope.

Séan's Ma was proving incredibly supportive. Immediately he'd told her, she'd come in from the Carragher family home out on the Ballymurphy Estate to see Máire, which, given their gypsy lifestyle continually moving around West Belfast, even just finding them wouldn't have been easy. While her own mother was grimly disapproving, Bronagh Carragher had welcomed her into their family.

And their wedding had been entirely Bronagh's arrangement; hiring someone she knew with a bus who made church trips for children to the seaside. They'd been wed at Corpus Christi by the old priest who'd taught Séan boxing, surrounded by friends neither of them had seen since school days, tracked down and persuaded by Bronagh. They'd driven off in a bubble of noisy happiness to the seaside like in the Cliff Richard movie – except theirs hadn't been a double-decker. And now Bronagh was doing everything an experienced grandmother could do to allay her daughter-in-law's fears.

Máire Carragher was frightened, but not for herself. She knew what she was into, committed in her trademark all-or-nothing style. But now they were three, and she was feeling desperately responsible for that new person.

The acrid smell of Duffy's soldering had thankfully dissipated. He hadn't thought to open any windows, and was now complaining about the cold. But she was feeling better, although without enough appetite to cook. Instead she made them both a pot of tea, and hoped they'd see Séan later.

By early afternoon it looked like evening, darkness drawing in with clouds and rain. Their subject had not returned. Headlights from passing cars reflected shiny-black from pools of water in the potholed road.

The buses were a distraction, their length obstructing part of their main arc of observation. They didn't stop unless a person flagged them down, but were few and irregular – the Sunday service. It seemed so much quieter than yesterday, when there'd been men coming in and out of the bookies, with the newsagent-cum-off-licence corner shop at the far end open until late on. Whereas today, the row of shops was dark and empty with, Straker noted inexplicably, the single bulb in the hairdresser's now off.

But then, at 4pm, the chip shop's neon lights flickered on behind the taped-up sheets of cardboard that covered the bottom half of its cracked front window. The top half was too misted up and grubby to allow them to see who was inside. No customers were attracted.

Straker was on stag. After four days, they'd identified most of the locals through cataloguing their routines: buying papers and cigarettes in the morning, drink at night, discarding slips of paper outside the betting shop, mothers taking very young children to and from school, men returning from work. These were the area's legitimate inhabitants. Any "players" would not be such creatures of habit; by luck they might recognise one, otherwise some kind of atypical activity would be their only clue.

The target flat's single light remained on. But in the growing dusk, it looked abandoned.

"*As quiet as the grave.*"

"Thanks for that, Tiger."

Their role was passive. This was unusual, because the 14 Intelligence Company "Det" people who usually did undercover surveillance were otherwise engaged.

Straker, with the Farmer and Hooves, had been rushed over here from Hereford in the early hours of Monday morning, only to be ignored by the RUC for 24 hours. They'd then been told to be ready for an RUC ops briefing, which didn't happen until the next day – the Wednesday.

The police had given them orders but no explanations; they said a PIRA meeting was "predicted", and if it took place, they were to photograph and identify the players. A police operation supported by normal Army units was on standby to make the actual arrests. Only Special Branch would know about the involvement of the SAS.

Unusual – but it had also been the same old rush-to-wait. Back in Hereford, Straker hadn't even been on duty. After a row with his father, he'd returned early to camp and been happily on his own in the Officers' Mess eating hot buttered toast on a quiet winter afternoon. This had been exactly one week ago.

Straker now saw a mother walking down their side of the street, pushing a pram along the pavement beside their building. She was obviously pregnant, wearing a brown woollen hat and a leather jacket. She stopped, dropping a half-smoked cigarette. Looking round, she pulled the pram towards her, then backed into their yard so she didn't block the pavement. She knelt down to take something from the wire shelf underneath the pram, her short skirt riding high up her thighs.

"*Nice legs.*"

But as she stood up, Straker's conscious mind slid smoothly into high-alert mode. He nudged Jacko and pointed. This was the same woman he'd watched this morning, but with the blonde hair up and different clothes.

He knew there was more, waiting as his tired mind processed the data. Three times the same woman – the first yesterday, without the pram, and he remembered thinking very particularly about her this morning.

"*Clean fatigue*," observed Tiger, using the Paras' term for a practice jump without weapons or equipment.

"Are you sure she's the same one?" whispered Jacko.

Straker nodded. Yesterday she'd been wearing a blue anorak and flared jeans, and had stood by the warehouse entrance, smoking. He remembered the care with which she'd stubbed out the butt.

This morning, the pram was the same: black with large wheels, a Spar supermarket bag hanging over its push bar. Her headscarf – tied under the chin, 1950s style – had made her look older and different. But also a short skirt and the same great legs.

"*Unforgettable... and now it's raining.*"

It was mostly always raining, thought Straker irritably. *So what?*

"*She changed the raincoat into a leather jacket...*"

Then he remembered pork-pie hat at the bus stop. He'd been there yesterday wearing the same black donkey jacket but without the hat. And he hadn't got on the bus.

Something's happening, Straker thought, his heart rate ratcheting up, *but I don't have enough information.*

It was very cold, not quite freezing. Despite the damaged roof keeping out the worst of the rain, they were teetering on hypothermia with just the shivering to fend it off. Needing heat, he fumbled in his coat for a packet of chocolate-covered toffee Rolos. He snapped off five and gave the rest of the packet to Jacko. Despite having been in his pocket, they were still cold and hard, like little round stones.

He put all five into his mouth and waited for the chocolate coating to melt. If you tried to chew too soon, you'd break a tooth. As they melted, he resisted the temptation to chew the toffee, and gradually swallowed the chocolate. Heat from the glucose spread from his stomach around his body like hot water in a central heating system.

Down on the street, the woman was walking across the road towards the chip shop, pushing the pram left-handed against her distended stomach, the plastic bag in her right. She lined the pram up parallel to the window, leaned over to check the baby, then went in.

It was always difficult to identify patterns of activity when watching an urban street. Successful terrorists worked very hard to appear random. They also minimised risk, only committing to an operation when confident of their own safety.

Jacko leaned across towards Straker.

"These fucking people…" he whispered, his breath sour with halitosis. "What kind of mother leaves their baby in the rain outside a chip shop?"

"*Clean fatigue…*" repeated Tiger. "*She's now wearing a bomber jacket.*"

Despite the Rolos, Straker felt the familiar metallic taste in his mouth. He took one deep breath and kicked straight into full-bore turbo mode.

The dialogue inside his head stopped, decision taken, clarity pushing aside both his anxiety and the tiredness. This was what he'd been waiting for, so he also felt an illogical sense of relief.

He fast-forwarded through what he'd observed:

"We watched their dry run this morning," he said.

"When?" demanded Jacko.

"Around nine. That same woman stopped by the entrance, checked the baby, then carried on."

Underneath the camouflage netting of his face veil, Jacko looked doubtful.

"What we're looking at now is the real thing," added Straker.

Jacko was still in slowed-down thinking mode: "What's the target?"

This made Straker impatient with him.

"Who's here that the IRA might want to take out?"

"You're saying we've been set up?"

Straker was thinking through what he now needed to do. Jacko's rather dumb question had interrupted this, making him even more impatient.

"It's a bit fucking obvious, isn't it?"

Straker had made the decision and was now picking up his Browning. He rolled onto one side to push it into its spring-loaded shoulder holster.

"What's obvious?" said Jacko, still fuddled with cold.

"Where we are," Straker spat back. "Directly opposite this supposed IRA meet, in this building – the only place from where we could observe it."

"What does that fucking pram have to do with it?"

Immediately Jacko said this, Straker could see he wished he hadn't.

"The pram's pretty obvious too," replied Straker gently. "Don't you think…?"

But there were no actual facts to back up any of this. Just burning certainty tipping into the fear that had now replaced his cold tiredness.

"When did matey across the road leave the flat?" asked Straker. "Has he come back yet?"

Jacko was catching up rapidly: "You reckon he left as soon as they completed the dry run?"

"That's what they usually do…"

Jacko squeezed his transmit switch. "This is One-Zero Alpha. All stations, any signs of the target?"

"We're eyes-on," hissed Straker. "The fucking flat's empty."

"She's inside the chip shop," said Jacko. "Nobody's dicked us up here… and in any case, what's she going to do?"

Jacko was still in the "nothing ever happens" mindset of long-term surveillance operations. His caution reinforced Straker's determination.

"I'm checking this out. It blows the op? So what, tough shit. Tell Zero, and we split right now, *rapido*."

Before Jacko could object, Straker pushed himself backwards into the centre of the roof space.

Behind, Sergeant Halliwell was on stag. Hooves Rendall was sleeping.

"I'm taking this to the street," he told the Farmer. "I think we're compromised, maybe plus an IED in a pram that's just been left outside the chip shop. Wake Hooves, take everything with you and get safe behind this building. Do it now. Pronto pronto."

He knelt under the eaves to open the trapdoor and lowered the ladder onto the first-floor landing. Hooves had woken as Straker began speaking and was stuffing his sleeping bag into a holdall.

Straker felt for the rungs, then lowered himself stiffly into the stairwell. He took off his gloves, then pulled off the woolly hat and stuffed the balaclava into his coat pocket. Replacing the woolly hat, he felt exposed and raw, his ears and neck suddenly very cold.

Stepping over the rotten treads, he got to the bottom of the stairs and slipped out into the rear yard, then moved along the side of the building to the front street. Legs still numb, he stumbled against a lamppost, waiting as a car drove past, holding the Browning inside his coat pocket.

The street and shops now seemed ominously and oddly quiet for a late Sunday afternoon – dark, with just the light from the chip shop. He ran in a limping shuffle across the road and peered over the cardboard sheets through the misted-up window – no one. The flat they'd been watching was two doors to the left, also dark and empty.

"*Matey's not coming back…*"

He knelt to examine the pram. She'd taken the carrier bag with her but, as Jacko had observed, left her baby outside. Or had she? The baby cover was zipped up tight. Without touching, he peered carefully under the pram hood. Any mother seeing a tramp doing such a thing would come rushing out. But nothing. Maybe it was her groceries?

The pram was parked side-on, touching the wall. It stood lopsided, weight pushing down the springs on its right-hand side – the side facing their observation building. What kind of shopping does that?

"*Heavy. Assume a bomb with nails and bolts,*" Tiger's radio SITREP voice said, spitting out the facts. "*No smell, so Semtex or gelignite. A pramful of it reduces our observation position to a pile of bricks…*"

Straker felt a stab of gut pain as all his fears surged into focus. He turned and gestured urgently up at Jacko, slicing his hand back and forth like a blade under his chin, then moving his fist up and down to signal urgency. He wished now he'd been more robust with Jacko. He could only hope they'd get out.

But for him, he now had to stop thinking about this bomb. There were plenty more immediate ways to get himself and everyone else killed – for example, being shot by anyone in the security forces who might come by.

He squeezed the pressel switch on his concealed radio: "Zero, this is One-Nine. Am foxtrot and have found suspect IED outside chip shop. Assume we are compromised. Withdraw all callsigns. Am entering chip shop."

To call an IED "suspect" was police-type radio speak. Straker was certain this was a bomb. But something specific was bothering him about the pram, only right now he didn't have time to work out what. Checking the Browning's safety catch was off, he entered the chip shop.

Like the street, it was deserted. He leaned over the counter, scanning the floor and into a brightly lit rear kitchen. No visible trip wires. He pushed through the counter's spring gate and ran to the back door, which he opened slowly, knowing he'd be silhouetted against the kitchen's neon lighting. He crouched down, then ducked out into the small yard.

A brand-new, seven-foot-high wooden fence shielded him from the alley.

He remembered the pram. The woman had checked the baby even though there was no baby.

"This is One-Nine," he muttered into his throat mic. "Don't touch that pram. Tell Felix she set a trembler."

"Felix" was the bomb disposal officer's radio callsign. His team would be on their way with blue lights and sirens in a small fleet of Land Rovers. They carried a library of files with the latest information about bombs. En route, they'd cross-reference any details he could provide.

Time was now running for Straker at half-speed, the outside world like a slow-moving dream. He kept thinking about his team, then cutting off the distracting thoughts.

The shops could give protection. But exploding prams made him think of babies turning into pigs and jumping down rabbit holes.

If I'm doing what they expect, we lose our heads, he thought. *So fucking concentrate...*

The yard was empty. He ran across to the wooden door at the end. This opened into the rear alley behind the row of shops. Its hinges and latch seemed OK – no wires. Kneeling low again, he reached up and eased open the latch, pulling the door open towards him.

He concentrated on whatever might be in the alley. To the left it was clear. He heard a very slight movement to his right. From the kneeling position he rolled forwards into the alley onto his left shoulder, bringing the Browning to bear with a two-handed grip. Light from the yard showed the pregnant woman squatting fifteen feet away. He noted the Spar supermarket bag underneath whatever she'd got beside her. She was triggering the bomb.

After long hours sweating into his respirator in the Pontrilas killing house, split-second facial recognition was second nature. Not shooting a 'hostage' – played by his comrades, was equally deeply ingrained.

The woman glanced up briefly. Recognition hit him like a splash of icy water, sending shivers down his spine. Her soft feminine features had looked so out of place among the hard-faced men of the "Players" gallery in the Det's ops room.

The Yellow Card Rules of Engagement stated you could only shoot a terrorist if they were armed, and your life was in danger. Recognition, no matter how accurate, wouldn't get you off the murder charge. They had to be armed, and your life had to be in danger.

He remembered the list of bombings she'd carried out: six dead soldiers and four civilians, plus schoolchildren disfigured by flying glass. But even though she'd earned her place on their wall, this wasn't a murder-trial-safe shoot. Plus, as earlier when he'd watched her from the building, instinct had been telling him she wasn't just padded out to look the part. He was now completely certain she was pregnant.

So he hesitated, knowing she was lethal, but he couldn't be totally certain what she was up to. And in any case, how could a pregnant women do this?

"*There's no time for a debate,*" said Tiger. "*Kill her now, or she'll kill you.*"

But Straker ignored the voice, instead shouting the statutory Yellow Card warning as he steadied the sights of the Browning on the centre of her body. His voice was guttural and dry.

"Army. Raise your arms above your head or I fire."

At this, she didn't even look up. She knelt in the filth of the alley, short skirt riding high, to hunch intently over something on the ground.

He really wanted her to do what he said, to give up, then stand there and scream abuse at him if she wanted. That would be just fine.

But instead she leaned forwards, focussed, terrible and urgent. Although in the greatest possible danger, she was indifferent to his lethal presence. He was suddenly quite certain that her lethality exceeded his.

He thought of being in a really bad nightclub – dark, dank, the smell of drains, stale cigarettes and perfume. One of those no-good disco encounters, but with the incongruous tang of gun oil from the Browning as it irritated the cuts on his hands from the derelict building. And in this moment she did look up, staring straight at him, burning eyes red with hatred.

As their eyes locked together, it was like looking down the wrong end of a telescope. He dropped into the looping dream. Time stood still.

His Browning had a seven-pound trigger pull. Just one calm and steady squeeze differentiated this moment from the previous tens of thousands of pistol shots he'd fired. Breathing steadied, as he automatically took up the pressure.

But in the millisecond of shock as her hatred had lasered into his brain, she'd triggered the bomb.

The explosion was massive. He heard no sound. There was just a hammer blow, like being hit by a train.

Straker didn't know whether he'd shouted the required second warning, nor if he'd even made the decision to open fire. He'd seen no weapon, just felt the certainty of death, which he now knew had been with him since the beginning of this cursed operation.

CHAPTER 3

Straker regained consciousness lying in the alley, ears ringing with pain, amid the acrid smell of burning buildings mixed with dust. It all seemed strangely familiar. But he couldn't remember why.

He got to his knees and took a torch from inside his overcoat. The darkness was misty with fine particles that made him cough.

The woman was lying on her side, face relaxed and very pale – perfect, like marble. She was bleeding out onto the weeds at the side of the alley. His bullets had hit her in the side of the head and again in the spine, just above the right shoulder blade. He checked her over – still breathing, but not for much longer. He rolled her into the recovery position, then stumbled to his feet. She'd been hunched over a controller of some sort. It looked like it was for a model aeroplane, with a telescopic antenna. Attached to that was a wire, stapled to the fence, then running up the metal post of a washing line.

"This is One-Zero, explosion, one serious casualty, send backup and ambulance."

He'd fired two shots, both fatal. Job done, move on. There was nothing he could do. But he couldn't help thinking that she'd been real even though the pram hadn't; a death of innocence, but not an ending, nor even a result. Pointless, and some kind of dreadful beginning. But he had no idea what he meant by this or what his brain was trying to tell him. So he forced himself yet again to concentrate; and so felt the flickering.

There was danger. This woman would have a partner – her own backup. He was vulnerable as long as he stayed here. He couldn't help her. She was dying regardless of what he did.

Behind him, every window at the back of the row of shops was blown outwards. The wooden fence had protected him from being lacerated by the glass.

His personal radio was dead. Then he realised he was deaf. They were probably calling him. But all he could hear was a howling, ringing wind.

He ran unsteadily further up the alley to where it joined the side street, which was also deserted. It was as if everybody except him had known this was going to happen.

He turned right and ran to the end of the shops, then right again along the street they'd been watching. The entire row was wrecked, with what remained of the chip shop and the flat above burning.

The road in front of their building had long, deeply gouged strips ripped out of the tarmac. The heavier side of the pram would have been lined with metal – nuts, bolts and large nails, improvised shrapnel to increase its lethality. Their observation building had taken the full force. Its roof was gone, the windows now huge holes among crumbling brickwork.

A jagged fear stabbed through the silent, howling numbness that surrounded Straker. He stumbled across the pitted road, then down the side of the warehouse to the open yard at the rear where he'd told his team to assemble.

By the side door, he suddenly stopped, raising his arms in the air and walking slowly forwards. This was a loading area and car park, with its own vehicle entrance from the street behind. As he got to the end of the building, the Browning was seized from behind and he was pulled to the ground.

"Take it easy, boss," said the Farmer.

"Where's Jacko?" asked Straker.

"Still in the building."

"What?"

"Hooves and me came straight down like you said. But he stayed in the OP."

"We've got to get him out."

"There's no point…"

"What do you mean, there's no point?" said Straker.

The Farmer looked over his shoulder at the building: "He was in the very front, where we all were. It's completely gone…"

The Farmer still held Straker by the shoulders, from when he'd pulled him down. "Anyway, it's pitch dark in there," he told Straker quietly. "You'd just get buried when the rest of the building falls down."

Straker stared at him. But the Farmer looked very determined.

"Listen, boss… You were right and Sergeant Major Jackson got it wrong. Let's just wait here until the cavalry arrive. They can do a proper rescue job – lights, JCBs, the full monty."

Straker's fear felt like he was being stabbed in the face with a broken bottle.

Fuck what's right and wrong, he thought. *The whole fucking thing's wrong. I've just shot a pregnant woman and left her and the baby to die. In there, Jacko could be dead or dying.*

But Straker pretended to be calm, and started counting.

"Yeah, OK, Farmer," he said quietly once he'd reached twenty. "That's fine."

They let him roll over.

Straker stood up and made safe his Browning, catching the round as it ejected, squeezing it back into the top of the magazine. He then reloaded. But he didn't make ready, pushing the pistol into the spring clip of his shoulder holster.

The Farmer knew what was coming next.

"Get onto Zero and start organising the Meet 'n' Greet," Straker ordered him. "You're now in charge."

The Farmer made no attempt to stop him as he entered the creaking blackness of the damaged building.

Volunteer Padraig Duffy was the trigger-point guard, watching for interference as Máire set off the bomb. He liked working with her, even though she'd now got herself married to Séan Carragher. But that hadn't stopped him from dreaming, and he still liked looking at her.

But Duffy had been caught out. He was too far up the alley, so when she crouched down by the fence, he couldn't see her. He'd heard Straker's two rapid-fire shots as the bomb exploded.

Now his ears were ringing, and he was disorientated. He'd got to his knees and looked up through a dirty brown swirl that caught in his nose and throat. Then through the dust, further down the alley he saw the outline of a black figure in a long coat moving forwards in a crouch, a torch in one hand, pistol in the other.

Duffy's overriding fear throughout this operation was of the other SAS men he was certain would be backing up their observation team in the warehouse building. So he stayed still and watched the figure go to Máire, kneel down and roll her over. He tried to control his panic. Breathing faster was sucking more of the particles into his lungs, and he really didn't want to start coughing.

Duffy stayed down and quiet, squinting through the dust and breathing through his woollen scarf. He saw the figure stand up and move quickly in the other direction, away from him towards the other end of the alley. Duffy didn't move until the man had disappeared into the dust.

Duffy had never been in such a dangerous situation. Killing Máire meant the SAS had broken cover from the hide, escaping the blast. The incredible coup of luring them into that building now looked like a set-up. Maybe they'd never even gone in there? You couldn't make assumptions with these people. He just wanted to run away.

Máire's blonde hair was smeared black which he knew would be dark red in daylight, but he didn't dare look closely in case she was still breathing. Her arm was lying over the radio controller, beside the slowly increasing pool. He wanted to avoid touching *that*; it was expanding. He couldn't bear to think that her heart might still be beating, pumping it out.

He knelt down to pick up the controller. But as he put it into its protective case, he felt her, sticky on his fingers. Remembering he'd have to face Carragher, he placed both hands flat on the ground in the middle of the still-warm pool. Then he stood up, tucked the controller case inside his coat, wiping his hands to make sure he'd got her blood on his clothes. He then sprinted in the other direction, past the chip-shop gate, back up the entry and out onto the parallel side street.

Straker entered the damaged observation building, scanning into the darkness with his torch. The air was thick with dust, reflecting back in the torchlight as a dull yellow.

"*Mustard gas on the Western front*," observed Tiger.

As far he could see, there was still space on the ground floor, but the ceiling joists were sagging downwards, with sporadic creaking sounds that made Straker imagine the building being alive, grievously injured and malevolent.

Jacko hadn't wanted to exfiltrate. In overriding the Farmer and coming back in to find him, Straker was working on the assumption that Jacko had nevertheless obeyed his order and moved back from the front of the building. If this supposition was wrong, he'd find nothing and could be crushed for his efforts. So he didn't consider this option any further.

Straker doubled over, coughing in the dust, sinking to his knees. To his left the creaking noises became heavy thudding sounds, as part of the stone side wall collapsed. He tried to imagine where Jacko might be in relation to their ladder down from the roof space and the building's staircase. If he'd still been up in the roof space, he'd probably be on top of the debris after it collapsed downwards underneath him. Straker forced himself not to imagine the effect of the shrapnel.

He shone the torch upwards, hoping it might reflect back the shiny aluminium of the ladder. But all he could see was Tiger's mustard gas, like a dirty, impenetrable wall. He moved further into the yellow to then see reflections from the aluminium, although only as brighter points of light under bricks, dust and timbers.

He tried to pull the twisted end of the ladder free, but it been crushed and buried under too much weight. He then started prising up bricks and throwing them into the clear space behind him. The dust concealed shattered roof tiles, which cut his hands. He felt desperation, then a sudden rising panic. Forcing this down, he realised what he was doing was not just pointless but could bring it all crashing down.

He now stopped, sweating with effort and breathless from not daring to breathe too deeply. He stood up once more, shining the torch carefully across the piles of debris. The yellow cloud was constantly shifting, as further falls of debris rattled down from the roof and upper walls. But then Jacko's face showed up white in the torch beam, further over from the ladder, underneath where the stairs had been.

Jacko was pinned underneath a door, which had protected him from the broken bricks and splintered roof tiles. Straker thought that, being further back than he'd expected, Jacko must have been withdrawing away from the front of the building. When the bomb went off, he would have slid down the disconnected joists along with the rest of the debris from the roof space.

Straker managed to get the door off, and was dragging Jacko unconscious towards the side door when the creaking increased. It was the last thing he remembered before waking up in the Military Wing of Belfast's Musgrave Park Hospital.

CHAPTER 4

As Duffy steadied his nerves to walk calmly to the safe house, he congratulated himself on recovering the controller. Being first in line for Carragher's retribution, that had been the critical action, more than worth the risk he'd taken.

Then, from inside the deserted safe house, after finding a power point to put the radio controller on charge, Duffy made a phone call:

"Just want to tell you where we are with this…"

"Hang on a second," came the reply.

When Carragher came on the line it was like he already knew.

"So tell me…"

"The package performed successfully, and I'm in position now as planned to make the rest of this happen. But I'm on my own. She's gone."

"What do you mean 'gone'?" said Carragher.

He couldn't think of what else to say.

"She's dead."

Then he'd put down the receiver, to sit shivering in the darkness at the bottom of a cold, bare staircase.

The Chief of Staff had picked up the phone then handed it to Carragher.

Duffy had sounded calm, hadn't acknowledged Carragher when he came on the line, and spoke with uncharacteristic slowness.

Now, Carragher was staring at the handset in disbelief. The little fucker had rung off.

His anger surged; he'd given him the good news then the bad news, but no questions, fuck off. Duffy'd set him up like a bad joke.

He handed the telephone handset back to the Chief of Staff, then opened the front door and stepped outside onto the pavement.

This was impossible. He'd talked to them both the previous morning. There was no way Máire could have been in danger, let alone get killed. He couldn't believe this.

These past couple of days Carragher had been on the move, no more than a couple of hours in any one place, bundled up for warmth in dirty clothes underneath a green-hooded scooter parka. The houses were empty and unheated, and they were moving too randomly and quickly to wash or eat properly. He was lean, with short black hair, and didn't like looking so unkempt.

He felt the flaring of anger and grief; then he shut it down – dead and cold. Outside on the pavement, the dark street smelled of low-banked coal fires, while unusually, the sky above had briefly cleared. A crescent moon sat bright above the silhouettes of chimney pots, its ancient, primitive light shining down on God-forsaken emptiness.

He'd then lost it.

The Chief of Staff, realising something was wrong but not what or how bad, had followed Carragher out of the house. He gestured over to Roxy, who was sitting in his cab, to get out quietly, and they followed Carragher to the end of the street. When he stopped and kicked in the door of a solitary parked car, they'd grabbed him from behind, forcing him struggling onto the pavement until he became still.

Back at the house, Carragher started thinking again. The plan had contingencies, but making them work would now be down to Duffy.

"In position as planned to make the rest of this happen" could only mean that he'd retrieved the trigger – which was good. So now he had to hope Duffy'd somehow find the balls to carry it through. The man was great at things that interested him, like geeking out on TPUs and trigger mechanisms, but not where there was real exposure, or street risk from security forces. He'd worked well enough with Máire these past two years, always as if trying to impress her – which was OK with Carragher so long as the job got done.

But Máire had been the reliable one, with the balls. So with her dead, what would Duffy do now?

Carragher picked up the phone and dialled.

"A fucking disaster," he said flatly.

The response from the other end seemed to calm him.

"Yeah, well… The first one worked, but Máire's been killed," he replied. "I don't know any more than just that, so I'm going down there."

Carragher stood for a few moments, listening. Then his face tensed up with anger.

"Of course I fucking won't. But you know I can't just sit here doing nothing. I won't fail you."

He slammed the phone back into its cradle, opened the door and shouted down the stairs: "Get Roxy outside, right now!"

He heard the front door open, a low whistle to alert the dickers, then a minute later the rattle of a diesel engine as the black cab arrived from where it had been waiting the next street over.

Just a couple of minutes after putting down the phone, Carragher was in the cab and they were pulling out onto the Falls Road.

There was ice on the double-glazed sliding door that led out to Breandán O'Donnell's neat garden. It was cold and dark, and earlier that afternoon a "Scottish wind" – his name for the bitter north-easterly – had been blowing sleet across the fields. He still had the phone in his hand.

O'Donnell was aged sixty-three, short, rotund, with grey hair streaked black like a badger and the gravitas of a university professor. Studious and apparently introverted, he lived quietly in a book-lined bungalow to the north-east of Belfast. His neighbours were the prosperous Protestant country folk of Aird Uladh – "the peninsula of the Ulstermen". They liked him. He was unknown to the police, with no jail time or even an arrest to his name.

O'Donnell was Carragher's boss, a Dublin staff officer relocated to the North and now PIRA's most senior liaison officer to the "Old" IRA. He'd recruited Carragher, then in 1977 took advantage of PIRA's reorganisation to set up his own independent, highly secret and extremely well-resourced cell.

He'd believed Carragher's bomb operation was certain to succeed, to be the attention-grabbing start of a new bombing campaign. The supposedly invincible SAS would be humiliated through the use of precision bombing with no innocent deaths, and he wasn't going to share the kudos with anybody else. But he'd stuck his neck out with this, which he'd never done before, and it made him frightened.

So now O'Donnell was thinking laterally. Regardless of whatever had *actually* happened tonight, the operation must be presented in such a way as to be a success – a positive narrative to keep his strategy moving forwards. It could not be judged a failure.

But Carragher had always been difficult to manage. Máire's death would make this much worse, which annoyed O'Donnell. Carragher being defeatist at this stage of the operation was self-indulgent and very stupid. O'Donnell wasn't going to be associated with anybody stupid. Despite this hopefully temporary ill-discipline, their plan remained in play. Cool heads and calculation were required, not grief.

So although O'Donnell hoped Carragher would sort himself out, the disaster contingency narrative would ensure Carragher took the blame.

The rear of the black cab was noisy, smelling of exhaust and disinfectant. The Falls Road was quiet, with only a few hurrying figures wrapped up against the cold; dark shadows anxious in the headlights, while flesh and blood stayed safe and warm in bed. The springs of the bench seat were shot, so Carragher sat uncomfortably slumped in the darkness, his mind trying to catch up. Roxy just drove, knowing when to keep quiet.

He'd needed to be on his own, driving around as if doing something. But in reality, he was keeping out of it – at least for the moment. OK, so they might get stopped by an Army patrol, and O'Donnell had been right telling him not to visit the scene. But he couldn't stay cooped up in that house with the Chief of Staff watching him like he was going to do something stupid.

Carragher preferred being on his own. But as the Belfast Brigade commander, using the headquarters bodyguard team went with the job. They moved to different houses sometimes every night, randomly, one step ahead of betrayal and the security force's observation teams. He'd cleared the decks for this, with no other brigade operations scheduled over the entire week.

He'd been listening for the explosion, which would be obvious from where they'd been just half a mile away. As its concussion had reverberated across the shining blackness of rain-slicked roofs, he'd looked at his watch and felt the surge of a strange kind of joy. It was dead on time, an auspicious way to start a new, far more deadly bombing campaign against the British Army – *his* campaign.

He'd then sat waiting for Duffy's call.

He thought again of Duffy's message, trying to stifle his fury. No doubt Máire was dead. But Duffy hadn't told him *how* she'd died, which would be precisely why the little fucker had rung off, to avoid being asked questions. So why had she been anywhere near the bomb? And what had Duffy done – or not done?

Carragher thought first of the explosion somehow catching her; but all his operations were planned to minimise risk. Duffy was one of the best when it came to the electrics, so the bomb could not have gone off prematurely. A random road traffic accident, maybe – some car in the darkness, a drunk driver? Or had she been shot?

At this, his anger surged again. Aside from being in overall command of the op, Duffy's job was to guard Máire as she triggered the bomb. She *had* triggered the bomb – he'd heard the explosion. That was a relatively safe job, which was the point of radio-instigated detonations. But *then* she'd been killed. And Duffy was still alive. So Duffy had failed to protect her.

With that, Carragher's anger seemed to implode, like being sucked down a drain into a void of total emptiness to became tiny, abandoned, worthless and vulnerable. This wasn't God's judgment. He already knew God didn't care for him. This came from deep within, from whatever kept him going. It was like he'd disowned himself. But how could you disown yourself? What terrible things did a person have to do to deserve that?

And instinctively Carragher knew the answer. He'd heard the hollow compression of the bomb's detonation. He'd known it was *their* bomb from the time and direction of the sound. Then out of all the emotions he could have felt, he'd *rejoiced*.

The heartless reverberation of the explosion had brought with it the instant of an awakening. Reaching out like a dream, Carragher's mind had connected with a small, gentle feeling that he knew to have been the dying. In his roaring moment of rejoicing, he'd specifically felt them both; and then for a few longer moments, the innocence of his child, faltering then fading.

And so, as with an alarm clock on a winter's morning, he'd woken from this dream. But not into the early-morning world where a cup of instant coffee was all it took to re-establish reality. He supposed his mind had been trying, in that instant, to prepare him for grief and mourning. But instead he'd woken into a world he'd created, in which people died according to his plans, including those he loved, and where he rejoiced as if these were great achievements.

So now he felt lost, drowning in his own corruption.

CHAPTER 5

Over the next thirty minutes, Duffy smoked roll-ups and watched the arrival of police and the Army from the safe house. They were predictable.

Duffy was thin-faced and skinny, like an anxious weasel with yellow teeth. He'd shaved that morning so as to look less suspicious, which hadn't worked.

Duffy wondered where the safe house's occupants had gone. It was spotlessly clean but bare and cold, with lino and a battered sofa with matching armchair in the front room, a crucifix and framed sacred heart Madonna print on the wall. They'd left milk, tea, sugar and a set of polished china cups on the kitchen table.

From observing previous bomb clean-up operations, Duffy knew the security forces would first secure an area for parking their vehicles and equipment. The SAS observation team building was by definition secure, and so the safest place. They'd set up their incident control headquarters beside it.

As blue lights flashed and armoured Land Rovers revved up and down the narrow streets, Duffy peered through a narrow gap in the curtains of the upstairs back room, looking across the yard and the end of the rear alley that led out to the road and the edge of the cordon. The remains of the SAS building were now lit up by sodium arc lamps, a diesel generator thumping. Armoured Land Rovers and Humber Pigs hissing with radios blocked the footpath. The cordon of soldiers guarded a row of moveable barriers, keeping back a gaggle of curious locals standing in the street behind.

Carragher had made a big point of ordering him to sit tight for at least a couple of hours. He'd been annoyed at this, as Carragher hadn't been too subtle in implying that he – Duffy – might be tempted to leave early. He'd kept looking at Máire as if relying on her to make sure this wasn't going to happen. Which had been when he'd realised that she'd known about this for months and that they didn't trust him – another bad moment in this shitty day.

Well, she wasn't here anymore – which was the one specific thing he wasn't going to think about right now. Only he could make this thing work, and success was the only way he could deflect the blame Carragher would soon enough be heaping upon him.

The forensic investigation vehicles were parking around the building. Eventually, once they'd finished, somebody would decide to allow the site to be cleared. So he waited for the bulldozers, backhoe loaders and heavy trucks to arrive. This would likely take several hours, so he went back downstairs to make that cup of tea.

A red-capped Royal Military Police corporal was sitting in a metal chair reading an out-of-date *Soldier* magazine. Straker was in a single room, rather than the main ward of the Army's casualty unit.

It was an effort for Straker to speak: "Where's Sergeant Major Jackson?"

The RMP corporal ignored him and picked up the telephone.

"Sir. The captain has regained consciousness."

"What time is it?"

The military policeman put the phone down and carried on reading.

A QA nurse came in and took Straker's pulse.

For a moment he was back in Seville, in sunshine. She had bright red lipstick and a beautiful flower in her hair. He smiled. She looked at him strangely. He got a grip of himself.

"What time is it?" he said again.

"Just before ten in the evening," she said.

It felt like he'd been unconscious for days: "On Monday?"

"No, Sunday," she answered, looking at him this time with concern. "You've only just been brought up here – less than half an hour ago, in fact..."

"Where's Sergeant Major Jackson?"

The QA looked at the RMP corporal, who shook his head.

"I'm sorry, sir," she said. "Just try to rest."

There were angry words in the corridor. A Royal Army Medical Corps captain with a stethoscope round his neck was remonstrating with an RMP major wearing barrack dress and gleaming brown leather shoes.

"You can't interview my patient until we've checked him over properly," said the captain. "Until then, you wait outside."

Straker raised his hand and pointed at the major. "Where's Sergeant Major Jackson?"

The RAMC captain pushed past the major and came over to the bed: "He'll be fine – he's just down the corridor, in fact. Some lacerations and burns, plus a concussion."

Straker felt a huge surge of relief at this news as his memories flooded back.

Jacko'd made it down the ladder, but when the bomb exploded he had been trapped under a door by some roof joists. Straker had pulled him free… Then, he supposed, the same thing had happened to him.

"So what's wrong with me – and why am I being guarded?"

"Concussion. But as for the guard, I don't know," replied the doctor.

Straker looked at the RMP major. "Am I in custody?"

The major nodded.

"Why?"

The major looked at him angrily: "Don't you mean 'Why am I in custody, *sir*'?"

Straker was already feeling nauseous from the concussion. An RMP major trying to pull rank on any captain was ridiculous enough, but from a staff officer fresh from "Slipper City" – the huge Army headquarters at Lisburn – was ludicrous.

"No, actually, I don't," snapped Straker. "If I'm under arrest, you have to caution me. So either do that or get the fuck out of here and take your monkey with you."

"You're out of order, Captain Straker. The RUC are on their way to interview you."

Straker kept his emotions flat. This was to be expected. He concentrated on the contempt he felt for this officer.

"So why are *you* here, and not my legal advisor?"

The Army Legal Service attended all RUC interviews. The RMP did not like being left out… But this was bullshit. There was something far more important than arguing to be done here, if only he could work out what it was.

I'll remember, he thought, *if I stop trying...*

The RMP major was talking again, less angrily now.

"Captain Straker, I'm actually here to help you."

"So tell me what I'm supposed to have done."

"You shot the woman who'd delivered the bomb."

"She was the bomber," said Straker. "She set it off using a model aircraft radio controller. I shot her, but she managed to trigger it anyway."

"She was six months pregnant. They couldn't save the baby..."

For fuck's sake. That's as bad as it's possible to get...

"She was a proxy bomber," the major continued. "Forced by the IRA to deliver the bomb in her pram – probably because they'd taken her other children. She was hiding until it went off."

"She doesn't have any children."

The major looked at him with a similar look of concern as the QA nurse.

"We're checking it out," he said gently.

"So that's the RUC story, is it?" said Straker. "I wonder who dreamed that up?"

The major's concern evaporated.

"You need to start taking this seriously, because very soon—"

"I recognised her," interrupted Straker. "She was Máire Carragher."

There was a silence. The major looked blank. He policed the Army, and so only rarely ventured out of Slipper City. Straker realised he knew nothing about terrorists.

"She's a serious hardliner. Séan Carragher's wife – you know... the Belfast Brigade commander."

"No..." The major shook his head with surprise and sudden confusion.

"Are you saying I got that wrong?" demanded Straker.

"I don't— *We* don't know about that," the RMP major rallied. "But we soon will.

"Regardless," he continued, "even *if*, in the darkness, you *did* see her well enough to make a positive ID, what was the Yellow Card threat? How could you genuinely believe an unarmed pregnant woman was going to endanger your life, and that you had no other option but to shoot her?"

Straker didn't respond. Maybe he *had* got this wrong...

"They found no weapon," the major continued. "And Felix says the bomb in the pram was detonated by a timer."

Straker could feel panic welling up inside him. He'd not been feeling right, but this was worse. The harsh neon strip lights overhead seemed to be flickering with a dry crackling sound that stank of disinfectant. He tasted bile and tried to swallow.

But then the weird dreams he'd been having in the frozen loft returned, in millisecond flashbacks like a strobe lamp. When you're bone-frozen cold and hadn't slept for days, your brain did strange things which you learned to accept. But this was reality.

He thought back to SAS Selection – psychological pressures that were harder than any of the physical stuff you were "invited" to do. This was why: the reality nobody tells you about.

But he wasn't going to lose it; especially not now. They'd done the job, and they'd done it well for the right reasons. He'd been as correct as it was possible to be; and, he believed, according to the Yellow Card Rules. So he remembered back to that quiet weekend in the Mess, before being summoned across the Irish Sea to all this dysfunction and unhappiness. He'd been enjoying the rugby, on his own, contented, hot buttered toast – at peace.

Slowly, slowly, he pulled himself back from the brink.

And then flashed up with sudden anger. How could this HQ staff officer be so cynical and amateurish? What gave him the right to think he knew better than the man on the ground? Straker had been there, eyes-on. Surely the explosion proved him right?

But another far more relevant question was, why hadn't he picked up the radio controller?

Suddenly Straker felt worse than he'd ever felt in his life. This wasn't what was supposed to happen. It was like being thrown into a very deep, dark well. He could feel himself spiralling downwards, into narrow black darkness and fear…

Down the rabbit hole…

He started counting, forcing his brain to slow down and take stock. *They'd got their theory and wouldn't want to hear anything else*, he thought. But he also knew there was something far more important. He needed to work it out – or just remember.

Straker liked being on his own. And right now he really *needed* to be on his own. But this wasn't going to happen. And once the

RUC arrived, things would get very much worse. His head felt like it would explode. He felt very sick.

"You're not going to get it, are you?" said Straker, speaking his thoughts out loud. "And it's actually very obvious. In fact, that's what's wrong... The whole thing was too bloody obvious."

"What do you mean?" demanded the RMP major.

"For starters, where we were in the building opposite. The only place from which you can overlook the PIRA flat and its front approaches. It's where an anchor OP *had* to be. Once you know somebody's watching a specific location, it's very much easier to spot them.

"Then there's the pram – which wasn't exactly covert, especially delivered right out in front of where we were."

"They've used prams before," said the major.

"Exactly," interrupted Straker. "It was obvious."

"Hang on," said the major. "You're saying Special Branch told the IRA you were watching the flat?"

"Certainly not. Why would they do that?"

The major flashed up with anger again: "You're making no sense, Captain Straker. Sounds like you've had a bang on the head—"

"Is that the Military Police diagnosis then?" interrupted a voice from the corridor. "It sounds much more to me like *you* need to start *thinking*."

Everyone turned as Jacko shuffled into the room, escorted by Hooves Rendall. He was wearing Army pyjamas and a black and white dressing gown, face red and blistered, collar-length hair patchy and shrivelled. He brought with him a strong smell of burning – as if, thought Straker, he had come directly from Hell.

Jacko stood in front of the RMP major.

"You and everyone else in Slipper City will go along with whatever Special Branch say, won't you?"

The major looked intimidated by this angry and very dangerous-looking person.

"So this entire crock of shit gets dumped into our laps. That's about right, isn't it... *sir*?"

The major went pale.

Straker gestured to the doctor. "I'm feeling ill. I need you to get rid of these policemen and check me over."

The doctor turned to the major, who shrugged, then pointed at the RMP corporal indicating the door. They both left.

The doctor closed the door behind them and came over to Straker's bed.

"Listen, chaps, all this has become a little too *busy* for my liking. We need to get everything settled down so we can do the medical stuff properly. My name's Michael Morton."

Jacko nodded his agreement. Morton and Straker shook hands.

"Thanks, Doc," said Straker. "But there is one thing we need to do first – get a message to my unit."

Jacko intervened: "The Farmer's on watch outside in the corridor. Forensic took our weapons, but he's still got comms with HQ."

Morton nodded. "He refuses to leave; a huge man wearing an ear-piece."

Straker nodded: "Can you get him in here, please?"

Morton turned to the nurse. "We need to keep people out of here. So strip Captain Straker ready for a full examination, and don't let anyone into the room until I get back."

Straker realised he was still wearing his wet clothing – less the woollen hat, overcoat, and filthy boots. He tried to stand up, then felt suddenly dizzy. The QA grabbed his arm and sat him back down on the bed, where all he could do was try to stop the room from spinning.

He didn't know for how long, but after some time, a huge and unconvincing-looking male nurse wearing theatre greens pushed into the room.

"Hi, boss. What do you think of my new ID?"

The Farmer, even though he'd washed his face and roughly shaved, looked nothing like an A&E medic, despite being exactly that in the Regiment. He grinned at the sight of Straker being stripped by a female nurse.

Outside in the corridor, there were raised voices. The Royal Military Police major burst in but then stopped, embarrassed by Straker's nakedness. The Farmer turned and looked very carefully down at him.

"You are so not allowed to be in here, major," he said quietly. "And you're leaving right now, aren't you?"

The major went bright red with anger, suddenly uncertain of his position, but realising he was out of his depth. A captain in barrack dress entered the room. The rank slides on the epaulettes of his woolly pully indicated he was Army Legal Service. He pushed the major out of the way.

"I'm Captain Straker's legal advisor, Captain Steve Riley."

The major retreated, shouldering past his corporal who'd been enjoying the drama. Dr Morton closed the door on them.

"Right, guys," said Dr Morton, "that's enough people in here. And now we really do need to get on with the medical stuff."

Straker nodded absently, then gestured to the Farmer. "Do we still have anybody at the bomb scene?"

"No, boss. After the front of the building collapsed and we'd dragged you and Sergeant Major Jackson out, the Army and RUC arrived in force. They took over and bagged our weapons. Hooves and I came here in the ambulance with you and Sergeant Major Jackson."

"What about the police cut-offs?"

"Nope – all out. The coppers seemed very keen to get everybody away from there asap…"

Straker realised that, apart from the SITREPs he'd transmitted before shooting Máire Carragher, none of what he'd seen had been reported. Felix and the forensic investigators would have only whatever was left on site from which to determine what had happened. The police narrative was wrong.

"Are you still in comms?" said Straker.

Dr Morton had been growing increasingly impatient and now pushed in between Straker and the Farmer.

"Captain Straker. Enough. I need to examine you properly…"

Straker looked vaguely at Morton, as if he'd forgotten who he was. But then, his attention suddenly snapping back into the present, he held up his hand like a policeman stopping traffic.

"Two minutes, please," he said. "I need to report to our unit. Then you can do whatever you like with me."

Straker transmitted a brief summary of what had happened and exactly what he'd seen, then lay back on the bed.

CHAPTER 6

Bomb disposal officer Major Robin Carlisle of the Royal Army Ordnance Corps, radio codename Felix, was having problems with the police.

"I've just heard from the Det that the SAS officer insists this wasn't a timer initiation."

"No way," said the RUC inspector dismissively. "They'd never use a radio bomb here."

"I'm concerned about what he's saying," said Major Carlisle.

"There's no evidence of radio initiation," said the inspector. "Just the crater and shrapnel marks on the road."

"This is *my* investigation, Inspector," said Major Carlisle firmly, "and there's no evidence of a timer."

"This is the city, Major," said the inspector patronisingly. "It's not like a country road where they're trying to hit specific Army or police vehicles as they pass by."

Felix knew far more about this than the inspector, but didn't rise to the bait.

"There's no need for them to use a radio here," he continued. "In any case, even out in the countryside, rather than have all the hassle of using a radio, they use very long wires and car batteries."

Major Carlisle was used to RUC officers presuming to know more about bombs than he did. And he didn't mind their obduracy. But he *was* interested in what seemed like a refusal to consider the SAS officer's eyewitness report.

"For PIRA to have their team near enough to this bomb to use a command wire would be risky," he replied. "And PIRA doesn't take risks without good reason."

The inspector shrugged.

"There's no need to take risks in urban areas," he said disinterestedly. "Damage and fear are guaranteed in here, with people and buildings so close together; they're not particular about who gets hurt apart from themselves."

"But this is West Belfast, Inspector O'Callaghan," replied Major Carlisle. "The buildings they damage here and the people they kill and hurt are their own. A timer bomb with no warning in the Republican heartland sounds most unlikely to me. Unless PIRA phoned in a warning that you're not telling me about…?"

Major Carlisle's unanswerable jibe made the inspector's ears tinge red and he looked away.

"The SAS captain's model aircraft story is nonsense," he muttered. "In Belfast, PIRA just use timers."

"OK," said Carlisle. "That's your theory."

"It's a fact," said the inspector.

"There's no evidence," continued Carlisle, "so I'm interested in why you're so certain of this – why you're so *insistent…*"

The inspector shrugged again.

"It's obvious. No need to go complicating things."

"Well, Inspector, I've asked you the question," replied Carlisle. "So if there's something you're not saying that backs you up, now's the time to tell me. Otherwise, I'm the expert and I'm keeping an open mind."

"Suit yourself," said the inspector rudely. "But we'll be clearing the site as soon as the plant arrives."

"Actually," replied Carlisle, "you won't be doing anything until I tell you I've completed my investigation."

The inspector was tired, needing to get home, but was not allowed to leave the bomb-site circus until the RUC forensics had finished. He'd already told them to wrap it up, and was about to tell Major Carlisle who was really in charge here, when the Royal Engineers troop commander walked across.

"Hello, sir," he said to Carlisle. "The earth movers will be here in ten."

"That's excellent. Liaise with Inspector O'Callaghan here about where to park up. You won't be doing anything until you get the order from me, in person."

This was another West Belfast Sunday night, now creeping over into yet another week. The RUC's senior officers were with their families at home, after morning church and the obligatory full-on roast with three veg and sticky pudding. But for most of the Army, over here on six-month tours with a week's leave in the middle, Sundays were the same as any other day.

More than twenty vehicles were now parked behind and around the remains of the SAS op building, illuminated by a string of harsh sodium lights on heavy duty tripods. The incident control point hummed with conversation and the clatter of electricity generators. Protected by a ring of troops in full riot gear with armoured Land Rovers, it was business as usual for the forensic specialists and Army bomb disposal and military engineers.

A square nine-by-nine frame tent extended from the rear of the Command Post Land Rover, neon light and radio noises escaping every time one of the watchkeeping staff slipped in and out of its overlapping curtain entrance. With everyone working, the explosive-detection dogs were given a break from their Land Rover's armour-plated kennels, proceeding to mark the territory with canine thoroughness.

These dogs, despite their purpose, seemed to bring with them a touch of normality. They hadn't been tasked, so were politely checking everybody out, tails wagging. A female Greenfinch police officer knelt on the broken tarmac to make a fuss of one of the dogs, a young German Shepherd. His handler, a corporal in the Royal Army Veterinary Corps, offered her a cigarette, explaining this was the dog's first operational outing. They drank dreadful coffee from the green plastic vacuum urns, eating sandwiches from the haybox all-day 'lunches' dropped off by the Royal Engineers quartermaster.

Major Carlisle's careful re-examination of the explosion point revealed nothing more than black burn marks. So he clambered carefully through the remains of the still-standing facade of the chip shop. The yard and its gate revealed nothing. He looked across to the ruined shops that stood between the bomb and where Straker said the woman had triggered it. He was pretty sure they would have screened a triggering radio signal from reaching the pram bomb's detonation circuit.

Carlisle could find nothing to disprove what the police were telling him. But he disliked their insistence – and Inspector O'Callaghan's manners – so he continued his search with particular diligence.

CHAPTER 7

"We're still too focussed on what's just happened," announced Straker after being examined. He looked unconvincingly vague, lying back on his pillows to stare at the ceiling.

"I shot the woman – Máire Carragher," he continued, speaking quietly. "And in the same instant she blew the pram by radio control, but now the controller is missing..."

Jacko and the Farmer looked at each other. Dr Morton backed off and stood leaning against the wall with his arms folded.

Captain Riley looked like he was about to tell Straker not to say any more. But then he seemed to understand where this was going, so he didn't. Whereas Jacko looked irritated.

"Only the IRA knew there was a controller," continued Straker. "So it was them who took it."

Jacko was worried. Straker sounded fixated on this mysteriously disappeared radio controller. Was this his cover story, which he was now trying to get established in front of the lawyer? Or was he being truthful, but had imagined it?

Jacko didn't mind either way, as he'd have shot the woman just the same. The positive ID would have been enough for him. Sort out the story later.

But Jacko could also see that Straker was looking ill and weak. He was sounding totally unconvincing. This scene wouldn't play well for either of them at a court-martial, so he needed to stop it.

He looked pointedly across at Dr Morton, who straightened up and moved to Straker's elbow.

"Leave it, Doc," said Straker. "I need to make myself understood."

"You need to rest," said Morton.

"I agree," replied Straker. "I feel ill and very tired. So don't interrupt me."

Morton shrugged. Jacko kept quiet.

"We're in West Belfast," continued Straker, who was now slurring slightly. "No commercial targets, unlike in the city centre. Plus apart from us, they're all friendlies. Collateral damage means killing your own people..."

"So what's your point?" said Jacko, as gently as he could manage.

"PIRA bombs in West Belfast are intended to kill security forces."

"Yeah, sure, boss – nobody's gonna disagree with you on that."

"And we don't know how long PIRA had been planning this op... It wasn't just cobbled together on the day."

Again, Jacko agreed with Straker's logic.

"That guy in the flat had been there for several days, making it look to us like something was happening," continued Straker. "So why did they run it like an opportunist hit – something on the spur of the moment, as if they'd just realised we were in there, with all the extra risk of delivering the bomb so we could see it?"

Jacko shrugged.

"And why, most of all, would they take the huge risk of going back to get the controller?"

At this, Jacko's heart sank. Straker *was* fixated on this idea he'd dreamed up. It wasn't going to work as a cover story because everybody knew radio-detonated bombs were too unreliable for PIRA to use in urban areas.

"So," continued Straker, whose voice was fading, making him sound confused and uncertain, "there's only *one* reason that the risk could be worthwhile."

Something about how Straker emphasised the phrase "one reason" stopped Jacko from interrupting. Captain Riley moved as if to say something, but then didn't.

Oh fuck, thought Jacko. *He's right – this is standard countryside bombing tactics. We are too focussed on what just happened. Like he says, we should be thinking about what happens next.*

Jacko's eyes widened like he'd been electrocuted. He grabbed the Farmer's elbow. "Give me your radio headset."

The Farmer must have reached the same conclusion as he swore quietly under his breath, then pulled the throat mic out from where it was concealed inside his shirt. He made a check call to the Det ops room then nodded to Jacko.

"Nines with Zero both ways."

The Farmer unclipped the elastic and handed it over.

Jacko pushed in the ear-piece and pressed the contact mic to his throat. The cable was still down the front of the Farmer's shirt, so they had to squeeze up close – a green polar bear cuddling a sunburned penguin.

"Hello, Zero," said Jacko, establishing comms with the radio operator in the SAS ops room. "This is One-Zero Alpha, sunray minor speaking. Who's the duty officer?"

"Roger. Is he *immediately* available?" he continued after a pause.

"Come on, come on," muttered Jacko, nodding his head with impatience. He leaned over to Straker.

"The Troop Sergeant Major's coming. I suggest you let me talk to him – at least initially…"

Straker nodded.

"Yeah, it's Jacko… We're at Musgrave Park…"

They were on the SAS's own encoded net, so he could talk in clear.

"We're both just about OK – stuck in here for a few days. Listen, much more important. You've got to get the police to evacuate that cordon and seal off the area, as there's another bomb in there, probably concealed in the rear of our building…"

Doc Morton looked anxiously across to Captain Riley, who nodded his agreement with Straker's and now Jacko's assessment.

"Yeah, correct," said Jacko. "Right where I expect SOCO's set himself up…"

The Army couldn't actually order the RUC to do anything, so getting everybody to leave wouldn't be easy.

"Well, that's as may be," argued Jacko. "But nevertheless, you're going to have to persuade them to get out of there asap."

Jacko's voice rose very slightly in volume, and he spoke noticeably slower.

"Listen, mate, take it from me, I'm still the man on the ground and you're still just doing nice comfy ops-room stags. Until you know any better, you do what I say. You know that— So what if I'm now in fucking hospital…?"

Jacko was now looking alarmingly angry. Doc Morton's anxiety made him look at Straker, who was now sitting calmly as if thinking about something completely different.

"OK… listen very carefully," said Jacko. "Our lawyer is standing beside me right now. So you'd better be getting this entire conversation written down verbatim in the signals log. Roger so far?

"Yeah, good. And if some fucker blows all those people up because you refused to take me seriously, you're shithouse paper.

"Yeah, I'm sorry too. But there's no time for any misunderstandings here…"

Jacko shook his head.

"Yeah, yeah, mate – so if I'm wrong, you know where I am. Just get on with it… And make sure the withdrawal is as covert as you can manage. For obvious reasons."

Jacko breathed in deeply, held it for a moment, then exhaled slowly and deliberately. He handed the radio harness back to the Farmer.

He then looked across at Straker.

"So, boss… Let's hope you're right."

CHAPTER 8

0200 - MONDAY 1 DECEMBER 1980

Duffy looked at his watch. He'd slept for a couple of hours, exhausted at the end of this long, tense day.

With a surge of adrenalin he realised Carragher had not phoned him back. It would have been a breach of security, but Duffy had half-expected it.

The night was totally dark, the streetlights not working. All he could see was an umbra from the sodium lights as a glowing backdrop to the rain.

The mechanism was simple enough; just one movement to power the bomb-end switch that fired the detonator. But these weren't factory-made, specific-to-purpose circuits with all the arming and safety mechanisms you'd see in a quarry explosive system or military munitions. They were cleverly modified, but home-made and tested only for function and not failure. Ensuring they didn't go off prematurely was impossible. This happened often enough to be an expected occupational hazard.

It was the Kraft Series Seventy-Three controller; a square, yellow-enamelled metal box with a black rectangle and the "Kraft" logo, two short joysticks and a telescopic aerial. Its user manual warned in red writing:

"*Remember: failure to fully charge batteries prior to each flying session may result in the model going out of control causing potential personal injury to others or to yourself as well as property damage.*"

Hence his first action on arriving at the safe house had been to connect up the battery charger. Duffy appreciated the irony, but the point was to avoid all *unintentional* dangers. Carragher rammed this message home on every operation, to minimise the numbers of innocent casualties:

"Indiscriminate IRA bombs are as dangerous to the Cause as

the British Army," he'd say. "We need to move from random terrorist bombings to precision attacks."

But Duffy found it fucking frightening. He'd much rather be working in a nice warm shed somewhere in South Armagh making these things, than being permanently scared to death delivering them. But you couldn't just do whatever you wanted. There were politics to becoming a bomb-maker. The top guys had been at it for decades having paid serious dues; bomb "factories" did not have extractor fans, and used shovels and cement mixers to mix massive amounts of weedkiller with diesel fuel and other noxious chemicals. They suffered respiratory and skin damage, and the chemicals regularly caught fire or randomly exploded.

Duffy's interest was the electronics, specifically methods of initiation – like this model aircraft system. With current technology, most of the time you just put fuses or timer units into bombs, which you placed, then ignited or set, and walked steadily away. It was different out in the countryside where you were trying to hit Army vehicles at the instant they drove past.

Duffy was too tired to feel any of the elation others said they felt at times like this. And also more worried about something going wrong with the controller.

So Duffy now disconnected the four-pin charger plug from the bottom of the Kraft Seventy-Three box, and walked upstairs to the rear bedroom. After checking that the transmitter switch remained in the "Off" position, he partially extended its telescopic aerial from the top of the box.

The controller could remotely activate up to six servo motors, rotating their little wheels clockwise or anti-clockwise. Its rudder circuit had triggered the initial pram bomb. From the elevated position of this rear window, Duffy didn't really need an antenna; but even so, after opening the window he pulled the telescopic aerial out to its fullest extent. Its green and blue radio frequency ribbons were stained with dried blood.

There'd been considerable debate about whether to withdraw from the bomb scene. Inspector O'Callaghan refused to believe there was another bomb. The Army had brought in their explosive-detection dogs, but he refused to let them search for a bomb that wasn't there.

Major Carlisle had already experienced Inspector O'Callaghan's keenness to clear the site. But now the inspector was reluctant to order the withdrawal as this would mean the forensic circus stopping work until it relocated, further delaying site clearance.

But the police SOCO, the Scene of Crime Officer, had refused to be held responsible if there was to be a second explosion. Immediately he'd learned of the warning, he'd ordered all his people away from the damaged building. The infantry company commander complied, expanding his cordon by another two rows of streets all round. The RUC told Republican community leaders to evacuate the rest of the houses. There were no protests. Everybody in Belfast understood this kind of thing.

Major Carlisle extracted himself from this bad-tempered situation and continued working, now alone inside the secured cordon. He took photographs and, as always, noted every thought in his notebook. His armoured bomb suit was too heavy and restrictive for clambering over rubble, so he'd left it in the 321 Explosives Ordnance Disposal Company main equipment truck.

He now focussed his attention on the firing point behind the shops. Regardless of whichever method had been used to detonate the bomb, this was where the evidence – if any had survived – would be found.

This time Duffy was going to activate the second control, for the servo that made the aircraft's nose go up or down – the Pitch. Carragher had marked the toggles with arrows of black paint. Judging by the bomb specifications Carragher had given him, Duffy expected the entire street and the car park behind the SAS observation building would be levelled – including the remains of the shops and severely damaging the line of houses on the other side of the entry where Máire had been killed.

Duffy was doing it by the book – as had Carragher in setting up the operation. The lightning conductor on the target building's chimney, the top of which Duffy could see, was the aerial, connected by the building's earth wire to the other end of the UHF radio connection, and had been tested by Carragher.

Duffy placed the fully extended aerial outside the opened sash window. The night air was cold and dank, with the oddly sweet smell of coalsmoke. But it seemed quiet, almost tranquil, the sodium halo from the arc lights picking out a silhouette of the bomb building's roof and chimney. He was glad he couldn't see the incident control point. And the sirens would arrive quickly enough to drown out the screaming.

Duffy was tired, but no longer anxious – blank, like the spare pages at the end of a user manual. He put his thumb on the right toggle. Carragher had marked the left-pointing arrow "B". Duffy pushed the toggle gently in that direction. Nothing happened, which felt to him like his heart had stopped. Panicking, he pushed it hard over, like he was controlling a German dive bomber.

This blast was very much larger than the first. It completely destroyed the SAS building. What remained of the row of shops collapsed backwards as if hit by an Old Testament wind.

The sergeant major of 321 EOD Company immediately cordoned off the second blast zone. He refused to allow anyone apart from the EOD team to enter until they'd completed a painstaking search with the three bomb dogs.

The young Alsatian did his job. Although afterwards, the handler wondered about exactly where the second bomb had been. He remembered standing at the rear of the building chatting up the policewoman while his dog took a break from the cage. They'd been smoking. He'd thought the dog seemed interested in something. But the young dog hadn't given the specific sign – which was to sit and not move. Instead he'd lifted his leg and pissed on the wall.

You couldn't report that.

The handler shivered, then deliberately put it out of his mind. This was just the start of their two-year tour.

Slowly the rest of the area was cleared of further bombs. They were very thorough.

The Company sergeant major's report estimated the bomb as twenty pounds of Semtex-H, built into the brick cavity of the derelict building's rear wall. He knew from similar bombs that had failed to detonate that the new mortar would have been smeared with old mortar scraped from the rear of building, carefully blended in to match.

"The initiation mechanism was probably concealed behind the original internal plasterboard in airtight plastic bags that prevented K9 detection. The installation had in all probability been facilitated several months earlier."

There was no evidence as to how either of the bombs had been detonated.

And Major Carlisle was dead, the last of his nine lives crushed beneath ten feet of rubble.

CHAPTER 9

Stanhope Chapman took the pre-arranged call on his STU-1 secure phone, in a soundproofed booth that in more civilised times had been the pantry in the small kitchen of his office suite. The voice terminal was a converted DTMF 5-line Western Electric telephone set, which rang like a normal phone.

"So it all got complicated," said the voice, with an unmistakable Antrim twang. "Our friends took the bait, which turned out to be even more poisonous than we'd imagined."

Chapman squeezed the PTT bar on the handset – the push-to-talk.

"I just heard about the second explosion," he said.

"That was the unexpected bit. Extremely well played, I thought. There should have been terrible loss of life."

"So why wasn't there?"

Chapman had learned to ask the questions then wait.

"An SAS captain saved the day."

Chapman waited some more.

"He seems to have worked it out, then managed to persuade everybody to evacuate the danger area before it blew."

"So he's home for tea and medals?"

"Aah, I really don't know about that."

"So where does this leave Mr Carragher's merry band?"

"Like I said, it's complicated. Depends on how he plays it. And also what the RUC decide they need to do about it."

Chapman briefly pressed the PTT to speak but changed his mind, clipping his Antrim source's next transmission:

"—a real mess. They need to be seen to be in control."

"Of what?" snapped Chapman.

"Of the Army. This looks like more Army undercover stuff."

"But she *was* the bomber?"

"I'd say so – and not exactly the mumsy type. But presenting her as a victim of the SAS gets them off the hook for having been duped. And as nobody except the captain knows what actually happened, it could work."

"So Mr Carragher isn't terribly happy."

"He is not happy at all. Plus he's got some presentational work to do himself."

Chapman got it. "This must have been a long-term set-up intended to prove his methodology," he said. "They need to impress the Libyans."

"They do," came the reply. "So I reckon without the captain, there'd have been a bloodbath – not to mention PIRA regaining its mojo. But the police aren't seeing it like that."

They never did, thought Chapman as he rang off, then walked through into his main office.

Through the plate glass he could look across the river towards the Palace of Westminster, where a huge Union Flag flew lazily from a gilded pole over the turrets and crenellations of the Victoria Tower. There would be as many perspectives to this as there were Honourable Members sitting on those green leather benches. The trick was never to comply with any of them.

At Musgrave Park Hospital, Straker was finally on his own, with just the Farmer as his improbable-looking nurse having been temporarily absorbed into the hospital infrastructure. The RUC had not arrived as Straker had expected, and Doc Morton had told him about the second bomb exploding.

"You're proved right," he'd added. "Vindicated."

Straker had stood up, gone completely pale, then collapsed awkwardly into the chair beside his bed.

"Was anybody killed?" he said.

Morton's disinclination to reply was obvious.

"Well?" said Straker.

"The bomb disposal major."

Straker seemed not to hear:

The police were over-extended, he thought. *Short-staffed over the weekend, looking for short-cuts and now too busy reacting. Clever PIRA planning.*

He knew he'd made a very serious mistake in not picking up the model aircraft controller unit – too focussed on his own safety he thought, not thinking laterally. And then he'd allowed himself to get preoccupied with getting the team out, and at the hospital, taking far too long to order the evacuation of the area. A second bomb was a very obvious possibility, especially as – unlike everybody else – he'd actually seen the controller.

Felix's continued site investigation could only have been to determine if the bomb had been initiated by timer or by radio. Which to Straker meant that the only person who'd been prepared to believe him was dead because he'd not been thinking straight immediately after the shooting. And now everybody else seemed to think he'd imagined the controller, or was lying about it to justify shooting Máire Carragher.

Despite trying very hard not to think about Máire Carragher, Straker was haunted by three images. The first: her appearance, pushing the pram, and how distracted he'd been by her really great legs – voyeurism prompted by boredom? But they were looking for anything that stood out from the rest. Would he have noticed her otherwise? Or then remembered her the next day? Voyeurism maybe, but it had led him to take action. It was a ridiculous scruple – but not to acknowledge it was dishonest.

The second image was poorly painted in weak neon light from the rear of the fish and chip shop, of Máire crouching, miniskirt around her waist, staring at him with eyes that seemed to glow.

And the final image: her like a doe, on her side and dying into a slowly expanding pool of black blood. This image was leached of emotion, with just the sadness of what could have been, oozing outwards with shiny finality across the dirt of the alley.

Duffy had been picked up by Roxy in the darkness just before dawn, on the corner of Sevastapol and Odessa Streets, just off the Falls. This was as previously arranged; and since triggering the second bomb, Duffy had thought of little else other than not showing, running, and his chances of surviving.

He had, however, kept the controller in its box despite the danger of being caught with it by the security forces. Carragher frightened him much more than they did.

Neither had talked, Duffy smoking nervously until they reached the safe house. As they clattered to a halt, the front door opened and Duffy was pointed upstairs. He dropped the cigarette to the pavement and stood on it.

The back bedroom was bare, newspapers blanking out the windows, with a small Formica-topped table and two chairs. Carragher was clean-shaven but gaunt and looked exhausted, bundled up against the cold in his dark green parka.

"Tell me all about it," he said, pointing to the chair on the other side of the table where he was sitting.

There was an ashtray, but it was empty and clean. Duffy suppressed his almost overwhelming desire for yet another cigarette.

Duffy's account was self-serving, but he stuck to the facts as benefitted him, trying to avoid anything that might sound self-aggrandising. Fear made him coherent, answering Carragher's questions clearly without stuttering. But he avoided looking directly at Carragher. Máire's blood still covered his hands and the front of his jacket.

"I only remembered about the radio controller after Máire died," he said. "She was face down in the darkness. There was a lot of blood, but I couldn't see much. I rolled her over into the recovery position and started doing CPR."

Carragher showed no emotion. Duffy had expected rage, so this was alarming.

"She'd been lying on the controller, so when I realised she was dead, I took it."

Carragher remained silent.

"I was expecting more SAS to appear," continued Duffy, "and Máire was dead. So I took it and carried on with the mission."

"You said you'd kept close to Máire…"

"Close enough."

Carragher just looked at him.

"I didn't see the SAS guy until after the explosion."

"That would be after he'd killed Máire…?"

"I'd come into the cut from the top end," said Duffy. "I was checking back for anyone following me."

"That's when the bomb went off…?"

Duffy nodded.

"This guy must have done the same thing," said Carragher.

"What do you mean?"

"After shooting Máire and immediately running away down the other end, like you just told me."

Duffy pretended not to understand.

"He must have looked around for anyone with her?"

Duffy stayed blank.

"You said you were close to her. So when he looked back you must have seen his face?"

Duffy couldn't work out if Carragher was saying he should have shot the guy, so he just nodded.

Then Carragher went blank, staring at the scratched patterns on the Formica table for what seemed a long time but was probably only thirty seconds or so.

"So what did you do after picking up the controller?"

Duffy was surprised at Carragher's apparent lack of interest in Máire's actual death, and tried not to worry about why this might be.

"You went back up the cut," said Carragher. "In the opposite direction to the SAS guy?"

"Yeah – straight to the safe house."

"But you said you'd cut round away from the second bomb?"

Duffy immediately realised his mistake. The safe house was only a couple of streets away, in line of sight to the chimney of the factory with the second bomb. In his initial panic, he'd run away, thinking only of distancing himself from the whole thing and ditching the controller box.

"Máire had decided it would be safer to approach the safe house from the opposite direction," he lied. "So I did a bit of a loop-round using the back alleys."

Once more, he waited to see if Carragher would accept this.

"So when did you leave the safe house?"

"I waited an hour after firing the second bomb," Duffy replied. "Until there were people out on the street. Then I walked back up onto the Falls."

"What route?"

"Leeson Street."

"And what did you do before the time to meet Roxy?"

"Hid in Dunville Park."

"And the radio controller?"

"That's why I hid in the park."

Carragher seemed not to understand.

"I gave it to Roxy," Duffy added quickly.

Carragher stopped asking questions and sat for several very long minutes, staring at him.

Duffy was now completely numb. Even the intense anxiety he'd been suffering since seeing the SAS man kill Máire was now smothered under a blanket of nervous exhaustion. So he stared at the Formica.

Eventually Carragher snapped his fingers and pointed to the door. Duffy got carefully to his feet, legs numb, only now realising how terribly cold it was in this cramped little room.

CHAPTER 10

MONDAY NIGHT 1 DECEMBER 1980

Carragher had contained his rage by stalking out of the investigation he'd so rapidly convened, leaving them staring at each other in confusion. After more than 12 hours there was nothing to show.

He'd returned to the safe house, to the other upstairs room to lie on the bed. After an hour of swirling, unwanted thoughts, he gave up and went downstairs, drank a tepid cup of black tea with sugar, then left the house. Ignoring Roxy, who tailed him in the black cab, he walked slowly back to the church hall to re-join his brigade command team.

He grimaced on entering the meeting room, which was rank with tobacco smoke. A wall-mounted Our Lady of Carmel presided over one end of the long wooden table, whose polished surface was now burned along its edges with cigarette grooves. Two huge pub ashtrays sat in the middle, full to overflowing.

Carragher wore a black cashmere sweater, a dark blue polo shirt and Levi's Sta-Prest trousers. He was fifteen years younger than his predecessor – just thirty-five, with the clear-cut look of a professional football club manager. When making his intentions clear, he could moderate the harshness of his West Belfast accent like he was being interviewed on television. But as his staff team was beginning to realise, in this first crisis since his predecessor's abrupt arrest and incarceration by the security forces, he didn't play games. And as he didn't drink or tolerate drinking on duty, these proceedings had been systematic and far more thorough than they'd expected.

Somebody had talked. But in West Belfast, PIRA activities were top-grade gossip, and everybody knew each other, so *everybody* talked. Which was why only a carefully selected few were privy to what Carragher was doing, and they knew to expect brutal penalties for telling anybody else. Security breaches were a threat to his authority. He'd made a couple of ferocious examples early in the tenure of his command, to get this over to the rest of the Belfast Brigade; later he released the story and some photographs to *An Phoblacht* to show the Republican community he was serious.

He'd then imposed a new type of cell structure, to limit what people knew. Only the ASU involved in a specific operation knew about it, and then only what they needed to know to carry out their part. The brigade staff knew only what Carragher told them personally. The quartermaster who supplied the weapons and explosives knew only what brigade staff told him to supply, and when to expect the weapons back. Discussions outside the command structure were discouraged in the strongest possible way.

However, for all that, the skill with which PIRA had just been outmanoeuvred could only have come from in-house knowledge. Except that this had been a totally secret operation known only to Carragher and Máire, with Duffy the team leader told only on the morning of its execution.

So even without Máire's death, the security breach alone was a grievous challenge to Carragher's authority. He'd made them fear him – but not, it seemed, enough to deter this traitor. He also knew there were people who hated him.

This long, stressful day and much of the night had been deeply unpleasant, a progression of uncertain, frightened Volunteers brought in to face detailed questioning. The "need-to-know" system guaranteed that the informant could only be one of them, so each felt the fear. The care and clarity with which Carragher had conducted the interviews filled them with foreboding. But nothing definite had emerged.

Carragher's fury and grief had surged like waves against a cliff, which he'd suppressed with icy determination. His reputation was on the line, even though his planning had been faultless. He'd played a long, patient game, from a year ago when he and Máire had rigged the building. He'd personally collected the Semtex, Cordtex and detonators from the Northern Command Quartermaster General over a period of months, skimming off small amounts from materials ordered for other ops. If the Northern Command QM had noticed this, the only person he'd have told was Carragher.

So nobody knew.

His appointment to brigade commander had not been popular, but even if somebody had dicked him to the security forces, they certainly hadn't been following him. Could they have followed Máire? *Unlikely*, he thought, as they both took precautions. In any case, the security forces wouldn't have held back, but arrested them.

And why, after the first blast, had the entire security force roadshow moved back a couple of streets and escaped the second bomb – which was by far the hardest for them to detect?

He'd told O'Donnell about his plan to lure the SAS to the flat, although *not* about the hidden bomb. O'Donnell hadn't liked the plan, saying he wouldn't risk the reputation of his top-level police informer to pass on false information. So Carragher then told him about the hidden bomb, after which O'Donnell agreed the potential gain was worth the risk, and to use his informer.

The day before the bombing, another Special Branch informer told them the police had learned of the meeting. Later that day, O'Donnell's informer told them the meeting was under SAS surveillance.

The meeting of quartermasters was totally genuine, a much-needed assessment of PIRA's very real arms crisis. It was cancelled at the last minute on the morning of the bombing.

And that same morning, after the makers had delivered the pram bomb, Carragher had gone alone to the ASU safe house, and with Máire, briefed Duffy about the hidden bomb. Nobody else had been there. Carragher had handed over his folder of notes, maps, the modification kit for the bomb trigger, and the radio equipment. And after that, with Duffy far too immersed in the technicalities to protest, and everything in place ready, Carragher had left them to put his plan into operation.

It had been as secure as anybody could have made it.

The day before, Carragher had told his Chief of Staff to get a pram bomb made. Late in the day he ordered it delivered to the ASU. The Chief of Staff been told nothing else, and even then, had not been told the target.

"In terms of how it was done," said the Chief of Staff, "with such a short timeframe, we were going flat-out to get the bomb delivered to the ASU."

He took a sip from a flat bottle of Coca-Cola.

"But within the ASU, Máire wore the trousers – she got stuff done. Recce, delivery, timing... it was all down to her. Duffy was the technical guy – and I should say that it was news to us until afterwards that he'd converted the timer circuit we'd installed to radio detonation...

"For all of us – brigade staff and the ASU – it was extreme last-minute stuff. Only us here on the staff even knew the original target. *None* of us knew about the rigged building. We got to hear about that from Duffy afterwards..."

The Chief of Staff felt some kind of eulogy might ease the tension.

"So this has to be said," he added. "Without Máire, we'd never have been able to do it."

Carragher knew all this. And yes, it had to be said – as if this was a fucking funeral. But he knew it was self-serving. They were all making excuses.

But instead of exploding with rage, he nodded.

"So, yeah – there was a lot to do, in very little time. It was top-notch security, Séan. Nobody else knew."

Carragher's anger flashed up once again, but only in his eyes like a strobe light. Again, he shut it down.

But this time he could see that the Chief of Staff had noticed, pretending to refer to his notepad as if it was a written report.

"Well," said Carragher quietly, "clearly somebody else *did* know..."

He waited for the Chief of Staff to continue.

"The Brits moved in too fast for us to see them. No sign whatsoever – just an empty building. It was only from the source that we knew they were there."

"The *source* told you they were in?"

"Yes – the day before, when you ordered me to organise the bomb."

"Hang on – so none of *us* saw anything to confirm that the SAS were in?"

"We put people into the area to confirm it," replied the Chief of Staff. "But to be honest, in the end we didn't. They were too well concealed. And at the same time we were sorting out the bomb."

There was nothing to criticise in how the operation had been carried out. Especially not the preparations, which had been as efficient as it was possible to be.

"So dear God," said Carragher, his voice hoarse. "Everything we knew was from this one source? We'd found out nothing for ourselves?"

Carragher could see that as the SAS *had* been there, the others thought this was irrelevant.

They were still deflecting – none of them was getting it.

Carragher had now interviewed everyone involved. Carragher's conclusion was that security had *not* been compromised, and the tip-off and subsequent intelligence from the RUC had been accurate. But all he'd found was fear, concealment and dishonesty, which had taken such a long time to unravel.

He'd believed they understood security and the new way of working. This had damaged everything he'd set up, especially as it encouraged his detractors. And without new evidence, he was going to have to take the blame himself. They would say he'd been clouded by ambition then cleverly played; something he could not deny even to himself. And all of this alongside the dreadful possibility of their being infected at high-level by a double agent.

Laying it all out chronologically, he thought everything that had gone wrong stemmed from their relying on this anonymous, supposed RUC source.

But they'd *all* been played. So realising that this was the deepest hole, Carragher stopped digging. He let the tension grow for a full minute before speaking again.

"So why was it that Máire delivered the bomb?"

"We thought that's what had been ordered..." said the Chief of Staff, with careful phrasing.

"And why the fuck would you think that?"

Nobody answered this loaded question. Opposing Máire had been daunting enough before she'd taken up with Carragher. Then, once she'd become his wife, it was safer to assume that whatever she said was with her husband's approval.

"So what you're actually saying is that she told you *I'd* ordered this?"

Again, nobody spoke. One more question answered.

Carragher again changed the subject.

"And now, what's with the tout who told us the SAS was in that building?"

"He's disappeared," said the Chief of Staff.

"What do you mean *disappeared*?"

Another uneasy silence.

"So bring me the person he was talking to."

The Chief of Staff looked across to the Intelligence Officer, who nodded uneasily.

"That was me," he said.

"So why in the name of fuck did you believe him?"

"He's trusted," said the Intelligence Officer uncertainly, knowing as he said it that this was a bad answer. "He's got credibility from giving us that fella who'd betrayed the Armagh bank job back in November."

Carragher's anger suddenly faded.

"We never did quite get to the bottom of that one…" he said quietly.

"That fella admitted to it, though, didn't he?" said the Intelligence Officer, then looked around the room for support. "When you's guys interrogated him – admitting he'd grassed out while arrested at Gough Barracks…?"

The silence deepened. That had been a bad interrogation, carried out by the South Armagh Brigade, with Carragher present as their guest. But they'd been told what the man thought they'd wanted to hear so as to stop the torture. He'd actually known nothing, and it had ended as badly as such things could.

"At least that's what I was told," concluded the Intelligence Officer, deflating into the silence.

Uncharacteristically, Carragher lit one of the Chief of Staff's cigarettes. After two slow drags he stubbed it out carefully, though not without difficulty as the ashtray was so full.

"So you believed him because he'd given us one of our own guys?"

"But the word was that the guy had confessed…"

"Well, he fucking didn't."

There was another silence.

Carragher saw the Intelligence Officer take a deep breath; then he seemed to change his mind.

"You've got something to tell us?" suggested Carragher.

The Intelligence Officer looked away.

"What were you going to say?"

The Intelligence Officer went pale, but managed to find his voice.

"Only one person knew enough to warn the security forces about the second bomb."

Carragher waited. He knew the answer, but needed somebody else to say it. Everyone else was examining the tabletop.

"You'd got us all thinking it was an opportunist attack, a quick hit in response to the tip-off. So with Máire dead, it was only Duffy who knew about the second bomb."

"And me," said Carragher.

"So, yeah," replied the Intelligence Officer. "That would be right."

The room was very quiet now. It was like the rest of the world had been turned off.

"We're volunteer freedom fighters," said Carragher eventually, "in an army of liberation. We shouldn't be wasting our time on this kind of thing. If everybody obeyed security protocols, there'd be no leaks and we'd know exactly where to look for the traitors. But because some people won't do what they're told, we have to waste all this time frightening and hurting people – some of them being innocent… It's no fucking good.

"For fuck's sake," he shouted, pounding the tabletop with both fists, then standing up with disgust as the contents of the ashtray spilled onto his Sta-Prest Levi's.

He pointed at the man guarding the door. "Get a dustpan and brush and clean up this fucking shit."

He was about to sit down, then he saw the ashtray had fallen from the table onto his chair. He picked it up and hurled it. Instinctively, everyone round the table ducked. It hit the far wall, shattering into large chunks of inch-thick solid glass. A poster was damaged – one of a young woman in a polka dot skirt and black leather jacket aiming a rifle round a corner, with the caption "Cumann na mBan" – *Join the Women's Army.*

Carragher pointed at it, then shook his head and sat down.

"And that's exactly what this is," he said. "Fucking shit…"

He leaned forwards, elbows on the table, holding his head in his hands. This was an uncharacteristically negative posture. The tension in the room relaxed very slightly.

"So who is the guy who killed her?" Carragher demanded. "British Army?"

Nobody spoke.

"And these guys in the sabotaged building – they *were* SAS, right?"

The silence continued.

"And nobody saw them come in? Do we even know *when* they came in?"

Carragher might as well have asked them about ghosts; raising the spectre of the British Army's anonymous killers. The SAS were wraiths, a dread mythological force that could not be opposed. They represented PIRA's ultimate fear that the British state was unassailable, the excuse for failure and defeatism.

This operation was to have turned all that round. Northern Command had badly needed a morale boost. Their fervent hopes for exorcism had clouded judgment. Instead of the devil being cast out in unidentifiable pieces mixed with brick dust, it had grown stronger.

Carragher sat up, stood slowly, then pushed his chair back in. The bogeymen should have been blown back to Hell, but they'd side-stepped death like they'd been dead to start with.

"It shouldn't be like this," he said quietly, as if to himself.

Too much time has been wasted, he thought. Other things needed to be done.

He was now totally calm, recharged, with venom in his voice.

"We're missing something here – like somebody's jerking our chain. This isn't over, and I want to know who these people are."

Carragher didn't want to call O'Donnell. But his inquiry was going nowhere, so he couldn't put it off any longer.

"I don't know what went wrong," he told O'Donnell. "The operation was completed by Duffy, but it seems like they'd known and withdrew their people to safety before he—"

"The one casualty was ours," interrupted O'Donnell. "Máire."

"That's another thing I don't understand," admitted Carragher. "It wasn't the plan for *her* to trigger the bomb."

"No," snapped O'Donnell, "but we can both see the reasons for it. Brave and direct, I'd say."

Carragher had to agree. But he didn't respond.

"You dropped it on me as being a failure just because Máire was dead, like you'd given up on it, when it was still up and running," said O'Donnell. "You need to find out what happened, Séan, without any further pissing around."

Carragher accepted this.

"You've missed something crucial," continued O'Donnell. "That's *your* error, and it's a long ways from being anything like good enough...

"Máire died doing her duty, Séan – she succeeded in her part of *your* operation. So to honour her memory, you need to sort this out."

O'Donnell put the phone down as he didn't want to hear Carragher's response. To calm the anxiety he always felt during confrontations, he sat for a moment, thinking. They'd been played, and unless Carragher could work out how, it would indeed be a disaster. One for which O'Donnell would ensure Carragher would pay.

CHAPTER 11

Immediately after the explosion of the second bomb, the group's lawyer had given Jacko, Farmer, and Hooves strict instructions not to talk to anybody. Although such legal advice was standard practice after incidents, the lawyer had caught their attention by adding:

"I mean absolutely nobody at all – regardless of their rank. Just tell them you don't know anything. This is one of those things that never happened."

The next day, the Monday, Farmer and Hooves were driven straight from Musgrove Park to Aldergrove Airport and back to SAS Bradbury Lines Barracks in Hereford.

But Jacko being a member of the Northern Ireland Group, coming to the end of a standard one-year posting, that evening – after a truncated twenty-four hours observation period in hospital, had been picked up and driven to their base. He'd changed into a clean set of civilian clothes, signed out an unrigged runabout, side-arm, and radio, then driven back out of Belfast to the police station they were using as control to re-join the country arms cache surveillance operation he'd been pulled off.

The NI Group was an amalgamation of the Army's 14 Field Security and Intelligence Company – the SRU Special Reconnaissance Unit, sometimes referred to by their previous name, "the Det" – an SAS Troop, RUC Special Branch officers, plus spooks from MI5. The Army tended to stick together, while SB and the spooks barely talked to each other let alone to anyone else.

When Jacko clocked into the makeshift ops room, he'd been taken aside by the SAS Troop sergeant major, an old mate, who told him quietly: "We heard what happened with your observation exercise. And since then, there's been a serious clam-up from SB."

"I had to picturise the duty ops sergeant major," said Jacko. "There was no other way to get him to order the evacuation. Is that part of the problem?"

"No, mate – not at all. He wasn't happy but did as you'd told him. He's now extremely glad that you insisted. That's totally cool. However, there's a much greater problem, Jacko, but I don't know what it is."

There was a knock at the door. The sergeant major opened it a couple of inches.

"No, and I'm busy," he said. "But I'll be with you in ten."

He came back round to his desk, sat down and waited a moment.

"So, my concern is making sure you don't get into any of the shit that I think is about to start flying around."

Jacko was taken aback by the troop sergeant major's certainty, so he kept quiet.

"If you're not here, Jacko, then there's nobody they can blame – for whatever the fuck the problem is. With you gone, we can say it was a police operation, they're in charge, we don't know anything about it so fuck off."

Jacko got that.

"All I can say, Jacko, is to get yourself out of here right now, straight back to Hereford. Don't talk to anybody and don't spare the horses. You're not needed here – certainly not on this op, which is winding down. And you're on Days-to-Do anyway."

Jacko must have looked surprised. The sergeant major continued.

"The OC and I have talked this through. You're good to go." He looked at Jacko. "But just leave, OK? Don't pack your stuff – we'll send it over. Keep totally away from Main Group HQ. And buy yourself a civ-air ticket so your name doesn't come up on the Green Army system."

So Jacko handed back his pistol and radio, drove to the main civvie Aldergrove airport, dumped the car in long-stay and caught the first BA-747 shuttle to Heathrow. At Euston station he called the RSM at Hereford, and then the Det chief clerk, telling him where to find the car.

He arrived back at Bradbury Lines to find a memo requiring him to take coffee with the ops officer. He walked quickly past that door, for a private session with the RSM.

"It's a cluster-fuck out there," observed the RSM. "But this is different. Captain Straker has upset somebody, but I don't suppose they'll tell us."

Jacko sat down in one of the two armchairs.

"Whatever the headshed might think about things having changed over there," said Jacko, "the security is still crap. Guys in the Det talking to Loyalist paramilitaries and SB trying to impress their PIRA sources."

"We'd hoped it would improve," said the RSM. "But they've got to live out there and we don't. It's their war."

"All of which means," said Jacko, getting straight to the point, "that we're outside the loop – which is what's bothering me with Captain Straker still being out there."

"He didn't hit it off with the RUC chief inspector…?" said the RSM.

"All he did was ask questions," said Jacko. "After a massive kick-bollock-and-scramble to get there, and no one telling us anything."

"Asking questions makes you the enemy," observed the RSM.

"The people in the briefing room just sat there," said Jacko, "while the chief inspector tried to blank him. But we needed answers to the questions Captain Straker was asking."

"So was this chief inspector the senior police officer there?"

"Yes," replied Jacko. "And he ended up giving Captain Straker the 'wind your neck in' speech. He actually said, 'There are times, Captain, when you just have to obey orders'."

Both the RSM and Jacko had been in these situations: you made your point, then got on with it.

"So afterwards, when the others had gone, Captain Straker told our ops watchkeeper that he'd report when we were actually in the OP, and ordered him not to tell anybody when we left base."

The RSM raised an eyebrow but kept quiet.

"We had a lot to do before we could go out," continued Jacko. "So whatever the cops might have wanted, there was always going to be a day or so delay."

"Was Captain Straker being difficult?" asked the RSM.

"That's what I'd thought," said Jacko. "But now I'd say the chief inspector's shite attitude made him cautious, so he was making sure we'd got lots of time to get properly set up…"

"For what?"

"Well," said Jacko, "with hindsight…"

They both sat quietly for a moment.

"So when did you go in?" said the RSM.

"That same night."

The RSM nodded.

"We organised very quickly and did a really slick insertion. Captain Straker then waited a full twenty-four hours before telling the ops room to tell SB we were in position."

"How long after that was the attack?"

"Late afternoon the following day."

The RSM stretched back in his armchair and breathed out slowly.

"So those extra twenty-four hours gave you time to ID the players?"

"We went in at 0300 on the Thursday. Captain Straker reported us in position at 0300 on Friday morning, by which time we'd ID'd the regulars and worked out the basic street patterns.

"We reckon PIRA started recce-ing later on Friday, before placing the bomb on the Saturday afternoon," said Jacko. "That extra twenty-four hours allowed us to differentiate the new people, which was how we called the attack."

The RSM sat thinking for a moment.

"That's very good work," he said finally. "So you think somebody in the ops room was talking to PIRA?"

"I think Captain Straker did – or he thought they'd gossip about it around somebody who was leaking…"

"And you?"

"I didn't at the time," said Jacko. "But I do now."

They both sat in silence.

"Sounds more like a Special Branch fuck-up to me," said the RSM. "Coinciding with a really well-organised PIRA set-and-forget bomb."

"I agree," said Jacko. "The second bomb must have been in there for months. They made it look like somebody detected us in the OP then put in a quick bomb attack. Brilliant, really – giving them two chances to take us out, plus a lot of other people."

"Yes – lots of potential egg on Special Branch faces," continued the RSM. "But nobody got killed – at least not one of ours—"

"Thanks to Captain Straker," interrupted Jacko.

The RSM stood up from the armchair and walked across to reopen his office door.

"Seems like a Special Branch problem to me," he said. "Maybe also with the SRU – but not our guys. So sit tight, Jacko, and make sure the Farmer and Hooves are squared away to do the same."

Jacko stood up to leave, but then turned back to the RSM.

"Why is Captain Straker still over there?"

"The Board of Inquiry…" said the RSM.

"An inquiry into what, exactly?" asked Jacko.

The RSM shrugged.

"Terrorist shot while setting off bomb. Bomb goes off, use of deadly force justified. Explosion of second bomb averted by perception and tactical awareness of Special Air Service, everybody goes home for tea and medals."

"Yeah, right," said Jacko.

The RSM just nodded.

"We're also trying to get an answer. But with power shifted to the police, we don't have the same influence as before. You were well-advised coming straight back."

"Bit of a shame nobody advised Captain Straker," said Jacko.

"That's with the headshed," said the RSM. "Way above my pay grade."

"He should be back here," said Jacko. "This never happened before."

"What never happened before, Jacko?"

"Any of us being made to stay behind – let alone the officer…"

"You said it, Jacko – that was before. This is now, and it's high-level politics – headshed stuff."

"That's not good enough," muttered Jacko. "And you know it."

Jacko was out of order, but even though the last thing he wanted was to fall out with the RSM at this stage of what was clearly a big problem, he found himself hoping he'd get a dressing down, so he could argue back and get this out into the open.

Careers were one thing, he thought. *But this was leaving people behind. We don't do that.*

"Well, yes, Jacko," said the RSM wearily. "It's not good enough. But early days. Let's see how this plays out."

Jacko then realised he hadn't phoned his wife. This was always the big moment, the tour over, when for a little while she could let go of the constant anxiety he knew she hid from him and their daughter. Usually, he called her immediately on landing wherever in the UK it all finished up. This was the first time in their ten-year marriage that he'd not done it.

Jacko treated his military life like it was another country from which he came home. Maybe a better analogy was a submarine; on operations he was underwater and incommunicado, returning to harbour and normal life. Whereas now, for the first time, there was an overlap.

Also, this had been a particularly toxic operation, and it wasn't over yet. He was already slated to become a Squadron Sergeant Major – which led to RSM and commissioning as a Late Entry Captain. Seepage from this could foul it up, and the politics to which they'd been exposed could remove him from the SAS – or even from the Army. But Jacko was being realistic. Part of the job was ducking out of these things any way you could.

The RSM's comment about there being nobody to advise Captain Straker bothered Jacko the most. This was unusual for Jacko. Experience in the SAS had rammed home the importance of self-sufficiency above everything else. You had to look after yourself because nobody else would. But then he remembered Straker going back into the wrecked building, and almost being killed saving *his* life.

So he made the call to Christine, his wife. She was at work, having done the school run.

"I'm back, the one-year tour done and dusted," he said, using his usual formula.

"Are you actually back in Hereford?" she asked, with her usual lack of drama after many such telephone calls from her husband.

"I'm in camp," he said. "But I've still got things to do."

Jacko knew Christine would be pleased to see him, but his long absences strained the mother-daughter relationship, so she'd want him to pick up their daughter from school – surprise her at the school gates. He loved doing this.

"So I suppose we'll see you sometime later then?"

Christine shared an office with other people, but he could hear the suppressed disappointment in her voice.

They were both disappointed; this was hardly the best homecoming.

CHAPTER 12

Forty-eight hours after Straker's admission, two plainclothes RMPs arrived at Musgrave Park Hospital, saying they had orders to take him to Headquarters Northern Ireland. Dr Morton refused, telling them Straker was far from recovered from the concussion.

"It's for his own safety," one of them said.

"He's being guarded here," said the doctor.

"That's against regulations," said the younger policeman.

"Hospital security is not your business," said Dr Morton. "Nor is Captain Straker's medical condition. You need to leave."

They left with ill grace. But Morton had known from the start that this was an almighty shit-storm in the making, so they'd be back.

He wasn't surprised when, that afternoon, he received a phone call from the RAMC colonel who commanded the Military Wing.

"We can't guard this officer in the hospital," he was told. "We don't have the resources. So as it seems he's got no actual injuries, he'll be better off resting in the Officers' Mess."

"That's for me to determine, Colonel."

"Yes, of course it is. But it's not in his interests to stay here."

"What do you mean?"

"Are you keeping him there because you think he's psychologically damaged?"

"It's far too early to say."

"Look, I know you're concerned with just the medical aspects. But our job is to look after our patients as military personnel – so they can continue to do their jobs."

"Yes, which is exactly why he should stay here under observation," replied Dr Morton. "If he has a stroke, or further brain bleeds that lead to memory loss or brain impairment, we'll be invaliding out an excellent officer."

"There's another dimension to this, which you won't know about," said the colonel. "He's a senior captain. I've been told he's passed the Staff College entrance exam even though he's not yet old enough to attend. The competition is fierce, and any suspicion that he's been affected psychologically would rule him out – which will be the end of his career."

"As I said, there's no indications of psychological damage."

"That's good news. So, you can discharge him now on light duties, pending further examination in – shall we say two weeks?"

Dr Morton thought for a couple of moments. He'd never experienced this level of clinical interference and he didn't like it.

"Captain Straker's been under forty-eight-hour close observation," he said. "I haven't examined him since that ended, because I'm still looking through his charts."

The last bit wasn't actually true.

"So you get on with that," said the colonel, "and then discharge him."

There was no way a staff colonel, even a former RAMC officer, gave such orders to a clinician. Morton dropped all semblance of politeness.

"Your attitude bothers me even more than Captain Straker's condition," he said.

There was silence on the line.

"Are you being leaned on?" Morton continued.

"Leaned on, *Captain* Morton…?" said the colonel with heavy emphasis on the rank. "What are you talking about? It's *your* attitude that is concerning. You are not being at all *helpful*."

Morton decided to push it.

"Captain Straker's inevitably top of the HQNI gossip agenda… But you're much too far out of order for this to be personal curiosity."

There was another silence, indicating that Morton was right.

"Look, Captain Morton…" The colonel had swallowed his anger, and was now trying to sound friendly. "We're not on a secure line here, so all I can do is remind you what Captain Straker does, and tell you that we have to take his security seriously…"

Morton thought quickly.

"OK, Colonel. Ethically I can't just discharge him – you know that. But I will agree to give him the option of discharging himself. If he decides to do that, it's his decision."

"That's more like it."

"But I will spell out to him the consequences if he—"

"One consideration please," the colonel interrupted. "Be very careful what you write in his medical records. He's obviously good at his job, and we're here to keep people like him working for as long as they're useful to the Army."

Later that day, Dr Morton examined Straker, then sat on the end of his bed for a chat.

"You were knocked unconscious – you think for only a few seconds, but we don't actually know for how long. You suffered thirty-six hours of altered perception, plus nausea, ringing in the ears, and headache.

"But I'm not writing that in your medical docs."

"Why not?" said Straker.

"I don't want to affect your career."

"How is my career affected by a bang on the head?"

"Head injuries are a particular problem for us," replied Morton. "Especially with people like you, as they can affect your reliability. You don't want that in your medical notes."

"That's nonsense."

"It might be, but with you, we don't yet know. This type of damage doesn't show up on a CT scan. Which is why I think you should stay here a while longer."

"But I've gone through the being-tired bit," said Straker. "I'm now bored. There's stuff I need to do, which I can't in this cramped little room."

"I understand there are things you need to do – which are none of my business. But you're my patient, so I'm very concerned about what other people want to do with you."

"What other people?"

"The RMP came for you yesterday, but I turned them away. Somebody senior thinks the Board of Inquiry is more important than your health – and that they can order me to release you to them."

"Why does that bother you?" said Straker.

"I can only hold them off for so long, Peter. And you're very vulnerable to further trauma injury – even if there's no force involved. You need rest, not questioning and further stress."

"It's not a problem for me," said Straker. "I've been proved correct in what I did."

"But aren't you worried?"

"I just want to get on with it. And no," Straker added. "Why should I be worried? We did our job, and I need to give my evidence to finish it off."

Morton sat for a moment not speaking, wondering if he should say any more.

"It's up to you what you do," he said finally.

He handed Straker a large envelope.

"This documentation gives you twenty-eight days' sick leave. You can go wherever you like – home, if you wish."

Morton looked hard at Straker.

"I'd go straight home – back to Hereford."

Straker just shrugged.

"Until your brain is fully rested – healed is a better way of putting it – you could have further bleeds. The tissue dies, and even though the damaged bits are too small to be scanned, this can mean memory loss and impairment of brain function – even a stroke. Nothing good. You really don't want to risk it. But what you do is now your decision."

Morton stood up.

"Painkillers mask symptoms, which is why I'm not giving you any."

He walked to the door.

"So immediately you feel you need them, get in touch with me. My bleeper number is written on the envelope."

CHAPTER 13

TUESDAY 2 DECEMBER

Arrosa Obregón walked from the entrance of the Queen's University School of Arts, English and Languages onto the cold pavement of University Square. Although she liked it here and agreed that it was indeed "grand" – one of the many English adjectives the Irish used in such interesting ways – Belfast in winter had a dankness that chilled her to the bone, making her wish she was back in Barcelona. Both cities shared the Celtic passion for freedom and cultural identity, but this dour Belfast cold was a very long way from the warmth and colour of Barcelona's streets.

The recently divorced professor of linguistics was standing on the pavement, shielded by the magnolia tree. He smiled, then walked across to join her.

"Doctor Obregón!" came a shout from the faculty entrance.

Cara, their pretty receptionist, was waving at her.

"You dropped one of your library books."

Cara ran down the narrow path, but stopped when she saw the linguistics professor, her pale skin flushing like a peach.

"It was on the floor in the hall. I guessed it must be yours."

Earlier in the week, Arrosa had watched Cara singing at one of the city-centre folk clubs. She was good. Afterwards they'd discussed music – but also men. In Belfast, as in Barcelona, harassment was a problem. The professor's name had been mentioned.

Cara was holding out a small volume of Spanish medieval poetry. But the professor interposed himself between them to take the book from Cara's outstretched hand, then turned his back on her. Arrosa took the book, then stepped past the professor into the faculty entrance where Cara was standing.

"This poet has many ideas for your songwriting," she said, turning the book over in her hands.

Her name was on the library stamp. Cara could have put it into her pigeonhole.

"The poet is Juan Ruiz," said Arrosa, resuming their folk-club conversation. "A priest who wrote of love among great ladies and also nuns; but also of the simpler pleasures of country lasses and the Moorish dancing girls."

The professor came up to them. Arrosa ignored him.

"Ruiz was jailed by the Inquisition," she continued, "so he has plenty of stories to encourage musical inspiration."

Cara looked up at the professor, then made as if to scurry back to her desk inside the building. But Arrosa took her arm, then handed her the book.

"I will collect this from you later, if that's OK? But for really accurate understanding you must get a good English translation. Our library has the one by Kane. Then maybe we can talk some more?"

Arrosa turned to flash a smile across to the professor.

"Cara writes very personal songs," she told him. "We're friends, so we share gossip as well as songs and Spanish literature."

The professor looked uncertain. Arrosa smiled at him again.

"Juan Ruiz would have appreciated Cara's most interesting stories. As would the Inquisition."

She noted the professor's uncertainty, and the grin that suddenly appeared on Cara's face.

"But I run late, Professor. So sorry, needing to dash…"

Arrosa picked up a large canvas shoulder bag, turning away with focussed but apparently absent-minded distraction.

Arrosa Obregón was five foot nine with green-brown eyes, slim but athletic with the muscularity and poise of a dancer. She did not conform to the scruffy informality of campus, nor to the dowdy respectability to which many progressed once they secured junior lectureships like hers. She was dressed warmly in a dark blue tailored jacket made of wool with black knee-length culottes. A silk scarf of vibrant red, blue and yellow was round her neck, long dark hair coiled into a single plait above her head, held in place by a freshly sharpened 2HB pencil, its rubber eraser blending perfectly as if it were costume jewellery.

She walked along the pavement, past iron railings where the faculty's splendid white magnolia hadn't yet been tricked into flowering early. When spring really did come – as she'd noted with sorrow the previous year, soon after she'd arrived here – it would be a mass of dead petals, shrivelled yellow by late frost. *This was the best part of this city*, she thought: a patch of well-maintained classical buildings with civilised squares and authoritative towers.

As she rounded the corner to walk north towards the city centre along University Road, she turned up her collar, hiding the bright scarf. She took a telescopic umbrella from her bag. Under the dome of its tattered black, her exotic but geeky "university" persona seemed to fade away.

A further 300 yards on, at the junction with the Lisburn Road, the civility of the university quarter also faded. Arrosa stepped into a space behind a telephone box where the pavement widened. The row of shops was run-down and partly boarded up, and yet there was an elegant three-storey hexagonal tower at one end. Stained-glass windows circled its imitation battlements, under a lead-spired roof topped by a medieval sailing ship weathervane.

She collapsed the umbrella back into her bag, then pushed open the heavy door of the phone box. Inside she shrugged into a dark blue cagoule, zipping up with the hood over her head. The glass panes were clear enough to observe people on both sides of the street. She watched faces while holding the tobacco-stinking handset to her ear. Then, after appearing to complete a call, she shouldered her way out to continue walking up University Road – a fed-up housewife making a phone call on a cold day.

She reached Bradbury Place then crossed onto Donegal Road to walk west for a few minutes, then crossed over to the northern side. After her change of direction, she did a quick check of the faces, then retraced her steps back onto the tree-lined Shaftesbury Square. She then wiggled her way through the smaller streets and squares around the back of City Hall, with its huge Christmas tree, crossing over to check behind her using shop windows as mirrors and onto Chichester Street, where she joined the search queue for the entrance into the shopping centre's twelve-foot-high barbed wire and concrete perimeter fence – the so-called "Merlyn Wall".

Nick-named after a previous Northern Ireland Secretary, it had twenty cage-like gates guarded by the watchful eyes of armed soldiers and specialist search teams. She stood impassively, waiting in line to enter the long, low search shelter, watching as a female Greenfinch finished patting down the woman ahead of her. She checked the faces, stoic and blank, enduring the mild humiliation of this process. Although, she did find it oddly reassuring – as was its purpose. She felt less likely to be attacked inside a fortress dedicated to shopping. But she felt little joy here, just lives blunted by weariness, cold, and the truly brutal intolerance of two opposed communities.

As she exited the far side of the search shelter into Donegal Place, a sudden gust of cold wind buffeted her from across the gardens in front of City Hall, a sound like a heavy blanket being shaken. For a moment the city seemed to fade away.

The cry of a seagull took her back to a quite different place, where she'd been free and happy, a moment of forgetting all this and simply being herself. Then it was gone, and the insidious anxiety that had been dogging her for this past fortnight surged into the gap opened up by this momentary lapse of focus.

Arrosa spent an hour wandering the shops, running a gamut of tinsel-lined windows and gift displays. Some shops had Christmas trees bizarrely hanging outwards horizontally at first-floor level from the walls; on some streets, lights dangled from electricity cables, stars hanging over the middle of the street. A laughably unconvincing horse-drawn "sleigh" made from a van chassis with large rubber tyres pulled by a blinkered horse made short trips up and down Royal Avenue. Its driver, in Father Christmas costume, was pinched with cold and far too skinny.

The handbag and body searches at department-store entrances allowed her once again to scan faces. At Leisure World, she was a mother looking for children's toys amid its crude piles of candy-coloured boxes, then she walked north via Fountain Street to leave by the turnstile at the top of Royal Avenue. After ten minutes of sitting with a dreadful cup of coffee in Smithfield Market, then several rounds of the market's souk-like alleys of stalls, she was finally satisfied that nobody was tailing her.

She re-entered the north segment to walk south along Royal Avenue and leave by the same gate she'd come in through – out onto Chichester Street. Then, just before re-entering Donegal Place, she stopped by the doorway of Burtons and took off the blue cagoule. She stuffed it into her bag, then pulled out a black headscarf which she knotted under the chin to completely cover her hair.

She'd memorised the faces. If any were the same, she'd double back, re-enter the shopping segment where she'd be safe, then after more of the same laborious precautions, go home using another route. Otherwise she'd walk along Chichester Street, where a black taxi would stop in front of her, and she would get in.

She walked slowly down Donegal Place, subconsciously hoping to recognise a face that would allow her to go home. But they were all strangers: pinched, pale, and preoccupied.

Since the very first meeting eighteen months ago, Arrosa had cultivated Carragher's driver. Their journeys to meetings were usually taken up by cheerful conversations about football, Arrosa enthusing about FC Barcelona. But today Roxy was sombre and uncommunicative.

They drove along the Falls Road then right into the narrow weave of terraced houses, taking random turns as Roxy watched his mirrors. She tried to catch his eye, but he wasn't playing. They stopped halfway along a deserted street and Roxy nodded for her to get out.

Something was wrong. The front door opened and she had no choice but to walk into the darkness, heart pounding. *This was how things went wrong*, she thought. It's not so much your cover getting blown, although that happens, but how you react. She constantly audited her procedures, so she knew for certain she'd not given herself away.

Something was seriously wrong here. On their previous meeting a week ago, she'd taken a risk asking Carragher for his views on the future, which she'd wanted to confirm today. Now she wondered if her question was the problem.

But that was as far as she dared to think about it. To show fear would be to confirm guilt for whatever was wrong. To save her life she had to act normal – choke back the fear and be her usual self.

"He's upstairs in the back room."

The Chief of Staff stood aside in the narrow passageway so she could get past and up the narrow stairs.

She forced herself to pause for a moment and look up at him, remembering the mantra: "*Be real, stay close to the truth; acting gets you killed.*"

"You look tired," she said.

He did look tired, and she was giving him a reason for why he might think she was worried.

"Yeah, well… We're a bit pressed, y'know? But it's OK."

He gestured for her to go up the stairs.

"D'yer want a coffee?"

She didn't, but nodded. Being offered coffee might be a good sign.

"Black, please."

She went upstairs, tapped on the door, then entered the small back bedroom. The window was blanked out by sheets of newspaper with a single lightbulb hanging down from the ceiling.

She paused as a flash of memory took her unawares – an interrogation exercise during IONEC at Fort Monkton, something she'd never before thought about. She took a slow, deep breath to get herself back into the moment.

Carragher was sitting at a small table with an empty ashtray in front of him. This struck her as odd as he didn't smoke. He didn't move, staring at the tabletop, so she looped her handbag over the back of the second chair and sat down.

There was no point trying to ignore this. If it was to do with her, she needed to address it head-on.

"Something's wrong," she said.

Carragher didn't respond, so she decided to push it.

"And you look terrible, Séan…" she said, using the quiet, concerned voice. "I'm sorry to say this to you, but it is true."

He looked up, bloodshot eyes ringed with exhaustion, pulsing out a single flash of pure hatred. She fought down a spike of adrenalin, and as she was about to say something she hoped might sound calm and soothing, there was a tap on the door.

"Two coffees, Séan."

"Yeah, thanks," replied Carragher. "Now get out."

The Chief of Staff put the tray down onto the table and retreated. In the cold room, steam from the mugs looked like cigarette smoke, making her notice that the room did not smell of tobacco. Carragher put milk and two teaspoons of sugar into his mug and stirred.

"You know what the Brit squaddies call this?"

Arrosa did know. Training with the SAS meant learning their language – another dangerous memory.

"They call it NATO Standard," he said, "like all those countries signed some kind of military agreement to drink bloody awful coffee."

She relaxed, then sipped her coffee, waiting for him to continue.

"Our work together…" he began. "We need to move things on, to get both our bosses fully committed."

"I think we're there," she replied. "Trust takes time. But I think you and me, we trust each other; and my bosses sent me because they trust my judgment."

She'd taken a risk in making this presumption out loud. But he could only disagree, and she could talk… But she was still very frightened. By deliberately avoiding talking about what was wrong, Carragher was making it clear that she was involved.

"We need to bring in the first shipments," he said. "As soon as possible."

So that's the good news, she thought. *But it's not the main news…*

They sat in silence.

"You and Máire used to meet up together," he said suddenly.

He'd caught her unawares, so she assumed he'd noticed a reaction and did not dissemble.

"Máire talks with me as a friend," she said quietly.

Carragher was leaning forwards, elbows on the table like an interrogator.

"But she doesn't want anyone else to know – we're girls together," Arrosa continued. "I respect that."

She felt Carragher's authority evaporate. She forced herself to continue.

"You said Máire *used to* meet up with me – this is using the past tense. So what's wrong, Séan?"

Carragher's head suddenly dropped, hiding his face in his hands.

"Máire's dead…" he said.

She hadn't expected anything like this. It took a moment to register, then a further moment as she curbed the involuntary *English* reaction she'd been about to make.

"Madre de Dios..."

She waited a couple more beats, utilising the genuine emotions that surged up from inside her.

"I am so sorry, Séan. Is this to do with... you know... her pregnancy?"

Carragher's voice was rough with emotion, sounding brutal as he tried to speak normally.

"No. And the baby's dead too."

Arrosa sat there, allowing herself to remember the conversations she'd had with Máire – about having the unexpected baby, her hopes for their marriage, talking about how they could live and work while also bringing up a child – so naïve and unlikely. And Máire always worrying that they weren't going to happen. Prescient.

But these were dangerous thoughts. Arrosa again focussed back into role. *Never ask questions*, she reminded herself.

"You're going to find out soon enough, so I'll tell you," Carragher said.

She'd shivered, imagining what would happen if he really could read her mind.

Back in the taxi, Roxy pulled over at the end of the road and stopped. He turned round to look back at her.

"Did he tell you then?"

She nodded.

"I've never seen him like this," Roxy continued. "He's always focussed on the next thing. Even when he's lost good friends. It's a war. We're soldiers, just do the job – do our duty. None of it's personal. At least, that's what he's always said..."

Roxy pulled out from the curb and onto the Falls, as if to stop himself from saying any more.

"He's not just lost a soldier," she said. "Not even just a friend."

They drove towards the city centre in silence.

"Sorry," said Roxy eventually. "I'm just driving. I'm not thinking. Are you going back to the college?"

They usually dropped her someplace from which it was easy for her to get where she next needed to be. Arrosa pretended not to have heard him.

"A wife… A mother and their baby," she said. "The death of innocents, a mother and child. How do you deal with that?"

Roxy stared straight ahead, the muscles at the back of his neck tight with anger.

"He's going to kill the SAS guy."

Roxy dropped her off outside the Grand Opera House on Great Victoria Street.

On her first trip with him the previous August, they'd chatted happily while driving back into town. Arrosa had said how much she liked the Opera House's oriental façade, and how it called itself a circus – "Cirque". But this time there'd been no chat. Roxy had nodded with Belfast's typically impassive but slightly menacing regard, then driven off.

Arrosa walked back down to Queen's, crossing University Square in the growing darkness.

Her previous meeting with Carragher a week earlier had been business as usual. She'd felt confident enough to lead him into discussing future plans. Whereas today, Carragher's devastating news and stark emotions, and then what Roxy had told her, cut into the world she'd created here like an axe to a wedding cake.

Carragher had been her regular contact; PIRA had kept her away from everybody else. He'd talked of being arrested by the British then jailed, and working with the Libyans. He knew his history, was well-read, and said he'd wanted to be a marine engineer. She'd thought him frustrated and impatient. She'd also met O'Donnell, whose careful, almost professorial manner she knew concealed something very different.

They'd compared Celtic similarities, and how the Provisional IRA's fight against the British had inspired ETA – the Euskadi Ta Askatasuna – to copy their tactics in Spain. But it was only in that penultimate meeting a week ago that she'd taken the serious risk of pushing Carragher on his ideas for the future.

She'd challenged him by saying Britain was not a fascist state like the remnants of the Franco regime still governing Spain, and that PIRA's real enemies were the Protestant Unionists. She'd quoted from the IRA Green Book.

"Your enemy is the British Army and the commercial interests of the British state?

"But even when or if you force the Brits out," she'd continued, "the Unionist oppression remains. So why don't you *negotiate* with the British government, and attack only the Unionists?"

"We'd still end up having to fight the Brits."

"Why?"

"The Unionist vote can bring down any British government. So they'll always take the Unionist side."

"So how can a united Ireland come into this?"

"I'd ask you the same about Basque independence..."

This was when Arrosa had decided to break her golden rule and ask a question for which she really did want an answer.

"We have a long way to go," she'd replied. "ETA must first to bring down the fascists and establish democracy. You already have democracy here. Which is why I'm very interested to know what you will do?"

Carragher had immediately understood.

"We do have democracy here," he said. "You're right enough. But maybe when you guys get to the same place, you'll find that there's no justice in it for *you*."

Arrosa had sat quietly, nodding as if she was thinking it over.

"The realistic strategy," he'd continued, "is to convince the British government that we're never going to stop."

She waited. Finally, Carragher had added: "We need to get back to bombing the mainland, but do it efficiently and accurately – without killing innocent people. The cock-up of the Birmingham pub bombings lost us a lot of our own supporters over here..."

Which was why PIRA leadership never admitted responsibility, thought Arrosa.

"We need to make Brit voters so frightened and sick of us that they force their government to make a deal with us."

As she ducked her head leaving Roxy's taxi, Arrosa realised she was shocked; and also unable to stop thinking about Carragher. She liked his respectful masculinity. Their meetings had always gone well, and over the first few months he'd introduced her to his inner circle – notably Máire, before the romance with Carragher had started.

With Carragher in her sights, to Máire, Arrosa was a threat. Arrosa had used this antipathy as an opportunity to engineer relationships, deploying laser-focussed empathy to disarm Máire, while being deferential and reserved towards Carragher. She'd also done a little flirting with Duffy, whose unreciprocated desire for Máire was obvious.

She'd liked Máire, who'd been sharp, ambitious and determined, besotted with Carragher but uncertain of how he felt about her. So Arrosa had offered herself as the outsider female, and they'd become friends.

But even though Arrosa had been invited over here by the IRA, and was ETA's official representative, she was still subject to the IRA discipline machine. They'd force her to talk, then she'd disappear. Hence never asking questions. But even though PIRA resuming mainland bombings was big news, she needed more.

CHAPTER 14

Carragher was exhausted, desperate for sleep yet tired all the time, kept going by anger. For the times it left him, he'd nod off, slumped back in a chair or with his head resting on the table to awaken feeling cold, ill, and empty.

But at night, in the early hours after he'd forced himself to go to bed, sleep would not come. Trapped in the interminable stillness, he was a prisoner to everything he wanted to forget, to all the memories he'd avoided over the years. He did sleep, but with dreams worse than the memories. These dreams were repetitive, meaningless, exhausting and deeply disturbing, images on a screen from which he was powerless to turn away. He rarely remembered anything about them – apart from how they kept looping back to the same start point; knowing there was no escape from the relentless repetition.

Although one time, after a noise from the street woke him, he did remember. He'd woken in the small hours to complete quiet and stillness, not only remembering but unable to forget. In the dream he'd been looking at a Madonna and Child, with all the sinister, out-of-scale background you'd see in a 15th century painting. There was a church, stunted trees, an odd-looking cottage with a river in front, and a rowing boat moored to a wooden jetty. This seemed like it should mean something to him, even though he'd never seen it before. Then the Madonna turned her head to stare at him, eyes shining with pure hatred. When he tried to look away, she handed him the baby, which was dead and broken. He then saw that the Madonna was Máire, and that apart from her eyes, she was dead too.

And as he woke, sweating and gasping for air, he remembered her broken voice: "You did this to us."

WEDNESDAY 3 DECEMBER

It was unusual for Breandán O'Donnell to have face-to-face meetings with people. Since Carragher had taken command of the Belfast Brigade, they'd talked only on the phone – brief conversations using call boxes, or veiled speech in case of phone taps. But if Carragher was losing it, O'Donnell wanted to know before anybody else, so needed to see for himself.

He ordered a meet at a quiet country pub off the A23 Ballygowan Road, ten kilometres south-east of Belfast.

Roxy had borrowed a respectable-looking Ford Cortina. His black taxi – one of many in West Belfast – would attract attention out in the countryside with its battered bodywork and the fumes from its high-mileage diesel engine.

Roxy drove past the pub, checking for cars parked along the adjoining lane. He U-turned back to drop Carragher off.

Carragher was impatient. There was a lot needing to be done without wasting half a day coming out here. He didn't know what this was about, but the anxiety of meeting O'Donnell did not sit well with the pain and anger that burned inside him. He pushed straight into the deserted bar, where the landlord stopped polishing glasses to point across to the stairs up to a private room.

O'Donnell was warming his legs beside a log fire.

"We're doing lunch," he said.

Carragher sat down at the round wooden table. The un-curtained bay window looked out onto wet sheep and a rain-soaked field that vanished into mist. O'Donnell left the room, returning with a tray bearing glasses and a jug of water.

"Tomato soup, then steak?"

"Sounds good," replied Carragher. "Whatever."

O'Donnell filled the glasses and sat down.

He decided to get straight to it: "I'm sorry about Máire…"

For a moment Carragher tensed up. But then he relaxed, and they sat in silence.

"I need to know…" said O'Donnell slowly, "how you are…"

Carragher looked up sharply. "I'm sorting this out."

"Fair enough," said O'Donnell.

After a minute of silence, he added, "So what have you found out?"

Carragher gathered himself to respond, but then stopped, staring at the bay window.

"There's no time for fucking about, Séan," said O'Donnell. "This is us, in this together. We both need to understand what went wrong, so we can do something about it."

After further contemplation of the misty outlines of the sheep, Carragher sighed deeply and reached for his water glass.

"This is very difficult, Breandán," he said. "I admit it. But I am working through it."

"That's why we're meeting," said O'Donnell. "We can do this together."

Carragher thought about this. "We?" he asked finally.

O'Donnell leaned forwards and touched Carragher's forearm, like a sympathetic relative. But then he jerked backwards as Carragher smashed the heavy water glass onto the tabletop. It didn't break, but O'Donnell flinched.

"Any more of this crappy 'we' shit," snarled Carragher, "and I'm out of here."

O'Donnell leaned back, his face blank. They sat in silence.

"It *had* all been going well," began Carragher, speaking carefully, as if he'd done a rewind back to the beginning of their meeting. "I'd found a sense of purpose…"

After the cliché, he grimaced.

"I really had. All those years… of uselessness, anger – the bloody shitty hopelessness of drifting."

O'Donnell waited for more, but Carragher had dried up.

"So," he prompted, "what was this *purpose* you're saying you'd found?"

Carragher had to continue; but he didn't like it.

"Everything, Breandán – getting married, commanding the brigade… And then the baby."

O'Donnell noted Carragher hadn't included their working together. But again he waited.

"I was even thinking about the kind of world the baby would grow up in, and how I didn't want the cycle to repeat."

"Your dad, then you?"

Carragher's father had been a welder at the shipyard, sacked when Carragher was seven.

"Same old same," said Carragher. "Although my job was in their drawing office."

Many Catholic men had suffered thus, to be left unemployed without options. And like some, Carragher had joined the Officials.

"Aye – cycles don't stop by themselves," said O'Donnell.

There was a knock at the door. The landlord brought in a plate of buttered sliced bread and two bowls of soup. Carragher shook salt and pepper into his, stirring until the granules submerged.

"Are you saying you've gone back to how you felt before…? As you'd said – useless and angry?" said O'Donnell. "I get that you're angry. But hardly useless."

"I don't need patronising, Breandán."

"So is that how you felt when you were banged-up in the Maze?" persisted O'Donnell.

"Patronised?"

O'Donnell waited.

"No," said Carragher. "Back then I didn't feel useless and angry. There was plenty to do in there, together with the others."

"Whereas now?"

"I'm in charge, Breandán – so yeah, there's still plenty to do."

"We'll get to that," said O'Donnell. "But right now we're talking about you personally and how you're reacting to the violent death of your wife…"

"Like I said, I'm dealing with it – what else can I do?"

Carragher looked hard at O'Donnell, who seemed to decide to go straight to the centre of it.

"It looks like you've given up…?"

This was so near the bone that Carragher didn't want even to *think* about it. But O'Donnell wasn't to be put off.

"You need to talk to me," he said.

Carragher really didn't.

He was in pain. He'd tried blaming other people, but that also made him angry. And O'Donnell was right. The pain came from everything – from life itself. Escaping the pain was to give up: on the Cause, other people, and even his tenuous, love-hate belief in God.

"Yeah – fair enough," replied Carragher quickly, suppressing another debilitating surge of anger, to drop back into an ambient sadness that leached away at his soul.

"Are you eating?" prompted O'Donnell.

Carragher rolled up a slice of the buttered bread, put it into the soup, then chopped the white dough into pieces with the edge of his spoon. A yellow slick floated on the flour-thickened orange surface. He spooned it down, then took another slice to mop up.

They sat in silence until another tap on the door, the landlord with a tray. He gave them two sets of knives and forks wrapped in paper napkins, a bottle of HP tomato sauce and small jar of Coleman's mustard. He gathered up the soup plates and left.

"It doesn't take long before you stop being hungry," said Carragher.

"What do you mean?"

"It's what the guys said… And also that hunger is easier than feeling the pain."

The landlord pushed back into the room, carrying two plates of steak, chips and peas.

"Anything else I can get you gents?"

O'Donnell shook his head, then waited until the man had closed the door.

"What the fuck, Séan?"

"You said we needed to talk," spat back Carragher. "So that's what I'm fucking doing."

"OK, OK…"

O'Donnell unscrewed the tomato sauce bottle and smacked the bottom with the palm of his hand. Nothing came out.

"So what's this pain you're talking about here?"

He smacked the bottle again much harder, grimacing as a large dollop of sauce landed largely on his plate, but partly on the table. He looked up to see if Carragher had noticed.

"Those guys I was banged-up with," said Carragher. "They'd nothing to think about except not seeing their families and all that life they're missing out on. It's a real enough pain – which you can't share with the others because you're all feeling it. It makes you lonely, which makes the pain worse."

O'Donnell pointed at Carragher's plate.

"You gonna eat this?"

Carragher picked up a knife.

"They say that after a week the hunger fades, and the pain goes with it."

O'Donnell carefully salted his chips, then poked one into a blob of tomato sauce.

"Hunger strikes are a waste of time," he replied. "By people stupid enough to get caught and put in jail."

"What else can they do?" said Carragher, ignoring O'Donnell's arrogance.

"Obey the rules and get early release," snapped O'Donnell. "So they can get back to being useful."

Carragher could have said, "What the fuck do you know?"

But instead, he thought about the hours he'd spent watching birds from the cell window – as they perched on the razor wire chattering to each other, wheeling together across the open sky. He'd imagined himself as one of them. There was no understandable purpose to their flying, burning hard-won calories simply for the joy of it. He knew that if he could fly, he'd do exactly the same.

"So you wanted to be free?" said O'Donnell.

O'Donnell apparently reading his mind jolted Carragher back to the present.

"Of the pain..." O'Donnell added.

"Yeah, at first I did," Carragher said absently. "Then I got used to it."

But he was still thinking about the birds. All they did was fly, seeming perfectly happy. As far as he could see, that was their sole purpose, and fulfilling that purpose brought them the joy they were so obviously experiencing. So was joy the reward for a life well-lived? And what might be the purpose of human life?

"What the fuck's the matter with you now?" interrupted O'Donnell.

Carragher put down his knife and fork. He looked steadily across the table at O'Donnell.

"So you think grief is selfish?" he said.

"No, of course I don't."

O'Donnell sensed the need to back off. He stood up and went over to stare at the fire. He pretended still to be talking about the Maze Prison hunger strike.

"But I can't think of anything more pointless than a suicide protest," he said reasonably.

"What – giving your life for the Cause?" said Carragher.

"Wasting your life for absolutely nothing," snapped back O'Donnell. "One of the few things on which I agree with the Church."

"The one sin for which there's no forgiveness…?" said Carragher.

"I'm not the Holy Father's advocate, Séan."

"But they're right," said Carragher. "If Catholics who killed themselves were allowed into Heaven, the Church's power over us would end."

"Suicides also hurt the people they leave behind," said O'Donnell quietly, repressing his anger. "They also kill their loved ones."

O'Donnell relaxed and let the heat from the fire absorb his anger. He then sat down and tried to focus on eating.

"It's what happens," he continued quietly. "You kill yourself; you kill everyone you ever knew. You throw God's gift back in his face."

Carragher just stared at him: "What the fuck are you talking about, Breandán?"

O'Donnell wasn't interested in what other people were thinking, only in how he could get them to cooperate. So he worked hard to match their moods, reflecting himself back at them as if he empathised. Now he suppressed a stab of fear. He'd been utilising the many hours he'd spent as a child listening to sermons – most of it nonsense. Other people seemed to believe this stuff, but not Carragher – at least, not right now.

So O'Donnell decided to change tack.

"D'you know the mural at the top of Lenadoon Avenue on the side wall of number 182?"

Carragher shook his head vaguely.

"It's one of those with Cú Chulainn, commemorating Volunteers from F Company killed in action."

The legend was that when Ireland's greatest hero was mortally wounded, he wrapped his entrails around a standing stone so he could die on his feet facing his enemies. In the murals, the corpse's head slumped down to one side, as a splendid raven stood on his shoulder.

"They're based on the bronze statue in the Dublin General Post Office," continued O'Donnell. "The one de Valera said represents 'the dauntless courage and abiding constancy of our people'."

Being face-to-face with Carragher, O'Donnell couldn't help but feel at a serious physical disadvantage. He hated to admit it, but he was frightened.

Lecturer mode conferred superiority.

"The puzzle for me," he continued, "regarding all these memorials, is that Cú Chulainn is obviously defeated and very dead, with only the raven still alive, sitting on his shoulder, triumphant like the sacred eagle of an ancient Roman legion."

"It sat on Cú Chulainn's shoulder to prove he was dead," said Carragher.

"True, but if you asked somebody who'd never heard the legend what the tableau means, they'd tell you it's all about the raven. To me it looks like she's about to start eating Cú Chulainn's eyes."

Carragher leaned back in his chair, stroking his fork as if gathering paranormal powers to bend it.

"This is Ireland's greatest hero, Seán. But we portray him like the dead Christ being eaten by a raven because that's what we've got here in Ireland. Old gods hiding behind Christian masks – mostly cruel, but at least they're honest.

"You've heard tell of the Morrígan – the 'Phantom Queen'?"

O'Donnell was now cranked up to full lecture mode. Carragher let him get on with it.

"She appeared to Cú Chulainn in the form of a maiden offering help. For some reason he turned her down – big mistake.

"The Morrígan foretells doom, death or victory in battle, shape-shifting often as a raven or crow, inciting warriors, helping bring them victory, striking fear into enemies. But she also foretells their death.

"The reasons for Cú Chulainn spurning the Morrígan aren't clear to me," he added. "But her side of it is obvious enough – stalking and thwarting him, then appearing as an old crone washing his armour in a river to facilitate his death.

"But oddly, having succeeded, she didn't revel in it as you might expect her to."

Carragher started paying attention.

"His killers were too frightened to approach the body," he said. "The raven came after three days to prove to them he was dead.

"Three days," intoned O'Donnell. "It's *always* three days…"

"We're taught the story in school, Breandán," said Carragher.

"Yes – *they* waited," continued O'Donnell, "but she waited too. Why did she do that?"

He turned away from the fire.

"She's there on both Republican and Loyalist memorials; official Irish state statues, coins, medals – Ireland's 'dauntless courage and abiding constancy' brought down by a vengeful woman."

He stepped back over towards the table.

"Or, conversely, she enabled Cú Chulainn's hero status through glorious death. Either way, it seems to me that the actual lesson offered here is that no matter the hero, vengeance prevails."

Carragher was suddenly stabbed by imagery from his dream; the dead baby's head and shoulders slumped sideways across the Madonna's forearm, a malignant presence rotting with hate behind her normally expressionless face.

This was a reality far removed from the empty comfort of Our Lady. It was certainly female, but older, its ancient wisdom unbounded by morality, and far more judgmental, demanding retribution.

O'Donnell sensed the change in Carragher, and immediately backed away.

"But that's legends for you," he said dismissively. "Take from them what you can, and leave the rest."

He then rewound their conversation, reverting back to what Carragher had been saying.

"You started talking about suicide, Séan. Which got a bit theological…"

Carragher nodded, his tension gone as quickly as it had manifested.

O'Donnell decided to push it.

"So is that your pain-relief plan?"

"I'm not going to kill myself, Breandán," said Carragher.

O'Donnell didn't argue, once again repeating what Carragher had said as if seeking clarification.

"But you're chasing some kind of dream that you think will make you free?"

Carragher didn't respond, giving nothing away. O'Donnell sat back as if relaxing; but he was being extremely careful.

"Those guys in the Maze," O'Donnell continued, "protesting at being treated like criminals... You know them well? They're friends of yours – yes?"

"A hunger strike is their only possible endgame," said Carragher, avoiding giving an answer. "And as I said, what else can they do?"

O'Donnell got up again, spinning this out. He added a log to the fire.

"You did – and it's pointless," he said. "We're soldiers fighting a war against very powerful enemies. You'll know that in the First World War, suicides were the guys who didn't want to be there, who didn't believe in the Cause. They'd no loyalty to the men around them. They just wanted out, any way they could, and nobody mourned them.

"The time of protest for us is long gone. It made things worse in 1969. Then we fought back. But now we need to operate with discipline and purpose."

He adjusted the position of the log with tongs, ensuring it couldn't roll off onto the wooden floor.

"But fighting's not enough. We need to be costing the Brits money, killing their decision-makers. Do you really believe a few of our people starving themselves to death will shame the Brits into changing anything?"

"But we're running out of explosives," said Carragher, thinking tactically. "Along with money and everything else..."

"It's being wasted, Séan, through having no clearly defined purpose. You can't be a heavenly choir unless you're all singing from the same hymn sheet. This is why the Brits are able to paint us as nothing more than a criminal gang."

O'Donnell was trying to engage Carragher intellectually, now adding a touch of flattery: "And you being our bomb expert."

"To me right now," replied Carragher, speaking very slowly, "it doesn't seem like it's a war, but something existential. It's a fight for survival... And my wife just got killed."

That last bit had slipped out.

O'Donnell sat still, saying nothing, allowing this to register fully.

"If it's a war we're fighting," said Carragher eventually, "it's not for *our* benefit. There won't be a united Ireland in *our* lifetime."

This was heresy, but it confirmed to O'Donnell that Carragher was still prepared to be honest with him.

"Then why are we fighting?"

"So future generations can live better lives than us."

"That's very vague."

"Yes, because although *we* call it the Armed Struggle, to the Brits we're still just criminals. But protest is all we actually achieve. We can't beat them. Like the hunger strike in the Maze won't get anybody released."

O'Donnell nodded. Carragher was right.

"But is bombing the right way to make our point?" said Carragher. "We have to work this out now."

O'Donnell didn't answer immediately, but sat back as if thinking, content that at last he'd got Carragher talking.

"We've always been too small to do this as a direct fight – with firearms," O'Donnell added after the pause.

"We're fighting against injustice, for what's *right*," replied Carragher. "So the way we fight has to be right too. Bombs kill innocent people – many of them *our* people, who won't then have children. So we're also killing the future generations we say we're fighting for."

"That's why bombs have got to be carefully targeted and controlled," said O'Donnell slowly. "As you and I have been doing."

"And what we're doing is not actually fighting a war," said Carragher. "Not really."

Carragher now sounded like he was talking to himself. He'd stopped listening, which irritated O'Donnell.

"And when they catch us," Carragher continued, "there's no firing squads. These days they don't even hang us. We're just common criminals.

"They're too powerful, so, yeah, as you say, there's so few of us that bombing's all we can do. Many of our people actually prefer bombs to bullets – less personal risk, and they don't care about civilians getting hurt."

Carragher was venting. O'Donnell listened very carefully.

"So how does this end?" said Carragher. "Even if our 'war', or whatever we call it, goes as well as it possibly could, we're still always going to be on the edge of losing the support of our own people. And it's going to take a very long time.

"We're wasting our people like casino chips – gambling with their lives. We need leaders who can end this before our own people turn against us."

"Agreed," said O'Donnell. "They are the sea; we are the fish."

Another tap on the door.

"Are you done, gents?"

O'Donnell looked pointedly at Carragher, who nodded.

"So, can I bring you cheese, or some pudding, maybe?"

Carragher shook his head.

"Two coffees," said O'Donnell.

After the landlord cleared the table and left, O'Donnell got up and stood by the window. Late afternoon sunshine had pushed back the mist, revealing small fields with uncut hedges across to a wood on a small hill. It was like a miniature world inside a glass dome.

He waited until the landlord returned with the coffees. Then, after the door closed behind him, O'Donnell sat back down.

"So this is you trying to get Máire's death out of your system by blaming the Cause?" he said.

"What the fuck, Breandán...?"

O'Donnell decided to push it.

"By saying it's all pointless... Is that you trying to free yourself of responsibility, so you don't feel so bad?"

Carragher clenched his fists and made as if to stand up. But then he leaned back in his chair, exhaling slowly.

"Right now, I'm focussed on just getting through each day, one at a time."

"Sure, I understand," said O'Donnell. "But this is not about *you*."

"I'm doing the job, Breandán."

"Yes, Séan. But you're not doing the part where you keep me informed. You still work for me, and I need to know what's going on with you."

Carragher didn't respond. O'Donnell was a dark, bedside-silhouette sort of father figure. But he was sober and calculating, unlike his own father, who'd stood over him in the darkness stinking of drink; but when sober had never threatened him.

"You see, Séan, I heard you're asking for the name of the SAS man who shot Máire?"

Carragher didn't react.

"Or was that just you talking?"

"It was just me talking," he muttered.

O'Donnell stood over him, waiting.

"But whichever ways we think about this," growled Carragher, resisting O'Donnell, "we need to stop this idea that we're being finished off by the Brits. Otherwise we might as well give up."

O'Donnell was unable to conceal his flicker of anger.

"If we don't make somebody pay," continued Carragher, "we'll lose respect. There's already too many fucking toerags taking Brit money."

Carragher stood up carefully and stepped away from the table, moving to stand and look out of the window. He'd thought working with O'Donnell would make him feel better about himself. It hadn't, and he now wondered if that was how O'Donnell wanted it to be.

He also thought of Máire; he'd played along with her in the beginning – who wouldn't? But in spite of himself, he'd got sucked into all her hopes and optimism, to marriage and fatherhood.

"That little fucker Duffy was there, and I wasn't… That's the bottom line on this," said Carragher.

This was O'Donnell's cue.

"It wasn't your job," he said.

"Duffy should have protected Máire," Carragher added harshly. "That was Duffy's fucking job."

"Duffy rescued the trigger," said O'Donnell.

"*After* Máire was killed…"

O'Donnell needed to get this next bit firmly established, so he purposely didn't reply.

"He's saying he tried to save her even with the SAS all around," continued Carragher. "So, yeah, Duffy's making me feel like a coward…"

Carragher was staring out of the window, talking quietly from someplace else – trapped in the mist of the miniature world.

"And the end result is that this SAS guy single-handedly defeated us – against all odds, as they say. That makes him the fucking hero."

"And you lost your wife and child," said O'Donnell equally quietly, trying to match Carragher's mood.

The fire crackled as one of the logs shifted.

"Heroes and cowards," said Carragher. "We can't tolerate that."

O'Donnell had to play this very carefully. Swift PIRA vengeance was required to get a positive narrative established for this whole fiasco. But assassinating an SAS officer could neither be swift nor certain. In fact, killing a specific UK-based soldier was so difficult that they'd never even tried.

Killing the traitor was all that was required, with Duffy the easily killed scapegoat who wouldn't answer back. But this had to be Carragher's idea.

They were both standing awkwardly, not facing each other. A seagull swooped onto the window ledge, making its guttural cry then diving back into the wind. Eventually Carragher turned away from the window as if from the edge of a cliff, to sit back down.

At the same time O'Donnell returned to the table, sat down, then leaned forwards to stare at Carragher, resting heavily on both elbows so their faces were close.

"So here's where I am on this, Séan," he said quietly. "The *only* name we're wanting here is the person who ratted us out."

Once again it seemed to Carragher that O'Donnell was reading his mind.

All the certainty he'd created by focussing his emotions on vengeance immediately evaporated. The buffeting of the wind outside rippled through the windowpanes like a blanket being shaken. A stab of fear cut through his gut, the smell of disinfectant mixed with cooking fat and boiled cabbage, as if he was once again a powerless Volunteer banged-up in the Maze.

"That SAS guy was doing his job," continued O'Donnell. "He'll go back home to get on with the rest of his life. That's how it is.

"But if you turn this into a revenge saga, you're risking other Volunteers' lives and *our* money to satisfy your vengeance. That's unacceptable.

"Whereas the traitor – *our* traitor – was betraying *us*, his comrades, for money… and will do it again. Until we find *him*."

Carragher knew this. But it didn't help.

"You've sidelined yourself by obsessing about this SAS guy," said O'Donnell. "We were actually discussing Duffy."

Carragher hadn't wanted to think about Duffy. It was too close to him having to think about Máire, the baby, and the dying.

O'Donnell decided to spell it out.

"They moved the cordon away from the bombed building while Duffy was waiting. He had a telephone in the safe house. Plus he was the only person apart from you and me who knew about the second bomb."

But Carragher had recruited Duffy. He knew all his foibles, including his resentment at Máire marrying Séan, then being left out of the bomb operation preparations. Duffy was clever and technical, not brave or cunning. He would never have dared to betray the operation.

"Much more important," said O'Donnell, "I want to know how the fuck it happened."

"I do too," Carragher said. "But killing Duffy buries the question."

"You're very certain it wasn't him…?"

"It wasn't Duffy."

"But you don't actually know, Séan – and that's a problem."

Without thinking, O'Donnell leaned backwards, away from Carragher.

"We're developing a new strategy to win this war, courting the allies we need," he said in his lecturer voice. "We must be seen to take action – to be strong.

"Leaders have to make decisions," he continued, avoiding looking at Carragher. "You're making us look weak."

CHAPTER 15

Straker wasn't actually discharged from Musgrove Park until the day after the talk with Dr Morten; after a restful night of unmonitored sleep. He'd not bothered thinking through the doc's suggestion that he leave Northern Ireland as it seemed pointless. He'd only have to return for the Board Of Inquiry.

And then, just after lunch, the same two RMPs returned to Musgrave Park Hospital, then drove Straker to Thiepval Barracks, Lisburn, the suburban fortress complex that housed HQ Northern Ireland.

On arrival, the RMP major explained to him that although he wasn't under arrest, he was required to give evidence.

"Hereford has agreed that you stay here until the inquiry's complete."

"Is this a military or police inquiry?" asked Straker.

"Military," said the major. "We're waiting for 321 Company's technical report on the two bombs. When that comes through, we'll hold a formal Board of Inquiry here in the HQ."

Straker nodded. The Board of Inquiry was standard practice. Keeping him here wasn't; but he was too tired to argue.

"So make yourself at home. You'll be here for a week or so."

That evening Arrosa looked completely different; all in black, a short denim skirt with thick black tights, mid-calf leather boots, wrapped warmly in a long black coat with a dark blue velvet collar. She looked across the huge, high-ceilinged room of the crowded pub to see the man she was meeting raise his hand briefly in greeting.

This was a toned-down version of her "goth going to gigs" look, for the rare occasions she adopted her "localised" Rós Ó Briain persona – completely different from the older vibe and oddly

European sophistication of university-mouse Arrosa. Rós Ó Briain was also one of her emergency options; Arrosa could duck out to the Ladies, and after five minutes applying mascara, diamante earrings and some vigorous back-combing, Rós would emerge – a quite different person with accent and banter that was just about authentic enough.

In this alternate persona, she wasn't trying actually to "be" a local, just to fit in with the generality of a polyglot university city with people from everywhere. But in any case, most of her time as Rós was spent talking to men, who had other things on their minds.

"Are you OK to sit here?" he said.

While waiting for her, he'd taken over two stools at the wooden bar that ran round the far corner of the room, opposite the door. Arrosa looked over into the pub's second, smaller room, which was darker and not visible from the entrance.

"I'd like a booth," she said.

"OK, you take it and I'll get you a drink," he said. "You're on the pints?"

She nodded, then walked into the back room, thinking how the booths' dark wood panelling and privacy resembled confessional boxes. Pouring her Guinness would take the best part of five minutes, so she took the time to think through how she was going to do this.

It was a move out of her carefully constructed neutrality, by which so far she'd avoided getting involved with the actual Troubles. She was also still deciding whether to take the risk of talking to Duffy, and hoped this evening's meeting might help make that decision.

She'd met this guy, Ciarán Moffat, six weeks ago at an Ulster Hall gig headlined by the English goth punk band Siouxsie and the Banshees. He wore scruffy student-style clothing, and even though his alertness and scanning of faces was well concealed, she could tell he was police; at first she thought Drug Squad.

She'd played down her "Rós Ó Briain" act and showed respect when he admitted he was police, emphasising that he was off-duty. They'd swapped first names and he'd given her his office phone number, then they'd arranged to go to gigs together. The last had been Hawkwind at the Ulster Hall on 13 November, after which they'd gone their separate ways deafened and happy. Her "Rós" character was intended for surveillance or for emergencies. It didn't have the same intensively developed background as Arrosa, so there was an element of risk in using it for a meeting.

Ciarán was intelligent and she enjoyed talking to him, Rós presenting herself as apolitical but firmly on the side of law and order – as she herself actually was. A consequence of this for her was confirming that he was Special Branch. She knew from other encounters how boastful they could be, and he was keen – hence meeting him tonight.

"Nice and quiet back here," said Ciarán, lowering the creamy-black pints onto hexagon-shaped Harp Lager mats on the booth's polished table. The glasses were straight, thick and proper, with the same harp logo but "Guinness" written underneath. In a good Irish bar, alongside all the shine and polish, the detail carries it.

As he leaned forwards, she caught a flash of an inside waistband concealed-carry holster. The butt looked like a black parkerised Ruger Speed-Six – of which she approved. The Ruger revolver was more reliable than the semi-automatic Walther PPK that most RUC still carried when off-duty.

She smiled up at him.

"I thought we could have a chat for once," she said. "As opposed to shouting to each other at gigs."

She'd already decided Ciarán was a decent guy – early thirties, married young and now divorced with no children, non-practising Catholic, mature enough not to push it with her.

"So how's your week?" he said.

"Everybody's packing up for Christmas," she said. "So it's parties and last-minute work crises. I'd imagine yours is rather different…"

He smiled.

"Christmas is bomb-threat season. Usually false alarms, but we've still got to do the work."

"With that crazy security fence, the city centre feels safe enough," she said.

"Yep – stops them walking the bombs in. Not many actual explosions, thank God. But a bomb alert means evacuation, stopping trade for several hours. The economic damage of a string of scares is much the same as an actual explosion."

"So how do you know when to evacuate everybody?"

"Pre-arranged code words," he said. "So we know it isn't just some nutter."

"I thought you weren't supposed to talk to terrorists?"

He gave her a weary smile.

"Aye," he said. "But politicians don't have to put bits of people into plastic bags. There's all sorts of stuff goes on just to keep the world spinning round, y'know?"

She did know, and returned his smile.

"In the early years," he continued, "when you were over doing your college on the mainland, we had hundreds of bombs going off every week. People were getting killed because bomb warnings were ignored."

Rós had shared a stripped-down version of her real bio with Ciarán in case he checked her out – which, with explanation, it would. She had Spanish parents, was born in England and had a UK passport in her anglicised name, "Rós O'Brian". She hadn't shared her Spanish identity with him. But even if it did come out, it was the exact same name; her Irish forebears the Ó Briains had emigrated from Ireland to Spain in the 19th century, to become "Obregon". She thus had three names – which happens often enough. Smoke and mirrors work best when combined with truth; the basic principle of distraction.

"The IRA minimises danger to themselves," continued Ciarán. "They're not so bothered about other people, though… But killing their own doesn't do their cause any good. So we talk to them, and accept the waste of time and money caused by false alarms."

This was RUC community messaging. It was part of Ciarán's job to put this over to the public. He did it well.

But tonight she was going to push him way beyond that, working on a principle she'd established years ago in Madrid – that all male police officers want women to think them free-spirited.

"Can I ask you something?" she said. "It's been bothering me for a couple of days, ever since a taxi driver pointed out a taped-off bomb scene out west."

"Yeah, of course. Where exactly?"

"I was coming back along the Falls Road; from this school initiative we've got running out in Whiterock. Just past Dunville Park, he pointed down a side street with lights and all sorts of Army and police vehicles."

Ciarán nodded vaguely – slipping, she thought, into professional blankness. But there hadn't been many city bombs over this past year. He'd definitely know about this one.

"He said there'd been a bomb gone off," she continued relentlessly. "But he also said that a pregnant woman was shot – he said *murdered* by security forces."

"This was a black cab – yes?"

Ciarán now spoke in the abrupt, slightly aggressive tone that can make Northern Ireland men seem unfriendly. She nodded. Ciarán remained blank and silent.

"I'd been thinking maybe there'd be something in the news. But nothing..."

He didn't look at her, seeming to be thinking it through.

She was taking a risk, but this meeting was nothing like as dangerous as talking to Duffy, her other option. Although she really didn't want to make Ciarán suspicious. The bottom line on that possibility was the risk of blowing her university cover. But it wouldn't be fatal.

There was also the possibility of her IRA contacts recognising Ciarán. But she was quite sure they wouldn't recognise *her*. And if anything went wrong, Rós Ó Briain would simply evaporate. At the end of the room in which they were sitting was a passage to the Ladies. Beyond that was the rear delivery door which doubled up as the pub's fire escape, opening outwards by a push-bar on the inside. Taxi drivers always stopped for her, and the Belfast Shuttle flew every hour until 10.30pm. Once at the airport, she'd be safe; and back in London by 0200.

"I hope I'm not being naïve," she continued, "but a pregnant woman being shot by a police officer sounds impossible, unless it was some terrible accident like a ricochet or something? Being pregnant is obvious, is my point. The police officer would know. And he would also know that the baby inside her would die too. It seems impossible that *anybody* would do a thing like that?"

Everything about Ciarán was genuine. He cared about his city, the conflict and his own community strongly enough to want to do something that might help. Not just by joining the police, but then enduring the sniping that even a non-practising Catholic would suffer from Protestant colleagues. He loved his music and was a true rock fan. And although he didn't partake, he ignored others smoking weed at gigs. All completely genuine; *he* was completely genuine. He was also, she thought, enlightened – possibly even progressive, a personal strength she recognised in herself, which made for the best sort of undercover officer.

But this could be turned into a weakness, which is what she was doing to him tonight – and required more than just fluttering eyelashes, empathy, and flashes of thigh. That aspect was working well; especially as they both genuinely liked each other. But more was needed. So her strategy was to turn Ciarán's enlightenment into the ambivalence she needed to leverage what she wanted from him.

"Did you believe this taxi driver?" he asked.

"Well, yes, I did," she said. "He was extremely angry. Shaking… which I'd never seen before."

Ciarán now looked uncomfortable, as if about to make a disparaging remark about the reliability of black-cab drivers. Rós pre-empted this.

"And then, just before I left the college to meet you, I heard a similar thing from a group of our students."

Ciarán made as if to laugh at this "corroboration".

"The thing is, Ciarán," she said seriously, "we have a good many students from West Belfast, and I personally know some of them have *those* sorts of connections… Being frank, this means I have to be very careful about meeting you. I shouldn't be, but that's how it is… You know that."

Ciarán nodded.

"I do," he said slowly. "This city's a rumour mill – impossible for secrets. So, yes, there was a bombing down there, but it was the Army who shot dead an obviously pregnant woman. She'd delivered a bomb – in a pram, would you believe it? She'd left the scene, but an Army captain shot her dead with his pistol from a couple of yards' distance. The bomb exploded soon afterwards."

"You said this poor woman had wheeled the bomb into position in a pram…?"

"Yes."

"And was trying to get away when she was shot?"

"Yes."

"And was unarmed?"

He nodded.

"So are they saying she *wasn't* the bomber…?"

He shook his head.

"There was talk of her being what we call a proxy bomber – somebody forced to deliver a bomb."

This was definitely something Ciarán would be permitted to say; presented as conjecture, were she a journalist.

She looked quizzically at him.

"The IRA would kidnap a pregnant woman and make her deliver a bomb?"

He shook his head.

"That's what they're saying."

"But you don't believe it?"

Ciarán didn't reply.

She thought he probably wasn't going to say any more, so she added: "Why didn't he just arrest her? Or maybe he recognised her as a terrorist? From ID photographs, maybe?"

"Well, that's the point," he said after a pause. "She was the *wife* of a terrorist – a guy called Carragher, who's a very senior player."

"So are you saying that makes it OK?" she said, forcing a touch of anger into her concern.

He leaned forwards, as if worried she was about to make a scene.

"No, just the opposite. Her photograph is on the list we send out to the Army, so, yes, the captain would have recognised her. But that doesn't mean he was allowed to shoot her."

"If he recognised her as the wife of a terrorist, he probably thought she would be armed."

"Yes, possibly. But none of us are allowed to open fire unless we actually see a firearm and believe our lives are in danger. The soldiers work to the same very strict rules. And the civil law applies to them, same as us."

She decided to remain silent. Carragher had told her with admiration how Máire had heard the officer's shouted warning, yet continued arming the trigger and detonated the bomb even though realising she was about to be killed. And Rós knew the Northern Ireland Yellow Card Rules for soldiers opening fire. They also applied to her.

"So he should have arrested her?" she said.

Ciarán looked like clamming up again. Which would be fair enough.

"Ah," she added. "But then the bomb exploded… She was a known bomber, so maybe the captain had been trying to stop her from blowing the bomb?"

Ciarán had got himself sucked into the combination of her logic and the passion of her disapproval, as she'd intended. He should have changed the subject, but didn't.

"The bomb was on a timer," he said. "Even if she was the bomber, shooting her wouldn't stop it."

"How would the captain know that?"

She then kept quiet, transmitting disbelief while keeping her face blank.

He responded: "Look, Rós, the captain has been working over here with the SAS for almost two years. The information is that he was running a hit team," he said quietly. "And Máire Carragher wasn't just Séan Carragher's wife, but a member of his elite bomb team."

He clammed up, and they both sat in silence.

"I shouldn't have told you that last bit," he said finally.

She remained silent.

"Look," he continued. "The only protection any of us have is the law. And over here, the law has failed. So we've got the Army on our streets, with their guns and all this random killing."

"I thought the Army was brought over to stop all that?"

"True. We'd lost control and couldn't cope. And the threat back then was to the Catholic community, from Prods who were burning houses to get people out of their areas. It all got worse when the Army arrived. You'd have been away at school for all that, but you know it, yeah?"

"Of course I do. But I also know how the Provisionals rose up from those ashes – you know, like the phoenix bird on their flag, to take revenge as well as protect the Catholic communities."

"*Vengeance is mine, saith the Lord*," observed Ciarán. "Old Testament..."

"And now you're telling me the Army are just as bad?" she said. "Or worse, actually..."

"What do you mean?" he said.

"The Army's our last hope of law and order, so them going round murdering people the same as the Provos makes them worse, doesn't it?"

She picked up her Guinness, looking down at the head, withdrawing herself from the hysteria she'd been generating by imagining it had shapes like a cloud, to say quietly: "But the soldiers you see on the streets... They don't *seem* like those kind of people, y'know?"

Ciarán nodded.

"True enough, they're not," he said. "And you're right, because it's just a small bunch of them doing these things. Most of the soldiers are fine – and doing a great job, I'd say."

They sat in silence for a few moments.

"I joined the RUC two years before all this kicked off," he continued quietly. "I started on the beat in Belfast City – y'know, going round at night on my own with a torch and nothing more than a truncheon in a special pocket in my trousers – like in the joke. And if you took it out you were supposed to file a special report..."

He shook his head. Seaside postcard humour wasn't funny anymore.

"We knew all the people. They talked to us; we were doing normal policing. Dealing with ordinary, normal criminals too. A different world.

"Whereas now we wear body armour, carry rifles and have to be surrounded by soldiers. People get beaten, even tarred and feathered if they're seen talking to us. And the Army get irritated when we refuse to go running round taking cover and acting like it's Dodge City..."

"I get how you feel," said Rós. "For me, returning home from boarding school and college, the changes seemed terrible. But what you're saying about the Army sounds crazy. Why would they have a team going round murdering people?"

"It's a military strategy," he said. "Developed over thirty years or so out in Kenya and Malaya – all those places where they had to deal with rebels and insurgents. They created special units imitating the terrorists, which did good work over there, so they brought them here after the riots in the early seventies. I'm not going to tell you any more than that, but it's one of those units we're talking about here..."

After the PIRA attack on the Army's Four Square Laundry intelligence-gathering operation in October 1972, this was common knowledge, even though the British Army had tried to downplay it.

"But if those kind of tactics work, isn't that good?" she said. "This captain *did* kill a terrorist during a bomb attack...?"

"Yes, but only by breaking the law himself, which makes him the same as a terrorist. To get us back to normal, the police have got to be in charge over here, not the Army. It's been a battle for our high-ups to get the politicians to see the danger. The Army says it's changing..."

"So what's going to happen to this captain?" said Rós.

"Well, like I said, even if soldiers obey their own rules, the Army is still subject to the law, just like the rest of us."

"I wondered what you meant by that."

"He's to be charged with murder, is what I've heard," said Ciarán. "Along with his team. Making an example of them, to shame the Army into stopping using colonial control tactics on UK citizens."

Rós guessed this was Special Branch rumour, but also that it had high-level approval for unofficial dissemination where beneficial. Ciarán was senior enough to do that, so she pushed a little further, looking troubled, putting her hand on his arm.

"Now you've explained, I still can't help thinking maybe this captain deserves the benefit of the doubt...?"

He shook his head slightly.

"I mean, this was an extreme situation," she continued, changing her approach. "As it must be *every* time you guys have to shoot at somebody – confusing, frightening, and incredibly dangerous. And the person this captain did kill was a terrorist."

Ciarán nodded.

"True... But there's reading between the lines on this, and I can't say any more, Rós. I don't actually *know* any more, plus I've said too much as it is. I hope you understand."

"Yeah, sure – not my business. But it seems a lot of people are upset about this, including me, I suppose. Are you saying this captain has done similar things before?"

Ciarán sighed. "No, *I'm* not, Rós, because I don't know. I was repeating what's being said."

He looked suddenly tired, as if distracted by other thoughts. Rós knew she had to stop.

"Let's go for something to eat," she said.

He nodded, picking up their empty glasses to take to the bar on the way out.

"To be honest," he said, pausing as she gathered up her handbag, "if I was over here as a Brit soldier, I'd be too scared of the law even to *aim* my weapon at anyone, simple as that. So this doesn't make sense to me either – like there's a game being played here."

She'd genuinely enjoyed her evening with Ciarán – a sit-down curry, then back to his high-ceilinged and rather nice flat for coffee and a grown-up snog. He actually lived quite near to her, just the other side of the Botanic Gardens, but she'd asked him to call her a taxi back into the city centre and was then dropped off without giving an actual address so she could "take a bit of a walk".

Her own flat was one-bedroomed and small, and like her office at the faculty, in the roof space of a large, beautifully decrepit Georgian town house. Converted from the former servants' quarters, the rooms were restricted by eaves, with windows set into the sloping slate roof like a huge doll's house.

She'd taken off her boots in the hall by the front door, carrying them in her left hand as she ran silently up the wide staircase to the first floor, pausing for a moment at the very top of her narrow staircase to listen for a moment. The hair was still in position in the door jamb, so she unlocked its well-oiled Yale and slipped inside. A table light illuminated each of the three rooms on plug timers. A quick room check, then she relaxed.

Last thing at night was the only time she allowed for herself – a few authentic moments before sleeping. She stripped off in the bedroom and hung her Rós outfit on a coat hanger, zipped up into a suit carry-bag that she pushed to the far end of the wardrobe. She changed into a set of black winceyette pajamas and matching woollen socks, then removed the mascara and lipstick and washed her face. The "Rós" big hair was brushed out, which she wove loosely into a single plait.

She checked the bird feeders outside her bedroom window: suet balls and sunflower seeds, with a water dispenser. They came at sunrise; the goldfinches were her favourites, even though they dropped more seeds than they ate. In a pang of uncharacteristic homesickness, at first glance they'd seemed like two-banded plovers, but with coloured-in red faces and yellow-streaked wings. She'd read up about their having longer, thin beaks for catching insects and extracting small seeds from thistles, so forgave their wasteful table manners.

It was cold up in the eaves, which she didn't mind; it was also quiet, above the street noise with no walking round above her head. Her only registered address was the faculty, so no one had ever ventured up her stairs. Against that ever happening, she'd dressed out the flat: a few posters – not Dalí, who instinctively she did not trust, but portraits. Ramon Casas's suggestively defiant lover Julia in a matador jacket, and Lluïsa Vidal's self-portrait – the only professional female painter of Catalan Modernism.

The flat was spartan; clean and bare, poised for immediate evacuation. But it wasn't actually hers – or anybody's. And at times like now, as she thought about who she was and the insincerity of her interactions with other people, this lack of identity and belonging made her feel sad.

CHAPTER 16

This wasn't the usual glass-walled senior police supervisor's office, looking out over rows of desks and telephones. Although it had been when Ciarán Moffat's boss first took over E5 – the Northern Ireland Special Branch's Belfast-based collation division.

Chief Superintendent Billy Flynn was happy spending the final years of his long and varied career "joining up the dots", as he called it, in Belfast. He thought of himself as dealing with a disease which he called 'Compartmentalitus' – a chronic, long-standing pandemic. Those infected denied having symptoms, avoided tests, then refused to be treated. Effective policing depended on the sharing of information, which wasn't happening here for reasons he completely understood. So he took temperatures, counted the dead, talked to the living, and tested the wells. The reports told him more by what they left out and who was doing the writing than each of the many reporting departments intended. He read everything and kept the jigsaw puzzle picture that emerged to himself.

E5 Collation was generally regarded as a back-room branch with no operational role. Chief Superintendent Flynn bent over backwards to help other branches, and when they reciprocated with information back that he was able to use successfully, he gave them the credit. This policy gave him anonymity within the system but, more importantly, considerable leverage. He knew most of the secrets; everybody owed him.

Chief Superintendent Flynn's real name was Seamus which, being American slang for detective and coupled with his southern Irish accent, hadn't seemed right when he'd started out as a rookie Belfast-beat constable. The "Billy" came from nothing more than the usual Loyalist piss-taking of an obvious southern Catholic, although in his youth he did have the long face and hook nose of the William of Orange murals. But he'd worn the nickname with such good humour that it had stuck.

"Billy" Flynn's early graduation to Special Branch in the 1950s had taken him out to Malaya and Kenya. He'd started in the barbed-wire sectors of Nairobi, identifying Mau Mau leaders, then alongside the British Army in Malaya where, early in that campaign, they'd removed their jungle patrol "Ferret Force" from police oversight, forming a series of jungle-fighting units from which the SAS was re-formed.

Flynn's most interesting work had been in Kenya, where their undercover teams infiltrated tribal areas, captured and turned Mau Mau terrorists, then operated what they'd called "counter-gangs" to capture more terrorists and demoralize Mau Mau civilian supporters. They'd also used what they called "pseudo-gangs" – undercover soldiers using terrorist tactics, weapons, and equipment.

Chief Superintendent Flynn's colonial experience was unusual, enabling him to see what was happening when others didn't. And so in the 1970s, the first decade of the current Troubles, Flynn had observed similar tactics being imported by the British Army into Northern Ireland. But as Brit soldiers couldn't infiltrate the close-knit Republican community, at first they'd been little more than a few soldiers out of uniform in civilian cars, taking potshots at PIRA Volunteers with inevitable mistaken identities and collateral damage. But then, as he'd seen in Kenya, they'd evolved a better structure with more sophisticated tactics, including "pseudo-gangs" emulating PIRA and even attacking Protestant paramilitaries, activating them against PIRA.

The Kenyan Mau Mau had been a brutal rebellion for which the police and Army could only use equally brutal countermeasures. The Army's undercover stuff hadn't been police work but had been worth trying, eventually proving effective, and hurting less people than some of the other tactics being used.

As he did now, Flynn kept most of what he'd seen to himself. He was a pragmatist; so now, with his own country destroying itself in civil uprising, he wasn't going to jeopardise anything that could reduce the violence, even though it might not always be entirely within the letter of the law.

But he also knew that brutality is itself a disease, infecting everybody irrespective of who starts it. Even the most closely targeted "official" violence by security forces spreads the disease.

The first change Billy Flynn had made on his appointment to E5 Collation was to plasterboard over the glass panels separating his office cubicle from the main room. He worked very hard at selecting exactly the right people, so the last thing he needed was to watch what they were doing. But even more, he didn't need them watching him. So now his office was a blank box with just the one small window looking out onto the flat rooftop of the building next door – cramped and claustrophobic.

It was early morning, the main office empty except for Detective Inspector Ciarán Moffat, who was at his desk hunched over files.

"Do you want a cup of coffee?" said Flynn.

Moffat looked up, surprised to see the Chief Superintendent.

"I'll make us both one," he replied.

"No, no, you carry on," said Flynn. "NATO standard?"

"Without the sugar," said Moffat, the Army "joke" having established itself even in the RUC.

An hour later Moffat tapped on Flynn's door. He noticed the care with which Moffat pushed it shut even though the main office was still empty.

"You look tired," he said, as Moffat sat down.

"I've been up most of the night."

"I thought you'd gone home?"

"Yes," said Moffat, sounding tired, "but I came back in."

Flynn took a cigarette from the packet he kept in his right-hand drawer then waited, tapping the tobacco end on the desktop.

"So," said Moffat awkwardly. "What's with this SAS guy – Captain Peter Straker – in the Máire Carragher shooting?"

The chief superintendent didn't answer immediately, although not because he resented the abrupt question as other senior officers might. He encouraged his officers to get directly to whatever concerned them, but he wondered why Moffat was asking.

"A captain of formidable intuition," he observed.

"That's not what people are saying."

"No. And some are probably embarrassed by his *percipience*."

He savoured the word; like "perception" but with undertones of "determination" and "action".

"Do you believe this proxy bomber idea?" asked Moffat.

"Do you?"

"Máire Carragher a proxy bomber? Being *forced* to deliver a bomb in her own pram? No, I really don't."

The chief superintendent nodded. "I doubt if she could have been forced to do anything," he said.

"Also the SAS hit-squad theory…?" continued Moffat.

"Theory?" echoed the superintendent.

"It can't be anything more than that," said Moffat. "I looked into Captain Straker's record – such as I could find. There's nothing, not even any suspicions voiced in the SB reports, despite his taking part in a lot of stakeouts and ambush ops."

"What about motive?"

Moffat looked up.

"For murder?"

"We've got to be logical. He had 'opportunity' and took it. So…"

Moffat had been struck by one report, parts of it actually written by Captain Straker, quoted verbatim by Special Branch as one of the eyewitness testimonies of the Narrow Water ambush at Warrenpoint the previous summer. Straker's observations had been measured and very detailed.

"He lost several close friends at Warrenpoint," said Moffat. "I read his report."

"We've all lost friends," said his boss. "As have many soldiers…"

"There was one bit," continued Moffat, "about him recognizing his former platoon sergeant from picking his face off a tree by the roadside…"

The chief superintendent sighed deeply.

"So you were up *all* of last night, then…"

Moffat nodded, then started absent-mindedly tapping his boss's desktop.

"That bit was very interesting," he said, still unconsciously drumming his fingers. "His reporting of it wasn't even slightly emotional.

"And he'd written out the guy's full name – Tadhg Gearóid Phelan, without his military rank but like on a birth certificate – even his place of birth and the names of his wife and children, before continuing with the report…"

The chief superintendent didn't say anything.

"His children also had Irish names," continued Moffat. "He'd spelled them all correctly, with even the fadas—"

"Where was his friend born?" interrupted the chief superintendent.

"Lickybeg."

"That's County Waterford."

Moffat nodded. "That's where you're from, sir?"

"Aye, right enough."

Flynn wandered over to the window and looked out into the pre-dawn darkness.

"I'm not too far down that same road myself," he observed.

CHAPTER 17

"Everybody's a traitor," said O'Donnell, his voice flat and expressionless. "It's only the price that varies."

"And you?" asked the voice on the other end of the phone. "What's yours?"

O'Donnell specialised in influence and contacts. Nobody asked him that question, and he hated being telephoned. Nevertheless, he laughed. "A united Ireland," he said.

This was one of the most senior "old" IRA people, a man he'd worked with in Dublin before moving north in 1969.

"Yeah, right," said the man. Privately they both believed the North was unlikely to become part of the Republic of Ireland in their lifetimes.

This phone call was Dublin imposing its authority. But those guys were out of touch to the extent of not even realising the possibility of a phone tap. O'Donnell had to accept the call – but he did not have to like it.

He put the telephone handset carefully back into its black plastic cradle, resisting the surge of anger that made him want to smash it down like an auctioneer's gavel. Taking his time, he put a grey gabardine raincoat over the top of his tweed jacket, wrapped a muffler round his neck, and left the house by the back door into the plastic car port.

The lane was quiet and very wet. After opening the low wrought-iron gates, he reversed his Hillman Hunter slowly out into the darkness then drove thirty miles south, through Newtownards and Downpatrick, into the fishing village of Ardglass and to a discreet public telephone box round the back of the main Quay Street.

"The sell-out is the most damaging aspect," said O'Donnell, resuming the call precisely one hour later, from a very clean phone box. "Outside the team, only three others knew."

"There's leaks all over like a sieve," said the voice. "The Brits know how to use their money."

"This is different," said O'Donnell. "We were played."

"So it's a good job nobody tried to boast about this to our foreign friends."

"That's because nobody your end knew about it," said O'Donnell bluntly. "Apart from you…"

There was silence as the inherent threat in what O'Donnell had said was noted.

"If we're to bring our foreign friends back on board," O'Donnell continued, "we need to impress them with our commitment."

"With them into suicide bombing?" said the voice.

"Whereas we know there's only the one virgin," replied O'Donnell.

"Yeah – over-expectation of something that isn't going to happen isn't much of a vice."

"They know that," said O'Donnell flatly. "But they are impressed by capability."

"As indeed they are," agreed the voice. "Like not making our own people drive suicide car bombs, but instead kidnapping a man's family then forcing him to make the delivery."

"They do coercion too," said O'Donnell.

But he didn't actually care. Bombs were equally dangerous to bomber and target alike. And religion was irrelevant. Nor did he care about Catholic theology condemning suicide as the only sin for which there could be no forgiveness.

"So, talking of commitment as we were, are the Maze hunger strikers going to end up dying?"

"We hope not," said O'Donnell blandly.

The dirty protest – and now this hunger strike – was an issue, but O'Donnell didn't want to talk about it. It was fine with him if jailed Volunteers refused to wear prison uniforms and went naked and smeared shit all over their cells – good luck to them. But here in the outside world, there were more serious problems to think about.

"You're hoping the enemy will take pity on them?"

"The guys are showing commitment," said O'Donnell, but he wasn't interested. "Getting banged-up is a fail. They're out of the game – not contributing."

"But is Gaddafi likely to be impressed?" the voice continued. "Thatcher definitely won't be, and she's just as fucking mad."

"It's a sideshow," said O'Donnell. "But let's hope they succeed."

O'Donnell's insincerity was backed by a detailed knowledge of both the Roman Catechism and Irish history. Hunger strikes were just as much a mortal sin as triggering a suicide vest. But in Ireland the Church had backed off from moral condemnation of hunger strikes, as they were quintessentially Irish, a pre-Christian tradition intended as a shaming protest that stopped short of death.

"What counts is what we do when one of them actually dies," added O'Donnell.

"Funeral with full military honours, I suppose."

O'Donnell didn't answer.

"Then pay for a couple of new Muriels?"

The voice laughed ironically. This disparaging mispronunciation of the word "mural" was a Protestant thing.

"I didn't think that down in Dublin you'd be watching *Coronation Street*," said O'Donnell.

"What do you mean?"

In *Coronation Street*, "muriel" was a malapropism frequently repeated by one of the characters when referring to a tasteless mural of mountains painted on her sitting-room wall. Protestants in Northern Ireland almost certainly watched it, disparaging the semi-sacred Republican murals as just one of countless sectarian insults.

"Never mind," snapped O'Donnell. "But Republicans up here wouldn't find that funny."

The "old" IRA, tucked safely away down in Dublin, paid no heed to the critical semantics that caused so much trouble up here. He'd taken the trouble to study all this, and thought them irresponsible.

O'Donnell had also studied Mao Tse Tung. Without the support of "the people" – those this man was disparaging – the revolution and PIRA were fish without water and would die. The Catholic Church had worked to a similar principle for centuries. Sinners had only to accept Catholic absolution for an infinitely renewable pass to swim in the holy waters of forgiveness. But they didn't have to stop sinning, and the Church was careful not to condemn PIRA and its supporters.

O'Donnell was quite clear that the Republican community support that kept Mao's PIRA fish-guerrillas alive was the same body of water as that for which the Church issued swimming tickets. Some PIRA leaders attended daily Mass; some priests worked for the Cause as well as for the Catholic community. There was no moral absolute. But care was required, which was O'Donnell's only interest in this, as Church forbearance depended on particular lines never being crossed, and suicide bombing was the other side of the line.

And they had yet to see how Rome would react to any of the Maze hunger strikers actually dying. But having juggled politics and diplomacy in its own favour since 1054, O'Donnell doubted that the Holy Mother Church would create problems.

"The Libyans value our expertise," said O'Donnell, returning to the main subject.

"We need to impress them. A few spectaculars are required."

"Yes," replied O'Donnell, "but we also need to send them somebody sensible to be our rep. Unlike that muppet you's guys had over there running things before…"

There was a silence. PIRA's previous representative in Tripoli had become too uselessly bizarre even for Colonel Gaddafi.

"Do that and you'll see…" said O'Donnell. "We'll get them back."

"Yeah," said the voice. "You are right, and killing that SAS team would have been a fierce start. So have you worked out what went wrong? I'd think you'd be looking at yer man for that…?"

This reference was to O'Donnell's long-term, exceptionally well-placed contact. O'Donnell didn't even know who he was – a careful, successful, purely telephone relationship cultivated over many years. O'Donnell imagined him as a man-about-Belfast, something to do with the university, politicians, police – wherever, whatever. Or so it seemed. High level, high achieving, a practising Catholic but closet Republican, a conduit who'd always been reliable and accurate. O'Donnell had used him to set up Carragher's ambush operation.

"He'd passed on the details of the meeting," replied O'Donnell. "We know the message got through because they put the SAS team into the building. Which should have been the end of them."

O'Donnell's contact was one of only a handful of people able to play one side off against the other, with one foot either side of the sectarian "river of fire". Most people attempting this got their bollocks burned, so O'Donnell considered it an appropriate metaphor.

"I heard yer man went down there, immediately after?"

This change of "yer man" now referred to Carragher.

"I told him to stay away," said O'Donnell. "Which, to be fair to him, he did. But he saw for himself how quickly they evacuated from around the bomb building."

The voice at the other end of the phone swore quietly.

"Instincts tell me we were betrayed," continued O'Donnell. "But I'm guessing not until after the SAS had occupied the building. Otherwise why would they have gone in there?"

"Perhaps the traitor told them about the first bomb, but didn't know about the one already in the building?"

O'Donnell wasn't interested in a discussion.

"If they'd known about either bomb," he said, "none of the security forces would have gone anywhere near. But listen to me – I'm sorting this out. Don't try to micro-manage this…"

There was silence. Then a quiet request, replacing the argumentative tone: "So what are you thinking?"

"About what?"

"It was yer man's plan – and then his wife who got killed."

At first O'Donnell didn't reply.

"That's another problem," he said eventually.

"Meaning?"

"I already told you he wasn't up to it," O'Donnell replied slowly. "But you wouldn't listen."

"Yeah, and we disagreed with you. But we still think he's a fine commander doing great sorting everybody out. And this operation showed genius – you said so yourself."

"You don't know him like I do," replied O'Donnell. "He climbed into marriage like it was a lifeboat. I told you he wasn't right for command, and I've been trying to keep him straight ever since. When this thing went wrong, he pretty much gave up."

"Yeah, but for fuck's sake, the man just lost a wife and his unborn baby…"

"That's just excuses," said O'Donnell coldly. "I told you he phoned me while it was all still going on. He'd lost it and I had to order him not to go steaming in and make things worse."

"Yeah, but he listened to you."

"We'll have to watch how this plays out with him. Unless you want him removed from command right now?"

"No! Of course we fucking don't – not that we can actually do that, for fuck's sake."

"Well, in that case, if you won't lean on Northern Command then you'll have to be the ones to unravel whatever he does next."

O'Donnell was suddenly sick of this discussion. Dublin was too far from Belfast to be relevant. Unless they agreed with him, he couldn't be bothered with them.

"And don't call me again, OK? Use the proper channels."

He felt his anger flashing up, so he put the phone down.

Outside the telephone box seagulls were crying out in the blustery night air, bad weather approaching. He walked back round onto Quay Street and into the marina chippie which sold fish off the boats from that morning.

Carragher had been proved right about it being a disaster, he thought. He was probably also right about their only suspect Duffy being innocent. The shame of this could be rationalised, even lessened by some plausible explanation. But the cost remained, and the sooner somebody was made to pay, the better – innocent or not.

After driving back home, O'Donnell sat for several hours in his north-facing study, staring out into the darkness. The positive narrative he needed didn't require him to do anything more than emphasise what was already there: the absence of civilian casualties, Máire's heroism, and the indiscrimination of the SAS in shooting a heavily pregnant woman.

He'd already primed *An Phoblacht*, which would put all that together with its usual brio, except that its over-the-top style was tolerable only to full-on Republicans and it came out once a week. Whereas O'Donnell needed immediate and argued coverage, that would be read widely across both the Republican and Protestant communities. He also needed it to make the UK national news which, if pitched correctly, would stir up the politicians in Westminster as well as over here in Stormont.

He picked up the phone again. He'd missed that morning's newspaper editions, but there was time for the Sixth Late Tele – the *Belfast Telegraph*'s evening edition – to interview Máire's family. But he also knew that the journalist he was going to talk to, before he did any work for his own newspaper, would call the BBC and sell them the story exactly as O'Donnell pitched it, getting it into this coming morning's national broadcast news cycle.

CHAPTER 18

Carragher never usually dreamed; or maybe he did, then couldn't remember. But now the circular, repetitive dreams were every night, exhausting and inexplicably frightening. Although, until tonight, the Madonna dream hadn't returned.

He avoided going to bed until the early hours, driven to it by tiredness. But no matter how late he left it, a couple of hours after falling asleep he'd be wide awake again, still exhausted. Unbearable anxiety forced him to get up in the cold and darkness, fumbling his way down to whatever sort of kitchen the safe house might have, to make tea if there was a kettle, cups etc. He'd sit and try to read, or stand with the lights off, shivering, looking out into a tiny brick-walled yard at the rear extensions of other blank-faced terraced houses where normal people were sleeping.

And tonight, she'd returned: the same church and strange, thatched house beside a river, the boat tied to the wooden jetty trailing an oar. This time he remembered a mountain in the background, jagged and black, covered in pine trees, with a splendid, shining raven staring at him.

The familiarity of this scene spiked his fear – random but also ominous, each object there for some reason he was supposed to understand. And then the Madonna beckoned for him to come to her. She sat on a wooden stool, the baby in her lap as if it were sleeping. But from the way its head lolled backwards he knew it was dead. He tried to stop himself walking forwards but could not.

She beckoned him closer, her skin like candle wax, eyes yellow with bright red pinpricks. As she spoke, he saw her teeth were broken. This time she said: "It wasn't you. It was him. Come closer and I will tell you his name."

He moved closer, closed his eyes, and she whispered in his ear. The knowing made him rejoice, all his fear and grief replaced by certainty. And then she kissed him on the lips as so many times before, exactly what he'd wished for. But then he opened his eyes to see her rotting face, mouth filled with blood, snarling at him. She then thrust the dead baby at him and he jumped backwards, falling, to awaken with the terrors of the night pumping through his veins.

She'd given him the name. But in the horror, he'd forgotten it.

Carragher knew these dreams came from the part of himself that he was suppressing. He also knew they would continue until he did something about it. The need was practical; he couldn't carry on like this for much longer, not sleeping or eating, shouting at people – or avoiding them, sitting on his own and brooding.

THURSDAY 4 DECEMBER

An Phoblacht had led with the story on its front page, plus a long editorial casting back through the history of British Army atrocities in Ireland. The journalist had also followed up O'Donnell's suggestion of including material from the Malaya and Borneo Emergencies, drawing parallels between the British Army's formation of undercover teams using the same brutal tactics as the Mau Mau terrorists, and the current SAS tactics in Northern Ireland.

Of the mainstream Irish newspapers, the *Irish News* had picked it up and done a well-researched article. O'Donnell's contact on the *Belfast Telegraph* had pretty much echoed *An Phoblacht*, although with less Republican outrage: a front-page splash with a photo of Máire looking innocently maternal, a scathing lead editorial about the need for police primacy over secret Army operations, and an op-ed thinkpiece on the opposing page about the unacceptability of using what it called "long-discredited Empire-building tactics" on British citizens in the United Kingdom.

The *Irish Catholic* quoted condemnation statements from its standard list of senior Churchmen, with the Archbishop of Armagh – the Primate of All Ireland – writing what O'Donnell thought to be a rather well-researched hue-and-cry thinkpiece combining theology and military procedures. His juxtapositioning of the sanctity of motherhood and the innocent souls of the unborn with the British Army's Yellow Card Rules of Engagement made uncomfortable reading for everybody who carried a gun in Northern Ireland – even though O'Donnell thought the theology ridiculous.

In London, the "innocent mother" photo of Máire was splashed with varying headlines: the *Daily Mail* raged about PIRA's irresponsibility in placing young mothers in harm's way, the *Guardian* earnestly demanded full disclosure by the Tory Government, and the *Sun* ran Máire's photo with the headline *SAS Shoot Dead IRA Boss's Pregnant Bomber Wife*. O'Donnell was impressed they'd managed to squeeze in the possessive apostrophe. The *Daily Telegraph* stuck to the facts provided by O'Donnell, with an op-ed about the dangers of the RUC seeming not to be in control.

Something to enrage everyone, thought O'Donnell with satisfaction, nicely deflecting attention from the unsatisfactory details. PIRA retaliatory action would still have to be taken, but the media shit-storm would give them more time to get that done. Taking the initiative like this also set the scene for shaping the eventual narrative into something positive.

Plus, he'd started a hare running inside the Stormont-Westminster and security force complex, to further confuse and complicate their already stressed inter-agency relations – especially between Special Branch and the Army. The Tory government would be unable to stop itself from interfering.

All this distraction was good news, but O'Donnell's urgent need was to confirm new sourcing for explosives, weapons, and ammunition to replenish their dwindling stocks. The new supply partner needed to be confident of PIRA's commitment and capability, which UK media were now trumpeting across the firmament as if it were gospel. To O'Donnell, with all the cynicism of a former altar boy remembering childhood Christmases, they seemed like the Archangel Gabriel announcing a new incarnation.

But O'Donnell was in no doubt that after his having claimed ownership of Carragher's operation, he'd be blamed not just for its failure, but also for PIRA being forced to stop operations. PIRA's operational commanders frightened O'Donnell, although none of them including Carragher would ever know this.

O'Donnell was a coward. He hated himself for it, and worked harder at avoiding blame than he ever did to safeguard success.

He worked equally hard at generating fear in others, which his long-standing mentor relationship prevented him from doing with Carragher. He couldn't confront him physically and, face-to-face, Carragher's unpredictability was too frightening. So long as O'Donnell saw advantage in the relationship, he'd jolly it along. But he'd ensure Carragher took the blame for whatever problems were generated in the playing-out of this situation.

Carragher never read *An Phoblacht* or listened to the news on either radio or the television. So it was the evening newspaper-vendors' posters that made him buy a copy, then to forget everything he'd promised to O'Donnell.

FRIDAY 5 DECEMBER

And then the day after the initial splash, O'Donnell's tame journalist had sought further details from his contacts in the Coroner's Office. The autopsy report included the gender of the dead baby. So he'd written a follow-up speculation piece about the little boy. The headline, accompanied by an enlargement of Máire's mumsy pic, read, *PIRA Leader's Son Could Not Have Survived SAS Gun Attack.*

"I want to talk with the intelligence officer," Carragher said to the Chief of Staff.

"He's downstairs."

"Get him up here now."

The Chief of Staff left the door open. Carragher listened to him go down, and the brief conversation in the kitchen. A different, more measured tread came back up the stairs.

"Has that tout been back in touch?" said Carragher, before the intelligence officer had even entered the back bedroom.

"The one that gave us the SAS men?"

The intelligence officer had learned to be less forthcoming.

"Yes," replied Carragher. "The one you said had disappeared."

"He has."

"And has he returned yet?"

The intelligence officer didn't reply.

"These people always do," said Carragher. "They only exist when they're being told something or passing bits of it on. In-between times, they're somebody different, which doesn't pay nearly as well."

The intelligence officer nodded.

"There's always a way of getting in touch," Carragher continued. "Do you know what that is?"

The intelligence officer didn't, but as that would be the wrong answer, he just nodded ambiguously.

"You're making me feel really fucking confident," said Carragher.

"I can pass the word," said the intelligence officer.

"You do that," said Carragher. "And can you guess what I want from him…?"

The intelligence officer nodded a second time.

"Good. And make sure he understands that I want that name soonest. He'll know it, and I want it. You fucking get it for me."

O'Donnell was in his conservatory on an uncharacteristically sunny morning – cold, but under a clear blue sky in which a flock of some hundred Brent geese were wheeling overhead in wavering lines. Their honking irritated him, and even though they'd be long gone by the time his frozen, empty vegetable garden was again producing, he imagined them like locusts, stripping it bare.

When the phone rang, he was already out of sorts and not enjoying his morning coffee.

"You've let things slip, Breandán," said the voice, with its heavy Northern accent.

O'Donnell didn't respond.

"I've got yer man talking to me, which is one thing. But he's come at me through somebody else, which is a whole additional cause for concern.

"But you know how it is," the man continued. "I'm happy. It's you who needs to do the worrying. Which is why I'm telling you this."

He rang off.

That was the end of O'Donnell's relaxed coffee morning. After a moment of intense anger, he returned himself to his normal state of cold indifference.

CHAPTER 19

Carragher was once again being driven south-east by Roxy, into the Ards. This was his second meeting with O'Donnell in as many days – highly unusual, so he knew he was in trouble.

"You've gone behind my back, Séan, which is unacceptable," said O'Donnell, speaking mildly, with great care.

The meeting took place at another country pub, but out the back, without food, drink, or preamble.

"I took the trouble to spell it out to you, so all you had to do was leave it – do nothing. But you couldn't manage that, or you didn't listen. Either one is bad enough, except that you've also jeopardised our relationship with the best source we've got inside the RUC."

The charge was delivered in a flat, slow monotone.

"Did you not think about the complications?"

This was rhetorical. Carragher didn't interrupt.

"Informers, contacts, whatever you call them – they're faceless so we don't know who they are, what they think, who they're working for, or whether they're even actually people."

They were standing facing each other across a high-ceilinged empty room out the back, half-filled with stacked-up chairs. Carragher didn't respond.

"You talk to a voice on the phone, and you don't know if that person is passing on a message from somebody else – it could be through a whole string of other people. The end person might be Margaret Thatcher for all we know.

"It seems I have to explain the basics to you – which I shouldn't have to be doing, y'know..."

O'Donnell looked around the room, which had an ancient, dusty-framed photo of a newly crowned Queen Elizabeth over the fireplace.

"We don't *do* what these people tell us. We don't even decide if we're going to *believe* what they tell us. We simply decide whether we're going to take any action in relation to what they say."

O'Donnell pulled one of the chairs across to the centre of the room, positioning it facing the window, precisely underneath the plaster ceiling rose from which a single bulb hung down on a one-metre electrical cable. He motioned for Carragher to sit down, then dragged a second chair over to one side by the window and sat down himself.

"And there's the relationship. This particular guy's been talking to me for decades. We rely on these guys, and they rely on us – and on the protocols."

O'Donnell was going through what he needed to say calmly and quietly, like a doctoral supervisor to a promising but unruly post-grad. But he couldn't discuss Carragher's jeopardising *his* source without anger creeping into his voice.

Carragher made as if to say something, but O'Donnell motioned at him to remain silent.

"You've put our man in jeopardy... or maybe the chain of people through which he gets to us."

Again Carragher made to say something, but was silenced.

"It's not for us to question that, Séan. He's made a strong complaint, so I have to act. I've no choice, and there's no comeback from this."

At this, Carragher did speak.

"So what are you going to do?"

"It's not me, Séan. This has come down from the Army Council – that's the level at which the complaint was received. I'm just the messenger."

O'Donnell turned away for a moment.

"Luckily, though, it's just me, the Council Chief of Staff and his Adjutant who know. They leaned on Northern Command, where your detractors were only too pleased to comply.

"There was nothing I could say – I was sidelined. So, yeah, Northern Command told me to tell you that you're relieved of command as of now."

There was a long silence.

"You're to get yourself back together, Séan," O'Donnell continued.

"Work through the emotions, and let's get us back to what we're both doing here.

"None of this is personal, and none of us is important enough for our feelings to count. It's emotions down the generations that have screwed Ireland. They've no place in fighting a war."

What O'Donnell had actually told the Army Council Chief of Staff was that Carragher was mentally unstable. He hadn't wanted to do that. Carragher was his protégé, and this would be passed on to Northern Command. But O'Donnell wasn't going to let other people's emotions get in the way of his plans.

Carragher sat hunched over beneath the bare lightbulb, leaning forwards with his arms on his knees. He was slowly clenching then relaxing his fists, staring at the floor.

O'Donnell wanted to leave as quickly as possible, but instead stood looking down on Carragher for a few moments, taking long, slow breaths, telling himself the lad would never bite the hand that fed him. It was like he'd made a dare with himself, counting down the seconds until he'd won.

Then, very slowly, O'Donnell nodded his head, as if agreeing with whatever Carragher was thinking. He turned away towards the door, but then paused to demonstrate his lack of fear. The young Queen seemed amused by this. He wanted to smash her dusty glass. But instead he walked slowly out into the yard.

O'Donnell walked across the rear car park to where Roxy was sitting in the borrowed Cortina. He pointed at him to get out and follow him round to the front of the pub.

"I've had to be the bearer of bad news," he said. "He'll be upset."

Roxy was deferential and nodded without saying anything. But O'Donnell knew he was Carragher's man, hence having this conversation out here in the open.

"I've a house in the Murph where nobody bothers me – and it doesn't get broken into, if you follow my drift. Here's the keys."

He handed over an envelope with the address typewritten on the front.

"The neighbours are helpful. They know me just as Breandán, so you can mention my name. But they know not to ask questions. There's tea and food in the kitchen."

Roxy also knew better than to ask questions. So when O'Donnell nodded to terminate the conversation, he turned away without a word and returned to the Cortina.

O'Donnell had moved into the Ballymurphy house after making his strategic move out of Dublin in 1967. He didn't like either the house or Ballymurphy, and wondered why they all didn't just leave – as so many had done.

But set against the dysfunction of the North generally, the Murph's disenfranchised, isolated community had a strange and very strong cohesion that he respected. Although his seniority within the Army was rumoured, he kept his distance from them and was himself respectful. He had others make it clear to the local PIRA cell that he was to be ignored, and from time to time he passed money to particular community leaders for the repair of roofs and other good works.

O'Donnell had parked his Hillman Hunter a little further down the lane from the pub where Carragher was still sitting. His Protestant dairy farmer neighbour had called its brown-beige colour "calf-scour". O'Donnell had assumed a joke, although he'd had to look it up: it was "diarrhoea affecting very young calves". His Hunter was one of the last assembled at Dublin's Shanowen Road plant; Rootes' top-of-the-range family model which he'd bought brand new after considerable research.

O'Donnell was a political history lecturer, initially at University College Dublin, and now a part-time Lecturer Emeritus at Queen's; an expert on the War of Irish Independence that drove the British out of the south, and the divisive cruelty of the eleven-month Irish Civil War which immediately followed. In the 1960s he'd seen the signs of similarly fundamental disorder in the North, and was now taking advantage of the opportunities this offered.

As he drove himself back through the narrow lanes, he reflected on the British Army and the support it had from the Protestant community. That was the big difference up here; the reason this would never be Ireland versus the Brits.

Eleven years ago, the British Army had been brought over as a short-term reinforcement for the police. At first O'Donnell had taken the same view as the old IRA leadership in Dublin; that deploying the Army was a political mistake by the Brits from which they could profit.

But the energy of the Provisional IRA as it broke away from Dublin control had prevented the withdrawal of the British Army, which had very rapidly developed new tactics – with staunch Protestant support. And so, early on O'Donnell had realised that this wasn't going to be a second War of Independence.

He turned into his own little lane, sign-posted to the dairy farm at the far end, then drove the Hunter into its plastic car port. The bungalow's side entrance into the boot room and then kitchen lined up exactly with his driver-side door, so he never got wet. As ever, rain was drumming on the car port's roof, splashing into the guttering and down the pipes, to a line of 176-gallon water butts across the back. O'Donnell was a conservationist, supported Greenpeace and grew organic vegetables.

Dusk was quickly setting in, motion sensors triggering lights around the house as he unlocked the side door and tapped his security code into the burglar alarm control box. He made a cup of tea and sat in his conservatory to watch the final fading of the light.

The dispassionate logic of the British Army frightened O'Donnell. Their undercover tactics and information gathering were formidable, despite power struggles between Army and RUC commanders, and some clumsy security failures early on leading to political censure. They drew on hundreds of years' experience and an endless well of clever strategists and leaders, backed by vast amounts of Westminster money.

O'Donnell had been a lone voice trying to change the strategy of this war they could never win. But PIRA chiefs hadn't listened, so he'd stopped sticking his neck out. And now, after a decade of evolution, the formidable British Army had brought PIRA to the brink of defeat.

Equally formidable was O'Donnell's personal ambition. In the late sixties, as a senior IRA staff officer down in Dublin, he'd realised the IRA's Marxist leadership would not help Catholics in the North when the violence began. He saw this as an opportunity, so in 1967 he'd quit Dublin for a teaching job at Queen's University Belfast, moving into Ballymurphy to establish Republican credibility, where he'd met Carragher. He'd then engaged with the Northern Ireland Civil Rights Association, which he'd correctly predicted would become the ideological epicentre of Republican protest. Protestant counter-protest would make the non-sectarian NICRA seem pro-Republican, a dishonest smearing of genuine protest which O'Donnell encouraged.

In 1969, during the acrimonious IRA split between North and South, O'Donnell had been one of the early joiners of the emergent Provisional IRA. He'd created a powerful niche for himself as the provider of combat supplies from the South, while keeping his former bosses in Dublin informed.

In 1972, O'Donnell had recruited Carragher from the Official IRA. After taking part in their botched bombing of the Aldershot Officers' Mess, he'd become disillusioned. O'Donnell sent him south to learn directly from the master bomb-makers, so by 1975 Carragher was an expert, working directly and exclusively for O'Donnell.

The high tempo of PIRA's initial campaign eventually tailed off, and by 1980 there was not much more than tunnel vision to show for eleven relentless years. Being both radical yet deeply conservative, PIRA leadership saw reducing the intensity of operations as defeatist. But dwindling resources gave them no other options.

This increased the delicacy of O'Donnell's position. Being PIRA's connection to Dublin and the massive resources of IRA funding and arms in the South made some people up here resent his independence and influence.

PIRA tactics had to change, but O'Donnell could only persuade. He needed a demonstration of unequivocal success to lend his allies enough courage to stick their necks out and support his ideas. But getting the recalcitrant to re-focus was just as dangerous as it was difficult.

The Army Council and the individual brigade commanders would mostly defer to O'Donnell; even so, being the lone voice of dissension was still dangerous. If this went wrong for him, they'd paint him as the unacceptable face of Dublin interference, and in the least-worst case scenario, he might have to move back to the South, having wasted thirteen years.

The other options were even less appealing. *If you're not with us, you're against us* always applied, no matter who you were. He knew how far it *could* go, so didn't take risks himself. That was for others.

Also, Breandán O'Donnell did not respect other people's emotions, causing as they did the repetition of mistakes. He thought them Ireland's Achilles heel. So Carragher's getting emotional and reporting "disaster" had greatly worried him. He was already out on a limb with some members of the Army Council and didn't like being frightened; that was not for him to suffer, but *his* currency to mete out to others.

O'Donnell thought Carragher's surrendering to his emotions weak and selfish. It was not *helpful.* He used this word a lot; everybody was required to be helpful, as an extension of the *If you're not with us, you're against us* mantra. It was similarly non-specific, yet sinister; O'Donnell used it to damn individuals without the need for evidence. Implying disrespect it also suppressed debate, another of O'Donnell's fear-induction tactics.

He did, however, trust his own judgment regarding character and capability – and Carragher was his protégé. His current weakness could only be temporary, but O'Donnell was greatly disappointed by Carragher's lack of self-control.

If they were to change minds, they had to succeed. Failure would only reinforce the intransigent in their determination to continue as before – and lose the war.

CHAPTER 20

PREQUEL – FRIDAY 21 NOVEMBER 1980

Captain Peter Straker was a Forces' brat, the only child of Army parents who were constantly abroad on foreign postings. After a disruptive succession of junior schools on military bases, at age eight he'd been sent away to boarding school – a prep school in Devon – then from thirteen onwards to Harrow, his father's old school.

Spending the holidays in sterile diplomatic compounds, with all the worry of having to fly a small boy halfway round the world on his own, didn't work for his mother. So despite her reluctance, he'd been farmed out to his godfather, an Army officer whose family farmed at Ardglenna in the north-west of Dungannon, a tight-knit village where he'd found a real home.

Back then in 1958, the IRA's border "resistance campaign" – Operation Harvest – was down to just a few shootings and occasional vandalism, like cratering roads. The IRA faced public hostility, with many of their own commanders calling for the campaign to end. The Cork command had actually withdrawn. That summer both the Irish and British governments closed their internment camps, saying the internees were no longer a threat.

Ardglenna village was far enough north of the border to have avoided direct involvement, although it had its share of "Army men". As a schoolboy Straker had known who they were; they'd been as friendly to him as any of his other childhood friends there. As in many other villages, there were also families in Ardglenna whose sons were in the British Army, a tradition on both sides of the border. The Irish have always made good soldiers. And everybody rubbed along.

Holidays at Ardglenna had sustained Straker throughout the loneliness of boarding-school, giving him a sense of family. His actual parents were too involved with chasing his father's military ambitions as a rising senior officer across the far reaches of the former British Empire.

But in 1971, Straker joined the British Army. Since then, his military career had revolved around Operation Banner – the Army name for its Northern Ireland campaign. For eight years he'd been either out there on operations, or training for the next tour.

But he'd never returned to Ardglenna.

Having known IRA Volunteers while growing up in County Tyrone, to Straker, PIRA could never be just the shadowy thugs imagined by his military colleagues. Nor were they the criminal gang portrayed by the security forces and the British government. These days, Ardglenna's IRA men were members of PIRA's East Tyrone Brigade, one of the most effective paramilitary groups in Northern Ireland.

But most of what Straker read about them in the Det's top-secret intelligence digests didn't equate to his boyhood memories. He'd thought deeply about this: the underlying injustice that drove them, terrorism and economic damage being their only recourse through being too few in number to fight the British Army directly.

True, they robbed banks and extorted. But this was to fund the war they saw themselves as fighting; a Second Irish War of Independence. Their objective was freedom from British rule, with the additional – and as they saw it, altruistic – aim of re-making all of Ireland as one socialist republic.

This, however, did not reconcile Straker to the terrible things they were doing. But he realised that the men he'd known probably felt the same way; as he'd felt similarly conflicted about some of the things done by the security forces.

A further complication was the warping effect of motivation, which Straker's experience now enabled him to see. Those giving the orders had motives that were often very different to those of the people directly involved with the carnage. The simplistic idea that "the end justified the means" was used by both sides to avoid thinking too closely about their effects on ordinary people.

Straker had seen the downward spiral in action; anger and disgust creating implacable hatred, justifying revenge, then even more of the carnage that started the cycle. Where it started wasn't important. But this process could disable good people, so Straker guarded himself against it.

Northern Ireland was ridiculously complicated, Straker's experience having taught him to trust his own judgment above orders or party line expectations. He took action on his own terms, with maximum efficiency, while accepting full responsibility.

But that meant there were orders he wouldn't obey – uncrossable lines. Over his eight years in the Army, he'd faced this dilemma with varying degrees of exposure. So far, he'd been proved right.

Soldiers in Northern Ireland were expected to act like policemen, which Straker thought was unreasonable. In August 1969, they'd been brought over in a panic when the RUC could no longer contain rioting in Belfast and Londonderry, initially to protect the Republican communities from Loyalist thugs. *Not* bringing in the soldiers, was thought at that time was to risk civil war.

But rather than making this a temporary measure, and using a withdrawal deadline to focus minds, the British Army had remained, rapidly becoming the adversarial focus of the newly formed Provisional wing of the Irish Republican Army. This revitalised the IRA's largely moribund "Cause", paving the way for PIRA's emergence as the world's most effective terrorist organisation.

Straker's first training in riot control, at the Mons Officer School in 1970, had been using banners and megaphones to order withdrawal, threatening to open fire, then shooting the ringleaders. This was from the British Army "peace keeping operations" manual, as used in the Borneo Emergency four years earlier, and in Kenya and Malaya, where the British Army had successfully imposed stability on native populations. Other techniques had also been brought forwards from that experience: intelligence gathering for example, and some of the techniques used by the Det and its discredited MRF predecessor.

But although Army tactics had adapted very rapidly since 1969, Straker remained deeply uncomfortable operating as a soldier in his own country against fellow British citizens. He'd wanted to be a soldier from early boyhood, and this ran against all his instincts and upbringing.

He'd started by reading about his father's cavalry regiment in the Second World War: the Western Desert, and fighting up through Italy. He'd then read about the Parachute Brigade's heroic holding of the Arnhem Bridge; desperate times, heroes fighting resolutely against a ruthless enemy.

But there were no such absolutes in Northern Ireland. Soldiers trying to be policemen, policemen unable to convict terrorists, the obviously guilty released to re-offend, leaks to Protestant paramilitaries who dispensed "justice" in lieu – and so on. Everything was blurred, very different to his boyhood vision; and as with most soldiering, you had just to get on with it.

Straker often thought about PIRA, and the mess they were all in. It made him realise how special those childhood years at Ardglenna had been.

Some likened the Troubles to an infectious disease. But Straker thought it more like a process in which everybody was robbed, himself included. And it was only after joining the British Army that he'd understood the full extent of what had been stolen from him.

On the Friday before he'd bundled off to Belfast for the surveillance operation, Straker had agreed to visit his parents. This was unusual.

When he'd removed himself from Harrow aged seventeen, he'd left home and never returned, even after the furore died down. But this was his mother's sixtieth birthday, he was her only child, and she'd persuaded him to come for the party she'd arranged for the Friday night and then stay over. This would mean seeing his father, which he really did not want to do.

But he had no excuse. It was the end of his squadron's on-call cycle, so provided he was on his bleep and could get back to camp within two hours, he was free until Monday. His parents' house in Wiltshire was precisely two hours away as measured by the Royal Automobile Club's route planner – which was how the MoD measured such things.

Straker kept an old MGB in one of the Officers' Mess single garages. Thanks to his being on call most of the time, it was used so irregularly that he disconnected the battery after each trip. It started third time lucky, and he checked the oil and water while the engine warmed up. The sports car was a convertible, white with a black canvas top. He had also a fibreglass hardtop, standing upright at the end of the cramped garage. But as swapping them over was a two-man job, he rarely used it. He disliked the canvas soft top, which was as flimsy as an umbrella, like driving around inside a dank little tent; so he kept it folded back beneath the tonneau. In any case, above 30mph there was enough of a slipstream to blow the rain away, and the car's blow-heater kept him warm below the waist.

He started the drive to his parents' at 0700, when it was still dark on empty roads. The dawn broke in front of him, clear and bright, and he was quickly through the Georgian respectability of Gloucester into wooded hills and rolling countryside.

The top of his head grew cold from turbulence, so he took a flat cap from the glove box, peak reversed to protect the back of his neck. At Cirencester there was commuter traffic, and Swindon was punctuated by a mile of red traffic lights and a burst of rain. But before getting too wet he was back on the open road, slipstreaming and dry.

After Swindon, the A346 started looking like the Roman road it was built upon, marching arrow-straight south, through rolling downland towards what for him was "Army country". To either side were military barracks, depots, and training camps, the parachute drop zone at Everleigh, then Ludgershall, Tidworth, Bulford, Larkhill, and the Salisbury Plain training area across to Warminster.

As the child of an ambitious Army officer, Straker had lived in many of these places, his father conforming to the official view that officers should move their families to wherever they were posted. It wasn't so much constantly moving from one Army quarter to another – the houses allocated to each rank were almost identical – but being taken out of one Army school and then the next day deposited into another. Being an only child, he'd been forced to lose and then re-make friends so frequently that by the time they'd sent him away to board, Straker had grown a protective shell.

As his father was promoted, the Army houses became larger, with a driver, housekeeper and even a cook. The two years in which his father commanded his Regiment, the 13th/14th Princess Royal's Lancers, had been the most fun. The tank soldiers befriended him, his father never getting to hear what they put him up to.

But after that, with his parents away on foreign postings in Hong Kong, Cyprus and Singapore, and him packed off to boarding school, he spent the holidays in Ireland with his godfather Rory at Ardglenna. His life then changed. He no longer had to fly out to hot countries escorted by air hostesses, to hang around diplomatic residences to be smart and polite at boring embassy lunches. He thought he'd escaped.

So today's journey was taking him back to before then, to those earliest days; from Collingbourne Ducis onwards, the red-bordered MoD road signs to either side of the long, straight road evoked a stream of memories that were not happy.

Straker had phoned his mother the night before. He'd remembered to ask if there was anything he could bring. But as ever, she'd just told him to drive safely and they'd look forward to his arrival.

"Your father's had some bad news," she'd added plaintively. "So he's a bit crotchety."

"I'm sorry to hear that. Anything specific?"

She'd laughed.

"Oh, nothing medical, darling. He'd never allow that."

"I'll arrive at coffee time if that's OK," said Straker, planning to stop in Marlborough to buy flowers, wine, chocolates, and a bottle of single malt for his father.

"Leave yourself plenty of time, darling. You know how he gets if people aren't punctual."

Plus ça change, thought Straker, who could quote word-for-word his father's lecture on punctuality being the politesse of kings.

"Oh, and darling... Your Uncle Rory and Abigail will be at the party. They've come across from Ireland because he's got some meetings in London."

His mother's voice was unusually animated, and this news had also cheered him up. His godfather Rory Ennis-Boyd didn't often leave Ardglenna. He was said to have once been his mother's lover, and was certainly the connection by which she'd met his father. Straker often wondered why Rory remained friends with his father, and guessed that they were making this a special trip for his mother's benefit.

CHAPTER 21

Coinciding with another shower of rain, Straker had driven through the open farm gate at five minutes to eleven. His father, in a trilby hat and Barbour jacket, was already standing there waiting to close it behind him. After a delay putting up the car's canvas roof in the rain, Straker was now sitting in the small kitchen, his mother serving coffee from the top of the AGA.

"I can't imagine why you don't buy yourself a decent car," said his father. "All that SAS and Northern Ireland pay puts you up to a lieutenant colonel's rate."

"You had a sports car when we first met," said his mother. "You liked it. But I didn't. When my hat blew away, you never stopped."

"I told you to wear a headscarf," said his father. "We'd have been late for the polo."

"My hat, your polo." His mother looked across at Straker with her usual slightly hysterical laugh. "I doubt if Peter worries about such things, darling."

"I wear a hat in the MGB when it's cold," replied Straker. "*And* a scarf."

"Peter's coming home for Christmas," announced his mother in a diplomatic change of subject. "For a really *good* rest after everything he's been doing."

Roland Straker looked sharply across at his wife.

"What do you mean, after all the things he's been doing?"

His mother had insinuated this invitation into their phone call, despite Straker having opted out of Christmases with them since they'd first farmed him out to stay at Ardglenna. He hadn't actually accepted.

"You know, darling," she said. "Northern Ireland and Peter training in case there's some terrorist attack."

"Need-to-know," interrupted Straker's father. "We don't talk about this sort of thing."

He then looked across at his son. "You can tell me about it later."

Ministry of Defence gossip kept Major General Roland Straker informed of the generality of his son's movements, although nothing specific. He passed everything he gleaned onto his wife.

"Actually, no, I won't," said Straker, irritated by his father's rudeness. "I'll say whatever I'm going to say to both of you."

"Need-to-know," repeated his father, fresh-scrubbed cheeks suddenly tinged with a flush of red.

"My squadron's on standby," continued Straker, ignoring him. "And training for counter-terrorist operations, which probably won't be needed."

"That's to be hoped," said his mother. "Isn't it, darling…?"

His father hadn't responded. And Straker knew he wouldn't leave it at that.

"Oh, and darling," said his mother, trying desperately to change the subject and in the process asking a thoughtless question, "Have you managed to get across to see Rory and Abigail Ennis-Boyd? I know they'd just love to see you again."

Roland Straker visibly bristled. Rory Ennis-Boyd was not only Straker's godfather, but his father's *bête noire*. Straker's mother's attempt at diplomacy was the worst possible change of subject.

Rory Ennis-Boyd was his parents' oldest friend, and as Straker's godfather Rory had been there for him when his father wasn't. Rory's wife Abigail had come on the scene when Straker was one, and wasn't his actual godmother, as that role had been given to one of his mother's sisters. Even so, she'd become a close friend to the boy, and was now also an interesting older woman; how Straker imagined the best sort of stepmother might be.

As a boy, Straker had noticed that although Abigail accompanied Rory whenever they met with his parents, she wasn't a friend to them like Rory. This was nothing negative, just that she was only there because of Rory, and to see Peter. He'd also worked out that his mother understood this.

The times they were all together were always strange. His father pretty much ignored them while his mother, in a fluster of desperation, focussed her efforts on mitigating Roland's rudeness. Abigail kept to her inscrutable half smile, Rory his well-practised bonhomie, both finding time to talk quietly with Straker.

Straker's father had joined the 13th/14th Princess' Own Lancers in 1939, when the Second World War was inevitable. Rory Ennis-Boyd was already a subaltern.

At the end of the regiment's Italy campaign, Rory volunteered for the Special Air Service. They'd not seen any more of each other until after the war.

Then, on the SAS's end-of-war disbandment, Rory was given command of a peacetime 13/14th Lancer squadron which, as he'd been away so long, Roland didn't think was fair. They had both then done staff jobs in London, which had been when Rory introduced Straker's mother to Roland. They'd married quite soon after that, with Rory as best man.

Rory excelled at Staff College and was given a prestigious brigade major job in Germany. But after six months he'd been called back to the re-formed SAS for the Malaya and Borneo campaigns, then commanded the 13/14th Lancers. This was a full four years earlier than Roland Straker. He'd then leap-frogged quickly over full colonel to command a brigade; at the same time, Straker's father was promoted to Lieutenant Colonel to command the Regiment.

The Ennis-Boyds had no children and treated Straker like a son, making a real home for him in Ardglenna's ancient house with its woodland, farm, and village. His mother seemed to have accepted this as benefitting her son. She'd thwarted Straker's father's demands for the boy's presence – particularly at Christmas, while feeling terribly guilty at not being able to provide him with that home. There'd been some in the Army who suggested Rory Ennis-Boyd's Irish background made him too much of a security risk to justify continued rapid promotion; he was said to have been slated for Chief of the General Staff, possibly the top job Chief of the Defence Staff. So when he'd suddenly retired to take up the barony and manage the Ardglenna family estates, there'd been suggestions that he'd left under a cloud. Roland Straker, with his usual sly discretion, hadn't contradicted the lie.

This had been in 1965, with the current Troubles brewing. Rory's father, the old Baron of Ardglenna, had made himself unpopular with other landed gentry and the Unionist government through his support of the Dungannon Campaign for Social Justice. Rory continued in the same vein to the approval of his tenants, although not the Unionists or their newly formed paramilitary group, the Ulster Volunteer Force or UVF.

So even though he knew they were coming, the mention of the Ennis-Boyds aroused the major general's ire.

"Are they still living in that falling-down old castle?" Roland Straker snapped back at his wife.

"Yes, darling," she said soothingly. "You know they are. And it's hardly falling down. It was redesigned as a Palladian mansion. It's just old – Stuart, I think."

Straker shook his head.

"It's best I don't visit them at home," he said to his mother. "All their people know what I do."

And so, after an uncomfortable lunch, Straker was summoned to his father's study.

"It really won't do, Peter."

"What won't?"

"Whatever you get up to isn't for general discussion."

"Exactly."

"That's not what I meant. Your mother is nervous enough as it is without you worrying her unnecessarily, and she's a terrible gossip."

"Whereas you expect me to tell *you*?"

His father snorted.

"And how might my mother have known I was on counter-terrorist standby?"

Major General Straker wasn't used to being taken to task about security. Especially not by his son – a mere captain.

Straker walked over to the window to look out onto his mother's small rose garden. She'd worked hard to make this cottage pleasant. But it hadn't been anything like the house his parents had hoped to buy for themselves after the grandeur of the huge Victorian villa that went with 24th Division, UK North – his father's last command before the system realised he'd reached the limits of his competence.

"As one of the Deputy Military Secretaries, what happens with officers is very much my business," said his father. "And, of course, the Military Secretary himself keeps me appraised of what happens with you."

Straker swivelled round quickly to shoot a look back at his father.

"He should do no such thing," Straker said. "What I do is nobody else's business. You know that."

"That's what *I* was trying tell *you* before lunch."

"Before lunch I told you that what I do, especially in Northern Ireland, isn't your business. Which is why I won't be telling you any different to what I tell my mother."

His father was now red with rage. Straker wondered what his bad news was, but as he suspected it involved not being promoted, he wasn't going to ask.

"What you do is most certainly Military Secretary business," Major General Straker spat back. "He told me that your time in the SAS is coming to an end – for which I am extremely grateful. Running round playing cowboys and Indians in Ireland, Oman, and wherever else isn't going to earn you a proper career. Time for you to get some real work under your belt. Let's hope you haven't wasted too much of it."

This was yet another replay of many one-on-one lectures from his father; different circumstances over the decades, yet with the same emotions, being browbeaten for no apparent reason.

"But what puzzles me," he continued, "is why you've been selected for the Staff College."

"What?" said Straker.

He'd taken the promotion and Staff College entrance exam several months ago, then totally forgotten about it.

"It seems you passed – although not by very much…"

As usual, his father had managed to throw him off balance.

"But you say I've been given a place at Staff College…?"

"You've been *selected*," said his father with heavy emphasis. "But not *given* an actual place."

"What does that mean?"

"My job as Deputy Military Secretary is to ensure that the Army's best people achieve high command. So you've passed the exam, which proves very little. But it seems that the selection committee thought you worthy of a place."

Straker's father was not a member of that committee, so knew nothing more than this.

"So does that mean I'm going there any time soon?" said Straker.

His father didn't know, but he wasn't going to admit that.

"The Army staff college at Camberley is for the top percentage of the officers selected," his father continued. "The rest go to foreign staff colleges, or the Navy and RAF. And even if you're one of those – which I don't know because I don't sit on boards for *junior* officers – you would in any case be the youngest student on the course. Sending you there would mean you taking a place that should go to a more senior, more mature officer."

This was similar to what his SAS CO had said when he'd told Straker to take the promotion exam. Except that he'd also told Straker to pass the exam early to get it out of the way.

"And being so young," his father continued, "I doubt you've got the maturity to get yourself noticed for one of the top jobs – which is the only reason for going to the Staff College.

"Plus you've no experience of armoured warfare, so I doubt you'll even *pass* the course, let alone excel."

Straker's SAS CO had also said that if he wanted to continue in the SAS and command a squadron, or have any chance of commanding the Regiment or becoming Director Special Forces, he had to do Staff College. It would be hard work, and he'd have to pass.

"So when would you think I might expect to be sent there?"

"I have no idea, given the SAS's apparent lack of career planning for its officers."

Straker didn't respond, to which his father added another jibe.

"Not for several years. Even they'll realise you're too immature."

Straker sighed to himself. Escaping being reliant on his father had been Straker's life mission as a child. Now, after fifteen years, he found himself back under the thumb.

In his adolescence, once Straker became physically strong enough, he'd simply walked away from these confrontations. The anger generated inside him had been hard to absorb, especially when he also then had to deal with his mother's hysterical attempts to justify his father's actions. Eventually he'd created an airtight, father-shaped box inside his head, into which he diverted these emotions.

But as ever, his father had succeeded in throwing Straker off balance, the point at which Straker would usually end these sessions. So he turned from the window and walked to the door.

Except that *this* time, he turned back to face his father.

"So what do you think I should do?" he asked quietly.

His father paused.

"What do you mean?"

They were both standing, Straker at the door, his father behind the desk.

"You seem to be saying that I shouldn't be doing this?"

"I don't think you should."

"But it's been agreed – by the Military Secretariat."

Straker was answering back. So his father responded with a threat.

"I may well look into that," he said.

"And why would you want to do that?" asked Straker.

There was no dignified answer to the question, so his father stayed silent, a small muscle below his left eye twitching involuntarily.

"You're trying to use your position to threaten me..." said Straker quietly, after waiting a few moments. "Why would you do that?"

Major General Straker didn't reply.

"Surely you've got something helpful to say?"

His father continued to stare at him.

Straker broke the silence, still speaking quietly. "As you know, a commanding officer isn't an expert in this – unlike you. Both my CO and DSF supported my Staff College application. I was shown their reports. And now you're telling me the Military Secretariat have passed me. So with your expert knowledge, what should I do – or what could *they* do?"

It was a seminal moment; Straker asking for guidance, showing himself willing to accept his father's wisdom.

But Major General Straker didn't like being taken by surprise.

"You've never taken any of the advice I've given to you over the years," he replied.

Straker just looked at him.

"Instead, you embarrass me by getting expelled from my old school, then you follow me into the Army, where rather than trying to make amends, you become one of the thugs. And now, because those people can't be bothered to do things properly, you come to me for advice."

Having hoped for something different, in this moment Straker realised how naïve that had been. So, as these confrontations usually concluded, he was rendered speechless.

"Just get out," said his father.

The party went as they usually did, with a few relatives and a boring collection of local nobs, his mother fussing nervously and his father doing the genial defence attaché act, handing round the canapés. Rory and Abigail arrived late and left early, but managed to catch Straker on his own for a private chat.

"Your mama said your father was upset about something; having a row with you..."

"It was that obvious?"

"No, Peter," replied Rory. "More like business as usual. Plus he's annoyed with us for arriving late and bringing your mum flowers."

Straker laughed.

"Your mama is always very specific," said Abigail. "So you should probably chalk up whatever you rowed about to your father's pre-existing dyspepsia."

"I'd call it permanent rather than pre-existing," said Straker.

"He's been caught by surprise," said Rory. "An interview with the Military Secretary which didn't go as expected."

"It's healthier to hope than to expect," observed Abigail. "Although in the Army both lead to disappointment."

Rory laughed. "The oracle has spoken!"

"Was it promotion?" said Straker.

"Yes," said Rory. "From major general upwards, it's political. If your face doesn't fit with the other generals, that's the end."

"He'd also expected the knighthood that usually goes with it," said Abigail. "Maybe that was the more important..."

Straker nodded. His father's ambition was grim and single-minded, taking precedence over everything else. He resented Rory's "unearned" title.

"The Army uses expectation to keep people hanging on," said Rory. "Folk who don't work that out early can only be disappointed."

After the Ennis-Boyds' departure, which Straker's father ignored, his mother persuaded him to stay over. But he'd left immediately after breakfast the next morning. His father had not appeared.

As a child, Straker would ruminate after rows with his father; an unhealthy playing-back of the conversation inside his head. He'd remember his father's expertly delivered disparagements, cycling through the responses he wished he'd made.

The drive back to camp had settled him back into a reflective, less emotionally charged sort of mood.

But he'd suffered too many of these episodes. There was never a conclusion, and they leached into his self-confidence.

It had to stop, he decided. This time had to be the last time.

And by Saturday afternoon Straker was back in Hereford. He'd put away the MGB (after disconnecting the battery), then walked across to the Mess compound, unlocking the security gate through the barbed-wire fence, then up concrete steps to unlock the front door. He informed squadron duty ops of his return using the hall telephone.

Everybody else had made themselves as scarce as possible within the rules, so Straker was now the only officer physically present on camp. His being deployed wouldn't disrupt anyone else – which was what the duty ops officer had said later that afternoon, just before telling the duty clerk to warn Straker off for the Belfast surveillance operation. He'd been eating hot buttered toast in the deserted Officers' Mess, watching rugby on television.

CHAPTER 22

SATURDAY 6 DECEMBER

Carragher was with Roxy, driving along the Falls Road, out of town to the Ballymurphy estate, with O'Donnell's house keys in Roxy's jacket pocket.

He'd been trying not to think too hard about the future, taking each day one at a time. But the sudden removal of his brigade command created too much empty time for this to continue. He supposed he'd still have to work out what had gone wrong, as nobody else was going to do that. But now there was nothing to keep the spectres at bay – the terrible madness of his dreams, and the revenge that had got him sacked and exiled.

O'Donnell had hung him out to dry, he supposed as a punishment, and would only take him back if it suited him. This exile was open-ended, possibly long-term, although he didn't think permanent, and he'd get no support from either O'Donnell or the rest of the Army Council. He could call on his old Chief of Staff, who was now in acting command of the brigade, but only as a last resort. So although living in O'Donnell's terraced house meant he hadn't been totally banished, he did have to think about his status regarding the Army, the local community, and the likelihood of being arrested. Specifically, he had several immediate problems to address before he could safely return to the Murph in any capacity.

Although only two miles from the city centre, this was a different world where the wind cut wet and cold. They turned right onto the Whiterock Road, with the sandstone pillars and iron gates of the city cemetery before them, their route now uphill into a mist that concealed the estate while emphasising the looming Black Mountain escarpment.

The first time Carragher had come up this road, as a twelve-year-old relocating from the Falls, he'd imagined this mist as clouds, with their similarly battered black taxi driving them up a road into the sky. His Ma had told him the Murph would be different to living in town, so he'd spent the rest of the taxi journey thinking about the new and mysterious tribe he was joining, sky people hidden from the rest of the world.

But after a few days, even though the people up here were certainly different, and most winter mornings were still and quiet as he'd imagined the sky might be above it all, these clouds tasted of coalsmoke – rich and dark like steam trains, but they made it so you couldn't smell anything else. They painted everything a nondescript shade of brown, and on some days made you cough.

But he was also to discover the special days, more common in summer, when dawn rose clear and bright. Their house was at the top of the Murph, so he'd rush out while the estate slept, across the fields up to the Ballygomartin Road, then further up, the steepness of the slope making him push down with both hands to power pistons in his knees.

These were good days from God, given to him personally as he was always the only person ever up here at dawn to see it. Up in the blue he had secret, private adventures: becoming a bird, granted sight of the wider world. So he'd evolved a protocol: packing his school satchel with water, biscuits and whatever else his Ma had as leftovers, then hiking up to specific lookout positions: a small outcrop from where he could see north-east across the city and the shipyards to St Helen's Bay and over the Irish Sea to Scotland; and another further round, looking south to the truly mysterious Mourne Mountains.

Some days he'd continue further up Divis Mountain, avoiding the service track to the ugliness of barbed wire and insect antennae of what they called the "KP" – a military broadcast station. There was a particular spot just short of the summit, sheltered from the wind. From up here the details and complications of the world fell away beneath his feet into the sharpest, most detailed tapestry, where he would try to imagine how, on such a day, God might feel.

The Ballymurphy council estate, at the base of the 1200-foot Black Mountain escarpment, comprised some 660 concrete houses crumbling with City Council neglect, on a 59-acre site at the top of the Whiterock Road. The Murph formed the centre of a square mile of similar housing estates: Moyard Park to the immediate north-east, where Carragher moved as a child, Dermott Hill, New Barnsley, Springfield Park, Sliabh Dubh, Springhill, Westrock and Whiterock – together known as Greater Ballymurphy.

The Second World War had ended with much of Belfast City bombed out, with nowhere for the returning soldiers to house the families they'd survived the fighting in order to have. Like most things, building materials were rationed, so the Belfast Corporation built concrete houses without insulation cavities. They added chemicals to make the concrete set faster, which weakened the steel reinforcement rods so the walls cracked. The houses were as dank and cold inside as out, with leaking roofs and draughts from poorly fitted doors and metal-framed windows. Their flimsy interior woodwork quickly rotted.

The layout of the Murph was planned by officials who knew best. Each terrace stood two metres back from the pavement. The terraced tiers should have been built across the hillside, southward-facing for light. Instead, the planners drew streets that curved artfully around a central space in concentric hexagons. This meant that the houses had to be built in awkward steps up the slope, in curved cul-de-sacs that prevented people walking directly anywhere unless they cut through each other's back yards. And despite the Murph's purpose being to house young married couples, they built no play areas, shops, or schools.

Twelve thousand people were moved into these "country estates", where they felt exposed and abandoned. Resentment and a sense of injustice turned quickly to vandalism and instability. Those able to move away were mostly Protestant, leaving just the poor families, which were mostly Catholic.

The original wire fencing lasted only a few years, rotting beneath rough grass and leaving ugly three-foot concrete posts. Low retaining walls of unpainted building block separated the house fronts from the pavement, which people tried to turn into front gardens. The planners also failed to provide direct footpaths across their artful hexagons. So fences were knocked down, with scrambles over walls and through people's rear yards; then, more recently, cut-throughs for those escaping from the security forces.

Even so, some people were able to make gardens, one man greatly enjoying growing then giving away the most beautiful flowers. However, a more common DIY alternative to gardening was "crazy paving" – smashed up bits of paving slabs taken from the dump and set in concrete.

Functioning streetlights were regularly broken to disadvantage the Army's occasional night patrols, although some were kept working for use by PIRA snipers. Ropes hung from lampposts as Irish maypoles or Tarzan swings, enjoyed by cheerful urchins.

The planners left large, open areas between some of the streets to give their drawings an impression of space and healthy country living. But in the built reality of the Murph, these open spaces became the battlegrounds where youths gathered to throw stones at troops and the police. The grass turned into mud and broken glass, with rubbish from the dustbins they emptied out to throw at passing security force vehicles, and burned-out cars and mattress barricades. These open areas seemed only to emphasise the Murph's isolation, and the bitter cold of the escarpment's wind and driving rain.

Roxy's taxi smoked its way up the Whiterock Road, past terraces of brick-and-slate houses on the right, with the stone of the cemetery wall to the left, before dropping down past St Thomas's Intermediate School for Catholic Boys. Its dour concrete façade had a low-ridged roof featuring a window-fronted hall in suggestion of a modernist church, which had likely been the Holy Father's intention. Séan particularly remembered the entrance, past a wall of school-milk crates, up five steps into glass doors and a foyer that smelled of school dinners.

Carragher had been happy here, playing on the football team and doing enough studying to remain in the exam class. He remembered the headmaster, Michael McLaverty, an accomplished novelist and short-story writer who loved geometry and sought fidelity, precision, and feeling in all things. McLaverty believed beauty could lead a person to virtue, but knowing there was precious little of it up here, insisted poetry be taught to all. Those imposed classes, though sometimes difficult, gave glimpses of a better world. But it never overlapped *their* world, and was easily overwhelmed by Murph tribalism and the effort required to survive. Less arcane pleasures were much easier to access, enhanced as they were by the bell-induced fear of the Catholic Mass.

Carragher had come to understand Mr McLaverty's perspective. But for most of his peers, aestheticism as exemplified by poetry remained a pretention, part of the pose they imagined middle-class life to be, for other people, somewhere else.

But there had been a street fight, when he'd challenged a much older bully who'd been pushing his younger brother around. It had been a ridiculous mismatch physically, Carragher smaller and slightly built, with half a dozen of the bully's gang in a circle taunting him. After knocking Carragher down, the bully had kicked him, then stood back to tell the others what he was going to do next. But Carragher's aggression has taken over; scrambling to his feet as if trying to run, then running at the bully in a flurry of fists. The bully had retreated and been knocked down, then as the gang tried to intervene, Carragher had lost control, repeatedly stamping on his opponent. A group of men had intervened, the bully taken to hospital with serious injuries.

The police had come asking questions, but as there'd been no complaints, they didn't come back. Even so, Carragher withdrew from the schoolyard and street life to the school library, while the parish priest's Corpus Christi Boxing Club taught him control and burned away the anger.

He remembered the No. 11 trolley bus, connecting the Black Mountain estates with the city centre – its strange hum and whining noises. At weekends when it wasn't raining, rather than reading in their crowded little house, he'd go into town, taking the No. 11 from the top of the Rock if he had the money. Sometimes down at the cemetery junction, when turning across onto the Falls Road, the trolley would stop dead as the overhead collector lost contact crossing over the high-voltage cables. The conductor would pull an enormous wooden pole from underneath, to reach up and push the arm back into place.

He'd started out returning to West Belfast, where they'd lived before being moved out to Ballymurphy for not paying the rent. But soon he was exploring other markedly different areas of what he found to be quite a small city. He also discovered that Protestants seemed different to Catholics and that they seemed able to recognise him just as easily. He wondered if this was some physical difference, or just a dislike of strangers. It was certainly tribal, and made the Protestant areas dangerous for him to explore.

But when the Ballymurphy mist cleared, he stayed at home. These were his "glory days" high up on the escarpment, when Carragher imagined himself a phoenix, reborn in flames from pain and ashes, rising above it all.

Working hard at school kept reality at bay. But despite suggestions from the geography teacher that he stay on for A-Levels with the aim of university, Carragher held no real hope of getting onto a degree course. On the Murph, such aspirations were resented. Work was something that made you sweat and paid you money.

Nevertheless, he could see that for those who could do it, study was a balloon that took those people up and away to a different world. So the geography teacher and Headmaster McLaverty had helped get him an apprenticeship in the drawing office of the shipyard, which sent him out to night school. In 1965, he qualified as a marine engineering draughtsman, and did his maths and science A-Levels, aiming for a place on the Queen's marine engineering degree course.

But he wasn't convinced he'd fit in at university. It looked to him like a middle-class, self-serving elite. The academic work was straightforward, but he didn't know if he could adapt himself to the rest of it. But this, as he realised, was a Murph-generated inner voice trying to protect him from disappointment. He decided to ignore it.

Alongside his labours in the drawing office and at night school, he'd made friends from the university in the pubs and clubs around the markets. Some of these new friends said they were working-class socialists; even that they supported the IRA because of its vision of a communist united Ireland.

However, these people made him feel even more isolated, especially when they argued – which they did often and passionately. The real and desperate problems of the Murph were for them nothing more than something to talk about; as not one of these people *did* anything. So he kept his thoughts to himself.

After three further years, Carragher completed the marine engineering apprenticeship and took straight As in Maths, Advanced

Maths, Physics, Chemistry, and History. The drawing office manager recommended him for a company-sponsored marine engineering degree.

But success brought attention. An anonymous executive in the personnel department realised he was a Catholic. So instead of sending him for university entrance interviews, he'd been sacked – during the chaos of the August riots of 1969.

From living happily in the city centre, he now realised he couldn't afford to remain there. Then, as Loyalist thugs took advantage of the housing protests to set fire to Catholic streets along the Falls Road and in other parts of the city, his Ma urged him to move back out to the Murph before the Greater Ballymurphy took on too many refugees – as thousands of homeless families were to do over the next few years. The community was well-organised and he was known, so by October he was back there again. He remembered his sense of guilt and failure as people welcomed him back.

He and Roxy were now driving past the house in which he'd roomed after being sacked from the shipyard. It was a grim, run-down terraced house, noisily exposed to the traffic constantly going up and down Whiterock – back then occupied by a broken-down old couple. He'd kept himself out of the Murph proper, living unhappily on its western edge.

He'd then understood his own father's decline into alcoholism, sacked by the shipyard eleven years before they'd done the same to him. He'd been one of their top welders. But whereas his father had blunted the rage with drink, Carragher had decided two things: not to become embittered, nor to lose hope.

CHAPTER 23

Roxy's taxi continued past the endless cemetery, its stone wall to the left running jagged and solid; now fortified by iron railings. Then Whiterock Road dropped down the hill past St Thomas's, the wall reduced to just two rows topped by solid coping stones.

Waist-high, running more than 600 metres to the far end of the cemetery, this was a boundary marker, built in five-metre-long steps down the hill. But now, rising from the coping stones were five-foot-high, black cast-iron spikes. They curved back over into the cemetery, with only the dead to keep from escaping.

Passing St Thomas's School to the right, the ground to the left dropped away, lines of graves seeming to vanish into the mist-shrouded rooftops of Whiterock Grove and the Turf Lodge. The gravestones were shiny black, bright with flowers and tricolours, the dead better tended than the living here, Carragher thought. He imagined them marching up the slope into the lowering presence of the Black Mountains.

The pointlessness of these neat graves and their serried ranks like regiments on a battlefield brought home to Carragher the massive transition he'd made since first coming up this road to the Murph as a child. Despite all his efforts to escape, this was where his happy memories were: early mornings up on the Divis, keeping his own company, of discovery, school ignoring the skivers' banter in the library gallery – and above all, of hope.

Whereas now, it seemed so naïve, laughable, and incredibly stupid to believe that hope was some kind of destination, rather than the drug that kept people in their place and the graves so well-tended. But what else was there? He'd truly believed the hope of his childhood, and in Headmaster McLaverty's conviction that virtue brought fulfilment. And he already knew what it was like to come back here, tail between his legs, defeated by the outside world, asking for readmission to the community he'd worked so hard to escape. Except that now, as a senior member of PIRA albeit in a complicated but hopefully temporary hiatus, this second return was far more dangerous and degrading.

Unable to suppress his first memories of coming up here as a twelve-year-old, the windswept enormity of his transition – his "fall from grace" – hit him like a punch in the face. That boy would have married his sweetheart, not got her killed. That boy could never have imagined the hatred and horror that would result.

Re-integration here now, was going to be very much harder than when he'd been sacked from the shipyard. The Murph was not "an IRA estate", having started out with both Catholic and Protestant residents, lumped together in the early days by the City Council as rent defaulters and the like. The Murph's remaining Protestant families were strongly part of the community, and feelings for the IRA were at best mixed. Back in the 1969 the IRA hadn't helped Catholics fleeing the burned-out streets of West Belfast, whereas community leaders in the Murph made it a safe haven – Carragher's mother Bronagh, a determined, public-spirited woman, was one of them. In June 1970, when PIRA reinforcements from outside tried to get involved with the Ballymurphy riots, Bronagh was in the deputation that ordered them out as troublemakers.

Even if it wanted to, PIRA could not guarantee Carragher's security here. Whereas his Ma was still a powerful force within the Murph, and would broker enough acceptance to keep him safe. The irony of this just added to the shame he was trying to ignore.

And despite everything, Carragher *was* going home, back to his tribe. This place was part of his soul. His return was bittersweet.

But Carragher's return was even more difficult for the Murph's local PIRA cell, complicated by their already uneasy relationship with Ballymurphy community leaders. So as Carragher had expected, they'd put out the word that he was no longer a senior PIRA commander – including, which was no business of theirs as well as being highly confidential, that he'd been sacked.

After descending the hill that runs down past St Thomas's, the Whiterock Road runs onto the lower slopes of the Divis. It was then uphill to the end of the cemetery wall, and so to the "top of the Rock", at the Springfield Road T-junction.

At the end of the cemetery wall, Carragher told Roxy to take the next right into Glenalina Road, which ran into the centre of Ballymurphy.

"Are you sure?" said Roxy.

On previous visits to the Murph, they'd worked on being anonymous, cutting round the top of the estate using the Springfield Road. Whereas Glenalina Road was like an entrance gate to castle Murph, with a mural on the corner commemorating the dead from the Ballymurphy Massacre nine years ago. An Irish tricolour hung in-between the two upstairs bedroom windows of the house on the other corner. Driving in this way, they might as well arrive with an escort of British Army Humber Pigs.

"I need to have a word with my Da," replied Carragher.

"Ah, shite. So you do," said Roxy.

Carragher hadn't thought this through, beyond the rather vague feeling that he needed to re-establish himself out here. He'd phoned his Ma, who'd not mentioned her misgivings. Carragher also felt an incongruous, verging on ridiculous need to go and see his father, who'd left them all twenty years ago. He still lived on the Murph, so in moving back here, Carragher felt he should define whatever their relationship might be.

Roxy'd responded immediately, opening his side window to hand-indicate the right turn into the estate. He'd had similar problems with own father, now long dead. He understood Carragher's legacy emotion. Maybe it was hard-wired.

They drove 150 metres along to where Glenalina Road ended at the estate's inner lozenge, the Ballymurphy Bullring – a line of shops with flats above. Built as an afterthought by Belfast City planners, this was the Murph's epicentre.

Carragher's father lived on the top floor above McGowen's Grocers, which was boarded up after a recent Loyalist firebomb attack. The smell of smoke remained, and although the shop doorway was blackened, there was no apparent damage to the floors above. People here knew how to deal with such things.

They parked on the corner outside McGrillen's Butchers, its window covered by a wire-and-steel-mesh cage. Carragher remembered it protecting nothing more than a life-sized white plastic lamb, and the telephone in the corner that everybody used because the outside phone boxes were long gone from being vandalised. He also remembered John Cossey's hardware shop, selling fireworks and squibs alongside the coal and briquettes everyone burned for heating – everything he'd imagined he could ever want from life.

There'd been a miniature television set on top of Cossey's cash register, price-tagged 2/6d. Carragher's Ma restricted telly watching, and he had dreamed of hiding away under the bedclothes with his own secret set. But after saving up the money and asking Mr Cossey to let him see it, he'd been terribly disappointed to discover it wasn't real, with just a roll of crude little pictures changed using a knob on the side.

The edge of the corner kerb was smashed, suggesting damage by a ram-raid vehicle driven at speed. There were no jewellery shops in the Murph. But that didn't mean it hadn't happened.

The wheezing clatter of the taxi's diesel engine stopping attracted curious stares from the dozen or so people shopping or standing talking. Roxy stayed with the cab while Carragher walked over between the shops to the darkened entrance of the flats, and ran up the four flights of concrete stairs. Gloomy daylight lit the stairwell through a six-foot-wide panel of grubby windows that reached to the top of the building. Some were broken, letting in the wind, or taped up with squares of cardboard.

Carragher banged on the door then listened carefully.

"I hear you," he shouted. "So open up."

"Whatever it is, I don't care."

"You will if I break it down."

There was shuffling inside, then a rattling of the security chain.

"Who the fuck is it then?"

"You know who it is. So just open the door."

There was silence, so Carragher twisted the knob. But before he put his shoulder to the flimsy plywood the door swung open, the lock's strike-plate having already been torn from the wooden frame.

One of Carragher's earliest acts of serious violence had been as a thirteen-year-old child, when his Da tried to take his paper-round money to buy drink. Soon after that, Carragher caught him doing the same with his Ma's social security. These attacks had shocked both his parents, after which their father left – this not long after their move out from the city to the Murph.

Now his father was a barely functioning alcoholic. He mostly stayed clear of Carragher's mother and the rest of the family, but sometimes came round looking for money.

The narrow corridor was dark. At the end, a small television showed flat racing.

"I hope you're not betting again?" said Carragher.

The lavatory flushed, Carragher's father emerging wearing a thick wool dressing gown that seemed familiar over the top of grubby pajamas.

"What's it to you?"

"The season finished three weeks ago. You're watching repeats."

The old man shuffled into the tiny sitting room to slump down on a broken sofa. A low table was littered with empty Harp cans and cigarette cartons, a full ashtray and half a bottle of Paddy Whiskey.

"Where'd you get that?" said Carragher.

"Some fella brings them up from Cork with the meat."

"You be careful. Too cheap, it'll make you blind."

"It's the good stuff. But you wouldn't know."

"You're right. I wouldn't."

Carragher was not a "drinking man", from back when he'd withdrawn from street life here. He stood looking from the window down into the tiny fenced-off yards behind each shop – bins, boxes, and rubbish, where night foxes from the hill would fight with the rats.

"So why am I here…?" prompted Carragher.

"You need something, right?"

Carragher nodded.

"Dead on," he said slowly, then continued staring from the window.

"I know where you are, son," said his father. "Being back here. It's not so easy, and now you need me to put out the good word for you… Am I right?"

Carragher laughed quietly. "Sure… That would be it."

His father nodded, then stood up with paternal authority.

"Well, it'll cost you, son. Nothing's for nothing."

"How much did you have in mind?"

"Fifty quid."

Carragher nodded and took a roll of cash from his trouser pocket, peeling off two five-pound notes and putting them onto the table. The old man started to protest, but something about Carragher made him stop.

"This is for nothing," Carragher said quietly. "It's for you saying *nothing* to anybody about me, or about Ma…"

The old man made as if to protest, but Carragher ignored him.

"It's easy. You're an ignorant old man. You know nothing anyway – not where I am or what I'm doing. Because you don't. And you definitely don't invent any of your usual shite."

"That's not a tenner's worth," said the old man quickly.

"I agree with you," replied Carragher. "It's not worth anything at all… The tenner is a sign of respect from me to my old Da – even though I know you'll only use it to get yourself banjaxed…"

His father tried to look affronted at this suggestion, then thought better of it. They both knew that the handing over of money was, like the visit, a symbolic act for others to consider – and, of course, talk about. And also that especially in his cups, Carragher Senior's word meant nothing – as a promise now, or whatever he might say to anybody else.

"I heard tell of you making up some shite about me and a problem with the Army," Carragher continued.

His father tried to looked puzzled, but failed.

"And I'll hear of any other nonsense you might be foolish enough to spread around. But if you forget yourself again, this next time it won't be me coming paying my respects…"

The old man flinched.

"Do we understand each other?" said Carragher. The old man nodded.

"This includes you talking about or contacting my mother."

There was a silence.

"And the reason it won't be me who comes back to see you is because you *are* my Da…"

The old man went very pale.

"But if you do need something," continued Carragher, then stopped talking. They looked at each other. "You pass the word," said Carragher. "Just that. Pass the word and I'll make sure you're alright."

The old man sat down heavily, to stare fixedly at the television. Carragher stood for a few moments more, listening to the silence while very slowly nodding his head.

Outside the block of flats Roxy was talking to two men.

"These gents seem very keen to know who I'm waiting for," he said to Carragher.

"Are they needing a ride?" said Carragher.

Both men were in jeans, the younger looking pinched with the cold but wearing a fashionable grey woollen jacket with a thick red, blue, and black stripe across the chest. He also wore bright-clean white socks and expensive-looking loafers with leather tassels.

"We know who you are," he said, looking contemptuously at Roxy.

The older one pointed at Carragher.

"Your Da told us you'd be calling. You'd better not have done anything to him."

Carragher stopped two paces from him.

"And what would that be to you, sonny boy?"

"We look after the people round here."

"Really," said Carragher. "Do I know you?"

The older man looked awkward.

"No reason why you should," he muttered.

"Anyway, it seems to me the people round here are looking after *you*..."

Local PIRA only survived because their communities refused to talk to security forces, whereas it was a continuing problem that some local PIRA Volunteers took British bribes – which Carragher had been addressing with some brutality over this last year. But these two were too far down the PIRA food chain to understand his sinister jibe.

The older man blundered on.

"You left your family behind here, so they're our concern," he said. "After you leaving and not even looking after your own father..."

"And now you've been fired," blurted the younger one. "You can't just come back here and think you're still—"

Carragher had glanced over to Roxy, who turned quietly and went round to the far side of his taxi. Carragher interrupted the younger man.

"I don't know what either of you's are talking about – and neither do you. So get out of my way. Unlike you, we've got things to do."

"You need to come with us," said the younger man, his voice now loud and pitching higher. People turned their heads to watch.

"And why would that be?" said Carragher.

"Gerard wants to talk to you."

It was then Carragher noticed the younger guy's eyes.

"That would be Gerard McComb?" said Carragher deliberately, looking across at the older man.

The older man nodded but didn't speak.

"Y'know, it's not for Gerard to tell me anything," said Carragher, "let alone send you two buck eejits giving me instructions."

"These are not instructions," said the younger man, tripping over his words. "They're official orders."

Carragher stood still for a few moments. The older man didn't move.

"Are you totally sure about this, sonny boy?" said Carragher, then suddenly closed the two paces he'd kept between them, pulling the younger guy down by the collar of his smart jacket. When he pulled back, Carragher pushed him so he stumbled backwards, then took the legs from under him with a vicious sweep kick to his left knee.

He then ducked sideways towards the other man, who was backing away while fumbling behind his coat.

"I'd leave that if I was you," said Roxy loudly, stepping round the bonnet of the taxi with a Glock 17 held low in his right hand.

Carragher ducked sideways out of Roxy's line of fire and behind the older man, lifting his coat to pull a heavy Webley Revolver from the waistband. He then walked over to the man on the ground, whose damaged left knee wasn't letting him stand. Carragher kicked him several times in the ribs until he rolled away onto his stomach. He knelt down and rummaged underneath his jacket, pulling out an old Luger P08 and discovering, as he'd suspected, plastic bags in the back pockets of the man's jeans.

Carragher stood back up. People had recognised him. For the moment they were standing back, but this had already the beginnings of a troublesome type of Bullring crowd.

"Let's get these two out of here."

*

Carragher sat in the back beside the younger man, who was able to sit up but probably had broken ribs. The older man was put in front.

"Drive us out round Ballymurphy Road and up Springhill," said Carragher. "I want to talk to the priest."

Roxy drove past Corpus Christi Church to the end of the road, turned round, then stopped outside.

"Gerard lives up Divismore Park, before the Springfield Road," said the older man.

"I know exactly where Gerard McComb lives," said Carragher. "He's next on our visiting list."

The older man was now looking worried.

"You both sit tight now," said Carragher, jumping out. Roxy locked the doors and turned to watch his charges.

Five minutes later Carragher was back, opening the rear door for the priest, who was wearing a dark grey raincoat over his thick woollen cassock.

The priest stood for a moment, bent over looking in, holding the black umbrella across his chest.

"Who've we got here then – all as mysterious as you could imagine…?"

"I told you, Father," said Carragher. "It's community business that concerns you as well as us."

"Well, as I see no obvious sin, I'll go with ye."

"Right then," said Carragher to Roxy. "Let's report as ordered to Commanding Officer McComb."

The taxi's diesel rattle brought people to the windows of the adjoining houses, although the street remained empty. Carragher sat in the back beside the younger guy, watching the drawn curtains of McComb's house. He noted a twitch in the downstairs sitting room, and the six-inch gap upstairs in one of the front bedrooms.

"D'you want me to drive round the block?" asked Roxy.

"No," said Carragher. "They've no reason to leave the house. Let's do this quickly. Just don't leave your gear in the cab, and we play it dead safe."

Roxy took the Glock from under his right thigh and stuffed it behind him into his waistband. He reached underneath his seat for the MAC-10 submachine gun, climbing out holding its spare 30-round box clip in his other hand.

These streets were usually busy with children playing, and people gossiping at the corners. A black cab stopping outside the house of the local PIRA commander was an event, so there should have been people coming out to see. Quiet streets meant trouble; Carragher knew the speed with which the cars of unsolicited visitors could be set on fire. Dickers at either end of the street would already have informed McComb, and judging by the twitching curtains, people were certainly watching.

Roxy had driven in so that McComb's house was to the left, their passengers seated on the side facing it. He got out and stood by his door.

Carragher turned to the priest.

"Why don't you get out first, Father?"

The priest looked at him questioningly.

"You know what we're about, Father – and I've brought you with us to keep this peaceful. So just stand yourself off a ways to the left so Gerard can see exactly who we are."

As the priest stepped out onto the pavement, Roxy opened the front passenger door.

"Get out," he said to the older man. "Then walk to the front of the cab and stand on the road."

Roxy then stepped round to the front of the cab behind the older man, dragging him as a shield across the pavement up the path to McComb's front door. Carragher grabbed the younger guy by the collar, pulling him out of the cab. Roxy battered the front door with his fist.

"Get McComb out here now," shouted Carragher, for the benefit of the neighbours.

McComb's curtains twitched some more, there were noises and talking inside the house, then the front door opened.

"We're obeying your orders to come and see you, Gerard," shouted Carragher. "And these two soldiers of yours have brought us."

"Why's the parish priest here?" replied McComb.

"You protect the community, Gerard," said Carragher. "And so does Father Malachy. You two need to work together."

"With all respect to you, Father, this is no business of the Church. You should leave."

"Everything that happens here is the business of the Church," said the priest, taking Carragher's cue and using his pulpit voice. "You'd know that, Gerard McComb, if you bothered with coming to church."

McComb swore under his breath and strode out onto the pavement, but stopped abruptly when he saw Roxy's MAC-10.

"OK, Carragher..." he said. "What do you want?"

"Why don't we deal with what *you* wanted when you set these two to take me when I went to visit my Da?"

"Nobody was trying to *take* you," said McComb. "I just thought we should have a wee chat, now you're back here with the rest of us."

"Including threatening me if I did anything to him, then trying to pull this on me in the street?"

Carragher showed him the Webley, then flipped open the cylinder and knocked the cartridges out onto the pavement.

"He attacked me," blurted out the younger man. "Then the other guy pulled a pistol."

"I've also got this one's crap old Luger in the cab," said Carragher. "You need to teach him how to clean it."

Carragher tossed the heavy Webley at McComb. He failed to make the catch, swearing as the hammer cut his thumb, the gun clattering down the concrete steps.

"So let's have this wee chat, shall we?" said Carragher. "Only I don't need the bit where you welcome me back home."

There was a silence.

"Fair enough," said Carragher. "And I *am* pleased to be back home, Gerard. Whereas..."

At which point Carragher turned to look round at the windows of the surrounding houses.

"We've got something *you* need to deal with," he shouted. "So why don't you get all your neighbours to come out and see?"

He nodded encouragingly at the parish priest, who realised that the more people became involved the safer it would be for him – and, of course, for everyone else.

So the priest beckoned forth the people from whence they stood at their windows, first from the next-door houses where they'd heard what Carragher had said; then the others from further down the street who'd realised something was happening, until a small crowd had gathered outside McComb's house.

"Well then," said McComb. "What's this *something* we need to deal with?"

Carragher pushed the younger man forwards, who turned angrily as if to swing a punch. Carragher stared at him for a moment.

"Turn out your pockets, son," he said.

The young man's anger evaporated immediately, and his face went deathly pale.

"Just do it," said Carragher.

He took out a cigarette lighter, a pouch of rolling tobacco, and Rizlas from his jeans pockets.

"Drop them on the pavement where everybody can see," said Carragher. "And now your back pockets."

He dropped a plastic bag onto the pavement.

"What's this?" said McComb.

"Mother's little helper," said Roxy.

"You know well enough what it is, Gerard," said Carragher.

"It's a prescription," said the younger man. "For my mam's nerves. I'd just picked it up from the surgery."

"So maybe you did…?" said Carragher.

McComb picked up the bag, which contained a hundred or so blue pills.

"Valium," said Roxy. "Ten milligrams – the strong ones."

Carragher prodded the younger man.

"And the rest."

Another plastic bag.

"And now your jacket…"

Two more plastic bags.

"What do we think?" said Carragher. "Say, four hundred pills? That's far more than even your fucked-up mam could need. And you're wearing expensive shoes."

Another silence.

Carragher turned to the older man.

"We might as well see what you've got while we're at it."

The older man went pale, then turned to run. Roxy clubbed him down with the spare magazine, then stood heavily on his hand.

"Why don't you search him yourself, Gerard? Or do you already know about this?"

Before McComb could recover, Roxy was tossing more plastic bags from the older man's coat, making a significant pile on the pavement.

Carragher turned to the priest.

"The Church makes a lot of money providing comfort to those in distress. These two guys are cutting into your profits."

He turned to McComb.

"And maybe this was also part of your service to the community?"

He then turned to the neighbours.

"The Army does not tolerate drug dealers. And nor should you. And I do not tolerate interference – to me, or to my family."

He then pulled the priest to one side.

"The Army's on a campaign against drug dealers – making examples," he said. "The best these two can hope for is kneecapping. But McComb may try to cover up for his likely involvement by killing them both. So you're their only hope."

"But you engineered this, Séan..." hissed the priest.

"Yes I did, but I'm not going to kill anybody, and I'm not going to turn the blind eye to drug dealing like you've been doing."

Before the priest could protest, he added: "You should thank me for bringing you into this. You play it right and the Church will be seen to do good work with both the community and the Army. The bishop's gonna love you, and McComb won't dare hurt you.

"And Father," he added loudly, so the people near could hear him, "you need to talk to the Bullring GP practice manager. If you wasn't the priest, I'd lay a bet with you that this lad here's into one of the nurses – forcing her, most likely. Let me know if you need any help sorting that one out."

The priest still looked doubtful, so Carragher spoke even louder.

"We all remember Mother Teresa, and her mission here back in 1971. She did good work, which the Church should have been doing but hadn't been bothered to. She put you and your bishop to shame. So instead of helping her as he should have done, he froze her out."

The small crowd were nodding at this. The international superstar saint's intervention had been an unexpected but massive boost to morale, along with the literacy and community services she and her nuns created over almost three years.

"We still need that help," continued Carragher. "So now we're gonna get it from *you*."

The priest nodded. The Church should have learned from Mother Teresa's intervention, but because she'd embarrassed them, nothing had changed.

McComb stood alone on the pavement, white-faced, staring sightlessly at the plastic bags. Then he turned back to his house. After a muttered conversation in the doorway, three Volunteers came out and dragged the two drug dealers inside. Carragher gestured at the priest to follow – which he did, brandishing his umbrella like a crozier.

But before McComb could follow, Carragher pulled him to one side, talking quietly.

"You're a fucking fool, Gerard," he said. "Northern Command is all over drug dealing like it's touting to the Brits. That's without what the Valium's actually doing to people who haven't got enough money for the electric meter."

Again McComb said nothing.

"You'll be lucky if you manage to separate yourself from those two shites. And note that I haven't actually accused *you*..."

McComb still wasn't saying anything.

"We *earn* people's respect," Carragher continued. "You can't beat it into them.

"Remember what I did to you, Gerard, back when you was seventeen? I stopped you bullying my brother, but you didn't learn."

Carragher shook his head, remembering the relief he'd felt on hearing McComb wasn't going to die.

"Whereas I learned to control my temper," he said, very quietly, as if to himself.

Carragher had waited, locked hidden away in the priest's kitchen for news from the hospital that could send him away to Borstal. He'd heeded the warning, withdrawing from street life, reading, and taking himself out of the Murph.

But it seemed he hadn't learned the lesson. O'Donnell had tried to tell him, but he'd refused to listen, with no priest or boxing club to curb his anger. What else could O'Donnell have done but sack him?

Standing now, outside McComb's terraced house, Carragher also realised that even though sorting out McComb had distracted him from the pain and grief, it was futile. He could not return to live here. He needed something that was worth doing.

He thought of the old priest who'd protected him from the police, and wondered if O'Donnell would bring him back like the Prodigal Son.

McComb sensed Carragher's distraction.

"Northern Command isn't going to listen to your fairy tales, Carragher," he snarled. "You're out."

Carragher allowed his surge of fury to flicker briefly enough to register with McComb, who backed away.

"Let's just say they're not going to listen to you either, Gerard. Especially not in relation to what they'll learn from everybody else."

He stepped closer, lowering his voice.

"But it's still there, Gerard. You try to cross me again, and I'll turn it back on."

Only now could Carragher go and see his Ma, which he'd been dreading. Like the other mothers on the Murph who shared a less binary view of the Troubles, Bronagh didn't like him being in the Army. But that wasn't it. With her, there'd be no avoiding the pain and grief.

It was getting dark as they pulled up outside her house, which had a Christmas tree with lights in the window, and a freshly painted front door. Roxy stayed with the taxi, and Bronagh took Carragher into the kitchen where they hugged.

"I heard you'd been to see your father," she said.

"I don't know how long I'll be here," he replied. "So I had to make sure he knows the score."

"He's harmless," she said. "Drinking himself to death."

"So how's you?" said Carragher, trying to change the subject.

Bronagh was fifty-five, had never smoked or taken drink, radiating a lean physical strength. She was ageless, an attractive woman of obvious capability. Her ten children had flown the nest, although living close by; she now both the Carragher matriarch and a force within the Murph.

But Bronagh wasn't going to allow the moment to be subverted by platitudes.

"How's me? Keeping on is how's me," she replied. "Happiness is mostly an illusion, and there's little enough of it in this world."

She pointed to the sofa, making him sit down.

"But you and your Da waste it like you'd never seen it before."

Before his father's sacking from the shipyard, together as a family they'd been happy enough. And after he'd left them, she'd made as decent a family life as she could. The others had moved out to get married, mostly back here on the Murph close to her with their own families. She had several grandchildren.

"She was a lovely girl, Séan. But you know that. And what's done's done, more's the pity…"

Carragher knew these weren't platitudes. Bronagh didn't do those. And what else was there to actually be said?

She sat down beside him.

"You know that grief's a process?" she said. "And that you have to go through it?"

He didn't respond. He'd known there'd be a conversation like this, which was why he'd put off coming to see her. His grief turned so quickly to anger, which he didn't want with her. And apart from the anger, he had no feelings.

"One of the problems is that we don't have the words," she said. "And most of us aren't used to talking about our feelings… Especially men.

"We let the Church organise these things – sitting there in rows all numb, the ancient words flowing over our heads. There's meaning in there for what we're going through, but as the priests tell us, we have to accept what they're saying – all of it, not just the bits we like."

Bronagh did go to church, although not as one of the priest's headscarf believers. And she hadn't made her children go.

"Priests make us feel better by telling us that everybody suffers the same. It's reassuring to be told we're not on our own, that grief and pain are just part of being a person. But they generalise. Priests do so much better if they know the people they're praying for."

"And we're the people who know Máire," she said. "We're the only ones who can mourn her."

She stood up and went over to the sideboard, where she kept a bottle of sherry, four glasses, and the best china tea set. It was photo-album time.

They sat long over the padded albums; formal photos of the wedding, and then the hot afternoon the entire party had spent at the seaside – even the bed-and-breakfast where Carragher and Máire had stayed that night after everyone else had piled back into the bus and returned to the Murph. Bronagh had photographs of every person in various stages of happiness – and some of obvious inebriation.

But also, unknown to Carragher, she'd given Roxy a Kodak Instamatic. He'd used up all the film and proved to have a good eye for documentary: focussing on Máire, especially the two of them together. On the beach, initially running barefoot in her wedding gown, then actually in the sea with her bridesmaids wearing a white Marilyn Monroe bikini. Roxy had remained outside the B&B all night, taking photos of them the next morning walking together on the beach, and through the bay window eating breakfast.

Carragher's unwillingness faded as they reminisced, until eventually Bronagh got up to make a pot of tea.

When she returned Carragher had closed the photograph albums and was sitting staring at the fireplace.

"So it's just you now," she said. "What's to be done with you?"

Carragher could see her sorrow, which made him feel worse than his own grief. Or was that because he'd learned to live with it?

But sorrow made him angry. It was pointless. There was nothing he could do about *her* sorrow, and so he didn't want her wasting time and energy on his.

"I'm stuck with this," he said, trying to broaden the focus.

"What do you mean?"

"In too deep."

"You know that's not true," she said. "You could just leave – to Australia, or somewhere crazy like Argentina. Nobody's gonna follow you."

He laughed.

"Find some mountain out there and sit on it," she said. "Start again."

"I did all that, Mam," he replied. "Look where it got me."

"The Divis isn't that kind of mountain," she said. "You should have escaped."

He didn't respond.

"And now you're killing yourself – just like your Da."

When Carragher returned to the cab, Roxy knew better than to say anything. He started the engine and drove down the hill to O'Donnell's house.

CHAPTER 24

SUNDAY 7 DECEMBER

So now, two weeks later, with time to kill amid the faded chintz of the over-heated HQNI Officers' Mess, Straker was thinking further about his strange vulnerability. Why had he asked his father for advice? He'd been hoping for something different, believing he'd become worthy of consideration. Although just a fleeting moment, he'd been trusting for no reason – a serious lapse of judgment.

Was he hard-wired to try to please his father? Was this why he'd joined the Army? He couldn't imagine that this might be so. His father saw the Army as a rigid hierarchy to be climbed for personal gain. Other people were little more than ladders. Straker's mother did her best to be a good officer's wife, whereas Straker was a liability.

Straker had never challenged the presumption that one liked one's parents; nor that he as a "normal" son might actually *dislike* his father. So it was a surprise to realise that he really did dislike his father – and that his father disliked him.

He immediately thought of his Uncle Rory, who'd seemed to understand Straker's troubled feelings about his father, managing to defuse the pain with some carefully timed, usually amusing remark. And of Abigail Ennis-Boyd, who'd given him a place that actually felt like a home.

But he could still hear his father's voice urging conformity while casting doubt on initiative and judgment. It was always there, generating hesitation and guilt.

"*His Master's Voice*," said Tiger. "*But you're not a dog.*"

The voice in his head was speaking softly, sounding as if he was smiling at Straker's youthful confusion.

"Too many voices," Straker replied.

"*Maybe so*," replied Tiger, "*but your father's voice will get you killed.*"

*

When on the Wednesday the RMP's had brought him to the Headquarters Northern Ireland Officers' Mess, they'd said it would be for "a week or so". At the time, he hadn't paid much attention to the vagueness of this statement. He'd been pleased to be out of the battered clatter of the military hospital, on his own for the first time since all this began.

But now, on his fourth day here, the mess' hunting prints, chintz sofas and over-heated public rooms seemed soulless. He felt imprisoned in corridors of dim shaded bulbs and dull carpet.

Mess Rules required members always to wear a jacket and tie, and after 7pm, suits or the equivalent (if women). So as his freshly laundered undercover observation clothes did not comply, he only got to eat or use the public rooms when nobody else was around. The mess manager's unconcealed disapproval increased after he'd asked to borrow some cash to buy a razor and have the NAAFI barber make respectable his "Northern Ireland" hair. Mr Beach, the Hereford Officers' Mess manager, sent over shoes, a suit, chinos, and a jacket and tie from Straker's room, which had not yet arrived.

On a Sunday the Officers Mess was free of the four-night London commuter civil servants, with a rolling brunch starting at the usual time for the watchkeepers and a buffet evening meal to give mess staff a break. Lulled into a false sense of imagining he'd have the place to himself, Straker had been relaxing in the anteroom when a burst of conversation in the hall interrupted his coffee.

He got up to find some thirty officers and wives in their Sunday best, he guessed having been to the garrison church. Some were entering the bar, others heading for coffee in the anteroom. The conversations stopped as they saw him, so he walked quickly away and up the stairs.

He lay on his bed, thinking about past operations. Normally they went straight back to Hereford, where things weren't considered finished until after they'd debriefed. This was always as immediate as possible: an accounting within the team of each operator's experiences, including their opinions, and analysing mistakes to a high level of self-appraisal. The report would be filed, then everyone moved on with no comebacks, and especially no divergence from the agreed narrative.

Straker believed the SAS selected the right people who then trained effectively to do whatever was required. But violence affected people differently, so in Straker's post-op sessions, each person got to say whatever they were thinking even if it seemed irrelevant – and especially if it was contentious. Unfinished business usually evolved into something worse, and people had to be able to work together in the future. So he always made sure every question was discussed until a team consensus could be agreed.

But despite having been a very violent and stressful operation, the post-op process hadn't even begun. And although the focus of the HQNI Board of Inquiry was an official drawing of lines, its purpose was not for the benefit of those involved.

Straker realised that he was doing the opposite of moving on but rather, dwelling on very unpleasant memories. He was also worried about the others; the Farmer would see Hooves right, but Jacko was still on his own.

Plus something else was bothering Straker; he was feeling quite different. He kept thinking back to how he'd been "Before", when the world had been better, brighter and he did not feel ill.

Logically, this "Before" would be prior to being blown up. He tied it down specifically to the afternoon of Sunday 23 November, fourteen days ago in the Hereford Mess, eating hot buttered toast.

So now he wanted, more than anything else in the world, to return to how he'd felt eating hot buttered toast. But then he remembered how, that afternoon, he'd been ruminating about his father, recycling the replies he wished he'd made during their last argument.

But even so, he now felt very different to then. And not in a good way.

That Sunday night, just in time for dinner, a large box arrived from the Hereford Officers Mess containing Straker's civilian clothes. It didn't improve things.

MONDAY 8 DECEMBER

Carragher had woken a little after three in the morning, to a strong south-west wind buffeting the front door and windows of O'Donnell's Ballymurphy house. For a moment the irregular vibrations and the Murph's characteristic smell of countryside, people, and coalsmoke was a comforting invocation of his boyhood, taking him back to a time when he'd believed there could be heroes.

He'd feared meeting his mother for what he'd thought she might say to him; that her loss might make him unable to bear his own. He now knew he'd underestimated her in thinking she might let her grief take priority over his. Seeing his Da had been different; a meaningless tribal ritual. Grief had destroyed his father a long time ago.

He'd made a pot of tea, drunk it black with three teaspoons of sugar, then finished off a packet of Rich Tea biscuits. He sat at the kitchen table, hunched into his dark green parka with the hood up over his head like a monk's cowl; that it might protect him from the dream that had forced him from his warm bed into the dankness of this bitter cold.

The dream had been the exact same tableau: medieval Christianity corrupt with putrefaction and hate. A Madonna, mockingly identical to Máire, was presenting her boy-child to him. But the boy's head and shoulders were slumped across her right arm in the ugliness of obvious death, a lifeless face with eyes closed.

He'd watched the blankness of her face, expecting her to speak. He'd prayed to God that she wouldn't, deeply afraid of the ancient presence he knew lived behind the mask.

But it had been the raven from his first dream that spoke – not using words, but saying everything that he'd feared to hear in a single guttural cry. It had then flown down from the pine tree to perch on the boy-child's shoulder, talons digging deep into his soft flesh.

Straker's fellow Officers Mess inmates – officially known as "inliers" seemed permanently miserable: a handful of married military staff officers serving over here without their families for personal reasons, short-tour watchkeepers doing shifts, and MoD civil servants flying in for lunch on Monday, then flying back to London on Thursday afternoons. For all its pretensions, it was nothing more than a dull, badly run hotel which only perked up on the rare occasions the general used it for official entertaining.

So the night before, wearing his newly delivered suit, Straker had ventured into the bar before dinner, to have the conversation suddenly stop around him. Even in a Parachute Regiment Officers' Mess bar, somebody would introduce themselves. But as they were all just standing looking at him, he said "Good evening" and ordered a pint of Guinness.

The barman poured the first half then put the glass aside to settle. The others went in to dinner. In the now-empty bar, Straker waited for the Guinness to be topped up, enjoyed the first taste, then took it with him across the corridor into the dining room. This was, he thought, almost certainly contrary to mess rules.

One place remained at the long table, next to a pretty young woman he guessed was a civil servant. She avoided eye contact. Then afterwards, when he returned to the bar, a staff officer he recognised from a Warminster School of Infantry training course drained his pint and walked out.

The next morning, Straker was reading the morning papers when a visitor walked into the otherwise empty anteroom. He was tall and looked to be in his late fifties, wearing a tweed jacket over a warm-looking pullover.

"You shouldn't be seen with me, Captain Straker, so let's go for a walk..."

The stranger spoke softly with a familiar southern Irish accent.

Out of sight of the Mess's public-room windows, the stranger introduced himself. "I'm Special Branch – which is all you need to know." This was said with a slight smile. "But you *do* need to know a bit more about what you've got into here..."

They walked around a barren-looking square of rose bushes, on a slippery flagstone path.

"I'm sure you realise that a lot of what *we* do is very close to the line that separates security forces from the terrorists. And we don't just fly in and out like you soldiers. We have to live here."

He sat down on a wet-looking bench, behind a well-trimmed six-foot-high hawthorn hedge.

"It's dangerous for us with our families... Most Republicans believe we're Loyalist sympathisers. Some even believe we help the paramilitaries."

Straker recognised this man – not by name, but by type. His career would have started back in the fifties, before the Troubles, as a bobby patrolling a city beat like any other police constable in the United Kingdom. Most RUC officers from that era felt betrayed. Armoured police cars, flak jackets and soldiers toting battlefield combat weapons had destroyed their world.

"You'll know that in June this year, two serving police officers were convicted of terrorist kidnap and murder."

He said this without emotion.

"Their statements implicated other officers in the planning and execution of shootings and bombings, and supplying Loyalist terrorists with weapons and critical information.

"I'm sure you've also realised that in order to get tip-offs like the one you guys were acting on, some of us have to be selectively 'helpful' to the IRA."

He's a chief superintendent or thereabouts – if he's even still in the police... thought Straker.

"We never met, by the way – just in case you feel like sharing anything I tell you, which I don't advise... And you won't see me again."

Those were the ground rules. Straker nodded his agreement, but then made the connection.

"So what's a Waterford man doing up here?" he said, challenging the stranger's domination of their conversation.

The stranger smiled, not even slightly ruffled.

"Not bad, Captain Straker," he said. "Nearer Cork, but top marks."

Straker waited.

"So you'll know somebody from down there?" he asked.

Straker was unable to conceal the sudden stab of emotion this generated. It was as if this large, quiet man could project electric shocks into his head.

Straker stayed silent.

"We're all supposed to be on the same side," the stranger continued, "but actually we're not... The stakes for some of us are too high.

"You Brits can afford to be straight. We can't. We're always juggling bad alternatives – like risking soldiers' lives to stop a bomb team that's killed a hundred people and will kill a hundred more; or to give credibility to a source who's very senior in the IRA."

"Are you saying we were deliberately set up?" interrupted Straker.

The stranger shook his head. "Nothing's ever that simple. The internal politics are complicated and very dangerous. No one person knows what's going on – only how the results can be made to look. Which is why I'm here now." He took out a packet of cigarettes. "Do you mind if I smoke?"

"No," said Straker.

He stopped talking and began performing a ritual: opening the packet, knocking out the cigarette, then twirling it while tapping the end against a box of Swan Vesta matches. The index finger of his left hand shook intermittently. He was delaying, maybe trying to cut back, postponing the moment of inhalation. Finally, he lit up, sucking smoke deep into his lungs with evident satisfaction.

"And on this occasion," he continued, "it looks like the IRA lost and we won... With the added benefit to us of Mrs Carragher's sad demise."

He took another deep drag, then exhaled the smoke away from Straker.

"You already know you were there on a tip-off..."

Straker nodded.

"Mrs Carragher was rather a surprise, and as you might expect, her bereaved husband is spitting vengeance..."

He looked at the cigarette for a moment.

"Our source is very high-ranking, so all this emotion is making his life difficult. We need to spread as much smoke and confusion over this as we can, alter how it looks, reduce the emotions, settle everybody down a bit..."

"I can see that," said Straker. "So how does this affect me?"

The policeman stubbed the barely smoked cigarette out on the paving stone at his feet.

He's definitely trying to give up.

"There has to be blame," said the stranger. "And you and your guys are the obvious choice."

Straker's anxiety surged briefly before he shut it down. This made him realise the extent to which he'd been denying the seriousness of his position. The RUC officer sat looking at him. Straker didn't respond.

"Republicans already believe freelance SAS hit teams are at work – you'll remember the MRF, and the ones we've uncovered in the RUC and Ulster Defence Regiment? And I'm pretty sure the IRA and UVF are trying to make some of their crime killings look like SAS work…

"Anyway, blaming you's guys stops PIRA thinking they were set up, and we – the RUC – escape the blame of being set up ourselves."

"Why are you telling me this?" asked Straker quietly.

"A lot of people over here think soldiers, especially Paras, are irresponsible. You do your tours then go home, no skin in the game. They'll believe this blame narrative.

"Playing this with a straight bat – or however a Parachute Regiment officer normally handles things – isn't how to deal with this."

They sat silently for several minutes.

"Like I said at the start," continued the SB officer, "some of us work extremely close to the red line. But although we don't get everything to go our own way, we do get things looking how *we* want them to look."

He paused and looked around as if he'd heard something.

"And also, there's a much bigger game being played. To the extent that none of us – at least, none of us over here – know the big picture."

Straker waited, hoping that this man's next few sentences might clarify this strange conversation.

"So maybe it's like a pawn who checkmates the king? Or takes out the queen but dies next move… But y'see, somebody set that up. Does the pawn know the plan, or is someone telling him what to do? Or does he work it out for himself?

"Anyway, this is *our* world over here – our game."

He picked up the cigarette butt as if removing evidence of his presence.

"But there are things *you* can do which we can't. No one'll tell you… but that's how this place works."

He stood up.

"We'd all be better off if we listened to God, Captain Straker. Did you know he speaks with an Irish accent?"

He then laughed.

"Anyway, I'm gone... Stay here in this lovely garden and enjoy the sunshine until I'm away. Good luck to you."

Straker sat in the garden until the sunshine was gone and he was cold. He'd been beguiled, and only later connected the man's accent with Tiger's. He knew not to take him at face value and yet the spell – along with the accent – had led Straker's gut reaction to do just that. So, as he had no other ideas, he began processing the implications.

Straker decided to write Jacko a detailed letter. He sealed it in a brown MoD envelope using a civvie postage stamp so it wouldn't go into the normal military mail system.

He thought he was probably being paranoid, but wasn't going to compromise his personal security. A letter could be intercepted and used in evidence against him. But using the civvie mail system was the only way to minimise the risk.

For the same reason, he didn't use the Officers' Mess post box but walked across to the main HQ building and posted Jacko's letter into the admin wing's main post box. It was full of blueys – free airmail letters to families, wives, lovers – from soldiers maintaining their connections with normality.

For a moment he was one of them, and felt comforted.

CHAPTER 25

The Farmer and Hooves were still feeling disorientated despite being back in camp at Hereford. The sabre squadrons were trying to get themselves off as early as possible for the Christmas break, while fending off the headshed's attempts at administrative interference and three-line-whip social events. The on-duty people were keeping out of camp as much as possible, willing their pagers to remain silent; the NAAFI was dismal and deserted.

They'd been ordered not to talk to anybody pending the Board of Inquiry, which the Farmer had further clarified to Hooves as meaning "not to *any*body, at *any* time".

"This is your first op of this sort," he said. "Camp is full of people wanting to know stuff they shouldn't. They already know something's happened, so we keep ourselves to ourselves. Maybe after Christmas leave they'll have forgotten."

So they'd walked out of camp through the housing estate and into town along Ross Road across the river, where now, mid-morning, they were lurking beside the heavily steamed-up window of the Cadena café. Hooves reckoned this was where some of the County Hospital nurses came for their breaks, but not the times.

The Farmer picked up a dog-eared copy of the *Daily Mail* from the bench seat of the next table. It was folded at the racing page, so he only saw the headline once he'd picked it up.

"We've made the papers," he said to Hooves, showing him the photo of Máire.

Without replying, Hooves walked across the café to the wooden rack where discarded newspapers were kept. He looked quickly at the dates, then brought over a selection.

"The *Telegraph*'s got it on the front page, continued on the back – *and* in the middle," said Hooves. "An editorial about the Army working behind the backs of the police."

"MRF," grunted the Famer. "Those cowboys fucked it up for everybody."

Hooves was still reading.

"It sounds like we're being blamed for Máire Carragher's death," he said.

"For fuck's sake," said the Farmer.

"Trouble is," said Hooves, "the *Telegraph* reflects government thinking. They're talking about how dangerous it will be if the police are thought to have lost control of the Army."

"Blaming Captain Straker?" said the Farmer. "The easiest option?"

"Which is why he's still out there," suggested Hooves.

"He definitely should be back here with us," said the Farmer.

"The headshed must be on it," said Hooves.

The Farmer shook his head.

"I wouldn't be so sure about that."

TUESDAY 9 DECEMBER

Straker had now endured five long days in the Mess, with no word about the Board of Inquiry.

He felt himself to be in two very distinct and hostile worlds: the darkness of the nights, and by day, "Slipper City", surrounded by office workers and administrators who experienced the Troubles second-hand from the reports they processed and occasional military visits outside the razor wire. The more adventurous might venture out into safe Protestant Lisburn, or on weekend trips to the deserted beauty of the coast. Some were even stupid enough to take sightseeing drives down the Falls Road.

Straker was an aberration. Miserable though it was, the Mess was their home, and despite mess rules requiring hospitality to visitors, everyone avoided him with varying degrees of politeness.

The headquarters' system of information restriction was rigorous, the most sensitive documents to be read only at desks inside a walk-in safe. Only the most senior people had any business knowing why he was here. But he'd been delivered here by RMPs, with his Northern Ireland hair and beard; and gossip was endemic.

That afternoon, two full colonels of the General Staff in barrack dress uniform came into the anteroom where Straker was drinking tea, stopped, then stared at him. One officer's scrubbed complexion flushed red as Straker caught his eye. But then his equally senior colleague pulled him by the elbow back out into the corridor.

As the Board of Inquiry was being run by HQ Northern Ireland, this level of antagonism worried Straker. Although the board's president and members were brought in from elsewhere, this did not bode well.

That night, Straker was in the anteroom drinking an after-dinner Guinness. He was desperate to sleep, but even more desperate to avoid his grim little bedroom and more of last night's dreams.

But then the female civil servant who'd ignored him on the first night came across to where he was sitting.

He stood up.

"Please don't bother getting up for my sake," she said. "I only want to ask you a question."

She had a slightly mocking tone; of his manners, perhaps, delivered in confident patrician tones – a posh girl.

He remained standing.

"Could I talk with you, please?"

He didn't respond.

"I'm not being judgmental," she said. "Not like the others."

"What others?"

She sat down at the end of the sofa beside his armchair.

"I'm from the Treasury, not MoD. And you don't seem at all like the sort of person they're saying you are."

He sat down.

"And what sort of a person is that?" he said.

"You just look very tired."

"I am."

A Civil Service fast-tracker from Oxbridge? he wondered.

"I've never met a man like you," she said, after a pause.

"What sort of a man is that?" he replied.

"You can't just repeat my questions," she said.

"I can," he said with a slight smile. "But yes, I'd say it's unlikely you would have."

"You made that sound rather disparaging," she said.

"That's your interpretation," he replied, "but it's based on the information you've given me."

In controlling her reaction, he caught a glimpse of the curiosity she was trying to conceal.

"If you asked *me* a question," she said, "I'd answer…"

Schoolgirl tactics.

"Good for you," he replied.

She continued as if she hadn't heard.

"I don't fit in here either."

Straker took a drink from his Guinness.

"Everyone over here is immersed in their own complications," she continued. "Even the political aides."

"A Belfast bubble," he said.

"Yes, but it's nothing like Whitehall. Each of us is here because of the violence. But it seems like the violence is just another topic."

"It might be like that in the headquarters," said Straker. "But not outside the wire."

She nodded, seeming encouraged.

"Absolutely, they make it about policy – how to work with the police, political control; or it's about logistics and costings.

"The guys over here are either working all hours," she continued, "or with their families in the married quarters. It's hard to relate to anybody."

An invitation? Straker didn't react.

"My involvement is with the costings part of all this," she continued. "It's frighteningly huge…"

He was probably expected to ask "How much?" but didn't.

"It's hard to see how the expenditure can be evaluated – set against targets, what those targets might be… Although that's an accountant's way of looking at it."

She was presenting herself as apart from the "others"; volunteering information, leaning forwards, speaking quietly as if imparting secrets, inviting him to lean in to listen.

This, he suddenly realised, was standard interrogation technique. She offered apparent indiscretions, matched with mirroring and synchronous behaviour.

He was irritated. If she was trying to work him, she wasn't doing a very good job of it; too amateurish for MI5, possibly Joint Services

Interrogation Wing – although far too naïve to be Intelligence Corps.

"And you're the first person I've come across out here who's actually done something," she concluded.

"There's plenty of us around," replied Straker.

She offered him a cigarette. He shook his head.

"Not in here there isn't," she said. "This headquarters is a crammed-in version of that military town in Wiltshire, except it's behind barbed wire and surrounded by Protestants."

"Tidworth?"

She waved the cigarette at him.

"Is that it? Probably… Doesn't matter. Whereas back in Wiltshire, they're at least part of the countryside. Here, it's disconnected from everything – totally unreal."

He now rejected the interrogator idea. She was just trying to get a conversation going. There was curiosity, also with loneliness perhaps, in this weird place.

"You're mixing with the wrong people," he said.

She took that as a joke, smiling. "I certainly am. And you're completely different," she added.

"I've had a haircut."

"No, I mean *completely* different…"

She reached over and put a hand on his knee.

He remembered a decade back to when he'd spent a week helping friends from Harrow whose heavy rock band had a best-selling album. They'd been on tour, and this was how the posh girls talked their way into the band's dressing room.

They sat in silence, she keeping her hand on his knee.

"So what *was* it like?" she said.

There it was; the conversation about the "killer" label. People were crass enough to ask, then judged you; mostly negatively, although sometimes ludicrously heroically, which was equally unacceptable.

But killing a pregnant woman was something else again.

"You haven't asked my name," he said.

He could see she already knew it.

"And," he added, "you haven't told me yours."

She looked flustered. "I'm Pandora," she said, "but I thought we were introduced when you first arrived?"

"There've been no introductions..."

She didn't reply.

"Which doesn't matter to me," he continued.

"Nor me," she said, as if that now brought them together.

"I see everybody avoiding you – not even talking to you," she continued. "So how does it feel?"

Even so, he didn't respond.

"What I meant was 'how do *you* feel'," she added.

The answer was that he felt as bad about it as she or anybody could possibly feel. The training prepared you for what you had to do, but not for afterwards, which you had to deal with by yourself.

He did need to talk, and felt tempted. But then he remembered how difficult a normal team debriefing could be, even among people of similar experience.

As the silence settled yet again, she became visibly annoyed at him not doing his bit to keep the conversation going. She'd be used to men falling over themselves to satisfy her curiosity, especially in an Officers' Mess.

"It's a perfectly reasonable question," she said.

The word "reasonable" pulled him back to the real world. There was nothing reasonable about any of this. He turned his stab of anger into an icy calmness.

"So you think I'm being *un*reasonable not telling you how it feels to kill a heavily pregnant woman?"

She'd been leaning forwards in the armchair. She now sat up straight, an abrupt movement, accompanied by a startled shake of the head.

"Or rather how *I* feel – as I'm not like you or the other people. Oh, and also killing the baby... How *that* feels," continued Straker.

He looked steadily at her across the arm of the sofa.

"Apart from being the subject of a classified inquiry, don't you think this is a rather personal question...?"

She looked uncertain.

"So me being, as you say, 'completely different from the others' is because I shot dead a pregnant woman?"

Her shocked silence confirmed Straker's statement. She now sat very still, as if terrified by what he might now do.

"Why is it you think you can ask me this?" he said, after a pause.

She made as if to rise, an involuntary movement away from him. "No," she said. "No, I just thought you might want to—"

"The only 'perfectly reasonable question' in this discussion is why you might think that," Straker interrupted. "Which is what the Royal Military Police will ask *you* if I make a complaint."

"Military Police…?"

He stood up.

"And no," he added. "I'm not interested."

She looked confused.

"You're definitely a Pandora," he said. "And also a voyeur."

She now looked furious.

"You keep this conversation to yourself," he continued. "I've had enough of the cold shoulder from everybody else in here. If I sense any more of it, I'll speak to the RMP and get you sent back to London."

He picked up the *Telegraph* and his Guinness, returning to his room and the dreams.

Tomorrow would be start of Straker's second week in the Officers Mess. So how much longer was the RMP major's prediction of "a week or so" likely to take? And had the Board of Inquiry even started?

He'd examined and re-examined his actions so many times, with such severity, that it now bored as well as horrified him. The "rightness" of the shoot cycled continuously like a self-generating report:

Two hits in the middle of the target as presented, under less-than-optimal conditions, standard double-tap…

As for his compliance with the Yellow Card Rules, he didn't remember pulling the trigger. So had he consciously fired, or did the bomb blast twitch off deeply ingrained muscle movements? He'd given one verbal warning, but not the required two, although he'd been correct in his assumption of the threat to his life.

It went round and round. He couldn't remember, the bomb had exploded, the woman and baby were dead – so what was the question?

After so many nights of being too fearful to sleep, Straker was both exhausted and desperate for diversion. Reading was impossible, the horror inside his head too vivid to be replaced by a world of words. A bottle of Bushmills might work, but would create another problem he didn't need.

He was generating unfounded fear, a panther that clawed randomly into his thoughts. When he was able to concentrate hard enough to logic his way out of the forest to calmer spaces, the beast pounced yet again, turning the mild surprise of any unexpected thought no matter how anodyne, into a trigger for intense anxiety.

The motto of the RAF's No. 1 Parachute Training School is "Knowledge Dispels Fear". But the dark power of Straker's panther came not from fear of the future, which would evaporate with reality and action, but from the past, and memories he couldn't change: indelible images, surreal and brutal. He'd locked them away from his conscious mind. But he'd no control of what happened further down in the darkness, nor of the panther's malignant mindlessness.

Straker's anxiety was physically painful, as with an injury. It was also tiring, verging on becoming unbearable – as he imagined a serious illness would feel. So should he phone the doc at Musgrave Park Hospital?

But Morton had been very specific. These weren't the headaches he'd warned him about, and Straker remained as disinclined to seek medical help as he'd been after the Warrenpoint bombings. He also remembered the doc's warning about the adverse career implications of this being written into his medical notes.

But it still felt like he was ill; and he wanted it to have a name. Other people suffering the same would mean he wasn't on his own – reassuring, although selfish.

His mother's birthday party, just eighteen days ago, now felt like another time in another world. He thought he'd escaped the HMV of paternal disapproval – and been glad. But its absence now worried him, as if he'd been disowned by his father which, given what had happened, was very likely if the Board of Inquiry found against him.

But was his father's voice in fact his own conscience? Did really bad people lose theirs? Could that actually happen?

This made him laugh. But it wasn't funny. He then thought about judgment, the "norms" of acceptable behaviour – even of sin and redemption; lines of thought he stretched long and wide inside his head, hoping to latch onto something solid. It was exhausting.

Straker was besieged by nonsense, trapped inside a doll's house of idiocy. He needed to do something. Maybe he should see the headquarters chaplain – an idea he rejected immediately he thought of it. He didn't need saving, and only the guilty talked to chaplains.

Straker tried only to worry about the things he could influence. But what other people thought was the one thing nobody could change. Nevertheless, the talking behind his back in the Mess was real, and their reluctance to engage with him was understandable. So could they be right?

"*Why is it important what these people think?*"

Tiger had returned, his other big cat, but soft-voiced like Irish rain percolating down to where the peat fire smouldered; logic asking the one question that extinguished all others.

But Straker's burning was too far down.

"These people" and their opinion of him was because of what he'd done and its fundamental unacceptability. They didn't know the details, which to them were irrelevant, because for such a crime there could be no mitigating circumstances.

Their revulsion could only be compounded by whatever he did now.

Straker was very angry. Ignorance was far worse than stupidity, the doll's house now a gilded carousel, its riders idiots waving their disapproval at him from prancing, blank-eyed stallions.

"*But do you even care what they think?*"

He paused for a moment. *Did* he care?

Then he decided not to analyse the question.

He didn't care, he *really* didn't. The question was the answer.

He didn't care what they thought. It wasn't about them not understanding – they never could. And he hoped the people who did understand were safe back in Hereford.

CHAPTER 26

Three days after Carragher moved in, O'Donnell arrived, dropped off from a car that departed immediately Roxy answered the door.

"How is he?" said O'Donnell.

Roxy didn't reply.

"It's me that's asking," said O'Donnell, standing back slightly.

Roxy remained implacably planted in the doorway.

"He's grand," he replied, "in the day at least."

O'Donnell wasn't going away.

"But you'll see for yourself," said Roxy after another pause, then stood to one side, holding the door so that O'Donnell had to push past him into the narrow hallway.

Carragher was in the kitchen with a mug of tea in front of him.

"That your wheels just drove off?"

O'Donnell sat. It would be an hour before his driver returned.

"So I'm getting everything calmed down," he said.

"With me out of the way?" interrupted Carragher.

"With you out of the way...?" queried O'Donnell, as if he hadn't meant that. "Well, yes, I suppose so."

"And is it?"

"Calmer than here," said O'Donnell pointedly. He'd thought three days of metaphorical death before this resurrection would curb Carragher. It appealed to his inner altar-boy. But he hadn't thought about it any more deeply than that. So the news of Carragher's dangerous foray back into Murph politics had surprised and alarmed him.

"You worry too much," said Carragher. "McComb's a gobshite."

O'Donnell had known trying to intimidate Carragher would be pointless. But arrogance still forced him to try.

"I've got *him* calmed down too," said O'Donnell.

"No," said Carragher, laughing at him, "*you* haven't. But the little wee shite's back in his hole and won't be coming out any time soon."

This wasn't to be a joyful reunion. Nor was there any likelihood of Carragher being grateful. O'Donnell felt rather stupid having thought that might happen.

"He's had a wee visit from the brigade, just to make sure," said O'Donnell, using his conciliation voice.

They sat in silence.

"So, yes, things have calmed down, and there's a lot to be done," said O'Donnell.

Carragher had known when O'Donnell's car pulled up outside that he was to be brought back into the fold. But there'd been three days of doubt in which he'd thought about how else this might go. As he'd said to his Ma, there didn't seem to be any point in taking massive risks to break away and try something new, only for the same thing to happen yet again. The Murph voice mocked ambition with good reason.

He'd no options. O'Donnell had always kept him isolated, which Carragher had liked for security reasons. But it made him dependent on O'Donnell. And his past ten months commanding the brigade had earned him enemies. So O'Donnell was Carragher's only way back.

This was history looping round again, stuck on the Murph with no prospects, then rescued by O'Donnell. He was indeed the Prodigal Son returned to the warm glow of paternal favour.

Except that Carragher hadn't walked away. He'd been fired, then abandoned – forsaken. He wasn't going to forget this.

They'd got down to the evaluation of mainland targets in terms of UK media impact and British prestige, and their relative danger and difficulty. Both agreed that PIRA's existing bomb cells, now dormant, were not to be involved – not even as sacrifices to distract MI5.

"London's got to be the focus," insisted Carragher. "It's the most difficult place to work, with the best security. But it's all high value. Good planning and staying independent gets us in and out. We'll be small, based over here, not there."

"Smuggling in the explosives is a massive risk. We'd have to do it for every operation," observed O'Donnell.

"True, but it keeps us away from the police and MI5," said Carragher. "Other people can drive the vehicles on and off the ferry."

There was no shortage of proxies who could be threatened or tricked into taking this specific risk.

"What's the timeframe to be ready?" said O'Donnell.

"No less than one year," replied Carragher.

O'Donnell looked surprised.

"That's because we need all the operations fully planned before we start – in advance, each one with alternatives, and all the materials lined up."

"We might have to compromise on that," said O'Donnell.

"Getting the materials is the problem," said Carragher. "The recces take long enough if you do them properly. But we haven't got anything like enough Semtex for a proper campaign."

They kept coming back to the failure of the SAS bombing operation. Success would have reopened the Libyan connection.

"We need the ETA relationship to start working," said O'Donnell.

"The girl is reliable," said Carragher.

"But is she serious?" said O'Donnell. "As in, do her superiors take her seriously?"

"I take her seriously," said Carragher.

O'Donnell laughed. Carragher looked at him without saying anything.

"You know exactly what I'm saying, Séan," O'Donnell replied. "It's important. If they take her seriously, they'll do this."

Carragher nodded.

"OK," he said. "So why don't we show her a shopping list?"

"I thought you needed to do the planning first?"

"It would be generic," said Carragher. "Calculated on five operations plus two diversionary bombs if needed, which we could recover and reuse. Just the total amount of explosive, detonators, and Cordtex. We'll make the initiation devices ourselves."

O'Donnell sucked his pencil, thinking it through.

"Concurrent activity…" he said finally. "And we won't wait for them to get the gear together. So in January we start the recces, to be ready for when they do deliver."

"We'll still need the full order before we start," repeated Carragher.

"OK," said O'Donnell. "I agree with you. This has to be relentless, timed precisely for maximum political impact."

"I'll talk to the girl immediately," said Carragher.

CHAPTER 27

WEDNESDAY 10 DECEMBER

Arrosa's latest meeting with Carragher had been completely different.

A week ago, his monumental self-control was in tatters; he'd seemed weak and capable of making mistakes, which she'd decided could only be a temporary situation before he regained himself.

Even so, today she'd been amazed at the improvement in his appearance and demeanour. He was positive, with purpose, and very detailed in all his questions, as if decisions had been taken and the period of waiting was over. Even Roxy was back to his old self.

But she hadn't forgotten the SAS man; what he'd done to Carragher, and Roxy's revealing indiscretion. The transformation was too much. It could only be a cover-up for the overwhelming fury and grief she'd seen just a week ago.

She also thought that Roxy's concern about Carragher personalising this would have percolated up to O'Donnell. That level of anger was too dangerous to all of them, and O'Donnell was terrifyingly perceptive.

Hunting down specific people was not a PIRA speciality, being far riskier than a normal terrorist attack. Personal attacks were usually only on police officers and Ulster Defence Regiment soldiers at their home addresses, which were easy enough to find. Whereas getting accurate targeting information on an SAS officer would be pretty much impossible, especially as he was certain to be back on the mainland by now. And realistically, attacking a guy that capable could only go wrong.

After their previous meeting, Arrosa had surmised that Carragher would either regain his self-control and give up this dangerous idea, or somebody else would stop him – probably O'Donnell. But as she didn't believe Carragher could have worked through all this in just one week, she decided he was doing a good job of suppressing his anger, and that he remained unstable.

This situation had considerable potential for danger to herself, and disruption to her mission. She again wondered about the extent to which O'Donnell was aware. Carragher had let slip how he felt to her immediately after Máire's death – as had Roxy. But although she wasn't going to underestimate O'Donnell, she was sure Carragher wouldn't have made the same mistake with him.

Which suggested that she knew something O'Donnell maybe didn't. She tucked that thought away for further consideration. If there was to be danger and disruption, she'd make sure it was visited upon others.

But for the moment Arrosa had to do her actual job; broker an arms deal for PIRA with her ETA superiors in Barcelona. Specifically, her purpose in this was to make an initial evaluation of the plan in conjunction with the people involved, which she would do honestly and to the best of her ability.

And in the process she'd learned about far more than just PIRA's planned resumption of UK mainland bombing, which Chapman was already expecting. Now she knew the scale of the campaign, its purpose, and that it was to be carried out personally by Carragher and not the sleeper teams who'd remained dormant on the mainland since the Manchester bombings.

Arrosa's intelligence value depended on her continued acceptance by both sides. Her job here was long-term, so she was not required to produce the sort of detailed intelligence that would enable arrests, or ships to be intercepted by the Royal Navy, or bank accounts to be frozen. Her job was simply to remain in position, from which over time she could piece together the overall shape of the networks – and as she'd done now, the strategy.

Other agents would do all the subverting and surveillance, leading on to seizure and enforcement action. This was work that could never remain hidden, exposing the operators. They were expendable, and so were protected.

Whereas protecting Arrosa was far more difficult. Anything additional to the personal security routines, cover stories, and relationships that she worked so hard to maintain would be anomalous and so make her job far more dangerous. People other than

Chapman would have to know of her existence, which was dangerous in itself, and their protection measures could give her away.

The single act of communicating was to do something outside her cover identity. It risked everything. As a long-term sleeper agent, the decision to communicate was the most critical one she could make. And although she knew her superiors would wish it otherwise, it was her decision, not theirs; one of the absolutes taught to agents during IONEC.

She was pretty sure she'd soon learn even more about this new bombing campaign. But although that might be a better time to break cover and communicate, she was going to do it now. Part of her training had instilled the process of continuous self-evaluation – of decisions, alternatives, routines, and ideas. This instinct was now telling her that she'd already made the decision to communicate with Chapman – over a week ago, while driving in the taxi back into town with Roxy.

Arrosa walked across to the side entrance of the red-brick and sandstone Graduate School, where she made a call from one of its public telephone kiosks; ten rings, then the click as an answer machine in London opened the circuit. There was no greeting, and she put the phone down after giving her two-sentence key. She then returned to the Language School, walking up several flights of increasingly narrow stairs to her tiny office in the eaves.

With two hours to wait, she marked some undergraduate poetry translations – awkward, uninspired attempts to recreate the flowing precision of Jorge Manrique's 15th-century funeral elegy: *Cómo se viene la muerte tan calando* – "And death comes softly stealing on, how silently!"

She remained distracted. Uneasy. There was nothing soft about this.

Her problem was equivocation – between concern for the SAS officer and the potential opportunity of this situation. Carragher would not have given up his murderous intention so quickly, and if the SAS man was warned of the threat to his life, the roles would be reversed, making Carragher the target. Warning the SAS man was important. But it had to be done soon, and she had no idea how.

*

Later, in the early evening, she walked down University Road, then Stranmillis Road, and turned right into the grounds of Riddel Hall, where she'd stayed after first arriving in Belfast. Nobody was following her, so she walked up the steps into the gloomy Victorian entrance, oak panelling smelling faintly of floor polish and boiled cabbage, along dim corridors past anterooms and the dining hall, to a deserted area that had once been the building's less formal back entrance.

Beside bicycles and bags of muddy hockey gear stood a row of rarely used telephone boxes, which she considered the most discreet in Belfast. She'd shut herself in to make a highly unusual telephone call to Chapman in London on one of his untraceable agent lines. Exactly two hours after her first call, following the verification and situation code phrases, they spoke.

"I heard they'd had a very busy week," said Chapman.

"Did you?"

Arrosa had initiated this call to pass on information. So she hadn't expected Chapman to say anything, let alone talk to her as if he already knew what she was risking this call to tell him.

"Yes. It seems everybody's been outplayed..."

A fair summary of the situation, she thought. "So you've already heard about this?"

"Yes, and I'm guessing that's why you've called."

"When did you know?" she asked.

"I heard about the meeting of quartermasters."

"What?" interrupted Arrosa.

This meant Chapman had been in the loop from the very beginning, in what was very strictly RUC, and so MI5, business.

"Yes," replied Chapman, "and I also heard that our police friends decided to take the bait."

Arrosa's work didn't cross over into Northern Ireland counter-terrorism, so she was surprised to discover that Chapman's interests apparently did.

"Are there other projects running that I should know about?" she asked.

Arrosa was now thinking outside the primary purpose of her intelligence presence in Belfast. She did not deal with the police over here – nor, as far as she'd been aware, did Chapman or anyone else in MI6 working on illegal arms trading.

"Actually, no," said Chapman. "But this incident gives us an opportunity to sow discord helpful to *our* cause."

Arms dealing generated huge amounts of money. Captains of UK industry were involved, some with knighthoods from the grateful nation – dangerous people, almost impossible to bring to justice. But justice was not MI6's concern. Involving police and the law meant exposing one's agents and methods to public scrutiny in the courts. So Chapman sought to understand enough of the connections of an arms supply chain to turn the criminals operating the market against each other.

"Is there a link?" asked Arrosa, trying to work out where this was going.

"With hindsight *now*, after the event," said Chapman, ignoring her question, "it seems the deal on offer to our friends had been too good to be true."

Chapman sounded supercilious. But Arrosa didn't mind, as this meant he was thinking across the whole range of the situation – whatever it was. Instead, she focussed on establishing which of "our friends" Chapman was saying had been duped, veiled speech being a standard precaution.

"The people I'm working with feel particularly aggrieved," she said.

"Understandably so," replied Chapman. "Because despite your people having done a good job, it seems *our* friends were rescued by one of *our* friends' contractors – an extremely capable person."

"Yes," said Arrosa, understanding that bit. "This is the person they're particularly keen to engage."

It was also, she realised with a start, the person *she* was most interested in.

"Your people were depending very heavily on this," continued Chapman. "So the failure has hit them very hard. Do you have any ideas why?"

"Yes," said Arrosa. "This is why I've called, after an interesting meeting with their principal."

"Yes," said Chapman. "The connection would be through him…"

Arrosa knew Carragher had been arrested for arms smuggling and sentenced to five years, serving two-and-a-half with full remission. But she had no idea what connection Chapman was referring to.

"He's said they'll be restarting work on the mainland, for which they need supplies."

"Did they say when?"

"They're looking for the usual raw materials," she said, "in a large bulk order. So I'd say they won't start until they get it."

"You'll send the details?"

She had mailing addresses, and a book of cypher code that only Chapman knew. The amounts on Carragher's shopping list would indicate the type of targets and PIRA's timescale.

"Yes."

"So they needed to do something impressive to facilitate this new supply chain?"

"Yes," she said. "That was part of it."

"And the other part…?"

"It's the effect on my principal – he's taking it very badly," she continued. "He wants to know the name of the contractor. He's making it personal."

There was a brief silence on the line.

"It's really unusual," she added. "It got him fired from his job…"

"So I heard," said Chapman.

"But although he's back in his normal job now, I'm pretty sure it's still a problem for him."

"He's not one to let something like that go," agreed Chapman.

"It could create opportunities," she added.

"Thanks for that," Chapman responded. "Most interesting."

Even though she knew the call was being recorded and Chapman would analyse every syllable, his apparent indifference to the risk she was taking in making it was disappointing.

"Specifically," she said abruptly, "I think we should make the contractor aware of this interest."

"That's also an interesting idea," he added brightly. "I'll consider whether we might get involved."

And then he rang off.

Afterwards, Arrosa felt cross but also uneasy. Her suggestion had seemed spur-of-the-moment, but now she realised it had actually been the reason she'd made the call. Everything else could just as effectively have gone into a communiqué. Warning the SAS captain was her only time-sensitive information. And Chapman seemed to have blanked the idea.

Then she thought about his last sentence. How could "*we*" get involved? Did "we" mean her and Chapman, or Chapman and other people, or MI6? And why should *any* of them get involved?

She swallowed her annoyance and analysed the rest of the conversation. Chapman said "the connection" would be through Carragher – and not O'Donnell, as she'd presumed, which was interesting.

Arrosa now remembered one of Chapman's tutorial-style explanations of how apparently disconnected information can be utilised. He'd been explaining how MI6 agents had "encouraged" PIRA's representative in Tripoli in the mid-seventies to behave oddly enough to lose Libyan government respect. He hadn't explained the nature of either his encouragement or the "odd behaviour". As well as discrediting PIRA, they'd achieved a reliable flow of intelligence, intercepting several munition shipments until Libya stopped supplying PIRA.

So four years later had PIRA been trying to get back into Libya's good books – impressing Colonel Gaddafi to re-establish Libyan arms supplies behind ETA's back? Had a deal collapsed because their attack on the SAS failed? Was this why Carragher suddenly needed the arrangement with ETA up and running? Should she challenge Carragher on this?

She had a lot to consider. Plus there was her instinctive resistance to Chapman's manipulation. He'd never tell her more than she needed to know, but she resented being played like a chess-piece.

During her field training their SAS instructors had repeatedly said "the man on the ground is always right until proved wrong". She was the agent in the field, and she played her own game. So she decided she needed to know more, particularly about this SAS guy. Duffy was the only person who'd seen him, and the only survivor of the operation, so talking to him seemed the logical next step.

But she didn't know enough about Duffy, and couldn't think of a good enough reason to talk with him, let alone be asking him about the SAS guy. Also, talking to him could be dangerous in itself, as Duffy was one of the people Carragher would be looking to blame.

But then it occurred to her that personal danger, and the consequent jeopardy to her mission here in Belfast, wasn't putting her off. For some reason, this SAS guy was more important.

CHAPTER 28

Not caring was liberating. Straker had actually slept, although he woke up still tired with a headache. It occurred to him that one of the drawbacks of not drinking, was having nothing to blame, and knowing how he felt wouldn't improve. But he was feeling distinctly better, like the relief after thunderstorms in the tropics, lightning taking the tension away to earth, leaving just the smell of wet dirt.

Although confronting Pandora had not helped. And now he felt sorry for her.

Straker came down for breakfast at 0830, with the living-in staff officers and civil servants already clocked into the HQ. One of the overnight watchkeepers was sprawled fast asleep across a sofa, so he took a cup of coffee upstairs to his room, deciding to analyse the strange conversation with his Special Branch visitor.

"This is our world over here," he'd said. "You need to understand the rules."

Deliberately melodramatic, this had been carefully phrased, containing a warning Straker knew he needed to understand. But in all his tours working over here, the only rule he'd latched onto was "if you're not with us, you're against us".

Being a Brit meant always being the outsider. As the Special Branch officer had also said to him:

"...there are things *you* can do which we can't. No one'll tell you... But that's how this place works..."

Straker had no idea what those "things" might be. He obeyed British Army orders, but had also to take account of many other factors, most of which conflicted with each other. There was endemic RUC resentment, Protestant outrage, Republican hatred, and two violently opposed religions apparently serving the same God. And on top of all this, Whitehall had suspended the

Northern Ireland parliament, and imposed government and laws which many people here did not recognise.

And was it down to *him* to decide what to do?

The SB officers' poorly defined riddle worried him far more than he thought it should.

He then realised why he was taking it so seriously. The enigmatic precision of the SB officer's County Waterford accent was to him as personal as anything could possibly be. In his head, Straker was replaying the policeman's sentences exactly as they'd been spoken to him, but hearing them in Tiger's voice.

This took him back to his first year in the Parachute Regiment – brand new, headstrong but uncertain. Tiger had never told him what to do, but was always there to be consulted, answering questions with the vagueness of a Greek oracle. Straker wondered if all County Waterford men were the same.

The SB officer had also said something about "not doing whatever a Parachute Regiment officer would normally do"; that "playing it with a straight bat" wouldn't work.

Thanks to Tiger, Straker knew exactly what this meant. With no personal military experience to draw on, play-acting the "Army officer" stereotype got a lot of young officers through. But Tiger never let him do that. With only Delphic wisdom from his platoon sergeant, young Straker's every decision had been a struggle, Tiger forcing him to think much harder than he'd otherwise have done.

Furthermore, in having to use his own judgment right from the start, he'd learned to do only what *he* thought was right. This cut through the crap and uncertainty, giving him confidence.

So now, being *told* not to play the Army officer made total sense.

Straker was worried about his usually reliable intuition, which always warned him of danger. It seemed to be malfunctioning. Even though he was resting and totally safe in this boring place, his danger-warning system was spiking constantly.

"*The train's rolling,*" came Tiger's voice. "*It's on its way.*"

He imagined himself as an automatic railway crossing, its barriers opening and closing at random. The warning bell was ringing, red lights flashing. Tiger liked metaphors, and mixed them with cheerful abandon. But he'd always been precise, and each one could often mean something completely different.

But then Straker had a quite distinctive *déjà vu*. As with the meaning of Tiger's pronouncements, it was elusive and easy to ignore, like incense in the wind.

"*I'm here to help you*," said Tiger, using plain speech for once. "*But you know that*."

So, yes, he'd been here before. But he'd forgotten – *probably deliberately*, he thought, having sorted himself out and moved on. *Déjà vu* was the warning; smoke from hidden fires, emotions triggering for no apparent reason. He'd wiped the memory connections; stuffed them away into a box. So they now seemed random and unreasonable.

"*Stop stressing. It'll bob to the surface…*"

A silent lake, the beckoning hand an invitation to cross dark waters, with nowhere else to go.

The process had started.

It came in the middle of that night, as a dream and yet completely real; the past he'd tried so hard to forget, despite it being just fourteen months ago.

A burning road edged on one side by tall trees and a stone wall, a wide river on the other, and a stone castle. Black smoke choked the air, ghost-like figures standing motionless or walking slowly and randomly, heads down as if in prayer or performing a ritual. The sound was of a mighty wind even though the air was still. He saw the silent figures were crying and knew that he was deaf.

A twisted black mass lay to one side of the road, with a steering wheel and two rear tyres. Then, further down, a recognisable lorry and Land Rover, wrecked and surrounded by charred debris. He saw movement and recognisable shapes, which he realised were people. Others were walking beside him, together into this vortex. He knew them but was afraid of them, his own dangerous tribe silently accepting his right to be there.

He heard gunfire, sirens, bells, and the noise of helicopters cutting through the haze of wind and smoke. He felt terribly sad.

But then a huge explosion further up the road sucked him from his feet into a black swirl, which he knew was death. It seemed to have come from the stone castle. This was when the dream returned him to the present, to the darkness of his room.

But there was no relief in knowing this was a dream. Instead it was a terrifying half-reality; a technicolour fury of deeply buried images flickering on the ceiling like a movie screen.

"*Don't be sad*," said Tiger. "*I'm still with you*."

Because this wasn't a dream.

He'd been halfway through his one-year tour with the Det. His team were doing surveillance down on the Eire border beside the Newry River, and on hearing an explosion north of Warrenpoint they drove down the A2 to investigate.

An Army convoy of one Land Rover and two four-ton trucks had been attacked with a 360kg ANFO fertiliser fuel-oil bomb hidden among straw bales on a trailer parked south of the Narrow Water Keep. The last truck was destroyed, killing six soldiers.

They'd arrived to find this was his parent unit, 2 Para, who fortunately recognised him amid the shock and burning debris. Soon after there'd been gunfire, then military reinforcements had arrived.

A Wessex helicopter evacuating the wounded was taking off when the second, larger bomb detonated – 450kg of ammonium nitrate plus nitroglycerine, and coal to add more energy. The helicopter was damaged but didn't crash, and a further twelve soldiers were killed.

Straker had been knocked over by this second explosion, uninjured but disorientated and deafened. He'd walked through the gloom towards the castle, seeing body parts hanging from the trees. Then, with all the other silent people, he'd spent the three hours until it got dark numbly collecting charred bits of people he knew from across several hundred metres of burned grass and dual carriageway.

Afterwards, 2 Para returned to their barracks at Ballykinler in County Down to complete the remaining nineteen months of their residential tour. He'd returned with his SAS team to the main Det base at Aldergrove for report writing, then redeployment west to Fermanagh.

For the remaining six months of *his* tour he'd not thought about this terrible day; nor thereafter until now. But he'd felt the exact same lethargy and pessimism as now, in the weeks that followed. And similarly lonely.

He'd been so lucky. Back then he'd hated himself for not feeling thankful. He still did.

It was hard to say precisely when, in process of these thoughts, he actually awoke. He sat shaking, partly with cold as the world outside grew light through meagre floral-patterned curtains.

"*Don't stress it, my friend,*" came the soft County Waterford burr. "*We all go there. And it's a hard coming. But you're not alone.*"

Straker walked over to the washbasin, intending to brush his teeth as if that might make everything clean again. He didn't like the haggard face that stared back at him from the mirror. It looked naïve and uncertain, as he'd been as a 2Lt and had tried so hard not to show.

But what should he do – get the hell out of Northern Ireland? He wasn't under arrest. And would the Royal Military Police be allowed to drag him back over here?

But then he decided he needed to be logical: Doc Morton had been right about the concussion causing headaches and nausea. Everything else could be summarised as his being uncharacteristically miserable, pessimistic, and negative.

The Officers' Mess sold aspirin, and it was warm while the world outside wasn't. More to the point, sneaking back to Hereford would be cowardly, maybe even to some an admission of guilt.

And unreliable – this in the clipped tones of his father's voice.

"I hoped you'd gone," said Straker to the mirror.

But his father was right. The Army was not his enemy; once all the statements had been read, the police would accept his use of force to have been justified. He should stay and finish this off.

He decided also to take the SB officer's warning seriously. So what was it *he* could do that "they" couldn't?

Well, for a start he could warn Jacko who was still over here, and the others he hoped were back in Hereford.

There were problems with this; HQNI staff had phones in their offices and the official mess phone was for incoming calls only and answered by mess staff. The two public phones in the hall could be overheard.

And what precisely to say to Jacko? He didn't believe they'd committed any offences, so didn't want to suggest they might have.

If as the SB officer had said, the police officer did want to blame them, would they accept the Army inquiry if he was exonerated? He didn't know. And he definitely wasn't going to tell Jacko or the other guys what to say.

Straker also thought about whether he should talk to his commanding officer at Hereford; he probably should, but was reluctant. The CO would know what had happened but couldn't interfere with the Board of Inquiry. So what was there to be gained by telling him about this mysterious warning?

He also thought about contacting Group, but quickly decided against that idea. The people he knew from his one-year Det tour had moved on, but remembering back to the start of their ill-fated surveillance operation sparked off the warning bells. The SB input had been particularly last-minute, bad-tempered and meagre. He'd mistrusted them then, refusing to say they'd even deployed until they'd been twenty-four hours in the building. Group were probably pissed off with him about that alone, and SB was integral to Group. So, yes, confiding in Group was not a sensible move. In any case, Straker preferred to solve his own problems.

But apart from keeping Jacko and the guys out of it, he wasn't interested in avoiding blame or the consequences. He'd done what was required, which the system would have to acknowledge.

That night after dinner, Straker walked from the Officers' Mess through the orange glow of streetlights along the road through the trees to the HQ building. From the front desk the duty corporal nodded disinterestedly, and he ducked down the stairs into the long, dark ground-floor corridor of the lower-security admin logistics wing. Unlike the fully lit ops corridors above, the log people worked normal office hours.

Finding an office that wasn't locked, he dialled Hereford Military and asked them to page Jacko. The operator took his number. He couldn't be certain his pager message would get through, or if Jacko would be able to return the call before someone spotted Straker and told him to leave this office. He settled down for what might be a long wait.

However, just five minutes later the phone rang.

"Hi, boss. I'm having supper with the wife and daughter."

"Ah," said Straker, taken by surprise. "You're home! That's great news."

But then he realised he'd interrupted Jacko's family re-integration – a very important moment.

"I didn't know," he added. "So I'm really sorry to disturb you. I hope everybody's well?"

"No problem – and thanks, boss, it's all great. And really good that you've called. Let me take this upstairs…"

There was a delay as Jacko unplugged the phone to take the call in a tiny bedroom he called his office.

"I was told by the Group Troop Sergeant Major to get out," he continued without preamble.

"That's good," said Straker awkwardly. "I was going to make the same suggestion."

"It's to do with our op," said Jacko.

Straker hadn't expected this. He felt sick. Had Jacko been sacked by the Det – because of not telling them what they were doing?

"Nothing to do with the SAS part of the Det," Jacko continued firmly. "They're all cool. And I've also had this from the RSM. But I've not spoken with the CO – he's keeping out of it."

"It's about the Board of Inquiry," said Straker. "Which is why I'm still out here. Did the other two get back OK?"

"Yeah – and they've been told by the Det lawyer to say nothing to anyone – literally, that our thing didn't happen."

"So that's my first point, Jacko – to make sure none of you come back out here even if the system orders you. They've got your statements. But you'll need to get yourselves well across the military law side of that with the headshed legal beagle. It's also important that you don't meet up and discuss what happened, or tell anybody else – no matter who they might be."

"Yeah – that's exactly what the Det lawyer said to Farmer and Hooves…"

"It's so nobody can accuse us of colluding to commit a crime."

"What crime is that?" said Jacko quickly.

"It doesn't matter," replied Straker. "Any crime. We've given statements, that's it. We mustn't discuss what happened."

"Right…" said Jacko hesitantly. "Is there something here you're not telling me?"

"Yes, Jacko… there is. But it's got no credibility rating, plus I can't say any more on this means."

"You've seen the newspapers?" said Jacko.

"Yes – and I'm now trying not to."

"I don't blame you. But a shit-storm in the nationals focusses everybody's attention."

"Tell me about it," replied Straker. "I might just as well have leprosy."

"So have you got some legal advice yourself?" asked Jacko.

"I doubt if I'll need it," said Straker. "But I wondered if you could get in touch with the Group lawyer for me – the guy who pitched up in the hospital? He seemed pretty straight."

"That guy wasn't from Group," said Jacko.

"So he'd be from HQNI," replied Straker. "Where I am now… and where everybody makes a point of not talking to me."

Jacko cleared his throat. "Look, boss, the RSM and I think what's going on is odd to say the least. I'm going to find out who that DALS captain was, and I suggest you do too – if you're allowed."

"I'm not under arrest."

"Well, yeah… But it seems to me you're not exactly free to go either."

After quick goodbyes Straker put the phone down, straightened the chair, and turned off the light. As he closed the door, he realised this was the first real conversation he'd had with anybody since leaving hospital. It made him feel lonely.

He noticed an office Christmas tree, its coloured lights reflected in the glass of the two heavy double doors. He'd been too preoccupied to see it on his way in, whereas now its tinsel and baubles seemed in gaudy contrast to the HQ's polished linoleum and gleaming brass.

Re-entering the Mess, Straker walked into the members' Christmas tree decoration session in the front hall. He supposed this must be the official HQ Northern Ireland Dekkie Day.

They were wearing fancy dress, being served mulled wine and mince pies by mess staff, and Pandora was up the stepladder in a red and green Santa's Little Helper suit. She looked across at him, reddened, then turned away. He went upstairs to his room.

The fake-fur-trimmed miniskirt looked good. A stab of unexpected regret plunged him into scriptwriting what he should have said to her. This place had nothing but memories he needed to avoid. Talking to Jacko, he'd been free – looking forwards, sorting it out.

He stared at the reflection above his washbasin – the mirror to his soul, judging himself as they'd now be doing behind his back. The key question was: could he have done it differently? Better, without killing the woman?

With hindsight, killing her hadn't stopped the first bomb and nobody could know whether she'd have been able to trigger the second bomb because he hadn't thought to take the radio trigger with him. And now, he couldn't use the second bomb as his reason for killing her because he didn't know about it at the time. He didn't even remember pulling the trigger.

But she was a bomber, he'd followed procedures, the board would vindicate him. Only it didn't feel like that, and he was circling yet again.

The HMV voice added its familiar disapproval.

The Army doesn't pay you to do what you *think is right.*

His father had avoided risk, keeping safe within the system.

You do realise following your own inclinations also means taking on the consequences?

Straker had always known this. Although the consequences now weren't anything he'd imagined.

But this is what happens if you can't be bothered to do things properly.

His father had slaved for years to master the Army's complexity, using that knowledge to further his career. He'd reached major general; so perhaps this criticism was fair?

And now you complain at having to account for your actions.

That *was* unfair. He *did* want to account for his actions. But this was par for the course. Throughout childhood, his father's put-downs had only worked when Straker took them seriously. But now, in these internalised dialogues, his father's twisting of the knife reflected Straker's own guilt.

And now morality; the chummy old Padre's talk over tea and biscuits at Mons Officer School, assuring the cadets that God didn't judge military killing as murder. It was just part of the process, not an end in itself; impersonal – and anyway, these days mostly long-range.

Straker knew from readings of the Old Testament lessons during boarding-school chapel that the actual theology wasn't so simple. Every killing, for example, was subject to divine accounting – this from Genesis; ancient laws from violent times.

The Bible metaphysics made sense; when warriors kill, the debt falls to the king or cause. But what they didn't tell you was that warriors were nevertheless doomed by their actions, although they might then be saved from Hell by God's audit.

So was this Redemption? And when exactly was it granted? Was there a delay, and did you go to Hell to wait? Even theology had process.

And was redemption ever withheld from warriors? He'd obeyed the rules and the Board of Inquiry would exonerate him. He had to believe that. But what about God? Would God grant him redemption?

This was real; he was in purgatory – but not, he feared, for the sort of sin that suffering could cleanse. Not yet damned, was he being shown the Hell that awaited him?

This brought him back to worldly considerations; this being so serious, would the military system support him? And if not, what could he do?

That last question sowed a seed. He always created alternatives for when plans went awry. So why wasn't he doing that now?

He remembered how yesterday his decision to stop caring what other people thought had made him feel so much better. Except that he'd not done anything about it. And making tonight's call to Jacko, he'd been his normal self, pulling things together and feeling effective.

Whereas now he was back up in his room, alone in this purgatorial Officers' Mess. He was in limbo, impotent, tormented by nonsense inside his head, being judged by office workers decorating a Christmas tree.

This had to stop. *He* had to stop. It, or he, was getting out of control. He needed action, to do something.

Not to be here.

CHAPTER 29

THURSDAY 11 DECEMBER

Stanhope Chapman was walking across Vauxhall Bridge Road from his flat in Victoria, taking the river route to Century House, the grim, 22-storey steel-and-glass tower on Westminster Bridge Road.

Chapman was aged fifty; tall, slender, and stylish, with an ability to walk briskly past people without them noticing what he looked like. His dark woollen suit conferred deliberate anonymity, beautifully cut to that effect by Hall Brothers of Oxford, tailors of tradition to six generations of shy dons. A black cashmere muffler concealed the lower half of his face, wrapped twice around his neck, and he carried a black leather briefcase.

Chapman paused for a moment at the centre of the bridge to look north across the water to the Palace of Westminster. A cold wind swirled suddenly up from the river, making him tuck the ends of his muffler down the front of his jacket. The collar was up, all three buttons fastened. Overly long hair flicked briefly across his eyes.

As Deputy C of MI6, the UK's Secret Intelligence Service, Chapman's purview supposedly began at Calais. Being part of the United Kingdom, Northern Ireland was strictly off limits. But right now, Chapman was listing to himself all the practical benefits of Northern Ireland becoming part of an all-green, united Irish Republic. Remaining responsible for its separation was far too expensive, costing the UK government a deficit of over £3 billion a year more than the taxes raised there. The UK also subsidised industry there, including the disproportionately large number of security-related jobs: the police, prison, and probation service employed over 10 per cent of all Protestant men. Northern Ireland depended on UK money and was being distorted by it, which Chapman couldn't see changing any time soon.

Being a part of the UK made Northern Ireland exclusively MI5 territory – the Security Service. The overall security agency budget was finite, with MI5 claiming increasingly larger slices of each year's pie; despite, thought Chapman, providing ever more evidence of their inability to understand how essentially *foreign* Northern Ireland was.

MI5 was focussed on trying to control what went on in Northern Ireland, rather than finding the compromises that Chapman knew were the only route to peace. Unlike MI6, they'd never had to adapt to the laws of other countries or accept foreign authority. Vested interests underpinned everything in Northern Ireland – including politicians and the police, who were not about to relinquish any of their advantages, especially not to MI5 spooks from London.

MI5's relationships with the other security agencies were bad-tempered. But Chapman also thought them undemocratic. They'd created an intelligence reporting system that showed the PM and Cabinet an MI5 version of events. Since direct rule was imposed six years ago, increased MI5 influence over decision-making had made government from Westminster much less effective than it might have been, and far more unpopular.

Chapman was supposed to protect the UK as a whole from terrorism. But clearly, with Northern Ireland being on a separate island, and with a long, convoluted border with the Irish Republic to the south, MI6 had to make special arrangements. To him, logically the only solution was to address this was as a joint MI5/MI6 project, which wasn't going to happen.

So Chapman focussed on tracing the flow of arms and explosives from abroad. Specifically, he did this in reverse; finding the people making the money, mapping the flow of funds, looking for the supply chains by which arms reached the terrorists.

But he didn't do this with the intention of putting people in jail. Because, quite simply, UK law could not protect UK citizens from foreign terrorist attack.

The legal system's protection of the innocent made successful prosecution of guilty gun-runners almost impossible. The offences had to take place in the UK – MI5 territory – with the offenders in custody. At trial, defence barristers would force MI6 to reveal their methods and the identities of undercover sources, then discredit them. Each trial shut down a hard-wrought chain of MI6 agents.

Senior British establishment figures were involved, plus certain of the UK's allies via extremely complicated links, often with political sensitivities. So arms dealers walked free; even after guilty verdicts, they knew which of their processes to change and the sources to kill. Sharing information with the police or MI5 was equally counterproductive.

So Chapman focussed on the long-term development of HUMINT (human intelligence) – grooming sources, information gathering, collation – then turning offenders, especially UK nationals, to become new sources. The arms trade could only work with reliable supply lines, which Chapman mapped in detail.

What *then* happened was a whole new arena for MI6. In most instances Chapman learned more by letting a pipeline run, so was obsessively secretive about these operations. It would take something of very great national importance to persuade him to jeopardise the operation of what he considered to be one of *his* supply lines.

Which was germane to Chapman's first meeting of the day; the report from Arrosa about the PIRA attack gone seriously wrong. She'd reported to him after her talk with Carragher; then, with her usual insight, assembled various bits of gossip. She'd been correct in her assumptions, but hadn't been able to obtain reliable corroboration. Whereas Chapman had, through his source codenamed "Cold Hook".

But although interesting, the RUC having been hoodwinked plus Carragher's possible instability, this was peripheral to Arrosa's purpose in Belfast. It could not be allowed to jeopardise her presence there.

Chapman was now proceeding into the office for a meeting with his team to work out what they should do about it.

Up in Century House, Chapman's team had been waiting for fifteen minutes in his large corner office after being summoned by his secretary. Senior section chief Ramsay and the grizzled Thompson sat in the two armchairs, while the younger Ambrose stood beside the window, where Chapman's splendid chess set was laid out as if in the middle of a game.

Ambrose usually perched on the edge of the coffee table clutching his notebook. But this time his attention had been drawn to the ebony figures on the board. With no sign of Chapman he'd started analysing the game, then without thinking, reached out and moved the queen. Thompson raised his eyebrows at Ramsay, who pretended not to notice.

"They're *still* waiting for you," bellowed Chapman's secretary from the outer layer of the security suite. Ambrose slid smoothly back down to his coffee-table position as Chapman swept into the room.

"The Provisional IRA intends a new phase in its war with us," he announced. "But we can't do anything about it."

The meeting now had an agenda. Ramsay stared steadily across to Thompson then down at Ambrose, like a sheepdog gathering the attention of his flock.

"At the peak of their UK bomb attacks six years ago," continued Chapman in lecturer mode, "they'd been doing one mainland bombing every three days. Nothing like the tempo of the early seventies in Northern Ireland, of course, but a very clear strategy which was succeeding."

"A strategy to create UK voter demand for action," interjected Ramsay. Chapman needed reminding that they'd been waiting for him.

"Yes – demanding that the Army be withdrawn from Northern Ireland," continued Chapman smoothly. "A strategy that required enormous effort by PIRA, and was succeeding to such an extent that our government wanted to find a political solution."

Chapman put his briefcase onto a table beside his desk.

"But then they messed up the telephone warnings for two pub bombs in Birmingham. Twenty-one innocent people were killed and almost two hundred injured. Their own supporters were so horrified by such ineptitude that PIRA stopped bombing the mainland altogether."

"They never dared even to admit responsibility," muttered Thompson.

"However, our collective view – by which I mean the Joint Intelligence Committee – cleaves to the misconception that security force operations have been preventing PIRA mainland bombings since 1974."

Chapman looked around as if expecting a reaction. The others merely nodded and waited.

"Whereas with Libya having stopped supplying them with explosives, and PIRA's UK cells lying dormant, I'm not sure I see what those 'highly successful security force operations' might be. But as we know, MI5 moves in mysterious ways."

This was Chapman's idea of a joke, but nobody responded. MI5 – and more publicly, the Met Police – always attributed reductions in criminal activity to the preventative effects of their actions. But everybody in the room understood the reality; that criminals frequently did nothing, often for no particular reason.

"Is that why the INLA was able to blow up Airey Neave?" asked Ambrose, whose questions were usually at least one logic step ahead of the current discussion, which could be confusing.

"Possibly," said Chapman, taking that extra step. "Although official complacency was less to blame there. The INLA are very efficient; plus they had a traitor inside the Palace of Westminster."

The Irish National Liberation Army was an offshoot of the Official IRA. The previous March, they'd assassinated the former soldier and shadow Northern Ireland Secretary Airey Neave in the Houses of Parliament car park.

Ambrose coloured slightly, realising he'd interrupted and that his question could be interpreted as argumentative.

"Neave posed a massive threat to the terrorists," said Thompson in support of Ambrose. They all wanted Chapman to finish this introduction so they could move on to discuss why terrorists were able to carry out such attacks in London.

"He'd have done a good job over there," agreed Ramsay.

"They used a mercury tilt switch," blurted Ambrose, recovering quickly.

This time everyone stared at him.

"In Mr Neave's car," continued Ambrose.

"They couldn't know when he'd want to drive home," he continued, "so they set the tilt switch's angle to the upward declination of the ramp so it would explode only when he drove up from the underground car park. I went over to have a look. The ramp's completely surrounded by concrete, like at Waltham Abbey where they test the rocket engines. Much less chance of killing anybody else..."

"Indeed an impressive operation," generalised Thompson solemnly.

Chapman walked round to his desk, glanced at the chess board, then sat down.

"All of which reinforces my view that PIRA is a long way short of being bottled up, although it does remain reluctant to risk another PR disaster like Birmingham."

"They can't drive in huge oil and fertiliser bombs to UK cities," said Ramsay. "Logistics requires them to use commercial explosives. And quarries or raids on Irish Army depots won't provide enough. It needs to come from abroad. And since Gaddafi stopped helping them in 1976 and they got low on funds, no foreign suppliers are selling them the other bits – detonators, Cordtex et cetera. But as our responsibilities stop at the UK border, we wouldn't even know if they were smuggling car bombs over on the Belfast ferry."

"Mainland bombing remains the best strategy for PIRA," said Chapman. "It's their only way to force the UK government into meaningful dialogue."

There'd already been several forced ceasefires, and some covert talks between senior British officials and PIRA.

"But PIRA leaders shot themselves in the foot by only discussing the uniting of Ireland," commented Thompson. "Making the talks their people had fought so hard to get completely pointless."

"PIRA strategy indicates distinct phases," said Ramsay. "From 1969, they were doing what the Army calls 'Insurgency' – fighting to take over the state. Then, since 1973, when as you've said, PIRA's operational tempo lessened, they've moved into what the military call 'Terrorism'."

"Yes," said Chapman. "And for our part we've been trying to discredit the IRA's political agenda, painting them as criminals while buying our way into their organisation."

Huge amounts of British cash were allocated to paying sources, touts, and traitors.

"But you've now got something a bit more tangible?" Ramsay asked Chapman, bringing the meeting to order.

"Yes – although I don't know what their new phase will be called. They already talk of the 'Long War' – so 'Extended War', perhaps? Summarising, there's a younger generation of leaders emerging who are from the North and take far less notice of Dublin; plus also a private acceptance that they can't actually win."

"Coinciding neatly with the British government's realisation that we can't win either," said Thompson.

"Quite," said Chapman.

"But the Unionists won't accept anything less than total victory," said Ambrose, unable to restrain himself.

"Blowhards," muttered Thompson.

"Protestant paramilitaries kill more civilians than PIRA," insisted Ambrose.

"Ethnic cleansing carried out by Protestants is one of the Northern Ireland doomsday scenarios," agreed Ramsay. "So the Protestant paramilitaries can't be ignored."

"And UK government needs the Ulster Unionist vote to get bills through Parliament," added Ambrose.

"We can't win, and neither can they," said Chapman. "But they can cause us such expense and commercial damage as to force us to take their political demands seriously. I'm talking about a new political dimension opening up here – of violence coordinated to support political demands..."

This *was* different.

"But far more specifically, my information is that PIRA will reinstate a UK mainland bombing campaign, with a new focus to the targeting – we think to kill Establishment figures: senior politicians and military commanders."

"Like Airey Neave, and PIRA's killing of Lord Mountbatten," added Ramsay, referring to the previous August when Earl Mountbatten of Burma – a great-grandson of Queen Victoria, the current Queen's second cousin, and uncle to the Duke of Edinburgh – had been blown up on his boat in County Sligo, in Eire.

"Two very impressive attacks," observed Thompson.

"Oh, they're good at it," said Chapman. "And remember how effectively those attacks re-focussed attention back to Northern Ireland?"

"PIRA don't seem to have quite the precision of the INLA," contributed Ambrose.

"Which is what I think they're working on," said Chapman. "And that brings me to something specific..."

He stood up from behind his desk and walked over to the east-facing window. From here could see across the river to the Palace of Westminster, where Big Ben presided over both Parliament and the four Great Offices of State.

This was Chapman's unconscious habit before saying something he considered questionable or risky. Last time, he'd started out by quoting John Donne: *Send not to know for whom the bells tolls; it tolls for thee.*

"This last week," announced Chapman, "PIRA mounted an operation in Belfast to kill an SAS team. They were able to fool the RUC into tasking the SAS into an observation position where a huge bomb was already built into one of the walls. But the SAS captain worked it out – he killed the bomber and evacuated his team. Then, guessing PIRA had a second bomb, he managed to persuade everybody to evacuate the area before it exploded."

"Righteous," muttered Thompson to himself.

"But what we have now," continued Chapman, "is a rather sad game, in which it looks like RUC embarrassment is to be assuaged by saying the woman the SAS captain killed wasn't the bomber. I expect the SAS will look after him – and he certainly seems well able to fend for himself. And we're not involved. But do I see opportunities here…?"

He came back from the window, as if his ideas had now received Westminster approval.

"Northern Ireland is hopelessly interconnected," he observed. "Manipulation is easy, although the results are unpredictable. And security is useless – pathetic, even.

"RUC secrets percolate down to Loyalist paramilitaries, while the concerns of hardline Loyalist leaders rise back up like temple smoke to guide the thoughts of Special Branch officers."

He paused, as if surprised by his own imagery. "MI5, the Special Branch, and Army intelligence are supposed to share information," he said, referring to the TCG, or Tasking Co-ordinating Group, in Belfast.

"Only they don't," interrupted Thompson.

"Then whatever they do *actually* share," he continued, "is passed into MI5's Joint Irish Section – the JIS – for analysis and passage to the JIC."

This was London's Joint Intelligence Committee, a Cabinet sub-committee which Chapman attended.

"So what we get is an incomplete and MI5-doctored version of whatever they decide we should be fed – and this is what JIC uses to determine policy. Poor Maurice Oldfield walked into all that like the oak edge of his Oxford college door."

The former head of MI6 had recently returned from Northern Ireland, framed by allegations of a homosexual liaison, after attempting to rationalise the intelligence process. As Oldfield's work threatened MI5's grip on the information flow, Chapman thought it reasonable to presume their involvement in Sir Maurice's apparent compromise.

"And as we're outside all this, we can't do anything to help."

Nobody wanted to discuss MI5's neutralisation of their former chief. Ramsay brought them back on topic.

"So what's happening to the SAS captain?" he said.

"He's being kept over there."

"Putting this on the SAS plays into the RUC's distrust of everybody," said Thompson. "If they can manage it."

"So this session is to get us thinking about Northern Ireland – yet again," said Chapman crisply. "Mainland bombing will kick off during this coming year and we need to be involved. Specifically, focussing on PIRA's need for commercial explosives and high-quality timer units."

"What about their sourcing ground-to-air missiles and heavy machine guns?" asked Ramsay. "For making rural areas more dangerous for Army helicopters…?"

"Yes, they'll continue with that," said Chapman. "But I think that assembling transportable bombs to use on us over here will be their priority, so ours is to make it as hard as possible for them to do that."

"You said the SAS captain's situation offered opportunities…" reminded Ramsey.

"Ah yes – thanks."

This was Chapman pretending to be scatter-brained.

"I think we should stir things up a bit. Unusually, the SAS captain has become a PIRA target – not something they'd normally do. So I'm thinking of using this to open up a rift between their top people."

Sometimes Chapman seemed like a trickster – almost mischievous, deliberately creating chaos as the means to his end.

"They really are remarkably exercised by this," he added. "Especially Séan Carragher."

Thompson looked up quickly.

"Carragher was a bomber in the Officials," said Chapman. "He quit to join PIRA in 1972 after the botched Aldershot Officers' Mess bombing. I'm fairly sure he'll be the key player when they start mainland bombing again."

Thompson nodded. "Fairly sure" meant "absolutely certain".

"The more we can make Carragher seem like a loose cannon, the better," said Chapman.

He then raised his hand to conclude the session. But as they all stood to leave, he added: "An interesting move. But it opens up the bishop. Checkmate in three."

Thompson chuckled, while Ambrose tried not to blush.

"My room in ten," ordered Ramsay.

After directing his team's thinking for this next phase, Chapman sat alone for a while working through precisely what he would do next. He'd mentally categorised this under the heading "Smoke and Mirrors".

Chapman wanted to confuse and further anger Carragher, plus complicate PIRA's betrayal investigation. He'd already fed information through his agent "Cold Hook" back to Carragher that the RUC thought the bomb was detonated using a timer – meaning they thought Straker had killed Mrs Carragher illegally. But Chapman couldn't tell if the RUC really did think that; although he knew from Cold Hook that it wasn't true.

Republicans were always complaining that Northern Ireland Coroners disregarded murders by the Army. So Chapman had concocted an additional deceit – that a Coroner had ruled Mrs Carragher's killing and the death of her baby boy to be illegal. Cold Hook would pass that on to *An Phoblacht* and the other Republican newspapers. Suitably outraged articles could only help confuse things further.

When you've got a piano, you might as well play it.

CHAPTER 30

Carragher's former Chief of Staff had asked him for a meeting. Carragher made him drive out to the Murph, which was dangerous for him, but Carragher wasn't making compromises.

"So, did you find the informer?" he asked.

"Not yet," said the Chief of Staff.

"Any more from your ops officer's secret source…?"

The Chief of Staff ignored Carragher's attempt at a joke.

"He stopped responding to the agreed communication protocols," he replied. "Which is why I thought we should meet – because today he got back in touch."

"What's that to do with me?"

"I thought you should know…"

Carragher's sudden removal from command had angered the Chief of Staff. Meeting like this, he was taking a risk. His loyalty to Carragher was the only reason he'd come.

"OK," said Carragher. "It's good to see you… So, what's there to tell *me*?"

"It was just a message – he gave it then rang off. He said a secret Coroner's inquest had ruled Máire's death to have been an unlawful killing."

Carragher felt a jolt of pain, and then anger.

"So fucking what?" he said. "Does that mean anything to you? It doesn't mean a single fucking thing to me…"

Máire's family were making the funeral arrangements, and he assumed there'd already been a post-mortem. But beyond that, he'd chosen not to think about it. Truth be told, he'd forgotten. Carragher had never dealt with the bureaucracy of death.

"Why would the British state bother?" said Carragher. "It's not like it's fucking news, and you say it's secret, so where does that get us? Does this mean delaying the funeral?"

"Possibly – or more likely they'll be releasing the body to the family very soon," said the Chief of Staff. "So we should probably start thinking about organising something..."

"You're joking, surely?"

The Chief of Staff wanted to off-load Máire's funeral onto Carragher, so he didn't take offence.

"Undercover security forces taking long-lens photographs?" continued Carragher angrily. "Ridiculous-looking Volunteers we don't mind losing sneaking out from the crowd and firing ragged volleys with rubbish weapons?"

Carragher couldn't attend the funeral even if he wanted to – which he really didn't. He'd be worth them trying to snatch, and would end up back in the Maze.

But as far as Carragher was concerned, Máire was gone. This was the past he was doing his best to leave behind. It made him feel irritated and unsettled.

"And what's all this about unlawful killing?"

The Chief of Staff shrugged his shoulders.

"It's unusual, granted, but I thought you should know. It's not like it's going to be in the newspapers."

This further irritated Carragher. False hopes of judicial revenge were not what he needed.

"Can you really see the Brits putting this SAS guy on trial?"

The Chief of Staff shook his head.

Carragher thought for a moment.

"So at least our police tout is still active?" he said.

The Chief of Staff nodded.

"But why the fuck should I care about what some Brit Coroner thinks? I get it that the police are pissed off with the SAS doing their job for them. But there's no way the SAS guy's going to wind up in jail, so what the fuck?"

"Maybe the police are making this into something," said the Chief of Staff.

"What – like showing the Army who's in charge?"

"Maybe," said the Chief of Staff.

"Makes no difference to us," said Carragher. "They've been punting around this accountability and police primacy shit for a couple of years now... And I'm not sitting here imagining that the police and the courts are going to do *our* job for *us*. Plus we need to find the traitor – or *you* do…"

Their conversation had finally arrived at the reason for the Chief of Staff being here.

"Finding our traitor is one thing," he said quietly to Carragher. "But we still need to find the SAS guy and take *him* out."

PIRA self-respect was at stake, as well as Carragher's personal need for vengeance. But admitting these feelings to each other was dangerous. O'Donnell had made that very clear.

Carragher's anger vanished.

"This informer comes and goes," said Carragher. "He's like a fucking wraith. I thought his vanishing meant he didn't want to get involved."

"Maybe this is him volunteering further services," said the Chief of Staff.

Informers only existed when they were doing their job. There was no point trying to understand what their motives might be. All you could do was pay the money, and do what you could with the information.

"Can we organise it so this guy deals directly with me?" said Carragher.

Carragher knew there'd be a price to pay for asking this question. But he didn't care.

The Chief of Staff nodded. It got him out of the danger zone.

"So give this guy my number, yeah?"

Carragher was later to realise he'd been played. Northern Ireland Coroners were not allowed to make so-called "short-form verdicts" – judgments about killings being lawful or unlawful – as could their peers in England and Wales.

The informer's message was pointless, nothing more than malign misdirection. Carragher should have spotted it.

Belfast was dank, cold, and Arrosa wasn't going anywhere. She shared teaching-staff relief at the student exodus, but not the self-satisfaction of those jetting out for Christmas in the countries they studied. So she was actively avoiding the contrived conviviality to which the School of Arts, English and Languages descended at the end of term.

Three days had passed with no word from either Chapman or Carragher. Today, her university-mouse, Spanish-mascot identity felt like a millstone round her neck.

She was distracted and unsettled, hiding in her tiny office up in the eaves. The pile of end-of-term essays Cara had rather hesitantly put onto her in-tray remained untouched.

Instead she was analysing the telephone conversation with Chapman. He knew far more than he was saying, so she needed to understand all the possible connections; plus she was becoming increasingly concerned for the SAS captain.

"They were depending very heavily on this operation," he'd said, "so the failure has hit them hard."

She'd thought Máire being killed was enough of a hit; but only for Carragher – and maybe Duffy. It wouldn't have upset O'Donnell. So she tried to evaluate this.

Máire had helped Carragher; but why exactly? Máire would have been ambitious to start with, but how calculating? Arrosa decided she'd been both; at first calculating and ambitious, but then she fell in love.

Whereas Arrosa couldn't decide if Carragher had loved the young and beautiful Máire. They'd shared the considerable danger of installing the building bomb, so he'd trusted her; and he'd certainly desired her, something which had now mutated into grief demanding vengeance – its most deadly form. But also, she thought, Carragher was more deeply affected by the death of Máire as the mother of his child. This was an anger he could not repress, greatly amplified by his guilt and regret.

What drove Carragher? Was it status within PIRA? He wasn't a hardline Republican, which in itself suggested he was self-centred and cynical, which she knew wasn't the case. That was O'Donnell.

In Arrosa's experience of ETA and now PIRA, she'd found that most terrorist operations involved some level of personal vengeance, which was what made civil wars so brutal. Most Volunteers had suffered violence and humiliation by Protestant paramilitaries, the RUC, or the Army. Equally, Protestant paramilitaries and members of the security forces had similarly damaging experiences. Wanting vengeance greatly reduced their capability, corrupting the control and balance needed by both terrorists and the security forces to carry out effective operations.

A closely targeted bomb attack to kill an SAS team was strategic, quite different to Carragher intending to kill a specific SAS officer, which would be unusual and exceedingly difficult to achieve. Carragher's impeccable planning required great patience, but could he control the anger she'd seen get the better of him? She hoped not, as emotion made him vulnerable. Furthermore, she was sure neither O'Donnell nor Northern Command would approve a vendetta.

And foremost in Arrosa's thinking was that if Carragher was to commit to his vendetta, *she* knew his target.

So now Arrosa considered why PIRA had, as Chapman insisted, been *depending* on this attack. Its failure had certainly hit them hard – so why exactly? She supposed it related to PIRA needing to impress whoever was to fund and supply them – ETA, the Libyans, or maybe somebody else.

So had Carragher been under pressure to pull this off in order to demonstrate capability? She doubted it could be as binary as that, with PIRA generally accepted to be the most capable terrorist bombing organisation in the world.

Chapman's focus was on supply chains, so this dependence was probably to do with arms deals, especially the acquisition of commercial explosives. Milk churns reeking of home-made ANFO would be a nightmare to smuggle across on car ferries. How much commercial explosive did they have now, and could they get more? How had Carragher acquired enough C4 for the sleeper-bomb attack? Maybe she should risk asking him where it had come from, as if it was a question from her ETA superiors.

But Chapman had also said he thought there might be something specific that involved *her*. So what exactly was she involved with? Máire, maybe – but that relationship had been speculative and purely personal. The ETA introductions she was making would create supply links between ETA and PIRA, which went through Carragher; but this did not *depend* on her. She kept strictly to being the honest broker, making sure she was never party to what happened after she made introductions. In her work for Chapman, all she needed to find out were the links in the chain. And nothing she'd seen suggested Carragher had been under pressure to deliver in order to impress senior people in Barcelona.

With Máire dead, Arrosa's only links to PIRA were via Carragher. His security was impeccable. She was out on a limb here – isolated, vulnerable, and borderline ineffective.

She briefly considered getting in touch with ETA in Barcelona, ostensibly to pass on the bad news of this past week, but actually to see if they knew anything. But as they dealt with other senior PIRA officials who might not even be aware of her presence in Belfast, and because anonymity was her only protection, she dropped that dangerous idea.

So Arrosa decided to take a walk round the campus, maybe have a coffee in the refectory. With luck there'd be nobody there.

But as she walked through the faculty's small reception area, Cara intercepted her before she got to the double doors.

"There's a fella been in just now asking after you, Arrosa."

Arrosa stopped and looked quickly through the glass doors past the bare branches of the magnolia tree. University Square was wet, windy, and cold – but now deserted.

"Anybody we know?"

"He wouldn't give his name. I called up but you were already on the way down. He's just now walked past, like he's waiting for you."

"Is he a student, maybe?"

"Dressed like one, but too old – maybe early thirties…? And doesn't look like university staff."

Arrosa didn't do random meetings, insisting colleagues phone her on the internal system. She stood thinking for a moment. Cara had good intuition.

"Let me nip out and see if he's still around," said Cara.

But Arrosa put out her arm.

"No," she replied. "That could look a bit strange."

Unfortunately the school did not have a rear entrance. So this was a problem with no good options.

"I'll be fine," Arrosa said brightly. "Thanks. Maybe this weather has sent him away. For once it is good for me!"

Outside the double doors, the path was slippery with rain. The magnolia's ungainly bare branches moved jerkily in the blustery wind.

Without looking up she turned left, walking quickly along University Square, past wrought-iron railings and three-storey Georgian façades to the corner of Botanic Avenue, where she turned left again past trees and the bright-red post box. She was huddled into the hood of her dark green cagoule, hurrying and apparently preoccupied.

But then she suddenly crossed the road to walk down College Green alongside the Theological College. Its car park and lawns gave her clear sight diagonally back across to the end of University Square, where she saw a figure wearing jeans and a duffle coat hurry round the corner and look anxiously up Botanic Avenue.

She ducked down behind a parked car. Then, as the man pulled back his hood to look around, she saw it was Duffy.

As Duffy turned away to look back down Botanic Avenue, she opened the black fold-up umbrella she'd tucked away under her cagoule and hurried east along College Green to vanish into the grid of university buildings.

Her worlds were overlapping. This was how you got killed.

CHAPTER 31

The next morning after the call with Straker, Jacko walked back across from RHQ to the deserted Training Wing. He automatically glanced at his pigeonhole and saw Straker's letter.

The phone call had made Jacko very uncomfortable. Over a week had elapsed since he'd left Northern Ireland, and although Jacko had spent much of that time avoiding people who wanted to know what had happened, he'd been trying not to think about it. There'd been admin to do, and he'd spent as much time as possible out of camp and with the family. It was what he always did between operations.

He'd pretty much forgotten about Straker. He'd rationalised this by telling himself that Straker was safe behind the wire, and would be dealing with whatever the problems were.

He now sat in an empty office to read the letter. Being safe back in Hereford, Jacko was on the outside of this problem – at best looking in. The letter emphasised Straker's vulnerability, and the reality that he remained very much at the heart of whatever this was.

Jacko now found himself doing what he'd never before done; allowing work to overflow into the precious time he preserved for his family. In fourteen years as a special forces operator, he'd never done this.

He decided to phone the Det, to see if their lawyer knew the Army Legal Service captain they'd met at the hospital. But after asking to speak to his mate, the SAS Troop sergeant major, he was connected to somebody who didn't offer a name and asked him a runaround of questions in a deadpan voice. Jacko instinctively disliked this person and put the phone down.

He then started dialling the numbers he'd got for Headquarters Northern Ireland. But this was worse; the registry chief clerk demanded Jacko's full name, rank, number, and unit before saying anything – which was not how Jacko operated. And the other numbers were answered by officers requiring standard Army-Other-Ranks-to-Officer telephone etiquette, which did not usually extend to the Officer doing anything to help the Other Rank.

By this point Jacko was annoyed, as well as sick of rotary-dialling long strings of military telephone-exchange numbers. Tight-fisted MoD. At home he'd got one of those new push-button phones.

Finally, he decided to abandon one of his most basic rules and pretend to be a Rupert. He phoned into HQNI's main registry, where all the admin people work.

"And a very good morning to you too. This is Major Jackson from Hereford Military. I need to speak with the DALS captain I met at Musgrave Park last week, please…

"No, I can't remember the chap's name. Things were rather hectic, if you know what I mean…

"OK – I'd say five ten, light brown hair, wearing barrack dress with an ALS stable belt and brown shoes.

"No, not boots and puttees – shiny brown shoes…

"Thin but fit-looking, maybe a runner…?

"Look, how many ALS captains do you have there?

"No, I can't wait until you get the sergeant major, this is urgent.

"Yes, I told you – Hereford Military. No, I can't tell you any more than that, but you can probably work it out for yourself. So how about you give me a name and a military telephone number?

"So you think you know who we're talking about but you're not sure where he is at the moment?

"OK, fair enough. Might I leave a message for him with my pager number, asking him to get in touch?

"Jolly good. Many thanks."

Jacko put the phone down with a sigh of relief. Life as a Rupert wasn't as easy as it looked.

This time O'Donnell contacted Carragher by phone, from a call box on a street corner behind Queen's Road, Bangor. Meeting face-to-face was too stressful, and he preferred seagulls and ozone.

"What have you done about Duffy?" O'Donnell said without preamble.

"Nothing," replied Carragher. "It's a Belfast Brigade inquiry, which is no longer anything to do with me."

"I told you to sort it out," said O'Donnell. "And that's exactly what I meant you to do."

Carragher remained silent.

"We have to find who betrayed us," continued O'Donnell, "then we have to make an example of them."

"I agree," said Carragher. "But like I said, it's no longer my responsibility."

"Duffy is your team," snapped back O'Donnell. "You need to sort it out. It's making us look like we don't know what happened – like we're weak."

"I don't know about weak," replied Carragher. "But we don't know what happened – except that Máire got killed."

This time O'Donnell stayed silent.

"Are you asking me for a scapegoat?" said Carragher.

"Fuck off, Séan. That's not what's happening here."

"Nothing's happening here, Breandán, which seems to be the problem for you. And as you said, Duffy's my team – in fact, he's all that's left of my team."

"Is this you being loyal and protective?"

"Fuck off yourself, Breandán. Loyalty's earned over time."

"There's a traitor, Séan. If it's not Duffy, who is it?"

"I don't know – and you don't fucking know either. All this demanding immediate action bollocks is politics, and I'm not interested in politics. You deal with all that."

"That's what I'm doing," insisted O'Donnell, realising as he said it that he was the one sounding weak.

"You're under pressure to resolve the embarrassment with enforcement action," said Carragher. "And Duffy's still the obvious choice for all your bigwigs…?"

O'Donnell didn't answer.

"Well, let's you and me agree this is a sticking point," continued Carragher. "It's not going to happen. If we're to progress like you've been saying, we need Duffy – and that's apart from the signal we'd be sending every other loyal Volunteer by killing him."

O'Donnell was silent for a moment.

"Well then, OK," he said. "I've told you what I think. But we're only putting off the evil day. This becomes a much bigger problem when we use Duffy for the next operation. If he *is* the traitor, then the same thing will happen again – for which you'll be responsible."

O'Donnell put the phone down.

Arrosa had retreated to her tiny office to think about men. Detective Inspector Ciarán Moffat was decent and capable, with less of the sort of baggage men over here tended to be carrying, plus he had a good heart. In the normal world, he'd be top-grade boyfriend material. Whereas for her, such a settled relationship wasn't worth the risk – although she acknowledged it would have been pleasant. So this particular morning Ciarán Moffat was just a catalyst for her thoughts.

Her strange life over here made everything complicated, although part of her success back in Spain had been the way she dealt with men. This had been one of the collateral benefits of her undergraduate degree at Cambridge – Spanish literature at Girton, one of the university's high-powered women-only colleges, whose motto translated to "better is wisdom than weapons of war".

She'd been as naïve as the other female students; an exotic minority among the equally naïve men, who were also schoolboy-immature. An older, handsome post-grad from Madrid told her he was a poet, two-timed her, then when she told him it was over, forced her from conversation into sex.

She'd been totally shocked, especially on realising that his composure meant he'd done this before, that there were other victims, and he knew how to get away with it. She nevertheless reported the assault to her tutor at Girton College, the man was interviewed by the Proctors, and nothing was done. He'd then stalked her and spread malicious gossip.

She'd never felt like this in her life; demoralised, powerless, stupid, unsafe, hopeless – as well as extremely angry. How could this one arrogant non-entity have for her degraded half the human race from being interesting people into potential threats?

Arrosa instinctively protected people around her, which she'd now realised began with protecting herself. Her desire to protect other girls from this man led her to overreact, a miscalculation that could easily have gone terribly wrong. Suffice it to say that the poet was humiliated, suffered considerable pain and was made to understand exactly why. He decided to curtail his Cambridge experience and return to Madrid.

So although the end justified the means, Arrosa looked back on this with guilt and shame. But she was still glad she'd done it. And thereafter she'd never again be as powerless as the "poet" had made her feel.

When the Secret Intelligence Service approached her, the part of their sales patter that had resonated most was their being the mighty but unseen protectors of both the nation and of their own people. She was keen to see what skills they could teach her, and liked the idea of being protected herself by such a powerful organisation.

She now knew that the SIS only recruited specific people, which they did with very carefully tailored approaches. She'd often wondered whether they'd known about her amateur "shame and persuasion" operation at Cambridge. It had certainly been a useful experience. In Madrid she'd dealt easily with similarly maladjusted men.

But Arrosa's problem, which she accepted, was that she'd never met a man who could hold her attention, who she respected, and with whom she could have a relationship like that of her parents – who were her yardstick.

Her mother had married at age eighteen, to be immediately pregnant with her older brother, then Arrosa eighteen months later. And now, despite the machinations of her SIS career, Arrosa still wanted to have a family, to share life as one half of a whole.

Aged twenty-seven now, she was almost a decade older than her mother had been when she'd married. She wondered if the life partner she'd imagined for herself actually existed. Maybe the criteria she'd drawn up for the father of her hoped-for children were too exacting? Plus, of course, there was her career.

But Arrosa knew too many strong, capable women who'd compromised themselves inside dysfunctional relationships. The biological urge to have children could do this.

Having no relationship at all conferred a different vulnerability, although still with age as the major factor. Her parents were as happy now, working their remote farm after thirty years and two children, as when they'd first met. She knew that level of happiness was possible, but not how it might come to her.

Nevertheless, she was still thinking through everything Ciarán had said, realising in the process that she was actually thinking about another man – this shadowy, dangerous SAS captain who'd done the unthinkable, breaking taboo to shoot dead a pregnant woman. It was however illogical that this should make him attractive to her, and inexplicable that she trusted him enough to believe his action was justified; which allowed her to admire his moral fearlessness.

Carragher's plan to kill the captain and his team had been innovative and sound. The RUC had been successfully duped, so it should have worked, except that this SAS captain had stopped it. However she looked at it, the SAS captain had reached beyond all the smoke and mirrors to do the right thing. He'd risked his life to save his team, including taking on the responsibility of shooting dead an obviously pregnant woman. As she'd said to Ciarán, how does a person do that? And the SAS captain had been right.

Alongside her growing interest in this man was her concern at the threats that were lining themselves up against him: Carragher's revenge was serious enough, but then also the RUC blaming him to assuage their embarrassment at being duped by PIRA?

If there was to be a murder charge, he'd be held in the normal prison system, not military custody, making it much easier for Carragher to kill him. And then there was Chapman's casual intention to use the SAS captain as a pawn in his bad-tempered struggle for operational parity with MI5. It was all so complicated and unworthy. The captain was like her, committed and doing whatever was required. They were both working for the same system of capabilities and values. They'd both made the same bargain, so the system owed them both its protection; but instead it was using him.

So she decided to get involved.

And then, with this decision made as she stared blankly at her shelves of poetry books and dictionaries, she experienced a strange moment of certainty. This came as a vision of the future.

She was back at home in the buffeting wind, listening to the seagulls on the brightest, clearest of days. A Land Rover came over the hill and started down the rough track to their farm. She did not yet know the man in the driver's seat, but she was certain that in time she would.

Concern for this man was well outside her remit. But then she thought of Carragher's vendetta being so far outside of his. If he could do it, so could she, the absurdity of this logic seeming to reinforce its truth.

Emotions created complications. But if those emotions were genuine, dealing with the complications was how you got to where the Universe intended you to be.

CHAPTER 32

It was now definitely "a week or so" after Straker's delivery to the HQ Northern Ireland Officers' Mess by the RMPs. But there was no sign that the Board of Inquiry had even been convened, let alone begun its work.

And so the next morning, after a cup of the Mess's stewed coffee, Straker resolved his debilitating and uncharacteristic indecision by walking out of Thiepval Barracks.

He looked warmly dressed verging respectable, his observation overcoat and woollen hat fresh from the dry cleaner. He strode confidently up to the barrier, waving vaguely when asked by the MoD policeman at the main gate about signing out, as might a visitor who'd already returned his pass to somebody else. But although the guards were less stringent regarding people leaving the base, he nevertheless walked briskly away from the heavily fortified entrance before anyone decided to ask questions.

He was familiar with the roads from the base into the adjoining town of Lisburn, but had never used any of the local public transport. So he headed for the main Belsize Road where he'd seen buses running, maintaining a purposeful stride up the hill until he was no longer visible from the sentry positions.

Out here the air was clear and very cold, with bright watery sunshine glinting off the wetness of the pavement. To either side were small bungalows which at the top of the hill became much larger detached houses with trees and front hedges. This area was prosperous, Protestant, and even without the military base, as stable as any place in Northern Ireland could be. The children were at school and everyone else profitably employed.

The vehicles passing him were military: Land Rovers and civilian-registered cars driving to and from the military headquarters after coming off the main Belfast to Dungannon M1 motorway. So although Straker was the only pedestrian, his overcoat and trilby rendered him invisible to the watchful eyes of the military personnel passing by; smart enough for this neighbourhood but boring, like a solicitor who didn't dare borrow his wife's car.

He was soon over the railway bridge and round a sharp bend in the road that led towards the centre of Lisburn. He remembered to take the next left by the courthouse, then left again onto the Belsize Road, which he knew ran parallel to the main A1 Belfast road and had lots of bus stops.

Straker's great escape had proved easy, and he felt much better for having done it. Forty minutes later, at Belfast's central bus station, he considered his options very carefully, deciding he should assume his absence had been noticed. If they'd actually posted him AWOL – absent without leave – there was a formal system whereby the RUC and military police would combine forces to find him. Aldergrove airport was guarded and closely monitored all the time anyway, so its passenger system would flag him up immediately. Whereas on the ferry he'd be one of the many foot passengers crossing to Birkenhead; from there he could travel by train back to Hereford via Liverpool Lime Street and Crewe.

Getting away from the chintz and central heating of the Officers' Mess made Straker realise how trusting he'd become – pretty much institutionalised. And as he got off the bus and stood shivering in a wind that smelled of seaweed, the events of the last twelve days seemed improbable, memories so unlikely as to be the product of an over-worked imagination. The real world was bright and busy.

But yet again he was waiting. This time he'd be a passenger trusting in Stena Ferries, rather than the Army legal system and in the continuation of this fine winter weather. But he was in the driving seat. Taking action felt right. He'd soon be back in Hereford with legal advice and the backing of the SAS chain of command. Plus he'd be among friends, which felt far more important.

The port was a wasteland, seagulls screamed overhead, as he tried to assess his situation. Out here in the ozone freshness and biting cold, he'd re-entered the real world, where Dr Morton's warnings about taking it easy and needing to rest were suddenly more serious, his tiredness real like blisters on a march, those to be taken seriously lest they cripple you. And the strange words of the Special Branch superintendent now seemed less lyrical, with far more substance than he'd thought at the time.

He wanted to be just in time for the morning sailing. Hanging around risked being noticed.

But he was pretty much home and dry. Eight hours relaxing on the ferry, then the anonymity of British Rail to Hereford with changes at Liverpool and Crewe. By close of play he'd be safe home at Bradbury Lines.

CHAPTER 33

Arrosa did the usual quick scan as she left the faculty – left while walking out of the front door, then right as she reached the end of the path to peer past the old magnolia tree.

A slight movement caught her eye; Duffy leaning against the fence opposite. He'd seen her too, the movement being his startled reaction to her sudden appearance.

As before, Duffy *appeared* to be on his own, so first she had to make sure that he *was* on his own – as in, not himself being followed. Her self-preservational instincts were catastrophising a PIRA assassination team using Duffy as bait to locate her. She turned left and walked fast to cross Botanic Avenue, where she ducked away behind a parked car to impose a moment of calm on herself, which out of hard-learned habit, she did in Spanish, like a mantra – "Ten calma, todo está bien."

Duffy had followed, but having lost sight of her had turned left and was now half-running away from her up Botanic Avenue towards the shops. He didn't know how to carry out a one-on-one follow.

She waited until he was out of sight behind College Green House, then trotted back to the corner, turning right and keeping to the right-hand side of Botanic Avenue. She couldn't see him now, so she walked across the road to look back down University Square where Duffy had come from. Both pavements were empty, so Duffy was indeed on his own.

She suppressed her relief, quickly deciding to do the reverse follow. She'd been considering contacting Duffy anyway, as he was the only person who'd actually seen this SAS guy. But she'd been prevaricating. Whereas now, Duffy contacting her was at his risk, not hers.

But before progressing this into an actual meet, she needed to get him under her control.

She ran back up Botanic Avenue to check the Mews behind University Square, then went forty metres further to University Street. Duffy was standing halfway along, looking uncertain. She ducked back behind the boarded-up bay window of the house on the corner and made a very rapid assessment; Duffy had no tradecraft, so to meet him she had to be sure nobody would see them together.

She shrugged off the cagoule, stuffing it into her bag. She then put on sunglasses, so when Duffy again looked back, he saw a smartly dressed woman in a tailored blue coat with silver buttons walking quickly towards him. Wearing sunglasses in December was ridiculously unusual for Belfast, which would be the only specific thing he'd notice about her. So by the time Arrosa reached Duffy, he'd already turned away and was walking towards the main University Road.

"Stay forty metres behind me, on *this* side of the road," she said tersely as she came level with him.

"Fucking hell," he gasped, stumbling away from her.

"Exactly forty metres," she repeated, striding past without stopping.

"Jesus fucking Christ…"

She turned right onto University Road, crossed to the other side, then walked briskly past the Victorian brick splendour of the Crescent gospel church where she crossed the road, ensuring he could see her, and entered the Crescent Arts Centre, which had a quiet coffee bar.

The large room was empty, except for the girl who managed the café. Arrosa took her mug of coffee over to the window. Through the condensation, she saw Duffy walking across the road; it looked like he'd delayed coming in until she was seated, which showed he was thinking. She took a paperback from her bag and pretended to be reading, looking up briefly as Duffy picked up his mug. The girl vanished into the kitchen, and Arrosa stood up and walked across to the far side of the room, round the corner away from the entrance and the windows. She sat down at another table, and Duffy took the chair opposite.

"I'd say this was a pleasant surprise if it wasn't so unexpected," she said.

Duffy shuffled awkwardly and undid the wooden toggles down the front of his thick woollen coat. He was sweating, and the empty café was warm.

"Yeah – well, I'm sorry for that. But I didn't have any way of contacting you."

Arrosa nodded, remembering meeting Máire for girly talks. She wondered if Duffy had known about those meetings. But as Duffy was now disobeying Carragher's security rules, this meeting was safe enough.

"I expect you're wondering why I've got in touch," he muttered.

"No, actually," replied Arrosa. "I'm wondering how you found out where I work."

This wasn't a real question. Having been at Queen's for more than a year, her name and office address were in the faculty student brochure. But Arrosa was playing alpha female over a beta male; she'd learn more by keeping Duffy off balance.

"Máire and I checked you out when you first arrived here," he explained. "But that was a while ago, so I had to ask your receptionist."

"She thought you were a stalker – was going to call the police."

Duffy blushed, then tipped two turns of the sugar dispenser into his coffee.

"So we must now hope that nobody has seen us come in here…?" she added.

Duffy nodded unhappily, then after another uncomfortable silence, spoke again.

"I was wondering if you've heard anything from Séan," he said.

Arrosa looked quickly up from her coffee, the sudden eye contact making Duffy flinch.

"What have my dealings with Séan got to do with you, Padraig?" she hissed.

She could see his flushed face blanch as he quickly looked away.

"No – nothing at all," he said. "I didn't mean it like that. You see, I haven't heard from him since… well, for over a week now."

"So?"

"Well, that's very unusual, you know. He's usually in touch…"

"Since exactly *when*, Padraig?"

Duffy seemed to deflate, then after stirring his coffee said: "Did he tell you what happened?"

Arrosa decided she'd pressurised him enough.

"Yes," she replied.

"Ah... So did you hear from him since then?"

"No."

She lied deliberately.

"Look, it's about the worst thing that could have happened. And with Máire gone, I'm now on my own. I can't get in touch with anybody."

Inside PIRA's cell structure, Duffy might as well be a solo North Sea saturation diver in a decompression chamber.

"So I'm wondering if you've heard anything..."

"What contact have you had with him?" she asked.

"I phoned him on the night."

"Yes," she said quickly. "He told me."

"Afterwards I split and laid low as planned. He then told me to meet him, with Roxy and the Chief of Staff standing outside the room like they were the prison guards, y'know...?"

He stuttered slightly, as if trying to tell it straight without emotion.

"I was concerned about *him*, y'know... But he was asking me all these pointed questions about why was it Máire who delivered the bomb and not me, and exactly where I was behind the shop – like he thought I hadn't been looking out for her."

He was on the edge of tears.

"I really cared for that girl. We worked together from way before Séan came along. He was the boss right enough, but she and I were close, y'know...

"I didn't think she should have been involved, being pregnant. But she wasn't to be left out... Ripped my head when I tried to say what I thought. So I just took it that those were Séan's orders."

Arrosa nodded sympathetically, wondering where this was going, but looking to learn what she could.

He'd entered a confessional flow.

"It was just the two of us. We didn't know the guys who brought the bomb. They just brought it in, then disappeared as fast as they could. Didn't even wait to see if I might have any questions. Just the two of us..."

She asked if he wanted another coffee. He nodded, so she got up and went round the corner to the counter. The girl refilled their mugs from an urn with a tap at the bottom, and shook her head when Arrosa took money from her purse.

"It's too stewed to be charging money for," she said. "And you can have those scones too, if you like."

Arrosa must have looked surprised.

"It's students come here," she explained, "but now they've gone home these'll only get stale. They're not too bad with a few pats of butter and strawberry jam."

They smiled at each other. She'd been remembered from previous visits, probably through leaving tips under her saucer.

She picked up the two mugs in one hand and the plate in the other, returning to where Duffy seemed like he'd fallen asleep. He looked very tired. She sat down and pushed the scones over towards him.

"You look like you need to eat something," she said in as motherly a tone as she could manage. He looked confused, then reached over to the next table where two knives and forks wrapped in paper serviettes were stood inside a water glass.

"Yeah, thanks," he said. "I haven't been out for the last couple of days."

"You should," she said. "Nobody's looking for you. You're safe enough."

He shook his head, then sliced open one of the scones.

"Right enough – but that's just for the moment. They'll be trying to work out what went wrong. Then they'll come for me."

His heat-flushed face had gone pale, and he was buttering both halves of the scone carefully as if trying to stop his hands from shaking.

"But you've done nothing wrong, Padraig. It was the SAS who killed Máire…"

"You don't understand," he interrupted. "There's nobody else to blame. I'm the only one, and with Máire gone, I'm completely on my own."

"You think you're going to be blamed?"

He nodded. She saw fear, poorly disguised self-pity and loneliness eating into Duffy's self-respect.

"So they think there was a mistake, and need somebody to pay for it?"

He nodded.

"So…" she said gently. "It's for *you* to work out what that mistake might be."

He looked up at her.

"I can't think of one," he said. "At least, not something I could have done…"

She waited.

"They could blame me for not delivering the bomb. But everyone understood Máire's determination. Even Séan accepted that. I didn't even know about the second bomb until that morning when Séan gave me the radio trigger."

A transmitter, she thought. Unusual with an urban bomb. Carragher hadn't mentioned that.

"Realising Máire had kept that to herself all those months made me feel sick. It would have been different if Séan had made her the team commander when he left. But he didn't… Just let me go on thinking I was in charge."

"So Séan needed *you* to make this work – yes?"

He nodded.

"He must trust you very greatly."

"I didn't think so at the time."

"But he'd spent over a year organising this, and then left it to you to make happen…?"

"Yeah, well, it was seriously last-minute – a pretty shit surprise. I really didn't need it, y'know? I like to have time to think stuff through."

"But he did trust you to do it?"

"Well… He certainly trusted Máire."

"Like you said, it was just the two of you. That's serious trust, Padraig – isn't it?"

She was really pushing the trust bit, trying to reassure him. But she suspected there was something else.

He nodded.

"They'd kept such a lot from me over a long time, him and Máire. But on the day, there was so much to take in – the maps and notes Séan gave me were amazingly detailed."

Arrosa made encouraging noises.

"You probably don't know, but UHF radio is very unreliable in urban areas."

Arrosa did know, but remained silent.

"UHF is used when real planes are talking to the ground – and also with model aircraft. You need unobstructed line-of-sight between transmitter and receiver. UHF means there's less chance of something else triggering a bomb, but buildings, trees, and vehicles can block the signal.

"So Séan and Máire had tested out every square yard of the area, plotting the dead spots. Séan had a street map marked up to show precisely where, and exactly how high, the trigger-point antennae needed to be; how they should be concealed. The target building's lightning conductor was its receiving antenna."

Arrosa nodded absently, pretending to be bored.

"And then the week before," continued Duffy, his voice rising in pitch, "Séan installed the antenna in the alley – just a wire up the fence and along a clothesline. He'd also hooked up the radio trigger unit and battery pack to the bomb in the back of the building. Batteries run down over time, y'know…"

"But once it was set like that," interrupted Arrosa, "couldn't something else make it go off – television, CB radio?"

"Premature detonation is always a risk, regardless of how you're triggering it," he replied. "Even if you're putting a match to a safety fuse. But yeah, out on an open park, another transmitter might interfere with your model aircraft. But the frequencies are set and extremely short range. Plus there's not too many kids living in West Belfast who could afford one."

"It sounds very complicated," said Arrosa.

"Yeah, Séan had worked it all out. His legendary reputation for successful bomb attacks is well deserved."

Duffy stopped talking for a moment.

"But I still don't understand why, with such a complex operation, we were so ridiculously rushed…"

Arrosa couldn't tell if he thought he'd said too much, so she steered him back to his original concern.

"So what might they think you did wrong?"

Her diversion had succeeded. Now she watched his geeky enervation be replaced by anxiety and anger.

"Séan suggested I delayed too long in firing the second bomb."

She raised an eyebrow.

"But that was just him looking back at what happened, y'know – with the Brit Army suddenly pulling out. It was him who'd repeatedly told me not to blow it too soon… Like he thought I'd lose my nerve."

"So you think that's what they're thinking?" said Arrosa.

"That I lost my nerve?" said Duffy, a surge of aggression replacing his rather plaintive self-justification.

"No," she said. "About why the Brits suddenly pulled out."

He sat quiet for a moment.

"Do you mean that I might have told them…? Is that what you think?"

Again the aggression, as if he was trying to intimidate her.

"I don't think anything, Padraig," she said flatly. "This isn't my business."

He slumped back in his chair like she'd punctured a balloon. She gestured at the plate of scones.

"You need to eat something."

She made this sound like an order. He sat up, reaching over to the plate again.

"The other factor in all this," continued Arrosa, "is the SAS guy."

Duffy's eyes flared briefly, as had Carragher's when he'd told her how Máire had died. Duffy dropped his head then nodded slowly.

"All Séan said to me was that this guy shot Máire," said Arrosa. "So tell me about *him*…"

Duffy smeared jam onto the top half of the scone, took a bite then chewed it slowly.

"This guy coming out of nowhere was when it all went wrong," he said finally. "One moment everything was going to plan. Then this black figure appeared wearing a long overcoat and hat. I didn't even see where he came from. He was just there, crouching down at the side of the alley."

Duffy was having difficulties telling this. Arrosa could see two things going on: strong emotions, but with very careful phrasing suggesting he wasn't telling the truth.

"I think I first noticed him when he shouted at her – she was head-down, connecting the transmitter. But then she triggered the bomb and everything disappeared into dust."

"So you didn't see where he came from?"

Arrosa was asking random questions, keeping him talking. She'd ask the real questions once he'd said what he wanted to say.

"I was watching the alley, so he must have come from the back of a shop."

"Did you have anybody watching the street out front?"

"No. It was just me and Máire. Too dangerous, in any case."

"So he could have come from out of the building you were targeting?"

"Yes."

"Alerted by Máire leaving the bomb in the pram?"

He nodded.

"I suppose so. But it was like he knew exactly what was going on."

He took a mouthful of coffee.

"The explosion took me by surprise. I was disoriented – I don't know exactly how long.

"I'd ended on my face – must have been trying to shield myself from the blast. When I looked up, I saw this black figure go over to Máire. She was down – wasn't moving. He was shining a torch on her. He knelt over her for a few moments then ran down the alley, away from where I was."

"Did you wonder why?"

"I wasn't wondering about anything. It was all too quick. He was really fast – like one of those blue lights you see flickering across a marsh."

Corpse lights... Arrosa felt a single shiver pass through her body. She could see all this very clearly. Duffy seemed transfixed.

"You were armed?" she said.

He paused, and she knew he understood the point of this question.

"I had a Colt .45 automatic."

"I'd have been terrified," she added.

"I was only thinking of Máire," he replied.

He clammed up. She sat waiting to see if he might reveal why.

"She'd looked at him," he said.

Arrosa waited. But then she had this image of Máire kneeling in the alley, her beautiful face staring up at the man who was about to kill her.

She'd liked Máire, and Máire had liked her. They'd both known it. She was lost for a moment.

Duffy was now looking at her, like their whole conversation had changed direction. Almost, she thought, as if he was trying to transfer how he felt about Máire onto her.

She steered him forwards in time, to after Máire had been killed.

"So you went up to her?"

"I wanted to see if she was still alive – if I could do anything for her."

The moment had passed. She wondered if she'd made a mistake steering him away from wherever they'd been going. She'd knee-jerk reacted, not wanting complications. So now he'd stopped answering again, dissembling.

"You must have been frightened that the SAS guy would come back?" she suggested, but he didn't appear to take in her words.

"I checked and she wasn't breathing. There was blood all over her head. It was dark so I couldn't see very well, but it was obvious she was dead. I turned her over and tried to stop the bleeding. There was a pool of blood..."

"You said he was like one of those blue lights...?"

Duffy was lying, and he wasn't listening to her.

"She was bleeding out. There was nothing I could do."

"You must have been terrified..." she repeated.

Duffy stared at the table while nodding his head up and down very slightly, like a dying bird.

"So did the SAS guy take the radio trigger?" she asked abruptly.

"She was lying on top of it," he said in a matter-of-fact voice. "I only found it when I was clearing her airways."

Another lie.

"So I grabbed it and went to the safe house. There was nothing more I could have done for her."

Arrosa nodded, then said: "Séan's feeling guilty that he wasn't there..."

She caught the slight shift as Duffy switched mode from self-justification to outrage.

"Yeah, he wasn't there. So how can he judge?"

"You completed the mission," interrupted Arrosa.

Duffy nodded.

"What was so important about it?" she asked.

Duffy seemed to flare up.

"They kept me out of it," he hissed. "But it's blown back on them both, that's for sure."

Arrosa nodded.

"It had some specific purpose," she said. "All that secrecy and preparation."

Duffy nodded, looking intense.

"Séan talks to me about working again on the mainland..." she said.

Duffy looked sharply at her. But she continued as if she hadn't noticed.

"You know why I'm over here. The C4, Cordtex, and detonators you use don't just grow from the ground like olive trees. Going back to bombing on the mainland can't even be thought of unless there's a reliable supply."

"That was another thing..." Duffy said slowly. "There's teams living over in the UK specially for that, guys who know the ground after blending in for years. Why take *us* over there...? It's a surefire trip to the Maze, or worse."

Arrosa let the silence grow. They'd been here long enough. She needed to break this up and go, but wanted to identify Duffy's main problem – beyond his simply wanting to talk to somebody.

"That SAS guy," Duffy said finally. "He would've killed me – and Séan too, if he'd been there."

He looked up at the ceiling. Arrosa saw his eyes had filled with tears.

"And there would have been others. But that one guy was enough. I know. I saw him."

He looked away, then picked up a paper napkin.

"And now Séan's going to kill *me*... unless I can do something."

Arrosa sat back without comment. Duffy was now exaggerating. He was too valuable for Carragher to kill, one of the rare electricians who could also design and make circuits for when the bomb factory's product didn't suit an operation, or was poorly made and dangerous – as happened often enough.

Duffy was genuinely afraid – but also, she thought, bitterly angry that Carragher hadn't acknowledged the danger he'd been in, or that he'd completed the mission. She thought this useful, as Duffy was right. He had saved the mission, and not killing the SAS guy wasn't his fault. Carragher disrespecting Duffy like this could only make Duffy disrespect him in return. And without Duffy, mainland bombing would not be recommencing any time soon.

Plus in Duffy she was seeing for herself the fear and dissension caused by PIRA's "SAS bogeyman" problem. She now understood Carragher's need to dispel it – and so his disappointment at the failure of this stunningly well-planned operation.

But Duffy's fear also made Arrosa feel strangely exhilarated. She imagined the black silhouette he'd described in the alley against the dust; its long overcoat and lethal certainty – the deathly blue light.

She reached out and took Duffy's hand. This was a modified version of the solicitation routine she used with male police officers.

"You're right, Padraig. Séan wasn't there. He ought to feel guilty about that, because maybe he should have been there with you. He was the boss…

"But it's not *fair* of him to put failing to kill the SAS team onto you. It wasn't *your* failure."

She squeezed his hand, trying to channel the strange elation she was feeling into something positive that might make him feel glad he'd sought her out.

"Is it a failure if you try to do something impossible? Maybe the only failure is *not* to try…? Maybe it wasn't anybody's failure.

"Well, you were the only one there, Padraig, and you tried. And you didn't give up."

She let go of his hand; managed to stop herself from patting it.

"It's unfair that Séan hasn't acknowledged your bravery. And it's stupid to play down the capabilities of the SAS to make you look weak."

This was a bit over the top, she thought. But Duffy nodded.

"So don't let him do that to you."

She made a play of looking at her wristwatch.

"I better go," muttered Duffy.

He looked up at her as if she was supposed to say something. He seemed disappointed. She paused, waiting to see if he'd go back there. But he broke eye contact.

"OK," she told him. "You leave first. But call me next time – you find my number, yes? Through the university exchange?"

Duffy nodded.

"Put up your hood," she added. "Walk straight to the door and don't look at the girl behind the counter."

He slipped quickly from his seat, did up the duffle coat and left. Arrosa waited a full five minutes, then took the mugs and plate to the now-unattended counter. She put a pound note into the empty tip jar, which she hoped would be all the café girl would remember.

She'd got what she wanted, justifying the risk.

CHAPTER 34

Straker had hoped the ferry terminal would be busy. But there were only a handful of lorries, hardly any cars in the vehicle lines, and no foot passengers. He bought a *Daily Telegraph* from the kiosk then walked across the passenger waiting area to the greasy spoon café. A blackboard outside gave him the bad news that the morning sailing was delayed.

A bell on the door pinged as he entered, and as no staff appeared he claimed the table in the corner away from the servery. From the window, he could observe the foot-passenger gate, with a large rubber plant between him and the window. He dropped his newspaper onto the Formica and walked over to the counter.

The emptiness of the terminal made him feel like he'd done something wrong, a distraction he needed to shake off. He ran through a quick assessment: a handful of people at the base would be put out by him having left, but he'd never been arrested. He was doing his usual personal security drills to make sure nobody interfered with him. It was what he did – preventative; not responding to any threat. He was safe. Everything would be fine.

The café's seaward-side windows were misted over with condensation, and a dusting of salt-streaked rime on the outside. A doorstep-size bacon sandwich washed down with a mug of Nescafé and condensed milk left him feeling fortified enough to sleep once he was safe on the ferry. But for now he remained alert, pretending to read the paper.

He was feeling a lot better. The black-hooked mind-loop memory of "what he'd done" had stopped, along with the guilt, anger, and self-condemnation. He was waiting for a ferry rather than something intangible, or for other people to make decisions, in a cheerful fug of lingering cigarette smoke, fried food, and warmth. He relaxed, which seemed so unusual that he wondered when he'd last managed it. He put the dates together in his head; the last time had been seventeen days ago – hot buttered toast in the Hereford Mess – an impossibly short period for so much to have happened.

The doc said to rest and let things settle down, which Straker had originally heard without understanding. The change was making him feel better – like a different person, as he'd been before. Once he was back in Hereford it would all fall into place. A couple of weeks' rest and he'd be his normal self.

So Straker sat, mind now contentedly empty, enjoying the warmth and clatter of the café. He made a start on the *Telegraph*'s cryptic crossword. Waiting at the counter for another cup of their oddly enjoyable Nescafé, the indifference of the young woman making it made him feel reassuringly anonymous.

Gazing blankly at the shelves behind where she was making the coffee was a two-metre rectangular mirror with "Jameson" in red letters and "Pure Irish Whiskey" underneath. He doubted the café served alcohol, so was speculating as to the mirror's origin when he saw his own gaunt face staring back at him, sunken eyes black-rimmed beneath the woollen hat. This took him by surprise, like the flash of a hidden camera. He wondered what mirror-land had done to that person.

He picked up the mug and returned to his spot behind the rubber plant.

Straker had always wanted to be a soldier, the sort of idealised boyhood dream that could never survive adulthood and the real world. And then he'd joined the Army to be that soldier: the most ancient of vocations, with a passion to do things that mattered alongside capable people.

But after being expelled from Harrow – or rather *leaving* then being expelled for absence – he'd thought about joining the French Foreign Legion. But as he'd been doing Spanish A-Levels, he'd hitch-hiked to Cáceres with the idea of joining the Spanish Legion. But reality intervened when a kindly recruiting *sergento* told him he'd be wasting his time, and to join the British Army instead. But as that would have required his father's permission, Straker went to Madrid and found work anywhere they didn't ask too many questions, and a beautiful older woman.

He'd kept in touch with his godparents at Ardglenna, but not his parents, despite his mother's pleadings on the telephone calls he'd made from Madrid. His father was now a brigadier, even more focussed on his career, and bitterly disparaging about what he called Straker's "failure" at Harrow. His mother vacillated between manipulative tears and taking his father's side. So he'd stopped calling.

Whereas his godparents Rory and Abigail Ennis-Boyd had remained in touch, staying neutral regarding his parents, and supportive of him – in both letters and phone calls. Rory asked careful questions about what he was doing and about life in troubled Spain, as the dictator Franco struggled to appoint a successor.

Then later, as Spain declined into recession, strikes, and student rebellion, Rory suggested he return to read Spanish at university. Rory's former college, St John's at Oxford, invited Straker for an interview. After a long conversation in Spanish about why he'd left Harrow, and the economy and student activism in Madrid, the Spanish tutor offered him a place with scholarship.

The week Straker turned eighteen and no longer needed paternal consent, he'd joined the British Army as a part-time soldier in 10 Para. His parents remained abroad, and as he'd done as a schoolboy, he spent much of his university vacation time at Ardglenna with his godparents.

It had been a serious decision to walk out of Harrow aged sixteen going on seventeen. He'd abandoned the gold-standard education that would have set him up for life. He supposed the fear he now remembered from that time was of rebelling against his father, and not knowing what the repercussions might be. But reaching that tipping point had been a long process, from well before teenage rebellion. And as had become clear, the threats by which Straker's father had forced him into obedience only worked back then because Straker had complied.

Thereafter, he ignored his father's raging about ingratitude and disloyalty. He'd been sent away to boarding school not for his own good, but to convenience his father's career, the MoD paying the fees.

Although back then, Straker still respected his father as a professional soldier with Second World War combat experience; who would soon be a general. But the real crunch for Straker had been realising that his father's disregard and disapproval of him had hardened into actual dislike.

But a thousand miles away in Madrid, the fear and uncertainty of leaving Harrow had been rapidly overtaken by the daily challenges of avoiding arrest, finding work, and becoming fluent in Spanish. Once free of the black cloud of paternal disapproval, he'd become his own person. And for those two years, he'd started each bright new day with an invigorating sense of newness, and a fascination which remained with him at Oxford.

Five years later, beginning officer training at Mons made him realise that all this had been personalised preparation for his life vocation. The boyhood soldiering dream had survived into the reality of adulthood.

He remembered that joining the Territorial Army had not felt like this. He'd been a private soldier with no responsibility. The hard runs and marches, relentless weapons training, and even the weighed-down sick-bag adrenalin of military parachuting had been fun – physical and immediate. The demands of soldiering were hard but straightforward. Mons officer training, on the other hand, was suddenly very serious – the life towards which everything else he'd done had been leading.

And so he'd blotted out the past, even suppressing the happy memories: life at Ardglenna; the fun, love, liberation, and maturity he'd found in Madrid; his friends at Oxford and in 10 Para. It was as if he'd needed to turn off all other aspects of himself to make the transition.

But why? Had it been too enjoyable, or too irresponsible to sustain? Or was it because he didn't want to regret the far more serious decision he'd made to commit to being a professional soldier and officer?

Now, twelve years on, he was wondering why he had even joined the Army. His life was a mess, emotions repressed, remembering corrupted by irrational fear, happiness a distant memory, facing all sorts of unhealthy consequences for having done his military duty.

He'd convinced himself at age 21, to be a warrior – to heed the ancient calling. But actually, had this been something far more depressingly fundamental – that he was still trying to appease his father?

Right now, Straker's life was anything but warrior-like. Had he been kidding himself? Wasn't this warrior notion just an immature pipe dream?

He then had another memory – of sitting here exactly like this, at this very seaport, thirteen years ago. He'd hitch-hiked over from Spain, tired from no food and lack of sleep – living from one lift to the next, with getting there as life's only goal. There'd been a wild sort of purity he thought, which made him smile. He'd been travelling to Dungannon to see his godparents after a heavy Trinity term of desperate swotting, examinations, and subsequent garden parties at Oxford.

At Birkenhead, he'd recognised some of his old friends from Harrow climbing stiffly from the back of a double wheelbase Transit van. They now had long hair and were looking as dishevelled and bleary as him – members of a successful prog rock band on tour.

He'd tagged along with them to their gig at a large summer music festival, to be very surprised when his godfather Rory and Abigail Ennis-Boyd appeared backstage, then to be even more surprised at them knowing everybody including the band's manager – until Straker realised his godfather was patron of the festival, raising funds for the civil rights movement the Ennis-Boyds had long supported.

His godfather had cut a striking figure; tall with immaculate white hair, in a dark blue linen suit that was cool yet conventional. Abigail had been equally ambivalent, the former senior officer's wife but far more stylish, circulating the sweaty drunkenness of backstage hospitality like it was a London cocktail party. His godfather had invited the band to stay with them afterwards at Ardglenna House.

The next few days had been a grown-up rock 'n' roll version of the happy schoolboy times he'd spent at Ardglenna: sessions in the Ardglenna Arms, the band even playing some of their own songs – a genuinely remarkable experience, especially in IRA country. Although the band didn't outstay their welcome, it was fair to say they left at exactly the right time, with local harmony not only preserved but reinforced by the distraction they'd provided.

That had been just a year after Rory inherited the Ardglenna estate from his father. This had entailed a hurried and highly unexpected resignation from the Army, as a major general slated for promotion, because running the estate was a duty the family had carried out for centuries.

The inheritance had been straightforward; the Will as expected, according to family tradition. But the new baron's first meeting with the estate accountant less so. Rory's most urgent task had been to realise enough cash to pay his father's death duties without jeopardising any of the villagers' jobs. After which he and Abigail discovered that parts of the house were in danger of falling down.

From a personal point of view, staying in the Army would have been the better option. One of Rory's last official engagements had been lunch with a disappointed Military Secretary, who'd offered him the role of Chief of the General Staff as a full general in two years' time. CGS ran the entire British Army – much more than a full-time job; whereas Ardglenna needed him to keep the dairy farm, bakery and sawmill operating.

For the band's last night, they'd had drinks on the lawn by the lake and then dinner, during which Rory made a point of talking with everybody. Afterwards he'd taken the nineteen-year-old Straker for a long walk and a private chat.

"Well done for getting back in with your chums from school," he'd said immediately. "And also for bunking off before A-Levels. That's why the tutors at John's gave you a place. Your father is apoplectic, of course – probably because he never went to university – and he'll react the same whatever you do, so it's not important."

This had been their first private conversation since Straker had quit Harrow. He'd been expecting criticism from his godfather, particularly for having refused to communicate with his parents. But instead he was being welcomed back home with celebration, like the Prodigal Son. Except that, though Ardglenna was his home, there was no forgiving father.

"*What's important is now, and how it makes you feel,*" interrupted Tiger, bringing Straker abruptly back to the steamy warmth of the ferry terminal. "*Take what's good, and don't feel sorry for yourself.*"

Straker was lost in the blur of condensation, staring through a window that made the outside world seem as indistinct as his thoughts. Tiger was as enigmatic as ever; and making total sense.

*

Twelve years ago, the windows of Ardglenna House had been bright with laughter. They'd been walking round the edge of the front lawn, in darkness beyond the pools of light.

"I particularly remember when you were very young," Rory had said. "Your mother was trying to get your father interested in baby development stuff – your first steps and words, talking, learning to read. But none of these things were ever good enough for him."

"All that... continued," replied Straker.

"It did," said Rory. "But you do know that's his problem, not yours?"

Straker had nodded, even though the years of paternal disapproval still rankled like something that had died.

"Most large organisations promote people like your father to keep things running," continued Rory diplomatically, as if trying to be more positive and make his comments less personal.

"They want a safe pair of hands who won't bring them problems. But people like him lack empathy and aren't creative – not the sort of people who will stand up and be counted. You are."

They'd been walking beside the fishing lake at the edge of the ancient oak forest that surrounded Ardglenna House. Mature trees stood above birches and hazels; rowan, holly, and thorn making the woodland dense and full of birds. With the shining crescent of a half-moon disappearing unpredictably behind clouds, they were picking their way carefully along the muddy path around the lake's edge.

His godfather pointed to several very dim greenish lights just inside the line of trees.

"As with many of the things I like," he said quietly, "glow worms are not supposed to exist in Northern Ireland. But you know that we keep such things to ourselves out here."

He'd already told Straker some of the secrets; the accommodations and wisdom of a many-centuries-old community rooted in violence.

"You're not your father," his godfather had continued. "You're a warrior, whereas he's a career man – like many in the Army; not actually a soldier at all. And he suffered an unfortunate war; you must remember we were all painfully young.

"He wasn't really one of us, although he tried to be. We'd all been at school together or knew each other's families, whereas he'd come from somewhere outside London – Watford, or was it Tring? Grammar school, quite bright, and I respected him for persevering – the Regiment desperately needed new officers.

"But he was badly injured in training and missed the desert – Tobruk, Alamein, and then the Salerno landings, joining us half-way up Italy, where he tried too hard. He did some brave things, although they were through lack of experience – trying to be the hero but not thinking it through. The men didn't trust him."

Roland Straker had told the young Straker stories of the war, but made Italy sound like horse cavalry charges in the Crimea: running free out in front of the division, hit-and-run gun battles, attacking the Germans before anybody else, capturing enemy officers and finding vital marked maps in hastily abandoned positions. He'd also revealed bitterness at not being awarded a Military Cross like Rory.

The boy Straker had thought this unjust, contradicting the ideals he'd believed should underpin military life – the honour of the regiment and the absolute heroism of warriors. And so a decade later, while in Aldershot training with 10 Para, he'd gone to the Prince Consort's Library and read the archived official Italian Campaign Regimental War Diary of his father's regiment.

The 13th/14th Lancers had been under relentless pressure from Divisional HQ to push on as fast as possible. The other recce troop leaders like Rory had worked hard to find alternate routes around the German strongpoints, often by themselves at night on foot, without the radios or firepower of their armoured cars. Four had been awarded the Military Cross, with several Military Medals for their men, and Distinguished Conduct Medals for the squadron commanders. Divisional recce had been a very dangerous game. Their commanding officer wrote about how much he deplored shoot-outs, as a waste of both time and the lives of his soldiers.

Even though by then they'd been estranged for five years, Officer Cadet Straker had been surprised by the disappointment he'd experienced on discovering his father wasn't actually a war hero. He'd wondered if this was the last vestige of hard-wired filial respect being mourned in its passing.

Rory's diplomatic assessment of his father's combat experience was not therefore, a surprise. It had put things in context, however – as Straker realised was Rory's intention.

"You *must* follow your own path," Rory had continued. "It's vital. Do not be swayed. Your father will never understand this.

"Integrity isn't just being honest or honourable. It's when everything connects and makes sense within you. It's about *your* values – being totally honest with yourself. And your values are nobody else's business.

"But you do have to think clearly about exactly what you want from everything you do. Be loyal and do your best, but make sure you're getting what *you* want from it."

The next morning there'd been a bleary breakfast then an early start. Straker stayed on with the band on the road to help out at a gig south of Dublin, before returning to London with them, and from there back to Oxford for Michaelmas Term.

Over those three years at Oxford, he'd thought more about his godfather's Second World War exploits as an early joiner of the SAS, a strange new unit whose aggression and apparent cavalier attitude many senior officers hadn't understood. Rory rarely mentioned it.

Back in 1968, the SAS was little publicised and, to outsiders, almost a historical footnote: responsible for Second World War behind-the-lines operations, disbanded after the war, then reformed for the Borneo and Malaya Emergencies. They were now fighting obscure battles in Oman and Yemen without the hindrance of unwelcome media attention.

Straker first heard about Rory's involvement through his father's disparaging comments – that regimental duty was more important than "swanning off to play cowboys and Indians". Straker had come to realise that Rory's promotion to command the regiment four years before his father, despite supposedly irresponsible adventuring, was the actual reason for his hubris. So four years later, when Straker joined the regular Army and started officer training, he'd already decided that the SAS was where he wanted to be.

Straker liked seaports, their freshness invigorating: ozone, salt and seaweed, with the purposeful smell of marine diesel. Sounds seemed to come from far away across the water: the distant percussion of tools on metal, the constant hum of ancillary engines powering ships as they loaded, and the slow beat of the small boats running between the quays through the rhythmic slapping of the waves.

Further inland, Belfast's older shipbuilding quays and dry docks were in quiet decay, the once-prosperous industrial complex where Irishmen had built the *Titanic*, HMS *Belfast*, and P&O's *Canberra*. The loss of this once-galvanising purpose was to be bereaved; leaving recession and hopelessness where so recently there'd been innovation and mighty achievement. It was sad, but the character of this port remained undiminished.

An unseen tug boat made mournful noises, the cries of gulls across the sky mixed wide with shouts from stevedores loading the ships. The warehouses sat dwarfed under a huge, wide sky over an endless sea, with only the idle cranes of empty docks in silhouette.

Out here, even in the lull between sailings there was a sense of constant activity, not just in this ferry terminal but right across the port. Its two-kilometre-long peninsula reached out into the Irish Sea, Belfast still offering itself to the rest of the world, attracting new energy, plus the old feeling of expectation that was now so notably absent in the rest of the city.

The tannoy broke into Straker's musings, and he stood up:

"The delayed ten-thirty sailing for Birkenhead is now approaching. The gates will open to allow foot passengers to disembark. Please remain behind the barriers until called forwards. We'll get you aboard as quickly as we can."

There was movement outside. A civvie car drove into the passenger area, stopping beside the passenger gate. Straker sat back down, watching carefully.

The disembarkation gate opened and a stream of people with impatience on their faces hurried off the ferry, heading for the buses.

"Will all foot passengers for Birkenhead now please make their way to the passenger embarkation gate."

Straker didn't move, remaining at his table, watching as a dozen people lined up behind the gate to show their tickets.

Two men got out of the civilian car. With a start, Straker recognised one of them as the RMP major, now dressed in civilian clothes.

Suddenly the rubber plant didn't seem so silly.

The RMP major was standing in front of the civvie car, scanning the line of foot passengers as they processed through the embarkation gate. He looked around to see if any more people were joining the queue. Straker recognised the second man in civvie clothes as the bad-tempered Special Branch chief inspector who'd tasked them for the surveillance operation.

The chief inspector looked at his watch, then pointed at the gate. The major ignored whatever he'd said, waving irritably then walking over to peer through the metal grille out onto the quayside, where the passengers were walking towards the gangway entrance of the ship.

An RUC Land Rover drove up behind the civvie car. A uniformed police officer got out and joined the chief inspector. Together they stood and watched the RMP major until the last foot passenger boarded. The RMP major then walked back to join them. The chief inspector said something and pointed at the vehicles. The RMP major shook his head angrily, gesturing at the café and toilet block, then over their shoulders towards the bus station. The chief inspector shook his head and both police officers got back into their vehicles.

The RMP major stood for a moment, flustered and angry. Instinctively, Straker lowered his head behind the rubber plant. The chief inspector turned the civvie car around then stopped beside the major who, after another bad-tempered exchange, opened the door and got in. Both vehicles drove away.

Straker sat thinking about this. This looked like a coordinated search, the police knowing the ferry was delayed and arriving at exactly the right time to stop him as he boarded. It looked like the major had followed the same line reasoning that had led Straker to come here. But not the police, so they were now rushing off to Aldergrove airport before the turnaround of the Heathrow Shuttle.

But what was the chief inspector from Group doing here? Were they behind whatever this was? But also, why hadn't they put out a general alert, so that other people could cover Aldergrove, the ports, and the railway and bus stations? Was this unofficial – just the chief inspector and the RMP major searching for Straker, the pair of them rushing around on their own, trying to predict his moves.

However, even though this needed analysis, Straker had now missed the morning ferry. Hanging around here for another nine hours to take the overnight sailing wasn't an option. He needed to get out of here asap – with a new plan.

CHAPTER 35

Jacko's pager went off half an hour later as he drove out of the camp gates. He did an immediate U-turn, driving back round to stop in front of the closed entry barrier. The MoD policeman was over the other side, chatting up one of the cleaning ladies, ignoring Jacko.

Jacko jumped out of the car and went into the barrier office to use the phone. The mouthpiece stank of cigarette smoke, a full ashtray on the desk.

"DALS, Captain Riley."

"Hello, sir. Sergeant Major Jackson, you rang my pager, so thanks for calling me back."

"They told me you were a major?"

"An easy mistake for them to make, sir."

"Right… Yes, and so it would be. Anyhow, how can I help you?"

The MoD policeman opened the glass door and pushed into the security office. "What the hell do you think you're doing?"

"Just a moment, sir. I have a little local difficulty."

Jacko put his hand over the mouthpiece and turned to face the overweight policeman.

"What does it look like?"

"You've no business barging in here…"

Jacko pushed him backwards out onto the step and shut the door in his face.

"Sorry, sir. Have you a few minutes for a chat? It's a follow-on from when you helped us a few days ago at Musgrave Park after the shooting – with the RMP major and my captain, Peter Straker…"

"Yep, I remember – I hope your burns have healed OK?"

"Yes, thanks. Nothing lasting. But yeah, you caught me just as I was driving out of camp. Can I call you back from my office?"

The MoD policeman was shoving and banging against the door, which Jacko had wedged shut with his foot.

"That's great. Thanks, sir. I'll call you back in the next ten minutes."

Jacko put the phone down, then stood back quickly so the policeman lurched in through the door.

"Where's your ID card?" he spluttered. "I'll have you charged for this."

Jacko pushed him aside.

"No, mate, you so won't. You checked me just now going out, so you should know who I am. And if you don't, it means you're not doing your job. When I need to use your phone, that's what happens. This is an operational base, not some cosy little ordnance depot where someone like you can do fuck-all one year to the next. Open the barrier."

Jacko shrugged off this flash of bad temper and stalked back to his car.

Back at the Wing, he dialled Captain Riley's number.

"That's a lot better, sir – thanks."

"I have to tell you, Sergeant Major, that I can't really say much about this. The Board of Inquiry is active, and its report will determine what happens next."

"Yes, sir, I realise that. But I need to tell you that Captain Straker asked me to contact you on his behalf. I take it he hasn't already spoken to you?"

"No, he hasn't."

Jacko needed to push things a stage further, so decided to take a risk.

"The thing is, it looks like the RUC have other ideas…"

"Well, it doesn't matter what they might think or want to do, this is an Army inquiry."

"For the moment, sir," said Jacko. "But with the newspapers stirring the pot, how long can that last?"

"If you're worried about Captain Straker," said Riley, "I understand he's in the Officers' Mess here."

"Yes, sir, I know, and I *am* worried about Captain Straker. The rest of us are back at Hereford, and we've been told categorically not to talk to anybody. The board's got his statements as well as ours, so I'm worrying about why he's being kept on his own over there. It's not what happens after SAS operations—"

"Is your worry for legal reasons?" interrupted Riley. "Or for Captain Straker's health?"

"Both," said Jacko quickly. He hadn't thought of that angle. "The doctor at Musgrave Park said he had brain trauma and needed to get back here and rest. He was very particular about that."

There was a short silence at the other end of the line. Then:

"OK, Sergeant Major Jackson, I understand. I'm going to read the file, then walk across to the Officers' Mess and have a chat with Captain Straker."

"Will you keep me in the loop, please, Captain Riley?"

There was a slight chuckle.

"I'll be restricted by legal professional privilege, so I can only do that if Captain Straker authorises it."

Jacko gave a sigh of relief.

"That's great, sir, thanks. Please page me whenever you can."

Straker's new plan was simple, obvious, and took one phone call – to Rory Ennis-Boyd, his godfather.

Ardglenna was the other side of Dungannon, and for them to drive across would take at least an hour. To avoid seeming like he was loitering, Straker ordered an all-day breakfast from the taciturn woman behind the counter. She took his money before telling him the cook was on a lunch break. He wished he'd not bothered.

He was mopping up egg yolk with the remains of the toast and starting the cup of tea that came with it when a familiar mud-spattered three-door Range Rover pulled up outside, carefully turned, then pulled over close to the café window. His godfather stepped down from the passenger side, pushing the front seat forwards. Straker abandoned his tea, left the café, and ducked quickly into the back of the car.

They drove out of the terminal, not speaking until they were through the M2 motorway interconnection and out onto the A12/M1 south-west. Then the driver turned his head briefly to grin at Straker – his godfather's gamekeeper, Ian O'Neill. A 12-bore shotgun was clipped underneath the cracked plastic of the dashboard, another in its sleeve alongside the transmission tunnel, butt almost touching the back seat. These weapons counted as agricultural "tools of the trade", and being ex-military out here, his godfather would also have a certified protective-carry pistol underneath the worn oilcloth of his ancient Barbour.

"Huge thanks for this, Uncle Rory," said Straker. "I hope it hasn't disrupted your day too much."

Straker's godfather half-turned to reply, the passenger seat's shiny vinyl squeaking slightly.

"Not much going on, frankly," he said. "Short days... We're finished spraying the wheat, and apart from repairing field walls and feeding the animals, there's nothing much until Christmas and New Year are out of the way. The bakery is flat-out with mince pies and barmbrack for the Belfast market, but all that happens without my involvement!"

Ian O'Neill grinned at Straker in the mirror but didn't say anything.

"So, a nice drive to the seaside was just what the doctor ordered."

The Range Rover's primitive heating was blowing noisily, and Straker felt suddenly very tired, the spiked anxiety he'd been fighting since the appearance of the RMP major suddenly falling away.

They were driving south-west along the two-lane M1 past wide flat fields, low trees, and farm buildings back towards Lisburn, retracing the route of Straker's bus ride that morning. They'd then loop south past the gaunt concrete towers of Maze Prison, the textile town of Lurgan, the southern shore of Lough Neagh, and into the flat peatlands of County Tyrone.

But as the prison's airport-like control tower faded into the distance behind them, Straker relaxed so much that he fell asleep slumped across the back seat.

Northern Ireland's winter afternoons were prematurely short, so he woke in the early dusk as they arrived at the back of Ardglenna House. The Range Rover's headlights illuminated the stone steps up to the scullery, where Abigail Ennis-Boyd was standing, as always wearing well-patched olive-green Army overalls.

The kitchen's two sash windows shone like a Victorian Christmas card, with skillets, pans, and ladles hanging down from racks along the far wall. It was like being fifteen again, returning home from boarding school for the Christmas hols.

CHAPTER 36

After Duffy's unscheduled appearance a week ago, Arrosa was being extra careful. She'd not been back to the Languages faculty, which was now closed for Christmas, and she hadn't heard from Carragher.

Her default as a sleeper agent was to blend in and do nothing. Her academic career – a real and demanding vocation in itself – gave her quite enough to do, so this inaction had never been a problem. Now she was making a point of being out and about as usual, but only in crowded places meeting people she knew, doing careful anti-follow drills. This was tiring, but she had no choice.

She was also worried and frustrated. At their last meeting two weeks ago Carragher had unexpectedly answered her questions so openly that now she was wondering if the lack of contact meant he regretted it. She was even considering whether she'd misjudged the meeting with Duffy – that he'd been sent by Carragher, and had reported everything she'd said to him.

She didn't know even if Carragher had regained his self-control, so had no idea what he would do: to her, to avenge Máire, and regarding whatever he was planning. Plus there was Chapman's insouciance, but above all, there was her concern for the SAS captain.

She remembered as a girl looking from her bedroom window across the sea as storms approached, swirling and fearful. The winds would hit their single-storied house, buffeting the windows, sleet clattering and howling across the galvanised tin roof. But she enjoyed the power of the storm's energy, imagining tapping off some of it into herself.

Arrosa's job was to survive storms, and not to be concerned with specifics. The danger she faced was from Carragher, which she could manage. Her standing instructions were to communicate anything requiring action and then go passive, not getting involved. But now she wanted to investigate further and make things happen, going against her long-term remit, which was uncharacteristic and dangerous.

When Carragher suggested another meeting, she'd been both relieved, but then anxious. Why would he take time out so soon after Máire's death to talk yet *again* to her – especially when he'd now be focussed on finding the SAS captain? She'd agreed immediately to the meet, but spent the days before it analysing the implications.

That morning he'd suggested a crowded bar in the markets, which was good. Along with the music venues, this was *her* territory, where she played socialist butterfly to the poseurs, activists, and perma-students of Belfast's left-wing community. Many of these people associated themselves with PIRA. So, she reasoned, Carragher would think it safe enough for *him*. She took reassurance from him having apparently selected a location where she'd feel safe – unlike their previous meetings at *his* safe houses in West Belfast, which were anything but safe for her.

She was exactly five minutes late. Carragher was sitting at a two-person table in the far corner near the rear door, with a clear view across the crowded bar to the main entrance. Out of the corner of her eye, she saw Roxy at the bar wearing his mod's scooter parka, clocking her in the mirror.

She went straight to the Ladies, removed the black overcoat, then after a minute in front of the mirror, slipped out and into the chair opposite Carragher as if she'd been there all night. She was in a muted version of her goth-going-to-gigs look, not the usual university-mouse guise by which the people she normally mixed with around here might recognise her. The big hair, tight jeans and black eye makeup were all anybody would remember.

He'd bought her a pint of Guinness.

"*Gracias*," she said.

He looked a whole lot better than a fortnight ago, clean-shaven and wearing a dark blue peacoat over a black rollneck.

"Christmas drinks," he said. "Partly corporate, partly social?"

"Slàinte Mhaith," said Arrosa.

Carragher nodded.

"*Feliz navidad*," he replied.

She smiled. "Is this one of your regular places?"

The bar had high ceilings and polished wood; it was dimly lit and busy with people preoccupied enough with their own mischief not to bother noticing anybody else. It was safe, plus Roxy was covering.

"They look after me here," said Carragher. "I have previous…"

Arrosa pretended not to understand.

"I'd come in here on my way home," he explained. "From the work I once had at the shipyard across the river."

Arrosa nodded, not showing the further relief she was feeling at this small revelation. He was trying to reassure her, at a safe venue, sharing personal experience. But also, for the first time, he was inviting her to ask questions, which she accepted.

"You built ships?"

"I was an apprentice at the shipyard, in their drawing office. I'd passed my A-Levels at night school and was selected by them to go to the university."

He picked up his pint, then set it back down again. "It's a common enough thing, though," he continued. "Once they realise you're a Catholic, the doors get closed on you."

He said this evenly, without the bitterness with which she'd been told similar stories by others.

"What happened?"

"It was fine in the drawing office, but out on the flats – where it's dangerous work anyway – there were 'accidents' – Catholics falling into docks, being pelted with rivets. Or threatened with guns… Happens everywhere."

"Other people have told me similar things," she said.

"Aye, it runs in the family," he said.

"Runs in the family…?" said Arrosa.

"It happens a lot here, down the generations."

"In *your* family?" she said slowly, turning the colloquialism into a personal question.

Carragher smiled.

"When I was a kid, two Loyalists with a gun threatened my dad on the docks. He'd been a welder throughout the war, making tanks and warships – and was not inclined to take any shit. He beat them up. That got him labelled as an IRA troublemaker, so they sacked him. He never recovered from being out of work.

"You see, hidden away in the drawing office, nobody'd got me for a Catholic. But when the drawing office manager wanted the company to fund me through the Queen's maritime engineering degree course, Orange Order alarm bells must have started ringing up in the personnel department. I got my cards. No Loyalist intimidation – just no job.

"I was really into the science – wanting to make something of it, maybe do research at the University."

"That's terrible," she said. "What did you do?"

"I couldn't afford to stay in the city, so I joined all the other Catholics who can't pay the rent and moved back out to Ballymurphy where my mum lives. It's a jerry-built concrete council estate, two miles out of town."

"Jerry-built…?"

"Means cheap and bad – 'jerry' maybe from 'Jericho'. You know, the walls that fell down when Joshua blew the trumpets?"

He shook his head. "This was exactly as my parents had done with the ten of us kids, eleven years before."

"Ten children!"

"Yep – I was number four, aged twelve when we moved out."

He looked around the bar.

"I used to come in here for the political craic, you know – after lectures at the college. It's still much the same, socialists and Republicans. Some people are both but it's not a given. I'm not a socialist, at least not anymore…"

He took another pull at his pint.

"When the orders for ships dried up, instead of the shipyard looking after their people, they did the capitalist thing of cutting costs to protect shareholders – sacking people. Totally stupid. That workforce could have made anything, as they did in the war.

"So by the summer of 1969 when the first riots kicked off, I'd become a full-on socialist. But socialism isn't going to solve what's wrong here. It might be the antithesis of Unionism, but why should a free and united Ireland be socialist?"

"In Barcelona, we have such discussions endlessly," responded Arrosa. "They can be difficult. But some people wish only for their own sort of freedom, which denies freedom to others. So I keep quiet. All I wish for is that we can each be ourselves."

Carragher took a long pull from his Guinness, placing the glass back down onto the beermat with exaggerated care.

"Politicising the really important issues only trivialises them," he said, then smiled.

"Anyway… I'm moving on – to the next thing, a change of focus. Or rather, pulling out of stuff other people can do just as well as me, getting back to finding my own role. Like we were talking about when we last met."

There was an awkward silence, as if that had been an unwise conversation – as perhaps it had been.

"So," said Arrosa, recognising the purpose of this meeting. "You're focussing on supplies…?"

"Dead on," he said. "For which I need you and me to understand each other."

This was a statement; that he'd moved on from grief. She could also see that he was making an especial effort.

She nodded but did not smile. A line needed to be drawn.

"I will of course make the representations," she said crisply.

Arrosa was deliberately avoiding mentioning Máire. Carragher was doing the same thing, totally professional, like this was a normal business meeting.

"I want to talk about where we are now," he continued, "in our campaign."

He looked across the bar.

"Some people, including the Brits, think we've been forced to reduce operations thanks to internment and the security forces bribing our people to betray us. They think we're fading and about to give up. Even our own people argue for ceasefire."

Carragher's objectivity suddenly slipped. She watched as he clenched his right fist until the knuckles showed white.

"But your people," he said slowly, "must not make that mistake."

She nodded, then took a lady-like sip of her Guinness.

"I'm only the messenger, Séan… and I do report with great accuracy."

She watched as he relaxed.

"As you do, Arrosa," he replied, after a pause.

His voice softened.

"So with me, things *have* changed. For one, I'm no longer looking after the Belfast people."

Arrosa kept quiet, wondering if he'd been sacked, and what might have caused that – had he done something, maybe to do with finding the SAS captain? And still no mention of Máire. She focussed on not showing any reaction.

"Now I've finally got the time to create those supply chains we've been talking about," he continued.

Arrosa continued to think fast, eyes down, grateful for the black eyeliner.

"Relying on the corrupt American mafia and eejits in Tripoli isn't getting us anywhere," he said. "And I can't plan based on whatever we might get from random raids of quarries in the South. We need the right gear, exactly when we need it, in reliably large quantities."

"So this is the new phase you'd mentioned?" she said carefully.

"It is. But that's all I can say about it here."

He'd noted her caution with, she thought, a flash of approval.

"This conversation is about where I am with this," he continued, "so we can move forwards. And it's strictly between the two of us."

Carragher is consolidating his position, thought Arrosa. *As in, making sure he remains the key point of contact. Is he trying to exclude anybody specific – O'Donnell, perhaps?*

He's also making this personal. Be careful.

"We're at a moment when things need to shift," Carragher said, "and we need to change."

Channelling his emotions. Utilising grief and anger to energise what he's decided to do next.

"Since the Birmingham disaster, we stopped bombing the UK mainland. Over here, we've replaced full-on bombing with specific attacks by specialist teams. But that won't make the North ungovernable. From now on we're going to get weaker."

He took a deep pull at his Guinness.

"Once a critical mass of our people realise this, they'll turn away from us. We can't operate without their support, so this is how we lose the war."

He'd stayed holding the glass, which he now placed carefully onto the beermat.

"That's *our* situation – we can't win, and that's how we lose. We're seriously disadvantaged. Whereas at the same time, the security forces can imprison any of us at any time, and they're running hit gangs that take out our people. Those guys are an extremely serious threat…"

The SAS captain casts a long shadow.

"But they're breaking the law," she interrupted, trying to get him to say more. "Does that not discredit them, especially with the moderates on both sides?"

"I'm not so sure about that," he said. "Moderate Loyalists just want the security forces to stop us making attacks. We're more the ones getting discredited – by *our* moderate supporters when we kill innocents."

"So what can you do?"

Carragher had tensed up again.

"Identify these gangs, then take them out," he said. "The security forces have a process, and the gangs are part of it. We need to make specific efforts to find them."

That's also personal, thought Arrosa. *So is it driving the creation of a new policy?*

"We had something similar back in 1972," continued Carragher. "When we took out a Brit Army undercover unit that was making hits – gathering intelligence using a laundry service and massage parlour, making their killings look like it was us."

"How successful had they been?"

"Very… And at the time I was sure they'd carry on with it, only more carefully."

"But until now, you hadn't been sure?"

Carragher went quiet, and Arrosa regretted her question. But then he sighed.

"It's actually very messed up. Which is why I'm getting on with doing my own thing."

He paused as if wanting to talk about something else, sounding suddenly very tired.

"In Spain," he said, "you have *no* democracy and you fight a fascist government that takes extreme measures. Here, we *do* have democracy, but our people are a minority with strong grievances."

"Getting on with my own thing," he said... So it is personal?

She knew better than to think about this now. Grind it all out later.

But why is he telling me this? Is it so I can report that he's no longer impaired by what's happened, so he can get his bomb operation running again?

Arrosa decided to match Carragher's candour.

"This is my personal view," she said. "I think it might help you here. ETA uses violence to force reaction from an unfair and unresponsive government. I think this is similar to your battle.

"Under Franco, we had the support of many anti-fascist groups. But now he is dead, I worry that ETA is still focussed on violence."

"Are things changing since Franco's death?" said Carragher.

"Not really. The Francoists remain entrenched, so ETA doesn't need to change either."

"Could ETA change?"

This was the question she'd been angling for – which she wanted *him* to answer.

"Terrorism can't make just terror," she said. "There has to be a message – it has to be violence with a message. And the violence must be controlled in all ways to match the message. Then, as the government reacts, your people must evolve. This is hard to manage and needs great discipline, with your people doing things they might not believe in."

Arrosa was getting into dangerous territory. She paused.

"Go on," said Carragher.

"But answering your question – no," she said. "ETA cannot change. We fight for a separate Basque state. That's our purpose.

"But only for between us, talking with each other here, this is impossible – even when Spain becomes fully democratic. The state could not allow it. This is my personal view."

She stopped talking.

"So if it's impossible, why do you keep fighting?" asked Carragher quietly.

"Me personally?"

"Yes."

"This is why I have this conversation with you, Séan. A fully independent *Euskada* is just as impossible as a united Ireland – or an independent Catalonia. We can both know this, privately for ourselves. But these are our personal views."

She hadn't answered his question, but Carragher looked away. An honest answer was as impossible for her to give as it was for him.

"I think you wish me to reassure my people," she continued.

As he nodded, she saw for a brief moment the enormous effort he was making to control himself.

"I will do this," she continued. "But I will keep our personal views from clouding the situation."

She paused, then spoke again.

"The things we do must be for an achievable aim. Otherwise we make people die for no reason."

Carragher nodded slowly.

"And all who remain," he said, "learn to hate."

There was a silence. Then Carragher drained his Guinness.

"We must change," he said. "Otherwise we lose the war."

Back in her flat, Arrosa assessed this conversation. He'd asked for the meeting, so he must be under pressure. But his grief and rage were now well concealed, and he'd seemed positive and forwards-looking. He hadn't mentioned Máire, but she sensed the depth of his anger and grief. He wasn't a psychopath, so the effort he'd made to seem unaffected would have been considerable.

She was now certain he'd been sacked. Stepping down voluntarily would have been too great a loss of status. And to resign because of grief was to admit weakness, which Carragher would never do.

His natural impatience and frustration had shown through, but he was planning well ahead. Was he using work in order to forget – work that would therefore have to be for the highest possible stakes? She decided he was, although she couldn't access the extent of O'Donnell's malign influence in this. This seemed like O'Donnell's policy, executed by Carragher.

But as she'd surmised several times already, Carragher had emerged from break-down and grief with convenient alacrity. He was now impressively together, just eleven days after the shooting dead of his wife and son – not to mention the insult and danger of being sacked from his command.

She didn't buy it. Carragher might fool O'Donnell, who wanted a compliant Carragher doing his bidding. But she didn't think O'Donnell human enough to understand the limitations of his ability to control Carragher. He relied on logic, whilst not understanding emotions. And Carragher's powerful emotions were primeval – Old Testament. Arrosa was now certain that vengeance was Carragher's prime motivation.

She decided to have another talk with Chapman.

"Have you heard any more about our contractor friend?" he said immediately their call began.

"Is there anything more to be heard?" she said, not immediately understanding who he was talking about.

Over this past fortnight Arrosa's thoughts had kept straying back to how the SAS captain had reversed the ambush. She'd tried to focus on other things but hadn't succeeded. It was as if she'd met him; as if he knew her. She'd rationalised this as stress generating a false emotional need.

"I meant about your principal's interest in our contractor friend," clarified Chapman.

"He didn't mention it," she replied. "Which is why I've phoned."

"So he's no longer looking for him?"

"I couldn't say. It's just not being talked about anymore – like it never happened. As if everything's normal and good – which it obviously can't be."

"Interesting."

For her it was more than just interesting. She felt as though she knew the "contractor", and even weirder was her strange thought that he was somehow aware of her. She wondered what he was doing for Christmas.

But she had to stay focussed on this call, especially now Chapman seemed interested enough in the captain to be asking about him. So she pulled her attention back to Carragher. There were things she needed to say to Chapman about him.

"He wants to reassure my people, and get the proposed contracts up and running," she said. "But regarding *our* contractor, he's also concerned that we might have other contractors doing the same thing."

"Why is he concerned?"

"Because he's very worried about the effectiveness of our people."

"That's good," said Chapman.

"It also means his people were taken by surprise."

"Ah, so they don't think it was our friends who set them up?" said Chapman.

"Correct," agreed Arrosa. "But I also think that our friends are covering up for their own mistake."

"I'm bound to say," said Chapman, changing the subject, "that our partner companies don't believe your contention that your principal intends to restart work over here."

"Partner companies" was Chapman's sarcastic way of referring to MI5 and the rest of the UK counter-terrorist infrastructure.

"That's disappointing. What do you think?"

"I have no reason to disagree with them. But obviously I'm keeping an open mind."

Chapman needed evidence to challenge MI5. But he "kept an open mind" to everything, which was his way of saying something wasn't a priority. This annoyed her.

"I hope you'll encourage them to take it seriously," she said. "If they fail to pick up early indicators, then knowing my principal, he'll be successful."

"Indeed," said Chapman blithely. "But there's no corroboration. In any case, should we give water to horses even though we know they won't drink?"

"What's happening here is serious," Arrosa snapped back at him. "It's a big change."

"But it's not our train set," replied Chapman, ending the call.

Arrosa remained annoyed at Chapman for the rest of the day. She imagined him as a court jester, wearing a hat with bells.

CHAPTER 37

FRIDAY 12 DECEMBER

After an early supper with nobody trying to make conversation, Abigail had suggested Straker go to bed. His room from school holidays, was above Rory's study. He found his winceyette pajamas under the pillow. Although it was cold, a heavy stone hot-water bottle warmed his feet and he'd slept soundly all night, with no dreams.

He'd woken cosy, warm under the weight of blankets and a thick eiderdown. Daylight lit the edges of the wooden shutters, so he'd slept late. In the high-ceilinged room, a massive cast-iron radiator did little to take the edge off the cold. He'd gone quickly to the chest of drawers to find his old work clothes folded neatly, now a touch tighter round the shoulders. His wool-lined slippers were under the bed. His leather work boots would be downstairs in the scullery.

Everything here started early, well before dawn at this time of the year, so this late nobody was around. He made toast on the AGA, with coffee from the percolator Abigail kept topped up at the side.

The wolfhound had nosed quietly into the kitchen as he finished breakfast, putting his large grey head on Straker's shoulder. After a few moments of silent communion, they'd both gone down the scullery steps, across the yard, and along the cobbled road to the implement shed. Ian O'Neill was already there, and gave Straker a list of things to be done. Abigail's two Jack Russells appeared, tagging along for the rest of the day chasing rabbits.

He'd driven the old Fordson and trailer round the 200 acres of the main shooting wood, topping up grain-feeders and water vessels. Some of the rearing pens had needed fencing repairs, and he'd replaced several posts. By dusk, with a break for coffee and a sandwich on his own in the kitchen, he'd done a good day's work.

The wolfhound had spent the day with Straker, ignoring the Jack Russells. Now, lying in front of the log fire, he and Straker were slumped together in companionable tiredness, the fire to themselves, wondering where the little dogs found such energy.

They were in the winter part of the house, in a small wood-panelled sitting room which led directly into the huge warm kitchen. The rest of the house remained bitterly cold and was rarely used, its ancient heating system barely capable of warming the elaborately carved Victorian radiators.

This winter sitting room had a huge stone fireplace in which the spit had once turned. Some original metalwork remained. Two oak benches with cracked leather covers sat to either side, on which Straker and the wolfhound were watching the flames.

This was his favourite place. And the woodland duties which had made him so agreeably tired had been his responsibility during school holidays.

"Thanks for sorting out the birds, Peter," said his godfather, walking into the sitting room from the outer hall passage. "I really needed this as a day in the office to get the accounts ready for the bookkeeper. Ian says you've done a great job."

His godfather wore a tattered covert coat to keep warm inside the house. He walked over to ruffle the wolfhound's neck, then dropped into one of the ancient armchairs, which absorbed him so he was more lying than sitting.

"Where's Abigail?" asked Straker.

"She's on a mission to bring the west wing back into commission. It's no longer in danger of collapse, but a long way off being habitable. I don't know what we'll do with it, but she's up there furiously sanding and painting. I suggested she might stop – at least while you're here. But she takes no notice."

"It's that lovely turret room, darling," said a loud voice from the hall, as Abigail strode in wafting cigarette smoke and closed the door behind her. "Obviously from when this place really *needed* to be a castle, with all-round observation and that door onto the roof. It's an eyrie, ideal for my cauldron and recipes."

"Can you give me the guided tour?" asked Straker.

"Double, double, toil and trouble; Fire burn and cauldron bubble," chanted his godfather.

"Cool it with a baboon's blood," replied Abigail.

"Then the charm is firm and good," said Straker, laughing.

"Well remembered," said Abigail. "And thanks for looking after the dogs. How did you sleep?"

"Untroubled by spells or witches," he replied. "So it works."

"Indeed it does, and we've Mrs O'Neill's walnut and carrot cake for tea, with roast beef from the farm for supper. I'll organise the tray."

Straker got up to help, but she waved him away brusquely and walked through to the kitchen, closing the door firmly behind her.

Rory extracted himself from the depths of the armchair to poke the fire and add a large log.

"We saw the newspaper articles," he said, concentrating on arranging the logs. "Somebody's making smoke. I suppose the facts as reported are correct?"

Straker nodded. "Although I haven't read much of it. But the lurid headlines I couldn't avoid are broadly correct – except for the speculation as to my motives and application of the Yellow Card Rules."

Rory slapped the bark dust from his hands, and stood for a moment in thought.

"To state the obvious," he said, "I can't see how you can be held responsible for Mrs Carragher's condition."

He went over to the huge sash window, looking out across the lawn to the edge of the woodland, as dusk turned into the early darkness of midwinter.

"As for her being where she was, doing what she was doing, that's her and Mr Carragher's business. The morality of *that* is nothing to do with you."

Straker reached down to stroke the wolfhound.

"Logic doesn't seem to apply," he muttered.

"Of course," replied Rory. "This is being hyped up to draw attention away from something else – people leaking on both sides. The media like victims and perpetrators so this story's ideal: pert, pretty, and pregnant… Whoever set this up knew what they were doing. And you've been ramped up as her executioner – good emotive stuff. Even the so-called *responsible* press hasn't been able to resist it."

The early twilight had faded. Rory reached over to where the wooden shutters were folded back into panels at the side of each window. Unfolding both sides so they closed, he dropped the iron latch, shutting out the darkness.

"It's terribly important to understand the moral dimension. Soldiers who keep to the regulations under which the state directs their services cannot be murderers. You know that."

Straker nodded. But knowing it intellectually was very different to believing it; or being able to set aside the guilt and other emotions.

Rory stood beside the shutters, now with just the flicker of flames lighting the room. As the shutter panels matched those that lined the walls, it was now as if the window no longer existed. There was a sudden feeling of warmth as wood replaced the coldness of the glass.

Neither of them spoke for a while.

"But, of course, that's not how you feel about it," said Rory finally. "Although in time you will."

He then sat back down in the all-embracing armchair. "Your mama was on the phone to Abigail."

Straker had been trying to remain detached, feeling melancholic. He now looked up sharply.

"She phoned up, distraught," said Rory. "Wondering where you were, and *how* you were... They'd seen the newspaper stuff."

"How did she think to connect that with me?" said Straker. "OPSEC – they didn't actually know I was over here."

"Your father, I'm guessing," said Rory gently.

Straker flashed up, instant anger bringing him back to the present.

"It's not his bloody business to know what I do."

"Easy," interrupted Rory. "There's a casualty reporting system back to MoD which Musgrave Park and HQNI will have triggered."

"MoD gossip," said Straker. "And he won't have been able to resist telling Mum how all-knowing he is."

Rory nodded. "I told her you were fine."

For twenty-four complete hours Straker hadn't thought about HQNI, that bloody dreadful Officers' Mess, or the Board of Inquiry.

"*HMV*," said Tiger, "*He'll get you killed*."

Suddenly the warmth and sense of belonging that had so relaxed him since being here vanished. He tripped brutally into analysis mode: now remembering the RMP major's anxious searching at the ferry terminal.

"They'll be looking for me," he said.

"I thought so," said Rory. "I think you should phone Hereford and let them know where you are."

Straker continued to think, asking: "Did you tell Mum I was here?"

Rory shook his head. "No, just that I knew you were safe."

"Did she ask if you'd seen me?"

Rory sighed. "Ah yes… I'm sorry, Peter. Yes, she did. She was upset – flustered. I wanted to reassure her, and so I did say I'd seen you."

They both sat in silence.

"I'd better phone Hereford immediately," said Straker quietly.

The wolfhound sat up suddenly, then growled. The two Jack Russells scrambled for the door, barking as if to force it open.

Outside in the darkness of the long hall, three heavy and deliberate blows reverberated from the thick oak of the front door.

"You stay there," said Rory. "Only strangers come to the front. I'll get this."

CHAPTER 38

FRIDAY 12 DECEMBER

One week after the second bomb exploded, the Officer Commanding 321 Explosives Ordnance Disposal Company was summoned by the RUC to a meeting at Newtownbreda, just outside Belfast city to the south.

Immediately the second bomb exploded, 321 EOD Company became responsible for sealing off the area; and they slowed everything down to ensure nothing further was missed. Their officer commanding had appeared on site to support the deceased Major Carlisle's sergeant major, who continued the work – which had become more like an archaeological dig.

They'd cleared several metres of brick rubble from behind the row of shops. The new wooden fence was intact, though blown backwards to lie horizontally across where the alley had been.

The sergeant major had supervised the lifting of the fence panel and found his boss's body lying face down beneath it, protected from the blast and flying bricks in the instant of the fence being blown over.

The sergeant major knew Felix usually tucked his camera inside the front of his combat jacket, so he rolled him over. His face and body appeared uninjured, suggesting he'd suffocated to death, or died of internal crush or blast injuries.

His combat jacket showed no signs of burn marks, and it didn't look like the camera had been affected by heat, although damage to the casing meant the film had probably been ruined by light. Even so, the sergeant major put it immediately into the light-roof bag he'd carried with him for when they found the body. He also found Major Carlisle's notebook, which he took back to their long wheelbase Land Rover to examine on a forensic tray under a bright light.

As usual, Felix had written brief descriptions of everything he'd seen plus his immediate thoughts – his official contemporaneous notes for when he had to testify at an inquiry or trial. There'd been nothing in there to support the SAS officer's story.

But then the sergeant major had been interrupted by banging on the locked door of his box-body Land Rover. The RUC chief inspector was demanding he hand over Carlisle's camera as police evidence.

Earlier that day, the sergeant major had listened in to Major Carlisle's conversation with this police officer. After six years over here as a bomb disposal officer, or ATO – ammunition technical officer – he'd worked with Major Carlisle for the last two. His major had died making this investigation, and as his sergeant major, he wasn't going to hand anything over to this person.

After a very bad-tempered discussion, the sergeant major had personally taken the camera back to 321 Explosives Ordnance Disposal Company's photographic section. He'd also spoken to their boss, the officer commanding the company, of which Major Carlisle's team was the Belfast-based unit. They agreed that the RUC's lack of objectivity was unprofessional, and the chief inspector was being unreasonable. The RUC wasn't capable of reporting on the technicalities of this attack, and 321 Company would stick to the protocols.

And now, one week later, the 321 Company OC took Major Carlisle's sergeant major with him to the RUC meeting at Newtownbreda, but did not – contrary to the RUC forensic officer's instructions – bring the evidence.

They were in civvies, driving a battered Ford Cortina, and after being halted and a phone call made, were waved through the security gates of the Belvoir Park complex to the south of Belfast, without even an under-vehicle mirror bomb check. They drove round the edge of the wire perimeter and into a small U-shaped drive outside the ugly concrete of the two-storey administration building. A uniformed constable was waiting, and escorted them to an empty meeting room before leaving without saying a word.

"Whatever this is all about, let me do all the talking," said the OC, as they sat down on one side of a long table in the centre of the room.

After fifteen minutes, the door banged open and three men in civilian clothes came in, followed by the escorting constable.

"You stay outside," said the first man. "We're not to be disturbed."

While the other two sat down on the other side of the table, he turned to the OC.

"Have you brought the evidence?" he said.

"We haven't been introduced," replied the OC.

"You were told to bring it."

The major shrugged.

"I have my procedures, as doubtless so do you."

One of the other men was the forensic team leader from the bomb site. He pointed at the sergeant major.

"That's the one who took the camera."

The OC leaned forwards across the table towards this man.

"Both Major Carlisle's camera, and the film inside it, are Army property."

The first man, who had not sat down, slapped the tabletop.

"This is a police inquiry, and you're withholding evidence. You are required to hand it over."

"At the moment it's an Army inquiry," said the OC.

"That's not how things work over here," said the first man. "We call in the Army only when we need you – it's called police primacy."

"Exactly," replied the major. "The police asked us to deal with those two bombs, so my headquarters ordered us in. Our investigation is part of that, with the camera and film being a vital part of our report."

The first man looked away for a moment, then sat down.

"We're trying to find out who did this," he said quietly. "But every day that passes makes it harder for us to do that. We need all the evidence."

The major nodded as if conceding this point.

"And you'll get it," he replied. "Once I've filed my report."

"I could have you both arrested for withholding information under Section 5(1) of the Criminal Law Act (Northern Ireland) 1967."

"No, you couldn't," replied the OC. "Plus you haven't got the forensic expertise, even out here at Belvoir Park, to investigate bomb debris. That's why we're doing it for you."

There was an uneasy silence.

"For my part," said the OC, "I'd like to know why you're so keen to get hold of Major Carlisle's camera and notebook..."

"Notebook?" interrupted the first man.

"Major Carlisle was very thorough," replied the OC.

The silence continued.

"OK, then," said the OC. "We need to get back – if only to prevent any further delay in finalising our report. I'm sure Headquarters Northern Ireland will forward it with all due urgency to the chief constable's office at Knock HQ."

"But we're the scene-of-crime office," said the first man. "You should forward it to us."

"So why are we meeting out here, and not back in the Belfast SOCO office at Queen Street?" replied the OC. "Belvoir Park is the forensic laboratory."

There was no reply.

"So did you expect us to hand over the film, which you could then develop here immediately...?"

The silence confirmed this.

"Let me just reassure you – the film survived, and we've developed it. You will be provided with copies of the prints and the negatives."

"We need the originals."

"And you should also know," continued the OC, "that we're carrying out a number of tests based on what the photographs have told us about how both bombs were triggered. These tests, when completed, will confirm what various Army witnesses have already told your inquiry. I'm giving you this as an advance on our report, to help your murder investigation."

With that, the two soldiers left the building and drove round the south of the city centre, up past the City airport to Palace Barracks in Holywood, on the other side of Belfast.

This situation was far more loaded than the usual kind of problems 321 Company had with the RUC. Twelve days ago at the scene, Major Carlisle had expressed his concern at the RUC's disinclination right from the very start to believe the SAS captain.

The tone of today's meeting suggested he'd been right. Now, rather than comply with these RUC demands, they decided to make absolutely sure that Major Carlisle's work wasn't ignored.

*

"Captain Straker?"

Two large men wearing overcoats pushed past Rory Ennis-Boyd into the cosy gloom of Ardglenna's winter sitting room.

"Yes?"

"You have to come with us."

Straker looked at them and stood up.

"Where?"

"To a police station where we'd like you to help us with our inquiries."

"Why?"

Rory eased past them into the room, then stood looking at the three interlopers.

"Captain Straker is a serving Army officer. You have no jurisdiction."

The older of the two turned to face Rory.

"We showed you our warrant cards, sir. Our investigation requires that we interview Captain Straker, who I'm sure is keen to cooperate."

"Your investigation does not supersede the military Board of Inquiry," Straker interrupted. "So let's get this clear – am I under arrest?"

"This is about the law, Captain Straker, which applies here the same as anywhere else in the UK, and we don't have to arrest you. We're requesting you come with us. It's going to be much easier for everybody, including yourself, if you cooperate."

"After dark, banging on people's doors without warning?"

Rory stepped forwards.

"I have to agree with my godson's assessment of this situation, gentlemen. He's entitled to be here, and you're not if I choose to tell you to leave."

"You invited us in, sir," said the older officer.

"And I can just as easily invite you out again."

"Unfortunately, sir, you can't—"

"Shall I call the police?" interrupted Rory.

The two police officers looked at each other.

"I mean Chief Superintendent O'Malley, who does have jurisdiction here. I don't suppose he's going to be terribly pleased about you two coming out from Belfast to threaten law-abiding people."

Abigail emerged from the kitchen, with Ian O'Neill close behind.

"We've closed the estate road, my lord," he said to Rory. "The woodsman saw an unidentified vehicle without lights driving past the sawmill."

"Thank you, Ian."

Rory turned to the policemen.

"We have a poacher problem. Strangers coming round after dark are not appreciated out here."

"We were taking normal tactical precautions," said the older officer.

"Really!" exclaimed Rory. "Against what, exactly?"

"It's standard practice when—"

"No, it isn't, especially not round here. You two are way out of line, and much further from Belfast than just the mileage might suggest."

Rory Ennis-Boyd was calm. But Straker could see that he wasn't going to give anything to these two.

Whereas Straker was growing extremely angry, stoked by knowing that the intrusion of these aliens was entirely due to him. Straker felt contempt for them, and wanted them to go away without further imposing on Ardglenna. They were part of the corruption of the Troubles – of emotion and pointless violence. Ardglenna was part of a much deeper life – the way things ought to be. These people could only damage what was important and good. He needed to stop this from boiling over.

Straker pushed aside his anger and shrugged to himself. He'd have to talk to them at some point. That was the only way to resolve whatever the problems were, and it would get him back to normal life sooner. He'd enjoyed the respite here, but once again, as back in the Officers' Mess, he'd soon become inert and ineffective. He might as well go with them.

Also, the questions they'd ask would give him at least some idea of where this was going.

"OK," said Straker, looking round at Rory, Abigail, and Ian. "I'll come. But you'll have to wait while I get changed."

"I'll get your clothes," said Abigail, following him out.

Up in his room, the curtains were open, a pale moon shining across the tops of the trees.

“Be on your guard,” she said, opening the wardrobe. “Nothing over here is simple, and there are many truths. But yours is the only one that matters. Believe that to make it so, and it will *be* so.”

They put Straker in the back of the car, then after taking country roads to Dungannon, drove back east on the motorway past Lisburn. But instead of continuing on the M1 towards central Belfast, they turned right onto the Hillhall Road – the B23 which then joined the A55. Then after twenty minutes they turned left, which was when Straker knew where they were going.

The three-storey flat-roofed brick buildings were surrounded by green-painted steel fencing with watchtowers and floodlights, shielded by forty-foot-high anti-rocket wire netting. They were waved through the two-gate security barrier, and drove down a side ramp into the main internal compound, parking beside a barred and meshed security gate.

This was Straker's first visit to the Castlereagh Holding Centre, even though this was where every terrorist he'd arrested had been brought for interrogation. The RUC officers ushered him through the entrance then departed, looking relieved.

Straker wondered if agreeing to this was the right decision.

Captain Riley paged Jacko early that evening. Jacko called him back and Riley got straight into it.

“I can't find him,” said Riley. “I went over to the Mess and nobody's seen him since yesterday.”

“Yesterday?”

“Breakfast, then nobody's sure. The mess staff don't think he was in for dinner. But they're not exactly helpful…”

“Maybe he's gone for a run, or the gym or something?”

“I've had the guard searching all over for him. One of them said he thought maybe he'd left camp.”

“Slipper City REMFs,” said Jacko disparagingly, referring to the people who never saw the frontline.

“Very unhelpful,” agreed Riley.

“So you think something's happened?” said Jacko.

“Yes. And I think you were right to be worried and get in touch with me.”

"Is there anything I can do from here?"

"Yes, there is. Take everything you've told me, immediately to your CO – maybe via the RSM so everybody's in the loop – and I'll phone the ALS officer in your RHQ. Tell him we've spoken and that I'm working on it at this end.

"First off, I'm going to get hold of Major Soames, the RMP officer who turned up at Musgrave Park. He may have knowledge of what's going on. Give me all your telephone numbers and I'll keep you posted."

Riley wrote Jacko's numbers into his notebook and rang off.

Two solid-looking men wearing boots and black overalls were waiting for Straker inside the holding centre. They escorted him along a wire-cage passageway and through an "air lock" of two locked security doors. They entered into a scruffy white-painted corridor, brightly lit with stairs at the end. They climbed several flights, also caged over like the reception area, and into an inner-locked security section. He was pointed into an empty room, where they left him.

He tried the door. It was locked. As the room was completely bare, he sat on the floor beside the single radiator. It was still warm, but after half an hour grew cold. There were no valves.

After several hours, the door was unlocked and a middle-aged man wearing a tweed jacket but no tie walked in.

"Sorry about this," he said. "We're not used to having guests. This is where we bring them initially. Except we don't let them sit on the floor."

He was deadpan and humourless. Straker just looked at him. He was in their world, and this was their game. It was being played with no witnesses. He also knew about the process of what happened here to suspected terrorists, and the initial softening-up to make them fearful. He wondered if they'd actually "process" him, and decided to let them make the running.

"*Although you don't have a choice*," said Tiger.

"We're just waiting for the rest of your team to get here," the man continued. "It makes more sense to have you all together so we can clear things up quickly."

Straker felt the first stabs of uncertainty altering the calmness into which he'd forced himself.

"Can I get you a cup of tea?"

Straker nodded, and the man left.

Nothing happened for a very long time; and there was complete silence. Then, in early hours of Saturday morning according to Straker's wristwatch, the door crashed open. A tall man came in. He looked younger than the first one, and was followed by a smaller, heavy-looking man.

"Don't tell me," said Straker. "You need to know if I take milk and sugar?"

They looked down at him.

"Holding unit regulations," said the smaller one. "We need to make an inventory of your possessions – things can go missing in here unless we do this."

"I wasn't aware that I was being held..."

"Yes, that's correct. But you're in here, so the regulations apply."

He was blank-faced, but with a slight edge of contemptuous hostility. Straker shook his head. Handing over his watch would mean he'd lose track of time. Disorientating him was the first step in the process.

Interrogation teams worked through playing roles. The longer the process ran, the less capable he'd be of working out the system they were operating. Straker decided to see if he could throw them off their game. He stood up.

"No," he said. "According to *your* regulations I shouldn't be in here at all. So you can go fuck yourself."

He addressed this at the thickset man who stepped forwards as if to kick him. The other hurriedly pushed past.

"Let me get you that cup of tea. You should have been given one when you were first brought in. Apologies for that."

Straker stared at him. Neither man moved.

"Both of you," said Straker. "Go fuck yourselves."

He watched them both carefully. The "good cop" immediately flashed up angrily, while the other turned abruptly and called a third man into the room.

All three jumped on Straker, slamming him against the wall then onto the ground. With his face pushed against the floor, they twisted his arms behind his back, fitted handcuffs, then removed his belt and shoes. His watch, money and wallet were listed on an official form then taken away in a plastic evidence bag.

This sudden take-down left Straker feeling nauseous, as he'd been during his first day at Musgrave Park Hospital.

He was left alone for several more hours. The room was now cold, Straker's hands completely numb from the cuffs. He'd started counting as soon as the men left the room; up to sixty, then adding one to the next sixty to make up the minutes and then the hours. As his brain got into processing the numbers, he felt calm again.

The older man in the tweed jacket returned, affecting surprise at seeing Straker wearing cuffs. He made a show of demanding that the "bad cops" return to remove them.

"Your colleagues have arrived, Captain Straker. Once we've got statements from each of them, we'll be back to you."

He made as if to leave, then paused at the door.

"But there's one small thing that's puzzling us. It's how you managed to identify Máire Carragher so quickly in the dark – before you opened fire.

"You were right, though. She *was* Máire Carragher, wife of the well-known IRA commander. Quite a score for the SAS Group's behind-the-bar trophy list…"

Straker reckoned it was now Saturday night. Along with the counting, he was also trying to keep in touch with his body clock's internal cycle. His blood pressure would dip to its lowest between 3 and 5am. That would make him feel really bad, but the thing he had to remember was that thereafter he'd feel better.

Despite the brightness of the overhead neon lights, he was sleepy. But every time he nodded off, the door opened and the thickset man kicked his feet – not violently, just enough to keep him awake.

At what Straker's counting reckoned to a couple of hours later, the door crashed open yet again, but this time a new man entered. He was older than the other two, although with the same blank demeanour. Straker guessed him as being more senior.

"Why are you sitting on the floor, Captain Straker?"

Straker looked at him, matching his lack of expression.

"The others are giving statements to us at the moment. I've got a few routine questions then you can all be on your way."

He shouted out into the corridor. The two others carried in a fold-out table and two plastic chairs.

"Sit down... Do you want a cup of tea?"

Straker shook his head.

"Suit yourself. I'm having one."

The man had a sheet of lined paper and a couple of ballpoint pens.

"Let's start at the beginning..."

"No," said Straker. His voice was an unfortunate croak, so he said it again.

"No."

"No what...?"

"You've got my statement. What else do you want to know?"

"That's not how we do things here, Captain Straker. We go through the whole thing from start to finish, in detail, so we can understand exactly what happened. Then we both sign the statement, and everyone can go home."

"I suppose it's pointless me insisting on the Group lawyer being here?"

"You're not under arrest, Captain Straker."

"Fair enough. So I'm not answering any questions."

The man looked at his watch.

"Here's the thing, Captain... By lying to us, you've got yourself and your team onto the wrong side of the law here. The tough-guy stuff doesn't work in the real world, and what we do safeguards the lives of ordinary, law-abiding citizens who are struggling to survive the Troubles. You've put yourself and your team beyond the law. Do you understand what I'm saying?"

Straker was slumped forwards on his elbows, holding his chin in his palms. The man jumped to his feet and pulled the fold-up table sideways, so Straker fell onto his knees.

"Look at you!" he shouted. "You're supposed to be a captain in the Special Air Service! We interview IRA Volunteers in this room who've got more pride and self-discipline than you. Stand up when I'm talking to you!"

Straker remained kneeling on the floor and kept his face blank, even though this performance was getting through to him.

"You've got no pride, have you? You can't even manage to look me in the eye... *Captain* Straker."

The man walked slowly to the door. "If I murdered a pregnant woman, I'd be ashamed – just like you. But I wouldn't be trying to put the blame onto my team..."

Straker was taking his time standing up, but couldn't prevent himself from reacting. It was just a flicker, but the interrogator caught it.

"They're going down alongside you, Captain Straker. All together in Crumlin Road, serving your sentences alongside friends of the IRA guys you've killed. Twenty years, probably... You won't survive."

He stopped at the door, then altered his tone as if sympathetic to Straker's situation.

"If you want to tell us what really happened – that you recognised Máire Carragher when you saw her on the street and then decided to kill her – I can't see any reason why we should detain your team.

"You can then argue that you thought she was the bomber and stick with everything else you said in your initial statement. We wouldn't argue with that, so we'd probably charge you with manslaughter. You'll get a couple of years – less with good behaviour. We'll let you do your time over in a mainland jail. I'll leave you to think about it..."

Straker's sense of identity and reality was weakening. He'd forgotten most of the SB officer's visit, but remembered the warning – that playing it like a Parachute Regiment officer wouldn't work. The interrogator's story felt like truth, a snake twisting guilt into his gut.

He'd stopped the counting, lost track of time, his plan forgotten. The natural early-hours drop in his body temperature and rhythms felt to him as though it was caused by the interrogator's insults and threats.

He felt extremely tired. The lighting seemed to be getting brighter. It was also very cold. He began shivering uncontrollably.

SATURDAY 13 DECEMBER

Chapman knew from experience the folly of trying to be clever. He'd walked down from Pimlico and across the river just as it was getting light, one step ahead of the city waking itself up for yet another day. He needed to re-examine what he was doing. These empty streets and the temporary early-morning silence of Century House represented the world as it really was, without the complications caused by other people. Its temporary emptiness gave him the clarity he needed to think.

Cold Hook was the product of decades of careful personal management by Chapman. Nobody else knew about him, although some who'd known Chapman since the early days, suspected he could be running an agent in Northern Ireland.

This current situation jeopardised Cold Hook's credibility – even his personal security. Chapman knew that stirring up confusion among people outside his jurisdiction, although interesting risked instability through their unpredictable reactions. He knew what he wanted to achieve, but needed to think through any detrimental consequences.

His secretary always prepared Chapman's coffee machine before leaving at night, which every morning he checked. He bought freshly roasted coffee in half pound bags, emptying what remained from yesterday's into an electric mill. As the beans reduced to the medium grind he favoured, he flipped on the percolator's water heater, then tipped the coffee into a new filter paper. Taking a bottle of full-fat milk from the fridge door, he walked across his outer office to their small kitchen, lit a gas ring, then stood watching the flame.

Chapman was a man of ritual. He took every step in the correct order with good intention. Experience had taught him that doing things properly, which others were wont to interpret as delay or prevarication, didn't just give him extra thinking time, but created a space in which the buds of uncertainty could unfold into identifiable leaves. He saw this as the universe reorientating itself, which it would do regardless of his actions. He always allowed time for things; there being no point reacting while the world was still changing.

Chapman's rituals created clarity amid complexity and confusion; like everything he did, they had a purpose. They also had to be perfect. There was, for example, no chance of a perfect *café au lait* unless the milk was added to the coffee at exactly that moment of expansion milliseconds before it boiled over, with a faint caramel taste of burning. It was the same with people and circumstances; success was fragile and easy to ruin.

Coordination, and so timing, was just as vital to create these sacred moments. Chapman turned off the gas and returned briskly with his precision-heated milk, the percolator jug full, his office rich with coffee smells.

He now cradled the hot mug in both hands and thought about this SAS captain, and whether to interfere with the RUC cover-up attempts. In order to pillory Straker and his team, Special Branch would have to stick their necks out a very long way. Chapman was intrigued to see if they'd go that far.

But more to the point, they'd also be enhancing the credibility of Cold Hook to Special Branch and MI5 – plus also to PIRA, convincing everybody that Cold Hook was *their* agent. Northern Ireland was characterised by hatred, which stopped people from making connections or thinking clearly, making them easy to play off against each other. And so this morning's coffee ritual was a typical Chapman invocation, imposing his will on their xenophobic world.

Specifically, he decided he'd gone as far as was wise in terms of actual manipulation. He'd now let things play out, from which he might identify new levers to future confusion. He would have backed off at some point anyway, because once PIRA's mainland bombing campaign restarted, it would be more important for MI6 to gather intelligence than stir things up.

But the SAS captain had excelled in that regard – a cat among pigeons of every feather. This was a singular, capable, authentic person who stood out amid all the lesser, mostly compromised people who populated this strange game. He was definitely somebody to watch.

But there was a critical judgment to be made here, as to how far to let RUC Special Branch take things before dropping a Chapman spanner into the works. But not just yet, as Chapman expected the SAS would look after their own. Although, in any case, the captain seemed rather frighteningly able to take care of himself.

Chapman finished off his breakfast coffee and stood up, thinking he might now take a stroll out to the French café where they'd be taking the first trays of croissants from the oven.

Halfway down, the lift stopped. For a few moments, in the silence, Chapman felt like he was in a cell. He shivered, remembering the desperation of his extended stay in Ruschestraße, the main Stasi headquarters in East Berlin, when he had to persuade them that he wasn't important. It had been one of the most silent, lonely places he'd ever experienced.

Then the compartment lurched, continuing down to ground level. The doors opened onto Century House's scruffy mezzanine, and a bright winter's day.

RMP Major Eric Soames had been the first military person to see Straker at Musgrave Park Hospital, so Captain Riley presumed he would be the senior military investigating officer in the Máire Carragher shooting case. He would therefore know what was going on; or if he didn't, he'd be concerned at Straker's disappearance from military jurisdiction.

But Riley also knew that Soames would not be cooperative, nor would he welcome Riley having involved himself with whatever was happening here. He needed to deal with Soames face-to-face.

Riley looked up Major Soames in the HQ phone directory, discovering he was a Grade Two staff officer in the HQ's massive G1/G4 admin and personnel division. He was not part of the 1 Regiment Royal Military Police's investigation structure.

This told Riley that whatever was going on wasn't part of the standard process. It might also explain why Soames had been at the hospital trying to interview Straker before Riley had even arrived.

Riley entered the military police registry office.

"Hi Chief, Captain Riley to see Major Soames. Can you point me to his office, please?"

The chief clerk, a staff sergeant, was sitting behind the largest of four desks, flanked by copying machines, two typists, and a private soldier busily shuffling sheets of paper into piles. They all looked up. The chief clerk's name was carved in gothic writing on a polished wooden sign at the front of his desk.

"Is he expecting you, sir?"

"No, he's not."

Army Legal Corps lawyers underwent the most rudimentary six weeks of military training alongside the Army's chaplains, veterinary surgeons, and dentists. Their value to the Army was as lawyers, not soldiers, so despite only very basic militarily training, they were immediately given the rank of captain.

"Ah, well, sir… I know he's very busy. Maybe I can help you?"

The typists were grateful for the interruption, and the private soldier was watching with interest to see how this inexperienced-looking captain would deal with the chief clerk's insolence.

"Of course, Chief," said Riley. "I was with Major Soames earlier – you probably know all about it…?"

"I do indeed, sir. The RUC officers came here to talk first to *us*, before Major Soames took them over to your Mess."

Bingo! thought Riley. You could always rely on the hubris of a chief clerk.

"So, is Major Soames back yet?"

"No, sir – he didn't actually go with them. Shall I let him know you're here?"

"No. Maybe Private…" Riley paused, looked at the young soldier behind the chief. He too had a name plate on his desk – Riley wondered if in mocking imitation of the chief's.

"Maybe Private Sutton can show me his office?"

Never underestimate a junior clerk. Private Sutton grinned, and before the chief could reply, he was out in the corridor beckoning Riley to follow. They walked past noticeboards, a row of military shields and a dusty rubber plant. Sutton knocked on a door then stood back to allow Riley to enter.

"Hi, Eric," said Riley abruptly. "You'll remember me from Musgrave Park?"

Soames looked up and frowned, then his jaw dropped slightly.

"Ah… yes. Thanks, Private Sutton, please shut the door."

"May I sit down?"

Soames nodded and waved vaguely at one of the two armchairs.

"You know why I'm here, then?"

Soames pretended to look blank.

"Have it your own way then, *Major* Soames. If anything happens to Captain Straker, your neck is very firmly on the line."

"What do you mean?"

"You do know he's recuperating from concussion, which was why he didn't fly back to Hereford with the others?"

Soames still looked blank.

"He could have another bleed. He's not allowed to travel."

"That's not why he's still here," said Soames.

"Really?"

"Yes, and you're not cleared to know about this."

"Well, I suggest you enlighten me rapidly before I take this to the GOC."

Soames tried to look calm but failed.

"You're out of order, Captain," he said angrily. "The GOC already knows. You don't think I'd just hand an officer over to the RUC off my own bat?"

"So you've handed him over to the RUC…?"

Soames flashed up angrily.

"This is an extremely serious incident. Captain Straker came over from the mainland after a request from the police for Army assistance. Right from the start he refused to listen to the RUC commander's orders. He then deployed without telling the RUC, and killed a pregnant woman—"

"The wife of the IRA's Belfast Brigade commander…"

"Exactly, which is why the RUC believe that was Captain Straker's intention all along – that he's running a murder squad. He was deployed over here before – for a year. The RUC are also investigating his actions during that time."

"I see," said Riley calmly.

"And yesterday he escaped from camp."

"Escaped? So was he under arrest?"

"No, but he was under orders to stay here."

"And where did he go – back to Hereford?"

"No, to County Tyrone."

"How did you find him?"

The major was growing increasingly impatient with being questioned.

"His father told us he was with some rich relative near Dungannon."

Riley realised this wasn't important, so switched his line of questioning.

"And where have they taken him?"

"He volunteered to help them with their inquiries."

"Did they tell him why?"

Soames remained silent.

"Did they arrest him – or even caution him?"

"He volunteered to go with them."

"So where have they taken him – which police station?"

"You don't need to know that, Captain."

"Like I said, Major Soames, playing it your way makes you responsible. You know what happens when officers countermand medical orders. For my part, I'll be looking very carefully at your role in advising Captain Straker to agree to this outrageous breach of his rights, as well as how your actions are likely to have affected the Board of Inquiry."

"Captain Straker agreed to go with them. I didn't advise him of anything."

Riley just looked at him. Soames stared back impassively. But a slight tic had started in the corner of his left eye.

"Well, actually, as a military police officer senior to him on MoD territory, you should have ordered him *not* to go."

"On what grounds?"

"So as not to jeopardise the Board of Inquiry."

Another silence.

"You need to stop resisting me, Major Soames. This nausea needs to be unravelled quickly before any serious harm comes to Captain Straker."

Soames stood up and looked out of his window.

"OK, Major Soames," said Riley. "One more question, then I'll clear off. Did the RUC contact you here, or did they come to you via the GOC's office?"

"Via the GOC's office, of course," replied Soames angrily.

"OK. A follow-up: did the GOC tell you to let Straker be taken?"

"Of course the GOC didn't—"

"The chief of staff, MA, or whoever – did they actually *tell* you to hand Straker over to the RUC?"

Soames turned around to face Riley.

"He wasn't 'handed over' or 'taken', as you put it. He volunteered."

"Listen, Soames." Riley dispensed with the politeness of Soames's rank. "I might look like a wet-behind-the-ears Army Legal Service graduate commission captain. But actually, I'm a criminal barrister fast-tracked to become a judge advocate general. Your professional lack of concern for the rights of an Army captain is of great interest to me, which I will be investigating once we sort this out."

Soames's tic increased slightly.

"So do you know where they've taken Captain Straker?"

Soames went pale.

Riley nodded.

"It would have been worse for you if you didn't. So now is the time to tell me."

Riley made a quick phone call on Soames's office phone to the home number Jacko had given him; he picked up on the third ring. As Soames stood and listened to Riley's side of the conversation, he grew paler still.

Then Riley took Soames up to the GOC's suite, ignoring the ADC and walking straight into the MA's office – a lieutenant colonel.

Riley got straight to the point.

"Captain Straker – the SAS captain…"

The ADC had followed them in, but the MA pushed him back into the outer office and shut the door.

"What about him?"

"Did you know that the RUC have taken him to Castlereagh?"

"He's helping the RUC with their inquiries."

"So you're telling me you knew that's where they were taking him? And you gave them permission to do that?"

The MA picked up the phone.

"Sir, I think you should come down to my office, please – yes, right now."

The chief of staff – a brigadier – acted on "summons" like this as if directly from the general himself. He walked straight in, then looked around trying to work out why he was here. The MA peered at Riley's name tag.

"Captain Riley's asking about Captain Straker."

The chief of staff swivelled back round to stare at Riley, quickly working out why a lawyer would be raising this issue.

"Police primacy," he said finally. "That means their inquiries take precedence over our procedures."

Riley kept quiet.

"I don't need to tell you why we've got to be transparent about serious incidents like this one. The RUC don't trust us – and there's been enough smoke over past years to justify their suspicion. So we're here to put an end to all that. Orders from the highest level."

"They've taken him to Castlereagh."

"I didn't know *that*," said the chief of staff, looking at Major Soames, who looked away.

"This is nothing to do with RUC–Army relations," said Captain Riley. "Captain Straker hasn't been arrested, so it was illegal for the RUC to have taken him anywhere. He's an SAS officer under military investigation after the fatal shooting of an IRA terrorist. His safety is a military responsibility."

The chief of staff stared hard at Riley, and when he didn't back down, glanced at the RMP major, then finally the MA, who shrugged his shoulders.

"It's getting late," said the MA wearily. "The GOC's had a long day and needs to leave soon to get ready for a dinner at Stormont Castle. So I don't want to bring him into this."

The chief of staff nodded.

"Agreed. So thanks for bringing this to us, Captain Riley. You did the right thing. I've got a meeting tomorrow morning with my counterpart at Knock, the RUC headquarters. If Captain Straker isn't back by then, I'll raise it with him."

The chief of staff turned to leave the office. Riley cleared his throat.

"Sorry, sir, this is far more serious. The CO at Hereford knows where Captain Straker's been taken, and he's certain to have taken that to the Director Special Forces."

The chief of staff's face tightened with anger, and he started to speak. The MA interrupted.

"How do *they* know?"

The Director Special Forces could speak directly to the Cabinet Office, who authorised the deployment of SAS units with the personal permission of the Prime Minister. The possibility that PM Thatcher might get to know about this had not occurred to any of them.

"The reason the SAS know he's missing is because I represent Captain Straker," Riley said, "and so I told them myself."

"What do you mean 'you represent him'? You don't represent anybody. You give legal advice to us."

"I'm a lawyer. I was asked to look into what's happened to Captain Straker. It's very clear he needs to be represented. So until you sort this out, that's exactly what I'm doing."

The MA glanced across at the chief of staff, who was now looking thoughtful.

Captain Riley continued.

"The SAS also know from the Musgrave Park medical reports they've been sent – copies of which we also have here in this headquarters – that Captain Straker is recovering from head injuries following the double bombing and could suffer a stroke and further brain damage at any time. I suspect from my conversation with Major Soames that the RUC have not been told about this."

There was a brief silence. Then the MA opened the door and shouted to the ADC, who was pretending not to be listening.

"Get the chief constable's personal staff officer on the line immediately, and tell the senior RUC liaison officer to come up here *right now*. I'll be in with the general."

The MA strode across to the GOC's door, where he paused.

"If he even makes the dinner tonight," he added to the ADC, "he's definitely going to be late. So tell the Secretary of State's office we've got an operational complication. But tell them nothing more. You've got that?"

Carragher was sitting at the kitchen table drinking tea. When the call came, he strode through to the narrow hallway where the newly installed telephone was on the floor, beside a brand-new Belfast telephone directory and the *Yellow Pages*. He had to squat down as the handset's curly lead was too short for him to stand.

"You asked we deal directly?"

The man's voice was deep with a strong Belfast accent, educated, but little indication of anything else.

"I did," he replied. "It's better if others don't know."

"It always is," came the deadpan reply.

Carragher sat down in the bare cold hall, his back to the wall.

"You'll have something for me?" he said.

"Your man is still in the North," said the voice very slowly. "He tried to leave, but in the end didn't."

Carragher picked up the dialler unit and stood up.

"What do you mean 'tried to leave'?"

"He was arrested, and I can tell you where he's being kept."

"Go on."

Every tout in the world was like this, lining you up for money, or for all manner of other motives and plays. And as Carragher wasn't paying him and this guy was anonymous, it could only be about getting Carragher to do something for *him*. Carragher was being manipulated, and both of them knew it.

"They've taken him to the Castlereagh Holding Centre."

"Aye right, of course they have," said Carragher contemptuously. "Where they'll be rinsing him until he confesses. That's what they do with all the Army officers who kill our people."

There was silence at the other end. Carragher was risking termination of the call, but he also knew this guy needed him to believe what he was being told.

The line remained open, but the caller wasn't offering anything more. It was Carragher who broke the silence.

"Castlereagh's a fucking fortress," he said. "What's the point of telling me he's there?"

Another silence on the line. Carragher used the time to answer his own question.

"OK," said Carragher. "So you need to tell me when they're moving him. Can you do that?"

"Stay by this phone," said the voice, then rang off.

Riley remained in the headquarters, sitting on a sofa in the corridor outside the GOC's office suite, despite being blanked by the MA. Eventually the ADC suggested he should return to the Mess.

"We'll let you know immediately there's any news."

Riley walked down the stairs into the G1/G4 complex. Major Soames was not in his office, and the staff of the military police registry office had packed up for the night, leaving clear desks and the lights on. Before going back up to the GOC's corridor, Riley wrote a memo to Soames advising him to get in contact as soon as possible.

But Riley had run out of ideas. He'd pulled all the legal levers he could think of, and as far as he could see, was now an "unhelpful" outsider to be ignored; even disciplined if he made any mistakes.

The GOC's outer office was now empty, the MA and ADC having shut up shop and gone home while Riley was looking for Soames. As downstairs, their desks were clear, with nothing to indicate if anything had been done about Straker.

"What are you doing in here?"

The GOC's duty clerk – a sergeant major – had come in from the corridor and was staring at him with unconcealed hostility.

"So they've all gone home," said Riley. "Did they leave any messages for me?"

"No."

"That's disappointing."

"And I need you also to go home – or wherever you stay," said the duty clerk rudely, a clear indication of how Riley was now regarded up here.

"Or I'll call the guard," he added.

"I see," replied Riley. "I wouldn't want to embarrass you."

The duty clerk didn't respond but stood aside as Riley pushed past him out of the office.

Riley went down to the far end of the G1/G4 basement to his own office, where he made a cup of instant coffee. Riley had very seriously rocked the military boat. His boss, the colonel legal, was not around, distancing himself with all the prudence of a lawyer safeguarding his military pension. He might even have flown back to the mainland on leave. And maybe, thought Riley, he would be sensible to do the same? Back off, go ultra-low-key to complete his time here. Get the tick-in-the-box he needed from the Director Army Legal Services at the MoD, then become a Deputy Judge Advocate.

Straker became aware of shouting and loud banging from the next interrogation room; somebody was very angry and demanding answers to questions. But although he knew this was all part of the interrogation process, and that these noises were almost certainly recordings, he found himself hoping not to have to face that interrogator.

But the question of his identification and shooting of Máire Carragher was troubling him, and he was reliving that split second of identifying her. He'd been right about who she was; but just the same, fighting to face down the certainty of the interrogator's analysis, he was beginning to disbelieve himself.

"*He's working you,*" said Tiger. "*It's what these arseholes do.*"

Straker then felt a flash of something different – a reality he could control. So he tried to analyse his circumstances rather than what these people were saying.

He compared this with the interrogation exercises they'd been put through at the Pontrilas training camp's interrogation centre. These people here hadn't yet hooded him, turned on the white noise, or forced him into stress positions – as the Joint Services Interrogation people did on their exercises. These guys would do all that with their usual clients, which indicated that either it was all yet to come, or that they didn't dare…

His shivering was getting worse. *This is a negative spiral,* he thought – shivering, then feeling frightened. But he wasn't frightened. Therefore he must be cold.

Looking around the room, he noticed air vents in the wall. He got up and walked over. They were gently blowing cold air from a hidden air conditioner down on where he was sitting directly below the vent. He moved the chair and immediately felt better.

It was probably very early hours on Sunday morning. But he had only his interrupted counting by which to judge. Depending on the time, his blood pressure would be nearing rock bottom, and so should soon be rising. This would also make him feel better. Plus they hadn't managed to get the "good cop, bad cop" routine working.

Straker now knew the process. What else could he deduce? Jacko, the Farmer, and Hooves?

Jacko was back in Hereford. And there was no way the RUC would have been able to order them to come here.

"*Tick tock,*" said Tiger.

Straker thought of them taking his watch, then of the interrogator looking at his own watch. They could only hold him here for so long. And in that time, they needed him to have signed a statement.

The door crashed open. The older man came in, carrying a file.

"OK... I've now got statements from your guys, although the sergeant major – Jackson – wasn't very helpful. He's saying that he told you she wasn't Carragher's wife, which we know isn't true. He's trying to save his own skin, which isn't going to work.

"But apart from that, what they're saying makes total sense – that you all identified Máire Carragher when she first appeared. Jackson confirms that her mugshot is on the wall of the Group briefing room – and a whole load of other Army ops rooms across the Province – so you'd all recognise her."

"That's bullshit," croaked Straker.

The man looked surprised. "Really? Do you want to see the statements?"

He opened the file and showed Straker the top sheet of a type-written form.

"I can't let you read them, obviously, but I expect you recognise the signatures?"

Straker didn't even bother looking.

"They also say that you ordered them to lie in their initial statements."

"About what?"

"About how you all discussed who she was... So you see, there's a choice here. If you confirm their story – which makes total sense – we can forget about them lying. Plus as I've already suggested, it would leave them out of this whole thing. I'm sure that's what you – as a responsible, caring officer – would want to do.

"Then, of course, your recognising she was a known terrorist excuses you for thinking she might be a threat to you. That's nothing more than manslaughter – if that, even – and I'm sure the Diplock judge would be sympathetic."

Straker knew this guy was spinning nothing more than bullshit. But he'd responded to his question. Then he felt a sharp stab of fear as he imagined a civilian trial and not a court-martial.

He *then* saw the other man had spotted the tell.

This guy was a lot sharper than the others – which frightened Straker. He felt suddenly disorientated and ill, fearful that he was now falling inexorably into the interrogation process.

Straker had a pre-prepared story for being captured by the IRA.

Having something to talk about without endangering operations or your comrades was an important psychological tool, keeping your balls out of the vice for a little bit longer. Under the right circumstances, a cover story could even be used as a fight-back weapon.

But these people were from his own side. Straker had nothing he could use against them. And he knew he was being lured into this conversation, and that showing his fear was a big win for the interrogator.

Straker was suddenly filled with an unbearable, dreadful conviction that he'd made a mistake. But he couldn't work out what that mistake was. He saw the image of the pregnant women and her pram, then her face as she lay dying after he'd shot her. This brought anger and dread, an unbearable combination he could not control.

Suddenly his burden of guilt and fear was replaced by a feeling of absolute clarity. *Heaven might well offer redemption to warriors*, he thought, *but only if you fight for it. That's the point, isn't it?*

He jumped to his feet, head-butting the interrogator before punching him in the throat, then went down strangling him. The last thing he remembered was being dragged off, and the first of the truncheon blows.

The interview room felt constricted, its centre brightly lit with dark walls; a box, like it was a black square on a chess board. He imagined the fingers of a huge hand reaching down to make the next move. But these faceless bloody people were just pawns. He was a knight.

CHAPTER 39

Major Carlisle's photos showed the remains of Carragher's extension antenna, which had run to the fence, then up onto the washing line and across the yard. 321 Company had carried out a series of tests with model aircraft controller transmitters, using similar wire-extension antennae. These tests showed that signals using a controller of the type described by Captain Straker in his statement could have triggered the first bomb, and that the second bomb could also have been triggered by radio.

So when the 321 EOD Company report was ready and had been exhaustively checked, the OC had personally delivered it to the Army Legal Service office at Headquarters Northern Ireland. The report explained in great detail the likely size and design of both bombs, as well as their detonation methods. The camera and copies of the negatives and prints were included, which later that day the ALS sergeant major signed over to the police.

The report itself was copied immediately to the chief constable's office at the RUC headquarters at Knock. Then – after a hurried dialogue between the chief constable, the head of RUC Special Branch, the colonel legal, the HQNI chief of staff and the GOC himself – the operational sensitivity of the report was upgraded so that it could not be shown to anybody else in the military headquarters.

That was when the colonel legal suspended the Board of Inquiry, telling its president in confidence that he didn't know when it would reconvene. The board members – staff officers from outside HQNI – returned back across the water to Headquarters UK Land Forces in Wilton.

This new security classification meant that the EOD report could not be passed down to the RUC SOCO team at Queen Street, Belfast. And so the technical details of this attack were withheld from the detectives working Straker's murder case, who continued their investigation without the proof that he was telling the truth.

And now, as nobody could see where this was going, they stopped thinking about it.

And so less than two weeks after the bomb attack, the RUC got what they wanted and the line of shops and Straker's OP building were bulldozed away, an inexplicable void amid the tight grid of Falls Road terraced houses. A progression of lorries, grinding their way noisily through the narrow streets, would remove every last trace to landfill, an acrid-smelling rubble of bricks, dirt, burned plastic, and twisted metal.

"Thanks for getting back to me," said Chapman blithely as soon as Arrosa's call was put through to him.

After the stress of tail-shaking and grim street telephone boxes, this annoyed her. And when he didn't say anything despite his having ordered this call, her irritation increased.

"You called *me*," she stated, after a silence. "But I have to say that I'm not happy with what's happening over here."

"How so?"

"You seem to know more about it than me, so why don't you tell me?"

Chapman laughed.

"I can always rely on you," he said. "I suppose I do."

"Do what?"

"Know more."

"Is that because you're stirring it up?"

He laughed again.

"I'm not sure what you mean by 'stirring it up'," he replied. "But with no jurisdiction, that's all I can do."

"What's particularly bothering me," she said, "is how so many people over here get to know things – and so quickly."

"That's the nature of the place," he replied.

"But is that what you meant by me stirring things up?" he added after a pause, the amusement suddenly absent from his voice.

"Yes," she said.

There was another silence, which this time she wasn't going to break.

"There *is* something I can tell you," he said finally. "Our contractor friend who interests you so much is in Castlereagh."

She didn't understand what that meant, so she kept quiet.

"They'll let him out soon enough. Apparently, he went on the run."

"He's been arrested?"

"I'm not sure of the technicalities, but they took him there last night."

"Is this why you called me – to tell me this?"

"The RUC are hellbent on stamping out the Army's undercover stuff," he replied, ignoring the question. "They're probably trying to teach the Army a lesson."

"You don't sound very concerned."

"I have no jurisdiction," he repeated. "I think the police are wrong, and we know historically how effective the Army can be. But this is not the Far East. It's UK politics driving this, not action, effectiveness, or results."

He'd abandoned veiled speech in favour of clarity, in order that Arrosa understand where he stood.

"In any case," he concluded, "the captain's people always take care of their own."

This was a massive sloping of shoulders. He wasn't responsible, but Arrosa did not respect his indifference to the injustice it seemed was being perpetrated here. Knowing should entail a requirement to do something about it. But this went against all her training – as he'd just made clear to her.

"So, as *you* know this," she said carefully, "it seems to me very likely that my principal will *also* get to know."

"Why?"

"That's how things have been going lately out here... People getting to know things remarkably quickly."

"I suppose so," he said. "That's Ireland for you. They call it the *craic* – as you probably told me."

And he rang off.

But Arrosa sat for a long time, both angry and thoughtful. Why had he told her this? Was she supposed to take some kind of action? She was, however, now certain that Carragher would get to know that Straker was in Castlereagh.

Unless she could leverage what Chapman had told her to increase her credibility, her long-term arms-trade intelligence mission was now sidelined. She was not getting drawn into Chapman's mischief-making.

But more than anything else, she was very angry; outraged that a hero who'd done his duty and risked his life protecting others was being treated as a criminal; disgusted with the Army for not protecting its own. Chapman's offhand refusal to engage seemed cavalier, and made her doubt for the first time whether MI6 would uphold their side of the bargain and protect *her* if this went sideways.

Jacko's personal rule was never to reveal anything more than the minimum needed to achieve what he wanted – especially to Ruperts. And he never brought problems to the attention of the hierarchy unless he knew exactly what was needed to solve them. Usually they took him seriously, then did what he suggested – but not on this occasion.

He'd done as Riley asked, and now emerged from the head-shed feeling over-exposed and slightly foolish. He found this very disconcerting.

The RSM had listened to him and asked questions for thirty minutes, and then taken him in for fifteen minutes with the CO. The ALS captain took notes. But they'd not said anything much in response, and to his self-disgust he'd not pushed it with them.

This was too far above his pay grade. He thought they'd know what to do, and would then do it. But they hadn't. So now, standing outside in the darkness of the potholed car park, he realised they'd been humouring him, which made him angry. He must have seemed naïve, he thought; lost in Rupert-land where his concerns counted for nothing.

It had been "Thanks for that, Sergeant Major, leave it with us…" And the RSM had even added a private little word in his ear at the end:

"Don't worry anymore about this, Jacko. We're already on it."

It was the "we're already on it" that got Jacko thinking.

He went back to his office and sat behind an empty desk; the overhead neon tube was much too bright for the tiny space. Even though the radiator was cold, the hoop-shaped hobbit house was too warm and stuffy. He opened the Nissen hut's four-pane window casement.

He thought briefly about going across to the med centre to talk to the doc about Straker. But as the Hereford Army Legal Service captain had not seemed anything like as concerned as Captain Riley, he decided not to risk stirring things up over there.

But he couldn't just leave it. Which was when Captain Riley paged him.

"They're not going to push it with the RUC," said Riley. "Maybe they can't – and they don't want to have a row protecting Captain Straker. So I can't get him out of Castlereagh any time soon. But I did speak with the doctor at Musgrave Park, who's extremely worried and spoke with his medic colonel."

"I don't suppose there's any lines of communication for Army medics to force the RUC to hand him over?" said Jacko.

"A combination of them, with me continuing to press, should eventually get him handed over. But as we don't know what this is about, it could take days – or God knows how long if they're serious about a murder charge…"

"Could the Musgrave Park medics talk to our MO, to force the headshed here to take it more seriously?"

"I can ask, but nobody seems very concerned about the medical side of this. I pushed it really hard this end. But something else seems to have become more important than Captain Straker's welfare."

That's the nub of it, thought Jacko. *Everyone else is thinking of themselves and backing off.*

"Even so, can you try that please, Captain Riley?" said Jacko. "It might give me another opportunity to stick my nose in – as I've just been told it's not my business."

After the call, Jacko turned off the lights and left the Nissen hut, locking the main door as he left. He was very out of sorts, and didn't want to go home to be grumpy with his wife and daughter, or to the Sergeants' Mess, where wise-arse people with snippets of rumours would try to pump him for information or take the piss.

Instead he walked across the big and mostly empty car park by the Paludrin Club, which – this being a Saturday night – had a line of girls queued up outside the wire waiting to be allowed in. He pushed past them and entered the club, then after ordering a beer, stood at the bar looking round at the alcove tables.

The Farmer loomed out of the semi-darkness and waved him over. He and Hooves were tucked away, low profiling, probably for the same reasons Jacko was avoiding the Sergeants' Mess.

"Not downtown, then?" said Jacko.

"It's going to be quieter in here tonight," said the Farmer. "And there might be some keenie tottie to chat up. I recognise a couple of nurses."

Jacko nodded to Hooves, who moved himself along the bench seat to make room.

"So what's on the schedule?"

The Farmer shrugged, and Hooves shook his head.

"Nothing," said Hooves. "It's like we're not back yet – neither of us is even on the nominal roll."

"Somebody decided you can't be sent off on anything new until whatever this is about gets resolved," said Jacko, then took a long pull at his pint.

"Yep," Jacko continued, "I'm on Christmas leave, and Captain Straker's in Castlereagh."

Both Hooves and the Farmer looked shocked.

"What do you mean 'in Castlereagh'?" said the Farmer.

"Arrested, admitted, banged-up – he's in fucking Castlereagh."

"Jesus H. Christ," said the Farmer. "He should be in hospital."

They sat in silence.

"So what are we going to do about it?" said Hooves.

"Do about what?"

"Getting him out...?"

The silence that followed made Hooves feel a bit stupid.

"He's right, though," said the Farmer. "He needs to be out of that place – and out of Northern Ireland."

"It's like nobody else is interested," said Hooves.

"That's because nobody else is," said the Farmer.

This made Jacko angry – irrationally so, because this was exactly what he was thinking.

"It's that caring, sharing time of year," he snarled. "But what the fuck can *we* do?"

The Farmer looked across the table at Hooves, who'd blushed and was glad it was dark.

"I don't know," said the Farmer in his slow, countryman voice. "But us sitting here isn't helping Captain Straker."

There was a silence.

"So I say we go back over," he continued, "and work things out from there."

"Christmas leave starts next week," said Jacko.

"Exactly," replied the Farmer.

Jacko didn't respond. He was thinking about his wife and daughter, and the presents he hadn't yet found time to buy.

"He needs a medic to bring him back," continued the Farmer. "I'm not exaggerating. And that's not counting for what they do to people in Castlereagh."

Jacko remained silent.

"He didn't hesitate," said the Farmer.

"We tried holding him down," added Hooves, catching on rapidly. "But that didn't work."

"What are you two talking about?" snapped Jacko.

"Going into that building when you was trapped," said Hooves. "Before he went in to rescue you…"

Jacko was still trying to think about the family Christmas that was waiting for him ten minutes' drive from the camp gates. His visualisation changed. As he'd done so many times in the past, he was now imagining his wife and daughter sitting round the tree, just the two of them on their own again.

And then he thought of the times on operations when he'd had the same visualisation, but of how they'd be if he never came home.

And then he thought of Straker.

"Peace on earth, goodwill to all men," he said finishing his pint. Procrastination was an ugly word. Rightly so.

"Stay here," he added. "I'm going back to my office to make some calls."

CHAPTER 40

The E5 office was empty, with just Billy Flynn and Ciarán standing talking. When Ciarán's phone rang, Flynn motioned to him to answer it.

"E5, Moffat."

"It's me," Ciarán heard Rós say. "Can you talk?"

As Ciarán looked up, Billy Flynn turned away and went back into his office, shutting the door behind him.

"Of course," said Ciarán.

"Some of those students I was telling you about are saying the captain is in Castlereagh..."

A set of questions sprang immediately to Ciarán's mind, which he realised had been there since his last conversation with Rós. But there was something about her downplayed urgency and immediacy that led him to quietly respond: "We already know."

"I thought Castlereagh was only for terrorists?"

"It's one of the holding centres for people suspected of terrorism."

"That's not what people say."

"So what might these people say, then?"

"Ciarán! You know what I'm talking about here. Don't treat me like a child. It's the central place where you run the interrogations of terrorists. OK, so maybe this guy should be investigated, but why would you treat him like a terrorist? He's obviously not one!"

"A crime may have been committed, which needs investigation," he said gently.

"So why was he taken there?"

"We don't know – but I'd like to know how *you* know about this...?"

"It's a rumour, Ciarán – you know, like when you told me he's likely to be charged with murder."

"And why are you bothering me with rumours, Rós?"

"Because I trust you. And this man needs help. You'd surely *expect* me to ask you if a person I knew was arrested and people were saying he was in Castlereagh."

A silence. Then:

"So, do you know this man?" he said.

This was the big question, and even the slightest hesitation in this instant would lead inexorably to Rós's cover being compromised – as she'd debated with herself continuously since her last telecon with Chapman.

"We already discussed this, Ciarán," she said angrily, using impatience to mask her fear. "And obviously, no!"

She quickly continued: "But the bigger question is, how do *you* know he's in there – is he in there officially?"

"No, it's not official."

She'd found the nerve. Ciarán's police voice changed back to a tired version of his own.

"He's been injured – inside Castlereagh, which they have to report. And my department sees such reports pretty much immediately."

"So why didn't you get to know he was in there to start with?"

This was one question too many. But Rós wanted to keep him on the defensive, and as this was probably on his mind too, she calculated that he'd answer.

"It sometimes happens," he said quietly. "It ought not to be like that. But you know – delayed paperwork, clerks off sick…"

"And when are you and your immediately-sees-everything department going to rescue him from these people?"

This sarcasm was delivered without acrimony, emphasising her disappointment and impatience.

"Tomorrow morning," he said.

She hadn't expected him to reply, so didn't immediately scream "why not tonight" at him – which was how she felt.

"Seven a.m.," he continued. "When the night shift comes off. He's being looked after by their doctor."

Rós left it at that.

Their instructions had been that the captain had to incriminate himself on tape, and also that the entirety of the tape had to comply with normal police questioning rules, with nothing defence counsel could use in court to suggest coercion.

By the time they'd got the captain under restraint, and the lead interrogator had received medical treatment, he'd calmed down sufficiently to realise the seriousness of the situation. But he wasn't paid to take decisions, just get results. So the captain was left with the doctor, to get got ready for another session once they'd been given the medical OK.

The doctor had been there all along, as required by regulations. But what none of them had realised was that after the take-down he'd filed a medical "damage" report – a PF09, which the duty clerk had faxed out, again as per regulations. The doctor and clerk had covered their arses.

So as soon as the lead interrogator realised this, very early on the Sunday morning, he phoned his boss, who was deeply unhappy at being woken. As the honorary president of Ards Rugby Football Club, he was not long abed after an extensive celebration of the day's win over Queen's University in the Ulster Senior League.

"I hope you're not calling to congratulate us," he said.

"No, sir."

"But I'm hoping you've got good news regarding our Army man?"

"It's a 'no, sir' to that as well, I'm afraid."

"So why are you wasting my time now? Phone me in the morning when you've got him incriminating the others."

"He's not incriminating anybody, sir. And we haven't got him to say anything to incriminate himself."

"Just keep at it, man. I really don't need this..."

The lead interrogator very much didn't need either this conversation, or to be still in the office when he should undoubtedly be in the sickbay. He was pretty sure his jaw was broken.

"This isn't why I called you, sir."

There was silence on the line.

"Are you still there, sir?"

The lead interrogator was having problems speaking clearly.

"Of course I fucking well am. Spit it out."

The lead interrogator decided to get straight to the point.

"He's been hurt – too badly injured to be kept here. The doctor is refusing to take further responsibility. So before I report the injuries, I'm giving you a heads-up."

His boss was drunk – as usual on a rugby weekend. And it was vital he didn't interfere.

"What do you mean, 'he's been hurt'?"

"He attacked me, and was injured in the take-down."

"How badly?"

"He's unconscious."

"How long ago?"

His boss had an uncanny ability to consume Bass and Bushmills. But although he could stand his ground and appear relatively sensible, he was unlikely to remember the details of this conversation. So the lead interrogator lied to him.

"Twenty minutes."

"Fuck."

"The doctor will say whatever we tell him, and it wasn't like we'd been at him for very long, or even made him adopt stress positions."

"So I take it he hadn't incriminated himself…?"

"He wasn't far off."

"You bunch of fucking eejits."

"He seemed disoriented and frightened enough to be processed…"

"Yet he manipulated *you*?"

"Manipulated?"

"Tricked you into using unreasonable force."

"I'd say that the captain proved to be completely unlike what he'd seemed during questioning, and as we observed him in the interrogation room during the waiting process periods."

"Save that guff for the RUC Internal Investigation team. Everything could have been glossed over except for you guys taking him out – for the simple reason that if this guy dies, you're all going down for manslaughter."

"We did nothing wrong. The schedule of questioning was by the book, furniture in the holding cell was removed, and the lights left on for the captain's safety. He attacked us and we were defending ourselves."

"If you think Internal Investigation will buy into that, then good luck to you's. You forget who this guy is…"

There was another silence.

"And not only is the interview unusable as evidence," his boss continued, "it could render you all liable for prosecution anyway, if the tape somehow gets to leave Castlereagh. Now fuck off and sort this out."

The lead interrogator hung up the phone, then reached over to switch off the tape recorder.

The rest of them were outside in the corridor. He told the doctor to make whatever medical arrangements he saw fit, and spent a terse ten minutes with the other two in his office.

He then instructed the holding centre admin team that the captain was no longer helping them with their inquiries and to let him go just before their shift ended, at 7am. They could inform the Army or do whatever else they needed to do – he didn't care.

He was very surprised when they told him the doctor had ordered that four hours ago. But it didn't matter.

He removed all documentation and listings related to the captain, placing the paperwork along with two reels of tape – one from his telephone conversation, one from Straker's interview – in an unmarked envelope that he put into his briefcase. Amid the shift changeover, nobody would notice the captain leaving.

The lead interrogator then telephoned another person he knew would find this interesting.

Immediately after the informer's call, Carragher sent Duffy down to Castlereagh to work out some reasonably safe way of getting eyes on the entrance. He'd then paid for a couple of dickers to join him.

Roxy was ready, now slumped on the front-room sofa watching a cowboy film on television, his feet comfortably resting on the black canvas gun bag. That was all they could do.

So by the time the second phone call came, Carragher was well and truly baited.

"He's being released at seven a.m.," said the voice. "That's it." And rang off.

Carragher was hooked. Somebody wanted him outside Castlereagh at seven the next morning. And that somebody knew he was going to be there. And the joke of it was that he *would* be there.

It was also laughably dangerous. A long street with the four-storey police barracks on one side and an industrial site on the other, with a large carpark. The police barracks' entrance was right in the middle, with its vehicle access gate to one side, surrounded by wire fencing and corrugated metal screening with spikes on top. There were security lights and an inner yard before you even got into the main parking area – like the outer bailey of a medieval castle.

The actual entrance looked like a miniature fortress in itself, with weapon slits along the front, bulletproof glass and all the rest of it. The whole street would be covered by some kind of surveillance and probably also gunfire from positions Carragher hoped Duffy would have ascertained by the time he got there.

Duffy had not been happy. But he'd been told what to do, and Carragher had no choice but to let him get on with it.

That night, as Carragher tried to get some sleep before joining Duffy outside Castlereagh, he had a quite different dream. He'd been wandering through a beautiful afternoon summer fair beside a tree-lined river and an American paddle boat, past women with elaborate hats parasols, strolling and talking. He realised that the purpose of this fair was to witness a hanging; then he realised as he walked around and people nodded to him, that he was the person to be executed.

Arrosa went back to her flat, but could not settle. She needed sleep, but once she regained the security of her own territory, the tiredness was replaced by anxiety. She'd really pushed it with Ciarán, and had been surprised when he'd answered all her questions. The information he'd given had only short-term value, but he shouldn't have told her. So did this mean he didn't consider her a threat? She'd succeeded in manipulating him, which meant she had to consider that he could be manipulating her.

Specifically, if she acted on his information and he saw her there, what could that tell him? This was not a fanciful question; he was a Special Branch intelligencer, in a senior enough position to release classified information to outsiders if he thought that might be advantageous. He would only do that with a very good reason, for a specific purpose. But she couldn't work out what that reason or purpose might be.

This bothered her. The more she analysed, the less satisfactory became the answers. There was no advantage for Ciarán – or at least none she could deduce from what she knew. But thanks to him, she now had a time and a place where she knew she could see Straker. Somehow this was more important than anything else, and she knew she had to be there. So she stopped thinking about it; at which point she decided she would go there for 7am.

Immediately she made the decision, her anxiety evaporated. This told her she'd done what her subconscious had been wanting, which usually worked out.

She set her alarm for 0630 – the 24-hour clock yet another military efficiency drummed into them by the SAS, and was asleep within seconds of her head touching the pillow.

CHAPTER 41

SUNDAY 14 DECEMBER

After the Máire Carragher shooting, the General's Aide had kept the general up to speed with the Board of Inquiry. But a few days ago, he'd asked the chief clerk for an update, to be told – rudely, he thought – that he was no longer on the distribution list; excluded from the paperwork. The MA was tight-lipped and preoccupied so he hadn't dared to raise this with him.

Now this morning, walking in darkness across from the Mess, the aide was thinking through what he'd overheard the night before. He decided he wanted to help the lawyer.

But as an acting captain on loan from the general's regiment – and not a trained staff officer – he was only supposed to know enough to ensure the general was smartly turned out and wearing the right clothes, with a brief about the people he was meeting. Sometimes he carried the general's case. The Royal Military Police bodyguard team handled everything else.

The aide took over the office at 0500 from the duty sergeant major, to be ready for when the MA arrived at 0600. Captain Riley was already there, hanging around in the corridor outside, as he had been late the night before.

The duty sergeant major made some disparaging comment about "instant captains".

"He's actually a substantive captain," the aide replied pointedly, who didn't like the duty sergeant major.

"Unlike me. Or is that what you were getting at, Sergeant Major?"

Hooves and the Farmer had received Jacko's early morning pager message with just enough time to organise themselves, then drive in the Farmer's civvie Land Rover the eleven miles out of Bradbury

Lines to the Pontrilas training area, where they parked round the back of the training hangar. When Jacko's headlights swept down the narrow access road, it was three hours before dawn, the car park empty, the whole complex dark and unoccupied, as you'd expect it to be so ludicrously early on a bitterly cold Sunday morning.

Hooves had the passenger window open by just an inch, listening for the helicopter turbine. He got out and ran across to the upwind side of the helipad, carrying a torch in each hand to marshal it in. The Farmer locked his Land Rover and walked to the edge of the rotor circle carrying a black holdall.

Once the Scout's four-bladed main rotor stopped turning, Jacko got out of his car and walked across to talk with the pilot. After a quick chat, he gave a thumbs-up. Hooves and the Farmer crammed into the back seats, while Jacko strapped himself into the front. They took off into pitch black, rising immediately to 3,000 feet, then turning with the street lamps of Hereford glistening like Christmas lights to their right.

"You two OK in the back?" said Jacko over the intercom, once they'd settled into their north-north-west course, flying into darkness. "You guys didn't have to come," he added.

"Yes, we did," said Hooves.

"What time is breakfast at the Little Chef?" said the Farmer.

Jacko turned and looked over into the back. Then he laughed.

"In need of a carb injection, Farmer?"

"I might fade away otherwise."

"So you stayed on last night in the club?"

"Actually, *I* didn't," said the Farmer. "But Hooves here trapped, so he probably needs one too."

"Well done, young man," said Jacko. "Hope my page didn't upset things. Although it's not like they play hard to get – but what do I know about that sort of thing."

They were flying over blackness, with just occasional chains of village streetlights, and dots of light from isolated farmhouses.

"What's the route?" asked Hooves.

The pilot, an 8 Flight senior NCO, pointed across to the left.

"Radnor's over there. We're crossing into Wales at Presteigne, on to Holyhead, then across the water to rendezvous at sparrow's with your Hertz rent-a-van at the civvie terminal at Belfast Aldergrove."

“This a training flight, guys,” said Jacko. “All filed and above board, with us as the cargo. But we’ll not be checking in with the Det, and our mate Andy here doesn’t know anything about that or anything else, do you, mate?”

“They don’t call us Mushroom Flight for nothing,” he said.

Riley had used up all his leverage, and although he’d made sure to be in the GOC’s corridor by 0500 when the office opened up, he didn’t have a plan.

He’d walked back down to his office for a think, when he saw the ADC wandering uncertainly along the deserted back end of the G1/G4 corridor, peering at door numbers. He had come down the fire-escape stairs, as if trying to avoid being seen.

Riley waved him quickly into his tiny office and closed the door.

“You’ve heard something,” he said immediately.

“Yes,” said the aide. “They’re releasing Captain Straker at seven a.m. this morning. Major Soames is going to get him.”

“Is that as in ‘releasing him to the custody of the RMP’, or just releasing him?” asked Riley.

“I don’t know, but Major Soames said he’d take some of his people down there with him.”

“What do you know about the Board of Inquiry?”

“Which one?”

“The one Captain Straker’s being kept here for.”

The ADC looked uncertain. “It’s being run by G4 Legal, so I thought you’d know more about that than me.”

Riley shook his head. “I don’t – and you’re right, I should,” he said.

The aide moved towards the door, then paused, turning back towards Riley and talking in a very low voice.

“I handle the briefs for all Boards of Inquiry,” he said. “The general doesn’t like being blind-sided by anything that might come at him from the chief constable, so the recorders keep us appraised of anything that looks like it might be of interest to the RUC.”

“While the board is in progress?”

“Yes,” said the aide, looking uncomfortable.

“So much for judicial independence,” observed Riley.

"Oh, we don't interfere," the aide said quickly. "It's just a heads-up – for information only."

"Let's not go into that," said Riley. "So you're saying there's been nothing across your desk about this board – even though it could lead to an SAS officer being charged with murder?"

The aide nodded.

"So they're doing it properly, are they?" said Riley. "This one time, letting the board do its job…?"

"I don't know about that," muttered the aide.

"Neither do I," replied Riley.

"What I suspect," continued the aide carefully, "is that the MA is dealing directly with SO1 Legal, then briefing the general himself – verbally only. And Colonel Legal's been in with the general rather more frequently than usual…"

These were Riley's bosses, who – since his declaration of legal support for Straker – had been noticeably and uncharacteristically silent.

"So we can take it that Captain Straker is unlikely to be allowed to return to Hereford – which is where he should be right now?"

Riley didn't wait for an answer, but picked up his phone and dialled Jacko's pager number.

They landed at Aldergrove in accordance with the civvie flight plan Jacko's mate had filed very late last night. The tower had queried the slowness of their approach, until the point at which they were visual when the controller realised they were a helicopter.

They landed in the civvie helicopter section, and the pilot pointed across to a white Transit van parked beside the small terminal.

"The paperwork's with the receptionist," he said. "I can stay here on the pan for a couple of hours max. The man with the clipboard comes checking at seven a.m. That's when they send a bill to the MoD. We come in like this sometimes, so it's not unusual. No one's going to know – at least, not unless some MoD clerk questions the extra cost."

The rotors slowed and stopped. The pilot reached up to apply the brake, then flicked through the sequence of switches to shut down the engine.

Jacko turned round to the Farmer and pointed at the van.

"I hope it's got the second row of seats," he said. "But just sign it out as quickly as you can so we can evaporate from here."

Jacko got out and stretched his back. The airport was cold and deserted, and once the engine was shut down, it was also quiet, with no aircraft on the main runway. As you'd expect, they were the only helicopter on the pan.

Hooves was fumbling with the rear door, so Jacko opened it for him. But instead of getting out, Hooves shuffled awkwardly across the seat, stepping over a large black bag, which was on the floor behind where Jacko had been sitting.

"Hand that out to me," said Jacko, but Hooves was already easing both legs down on the skid. "What have you got in there?"

"Just radios and a couple of other things I thought we might need," replied Hooves.

"Let's get clear of the aircraft then," said Jacko. "The sooner we're gone, the better."

Hooves turned back to the rear of the Scout, seeming to be struggling with the bag, which he finally heaved over the skids and set down on the concrete.

"Hang on a sec," said Jacko angrily. "Is that what I think it is...?"

He strode over and opened the double zip.

"For fuck's sake, Hooves. Do you have any idea how many rules you've just broken?"

Hooves shrugged his shoulders.

"Breaking a few more isn't going to make much difference," he replied. "Having is a lot better than wishing..."

Jacko's reply was interrupted by the return of the Farmer, who reached over into the bag and helped himself to a Browning and three loaded magazines.

Then Jacko's pager went off. It was Riley's number. But having been out of range during the flight, the page was over ninety minutes old. He swore to himself.

"Get us out of here asap, Farmer," he said. "And stop at the first telephone box you see."

CHAPTER 42

Carragher and Duffy were sitting just thirty metres from Castlereagh's fortified blockhouse entrance. They'd broken into a van in the industrial vehicle park just across the road, and were looking from across the road at Castlereagh's main entrance. Alexander Road was cold, dark, and deserted, and would remain so until the shift changeover. The gatehouse's bulletproof windows reflected the glare of the security lights.

A metal mesh surrounded the entire complex, higher than a tennis court, designed to detonate anti-tank missiles harmlessly in the air and preventing penetration of the walls. But illogically, the blockhouse itself wasn't protected by the mesh. One of their Libyan RPG-7s would destroy it.

Also, the gate's security lights were designed for checking vehicles coming in and out but not for perimeter security. This created two bowls of bright light: one in front of the gatehouse, and another just inside the outer vehicle gate, illuminating the search bay in front of the second inner gate. These lights blinded the security guards. No one could see them. Duffy had done well.

Carragher knew coming here was foolhardy. And now he was here, he was regretting it. But there were many more reasons for delay than for getting on with it; and this was his only chance to see the SAS captain. He stopped thinking about it. But if ever there was a place in Belfast not to go, Castlereagh was it.

"I can't see the two dickers you'd said would be here," muttered Duffy in his whiny, complaining voice.

"If you're scared you can fuck off," Carragher snarled, his own fear making him far more angry than the comment warranted.

Duffy had the sense to remain silent.

"So what's with the surveillance?" said Carragher, making an effort to be civil.

"Two Philips CCD cameras," replied Duffy. "Both covering the entrance. One might be a dummy but probably not."

"Patrols?"

"None that I've seen since getting here."

Carragher nodded. There was no need for the RUC to waste resources in this Protestant area.

Alexander Road was a huge dogleg joining Montgomery Road and Ladas Drive, speed-bumped to deter car bombers. These two roads were their escape routes: via the A23 onto the A55, then away south-west; and north-west to the A20 heading east out of Belfast.

"Vehicle traffic's been just vans and trucks for the industrial estate," continued Duffy. "It's now closed for the weekend. The next vehicles will be the screws coming on duty. They drive straight in through the security gates."

The buildings were set back from the road, shielded from view by twelve-foot steel fencing with spikes.

The van Duffy had broken into would not be used again until Monday, when they'd be long gone. He'd got in through the college playing fields behind where they were sitting, cutting the wire fencing into the rear of the car park. He'd brought Carragher in by the same route.

"They're bringing him out at seven a.m.," said Carragher. "I need you to confirm it's him."

"They'll do that in a vehicle," said Duffy. "Anyway, I only saw him in silhouette, at a distance."

"You told me you were close to Máire," said Carragher.

"I was, but there was all this dust everywhere, and I didn't see him until she blew the bomb, otherwise I'd have stopped him."

Carragher just nodded, refusing to let Duffy's weasel whining get to him.

"You're the *only* person who's seen him," Carragher replied, with a lack of expression that sounded far more threatening than his previous anger. "And once *I've* seen him, you'll be off the hook."

Carragher relaxed. Having forced the passenger seat back as far as it would go, he couldn't be seen, even if a patrol was to shine a light across the vehicle park.

They settled into the cold mindlessness of waiting. Carragher tried to think of this as yet another stakeout – one of countless recces for operations that mostly never happened. He'd rationalised the risk as part of obeying O'Donnell's order to kill Duffy. Once the SAS captain was identified, Duffy would be expendable.

But Carragher didn't want to kill Duffy. He wasn't their traitor, and he'd argued with O'Donnell that the bombing campaign needed him as the electrician.

But Carragher knew he needed to stop obsessing about the SAS captain. He'd already made one mistake telling Duffy he'd be off the hook once the captain was identified. He hoped Duffy hadn't noticed that.

But Duffy knew all this, and prompted by the conversation with Arrosa had already worked out where he stood. His aim was to get back to normal team duties. But although he knew a resumption of operations was planned, things could never be the same as before Máire joined them. Carragher was too disturbed, and even worse, didn't trust him anymore. Duffy needed to rectify this or Carragher would kill him.

Duffy was losing it; fearful of Carragher, but as an even more unbearable complication, unable to stop thinking about Máire. In life, even after she'd started going with Carragher he'd imagined being with her. But now she was dead, this had become much worse – as if her no longer being in the real world had unlocked his imagination.

His dream Máire was relentless, promising him everything – except her being dead turned it into a horror show. She was more real to him in death than she'd been in life. He'd thought about little else. He didn't care. Knowing he was lost was now a commitment. He was very fucked up.

There was an unpleasant logic to this. Máire hadn't seen him as a man. Then, in the moment with Máire's killer, he'd felt quite literally emasculated. Fear had chopped off his balls, and now he felt like Carragher's castrated mongrel. But he didn't dare to hate Carragher, despite Arrosa telling him how unfairly he was being treated.

Duffy had once imagined himself with both Arrosa and Máire – them together and him being invited to join in. And there'd been a moment with Arrosa back in the café when she'd seemed to become Máire. He couldn't forget this; her urging him to prove

Carragher wrong, this Arrosa-Máire offering him everything, as if this would satisfy them all.

Waiting for Jacko to return his page, Riley had fallen asleep. When the phone woke him, he was shocked to find it was after six.

"They're releasing him at seven a.m. – that's all I know," he said to Jacko. "Major Soames is going to get him. But I really don't like that idea so I'm going down there myself."

"Can you be outside Thiepval Barracks in half an hour?" replied Jacko.

"Yes, but—"

"Good, 'cos I'm at Aldergrove with backup. Walk out of the main gate and turn right up the hill into town and we'll pick you up – a white Transit van. We'll be coming towards you, and will do a three-point turn to go back the other way towards Belfast. Then you get in – OK?"

Riley put the phone down and ran out of the HQ to his room in the Officers' Mess, where he changed into civvies. It was raining, so he wore a large cagoule with running shoes so the guard would wave him through.

He was halfway up Magheralave Road when he saw the Transit. Its sidelights flashed once then made the turn. He continued jogging until it drew ahead of him and slowed. He recognised the Farmer driving, then the side door slid open and he was pulled inside.

"Very athletic," said Jacko. "Squaddies are the only people daft enough to run the streets round here."

"Exactly my logic," replied Riley. "The gate sentry didn't even log me out."

"Touché," said the Farmer in the most un-French accent imaginable.

"Fair enough," said Jacko. "And just so you know, we don't have a game plan. The best possible outcome would be if nobody gets to know we're here."

Riley looked puzzled, so Jacko looked pointedly across at Hooves.

"There are understandable and possibly legal complications."

"Don't tell me anything now," said Riley quickly. "We can sort stuff like that out once we've made sure Captain Straker is safe."

"That would entail him going with us rather than the military police?" asked Jacko.

"It would."

"I have an idea about that," continued Jacko. "But let's see how this develops."

"There's a security clampdown – no vehicles in or out," Moffat was told as he and Chief Superintendent Billy Flynn tried to drive through the Castlereagh security gates. "But you's can come in on foot."

After parking the car down Alexander Road, they were allowed through the mini-fortress street entrance, but then kept waiting in a wire-mesh cage by the main door before being escorted into the building.

They locked their side-arms into a weapons drawer then walked up several flights of open steel stairs. At the top of the building they went through double doors into a highly polished lino corridor with numbered green steel doors to either side. The whole place seemed empty, with no noises or other security staff.

The escort unlocked one of the green steel doors. It opened outwards, and he stood aside for them to enter. Moffat remained in the corridor leaning against the door, while Flynn stood in the doorway without entering the room.

"You both have to go in," said the escort.

"No, we don't, son," replied Flynn. "And you're not going anywhere either."

Their escort shook his head.

"I can see from where I'm standing here, this man needs medical help," said Flynn. "You pick up the corridor phone right now and tell your control room that Chief Superintendent Flynn says the doctor is to come up here immediately. Then you move away from this cell and wait twenty feet down the hall."

Flynn motioned Moffat to stay at the door while he went in to take a look at Straker.

"We're the white knights, Captain Straker," he said. "You shouldn't have been brought here, and we're getting you out."

Straker rolled over and stared blankly at Flynn. One eye was leached completely red, almost closed from puffed-up, shiny blue bruising. A deep cut on his cheekbone would need stitching, and his forehead was grazed as if by coarse-grade sandpaper.

"Do you understand me?" said Flynn.

Straker said nothing, the blankness on his face seeming to change slightly into an impassive mask.

"He doesn't believe you," said Moffat.

"I'm Chief Superintendent Flynn, and this is one of my officers, Detective Inspector Moffat. I run the Special Branch collation unit, which is how we got to know you were here. We're nothing to do with RUC Castlereagh. Us being here isn't part of what they were doing with you. Your interrogation is over. Do you understand that?"

Straker's impassivity altered very slightly, but the mask remained in place.

"It's over, Peter," repeated Flynn. "I know your name from the files I've been reading – and I think you probably recognise me from when I paid you a visit last week."

Straker nodded, although the mask remained in place.

"So we're getting the doctor to you, then we'll escort you out of here."

The roads were empty, and they'd just about enough time to cover the eleven miles to the Castlereagh Holding Centre.

"Our job is to make sure Captain Straker is safe," said Jacko. "But this whole bloody episode has been nothing but unpleasant surprises. We need to be ready for anything…"

"Which, thanks to Hooves, we are, Sergeant Major," interjected the Farmer, who only used people's ranks when making a point.

Jacko didn't rise to this, just nodded and pointed at the city map he'd been studying.

"So we'll go to the southern end of Alexander Road, drop Hooves off to do a steady walk-through from that end. We'll drive around the school to the other end of Alexander Road where we'll be able to see down to the entrance. They'll also be able to see us, and unless they're complete numpties, a white van isn't going to remain unnoticed for long. But we'll play it by ear, ready to drive down there, go in on foot – or whatever."

Jacko turned to Riley.

"But you're in charge of negotiations… which is all that's actually going to happen here."

"That means I need to be at the gates when the RMPs arrive," said Riley.

Jacko nodded. Riley was going to have to get out of the van at the top end of Alexander Road – and what, walk down from there on his own? He didn't like that idea.

"How about Captain Riley walks up with me?" said Hooves.

"And we'll be the cavalry ready to ride in," said the Farmer to Jacko.

Jacko looked at his watch.

"OK, and let's do a comms check right now before we get anywhere near the police barracks. And everyone be ready to leg it at any time – which means taking everything with us and abandoning the van."

The Farmer looked across at Jacko.

"Which would be why you got me to sign for it?"

"What name did you use?"

"Good point," replied the Farmer.

"We can report it stolen," said Jacko.

"Of course we can," said the Farmer.

Hooves scrambled to the rear of the van to mutter into his throat mic. In callsign order, they each clicked their transmission pressel switches.

"We're all clear both ways," he said.

"But let's all agree," said Jacko, looking pointedly at the lawyer, "we don't expect trouble or the need to do anything. We're just taking precautions…"

Arrosa tied her hair back underneath a thick woollen climbing hat. She wore it inside out so the pom-pom was underneath. It made her head look larger, but was warmer.

After opening the bedroom window to bitter cold and sleet, she pulled a fleece-lined jacket over her long-sleeved Lifa thermal top and tights, then shrugged into a battered blue Gore-Tex jacket with its large hood. The Ron Hill tracksuit trousers were skin-tight with no insulation, but even so, her running gear was too warm for much of an actual run, but for if she had to go static and observe without getting hypothermia. On a string around her neck she had a plastic envelope containing £500 in big notes and a passport; and the key to her flat.

She jogged slowly through empty streets, squinting against the sleety wind across the Ormeau Road Bridge and left along the side of Ormeau Park down to Ravenhill Park, to approach Castlereagh Barracks from Ladas Drive to the north. There were no bus shelters, so she tucked herself behind the pillar of the Ace Garage's Esso sign and took a long look up towards the junction with Alexander Road, and the flat roof of the barracks to the right.

A white Transit van came up Ladas Drive from behind her, moving slowly with its windscreen wipers brushing away half-melted snow. The passenger was looking across to the right. The van pulled over just before Alexander Road and sat parked on the corner facing oncoming traffic.

She looked at her watch, then continued jogging up Ladas Drive, crossing just in front of the Transit, then down Alexander Road towards the Castlereagh entrance. In her peripheral vision, she saw the driver of the Transit turn his head left to watch her. He'd be watching her all the way down the road – which was what happened when she wore the Ron Hills.

CHAPTER 43

"Why are they insisting I leave at seven a.m.?" said Straker.

He was sitting on the side of the prison bed, feeling light-headed having leaned down to tie his shoelaces. The doctor had cleaned him up, taping a couple of cuts for stitching elsewhere, then made a hurried exit.

"They have a process," said Moffat. "And it's better for us to wait here in the warm than to argue with them out at the gatehouse."

"Is that prison officer still outside?"

"Yes – we need him to unlock the doors."

Straker sounded anxious, so Moffat added: "But he can't hear what we're saying."

"And they told you to come here and pick me up?"

"Yes," said Moffat.

"At seven a.m.?"

"That's what they told us," said Billy Flynn.

"And they didn't let you bring in a vehicle?"

"There's some kind of alert," replied Moffat.

Straker went back to rubbing the side of his head, which hurt. He stopped and examined his fingers for blood. "You said something about the shift changing at seven," said Straker.

Billy Flynn wanted to give Straker his reassuring smile, but the captain was staring blankly at the floor.

"It's the same at any police station," he said. "Handing you on to the next shift for *them* to release makes more work."

"Getting rid of the complications..." said Straker.

"And there's that," said Flynn.

"Most of the staff drive in, so how's this shift change going to work?"

Straker was talking quietly as if to himself, distracted, like he was reading from a list.

"With this alert, where will all the staff park their cars?" he continued. "Or was that just for you – so that we have to walk out on our own? How far from the gate is your car parked?"

Flynn looked at his watch.

"It won't be long now, Captain Straker. A little more patience and we're gone."

"Are you both carrying?"

Moffat looked at Flynn.

"Aye, we are," said Flynn. "Or at least, we will be when we escort you out of here."

Duffy had seemed very anxious. When two long-wheelbase Royal Military Police Land Rovers arrived, he wasn't in the van. Carragher assumed he was taking a nervous piss.

As it was now 7am, so it looked to Carragher that they were here to pick up the SAS captain. The informer's information was once again proving accurate.

But the RMPs weren't being allowed through the gates, so their vehicles were obscuring Carragher's line of sight to the gatehouse. He crawled over the seat and let himself out of the rear door of the van, to crouch beside the left rear wheel, deciding how close to the wire fence he dared go in order to see.

But then a movement caught his eye, in the darkness off to his left.

The military police Land Rovers had blocked off some of the yellow glare from the gatehouse lights. In this half-darkness Carragher could see Duffy fifteen metres away, beside the fence.

He now saw a hole in the wire, Duffy creeping through it slowly and carefully. Somebody obscured by the bright light on the other side of the vehicles started shouting in an Army kind of way, causing Duffy to freeze.

Carragher got ready to run backwards into the darkness. He imagined searchlights pinning them down like moths.

But this seemed to be a dispute between the RMPs and Castlereagh guards, so Carragher remained still.

Duffy began moving again, pulling himself carefully and slowly through the wire onto the pavement. He reached back into the darkness for what looked like a small canvas satchel.

He leaned over this for a few moments, his back to Carragher. But then as he tied a length of wire around his right wrist, Carragher realised what he was looking at.

The satchel could easily contain enough explosive to wreck the van Carragher was hiding behind, as well as the RMP mini-Pigs and the Castlereagh gatehouse. Although he didn't think Duffy mad enough to make a suicide attack, he decided not to wait and find out.

And then there were shots, two very fast double-taps.

So Carragher ran for his life, across the car park and out through the entry hole they'd made in the security fencing. The explosion was shockingly loud even though he was expecting it. He didn't even look back.

Straker was moving with deliberate slowness, from his cell and then down the green lino corridor.

"*Green mile. Dead man walking*," announced Tiger.

Straker's brain fog evaporated instantly. He still felt very ill, but his confused lethargy was replaced by an avalanche of ice-cold fear.

"*At Crumlin Road, they used to do it at eight o'clock in the morning. On the dot.*"

As they approached the gatehouse entrance, Straker baulked like a spooked racehorse. Major Soames, in a flak jacket and bright red RMP beret, was getting out of an armoured Land Rover with two armoured Humber mini-Pigs parked behind it.

"*The tumbrils await, my Lord*," said Tiger.

"We'll sort this out, Captain Straker," said Flynn reassuringly.

But Straker didn't seem to hear him, lunging backwards away from the gateway.

Moffat grabbed his arm. "There's nothing to worry about, Captain Straker."

The whole point was that vehicles didn't stop outside this gate where they were vulnerable, coming straight into the inner keep compound to be searched. But the two gate guards weren't letting them in.

Straker watched as more military police climbed out of the vehicles. He turned and asked Flynn and Moffat: "Do you both have weapons?"

Moffat looked questioningly at Flynn. Straker had been standing beside them when they'd unlocked the weapon tray.

But Straker was now staring beyond the military police, to the right of where their vehicles were parked. Four tall corporals in flak jackets and drill-pig slashed peak hats with bright red tops were standing like statues, brandishing submachine guns.

Major Soames saw Straker and moved forwards to the gate, where one of the two guards stopped him. Soames didn't like this, and a loud, bad-tempered discussion began.

But Straker was ignoring Soames and the argument, scanning anxiously across the road into the darkness of the vehicle parking area. Flynn noticed this, then saw a sudden change in Straker's posture.

"One of you, give me your weapon," Straker demanded.

Moffat didn't respond, so Flynn took the Browning from his shoulder holster and placed it butt-first into Straker's outstretched hand.

"It's made ready," he said.

Straker, who was still staring out of the gate, didn't look down but took the Browning and pulled back the slide. A round flipped out of the chamber onto the ground, and he controlled the slide's return to feel the click as the next round loaded. Never trust anybody else's weapon. He moved quickly forwards towards the gate.

Moffat tried to stop him, but Flynn pulled him out of Straker's path.

One of the military police corporals had heard the Browning being cocked and raised his SMG, even though Straker was hiding the Browning down by his side. Straker ignored this, and as he reached the gate stepped suddenly to the left, crouched, and raised the Browning into a firing position.

The RMP shouted a Yellow Card warning at Straker, who ignored him, shuffling forwards still in a crouch, looking off to the right.

The RMP started to shout the second warning, then remembered he'd not cocked his SMG lest it go off accidentally during their vehicle journey.

Straker squeezed off two rapid-fire shots, deafening hammer blows that felt to him like history repeating itself.

The RMP was fumbling with his SMG's working parts, the other three RMPs flinching away from the noise.

But the target was moving. Straker fired a second double-tap as the target vanished behind the Land Rovers and back into the darkness, running, fleeting, a blur of action.

Then Straker saw a curved arc of smoke, a grey rainbow illuminated by the security lights in the air over the roofs of the vehicles. Its pot of gold was a satchel that lay between the gatehouse and the Land Rovers, smouldering and hissing like a bag of snakes.

Straker half stood, lurching back into the police compound. Flynn was already taking cover, but Moffat was still trying to work out what was going on. Straker knocked him to the ground beside Flynn, behind the brick pillars of the gate.

The intense concussion of the explosion turned the world suddenly black. A blanket of noiseless, slow-motion numbness descended on Straker with horrid familiarity.

They'd dropped Riley and Hooves off at the bottom of Alexander Road, then driven round onto Ladas Drive and back up to Alexander Road where they were parked and looking right, down at the barracks entrance.

The Farmer looked left past Jacko and whistled quietly to himself.

"You can run, but you can't hide," he muttered, as an early-morning athlete in Ron Hills with great legs trotted past, the rest of her bundled up in blue Gore-Tex.

But then, on Alexander Road, two RMP Land Rovers drove round the bend into view from the other end, pulling over onto the pavement beside the gatehouse.

"We're just in time," muttered the Farmer. "Do you see Hooves and Riley?"

"Not yet," said Jacko, as he lifted the binoculars to see a big RMP major in a flak jacket and bright red beret get out of the first car. It looked like they were being refused entry. The major began remonstrating with a police guard.

And so he missed seeing Duffy creep out from the wire fencing.

But when Duffy stood up and threw what looked like a school bag over the top of the Land Rovers, Jacko ducked down behind the dashboard, pulling the Farmer down with him.

The explosion rocked the Transit. Thankfully, its windscreen remained intact.

Arrosa was running very slowly, trying to work out what she was actually going to do. She crossed to the right-hand side of Alexander Road so she could see into the gatehouse entrance, noting as she did that the passenger of the Transit was lifting binoculars to his eyes. White-van man checking out her bottom? In that split second, she really didn't think so; but then she saw the arrival of the military police and stopped running to watch. She could hear raised voices over the top of the vehicle engines.

She was just thinking how this confirmed what Ciarán had said, when she saw Duffy creep from the darkness and throw the satchel. And all at once she felt terribly, massively angry.

In wanting to see Straker, she hadn't seriously considered that Carragher and Duffy would learn so quickly about his release – and certainly not in time to attack him. But then fury at Chapman and all the self-centred machinations of this grim little city suddenly evaporated.

The satchel started fizzing as soon as it left Duffy's hand. He'd somehow triggered a time fuse so he could get clear.

She sprinted left across the road and threw herself down to the kerb, hands clamped over her ears, chin and elbows on her chest, legs up in a foetal ball trying to squeeze as much of herself as she could into the eight-inch step between the road and the pavement.

CHAPTER 44

The Farmer did a tyre-burning three-point turn. He wasn't going to drive head-on into a second bomb. He reversed the Transit as fast as it would go, to where black smoke was already billowing.

One of the Land Rovers had been blown onto its side, and although the other was still on the pavement it was black, tyres burning, glass gone. There was smoke, screaming, groaning, the stink of burning plastic and oil, and a strange baked chemical smell – the smart arrogance of the military police patrol turned instantly into blackened rubbish.

Jacko found Straker inside the gate entrance lying on the ground behind the left-hand pillar. He lifted him up by the shoulders, then pulled him out of the gate, away from the smoke towards the van.

"We need to fuck off asap, boss," he shouted in his ear. "The cops will be coming out of that building like rats from a drainpipe."

The Farmer jumped out of the Transit, looming over them both.

"Here, Farmer, grab the boss and let's fuck offski."

But the Farmer shook his head, then looked at Straker, who nodded at him.

"We stay," Straker muttered, pulling back his shoulders and looking around.

"There's no time for this, boss," said Jacko.

The Farmer turned away and shouted across to Hooves who, with Riley, had taken cover when the bomb went off, and was now running up to them.

"Get the medic gear."

"For fuck's sake," snarled Jacko. "The whole fucking world will be here in a minute. What good can we do? We need to go – right now!"

"No," said Straker. "Right now, we need to keep people alive."

Hooves was rummaging in the back of the van.

"Hang on," shouted the Farmer, and reversed the van the final thirty metres to the edge of the black, billowing smoke.

Hooves cracked open the back door, dumping the medical kit onto the ground, coughing uncontrollably as heavy black fumes rolled in.

The Farmer pulled on a thick pair of leather gloves and was out of the driver's seat and into the wreckage, hunting out bodies from the blackened plastic and metal.

"Ignore the screamers," he bellowed. "We have no idea how many people are here. Find the quiet ones before they bleed out. Drag them clear."

They ducked instinctively as a magazine of 9mm submachine-gun ammunition cooked off with sporadic firecracker noises.

The Farmer wrenched the door completely off the first mini-Pig, dragging two inert soldiers from the back by the collars of their flak jackets. They were limp but apparently unmarked, the bright red tops of their khaki cheese-cutter hats oddly smart amid the filth of this destruction.

Riley had recovered quickly and was obeying the Farmer's orders. He'd found Major Soames beside the gatehouse, where it seemed the wall had diverted some of the blast. Jacko ran over and they dragged the unconscious major over to where the Farmer was lining up bodies.

A police officer had come out of the gatehouse and was fussing over one of his colleagues who'd lost a leg and was writhing in agony.

"I told you, ignore the screamers," shouted the Farmer. "We know where they are. But the quiet ones are actually fucking dying. So drag them over here to me RIGHT NOW!"

Hooves had pulled the combat medic pack over to where the Farmer had set up his triage, and was ripping open vacuum-packed field dressings, laying them out in a line on the pavement ready for application.

He moved over to one of the RMPs from the second mini-Pig, checking his neck for a pulse.

"Leave him, Hooves, he's gone," shouted the Farmer. "But cut the top off this guy. He's pale, like an abdominal bleeder – maybe a bit of metal got under his flak jacket."

*

Billy Flynn also recovered quickly. He was now thinking fast about what he was seeing. Clearly, some capable people were taking the right actions, so he didn't need to interfere with that – whoever they might be.

So instead he focussed on the next thing, realising as he did the total fucking disaster that was about to envelop them all.

He grabbed Ciarán.

"Barge into the gatehouse waving your warrant card, and get on the phone before anybody else does. They'll have the alert numbers on the wall – tell them I'm personally in charge of the situation. We need three ambulances and roadblocks around the whole area. But tell them we're secure within it – make sure you insist on this. Then give them as much casualty detail as you can."

Flynn walked back through into the barracks yard, waving his own warrant card above his head as armed police officers ran from the building towards him.

"No guns, boys," he shouted, intercepting Castlereagh's Rapid Reaction team before it made things even worse.

"The gate is secure. We need stretchers, the doctor, all your first aiders, and ambulances. Do what I'm telling you. Do it right now."

But instead the team commander ran at Flynn, brandishing his Ruger Mini-14 assault rifle, shouting for him to get on the ground. Flynn, who was taller by a head, simply took the weapon from him, throwing it away to one side.

"I'm Chief Superintendent Billy Flynn," he shouted. "Do what I'm telling you. This gate area doesn't need you. Secure the rest of the barracks perimeter from inside. Do it now."

He bent down and picked up the team leader's Ruger.

"Just make sure none of the prisoners escape," he said quietly as he gave it back to him. "And keep everybody calm."

Already, police and ambulance sirens were coming at them from all directions.

Flynn walked back to the gatehouse, where Straker was kneeling beside the police officer with a missing leg, using two hands to squeeze the stump, trying to stop the bleeding. He noticed a female in a blue mountain jacket rummaging in the medical pack, then running over to elbow Straker aside so she could apply a tourniquet. Behind them, where bodies were now in a neat line, a young guy had bags of saline drip tied up to the security fence, and a huge fair-haired man was inserting a cannula into one of the RMPs.

Flynn looked around and noticed a stocky, bad-tempered-looking man standing beside the white van, staring intently away from the confusion through the wire-mesh fence of the secure vehicle park. This man held a Colt AR-15 by his side, its butt retracted so it looked like a large pistol.

"I'm Chief Superintendent Flynn," he called out cautiously, standing very still.

The man's head swivelled, but the AR-15 remained pointing at the ground.

"I heard. Thanks for heading off the goons."

"You'll be one of Captain Straker's people, I take it?"

The sirens were growing louder, seeming to surround them with their urgency.

"Correct, and with the world about to descend on us, I'm wondering if we might remove Captain Straker from all this?"

"It's your van?" asked Flynn.

Jacko nodded.

"It's about to get hemmed in," said Flynn.

"Maybe we could just walk away?" said Jacko.

Flynn nodded. "If that's your preference?"

"It really is," said Jacko.

"How about my inspector goes with you in the van – to get you where you need to be?"

Jacko looked uncertain.

"You've got… weapons and so on," said Flynn. "We were getting Captain Straker out when this happened. He'll tell you. Detective Inspector Moffat answers to nobody but me."

Jacko nodded. Being picked up by the Army or RUC, with their small arms and whatever else Hooves had brought, would be complicated; especially when it was beginning to look like they might get away with this.

"Tell the follow-up to get a dog through this fence over there where it's been cut."

He pointed to where Duffy had scrambled back through, leaving the wire sticking out.

"The bomber's gone, but the dog'll tell you how he got away."

Flynn nodded and went back to talk to Moffat, who was still in the gatehouse.

"Bit of a shit-storm coming our way," said Moffat.

Flynn nodded and dialled out on the other phone.

"This is Chief Superintendent Flynn. Get me the chief constable. Of course I know what fucking day it is and what time. Get him on the line NOW."

He saw Moffat peering out through the bombproof glass, noting his surprise and then concern at whatever he was seeing. Then the chief constable came on the line.

"Sorry to bother you, sir, but I need you to transmit some immediate orders to everybody responding to the Castlereagh incident. You don't know about it? OK, I'm on the spot and in charge, and I'll brief you once you've ordered the Army and the duty superintendent to defer to me in everything.

"You do that now, please. I've got a lot to sort out, but I'll have them keep this line open for you."

Flynn turned to Moffat.

"What's happening?"

"That nurse out there," he said. "Does anybody know who she is?"

"Looks like a medic out for a quiet Sunday morning run," replied Flynn. "She knows what she's doing."

Moffat nodded, but looked uncertain. Flynn handed his phone to the remaining gatehouse guard.

"When the chief constable comes back on the line, give me a shout," he said.

He pulled Moffat to one side and explained about the SAS.

"And have a quick think about this," he added. "If all these people hadn't been here, imagine where we'd be right now..."

Moffat looked uncertain.

"It's not *who* people are," continued Flynn, "or even what they say. It's what they *do* that counts. Nothing else is important."

Carragher ran along the lane, then cut right across the top end of the playing fields. But when he reached the bushes by the fence at the far end, he realised somebody was a couple of hundred yards behind him. He dived into the bushes and waited.

As he gathered his breath, fury took over from the adrenalin. It was Duffy, the little fucker. He'd planned this behind his back, and as far as everybody else would see it, with his approval. And now it looked like he was returning to where Roxy was waiting – as if this was what Carragher had ordered, something for which Carragher would now be responsible.

So when Duffy came stumbling across the muddy grass to the kid's scramble entrance to the playing fields, Carragher rose from the darkness and punched him hard in the stomach.

"What the fuck were you thinking?" he snarled at Duffy, as he writhed on the ground, vomiting.

Carragher was already holding his M1911; you couldn't run with one and a half kilograms of Colt stuffed down the waistband of your trousers. He now stood over Duffy, waiting until he stopped moving, intending to shoot him in the head.

But at that point, as the sirens came at them from all directions, he realised the futility of executing Duffy. Apart from the noise of a gunshot so close to so many angry policemen, killing him created problems; plus, and he really hated to admit it, he still needed Duffy.

So another narrative formed in his head; that this was the demonstration. A far more personal, committed type of bomb attack, with no collateral damage to ruffle Catholic sensitivities, carried out by operators who planned to live and fight another day.

O'Donnell would buy that – as would the Libyans. And there'd be lots of money to be made running training courses in warm countries, showing them how to do it.

It also got Carragher off the hook of Duffy being the traitor – as quite clearly such bravery, encouraged by Carragher's leadership, proved he was not untrustworthy. It didn't even matter if Straker hadn't been killed, although Carragher thought there was a good chance he had been.

This might well satisfy everybody.

So Carragher put the Colt back into his waistband and helped Duffy to his feet. Roxy was waiting at the top of Mayfair Avenue, and they were gone before the Army sealed off the area.

CHAPTER 45

Moffat did a great job getting them out of the Castlereagh traffic jam. They didn't even have to dump the Transit.

Moffat drove, then co-opted the first uniformed police officer that stopped them to sit beside him in the passenger seat, getting them waved through the roadblocks. The others were jammed into the back seat with the radios and weaponry at their feet, Hooves standing in the rear, hanging onto the back of the seat.

Once they got clear of the roadblocks, Straker wanted to go straight to Aldergrove.

"If the Scout's still there," he argued, "that gets us out of here and gone."

But the Farmer wasn't having any of it.

"We go to Musgrave Park, please, Inspector," he said, looking pointedly at Jacko, who nodded.

They sat in the hospital car park ignoring Straker's increasingly incoherent objections, until Doc Morton came out with two orderlies and a stretcher.

"He stays here for twenty-four hours' observation," said the doc, after stitching up Straker's cheek and head wounds.

"We'll all stay," said Jacko, then went to make a couple of phone calls.

One hour later a battered Range Rover drove into the car park, stopping beside the white Transit. After a careful conversation, Jacko entrusted the potential embarrassment of Hooves' large black canvas bag to Ian O'Neill.

Captain Riley was ordered back to HQ Northern Ireland, collected from the hospital by a Land-Rover team of RMP bodyguards. After a long conversation alone with the general, the protection team returned him to Musgrave Park.

He talked with the doctor and Jacko in the corridor outside Straker's room.

"There are problems," said Riley without preamble. "I'll tell you what I told the general – that my legal advice remains as it has always been, and that Captain Straker must return to Hereford as soon as possible. Once he's there, the legal process can run its course without further local complications."

The doctor made as if to protest, but Riley gestured for him to wait.

"So although the general won't agree to that, the RMPs *have* brought me back here, and nobody's harassing you or Captain Straker."

"They can't," said the doctor. "Even my boss has backed off."

"Exactly," said Riley. He then stopped talking, waiting until the others caught up.

"So if you'll allow me, I have a plan…"

There was a silence.

"Spit it out, then," said Jacko.

"OK," said Riley. "Firstly, I understand Captain Straker should be kept under clinical observation for one week?"

"That's correct," said the doctor crisply.

"And the Farmer's been doing this for the last twenty-four hours?"

"He has."

"Meaning he knows what to check, symptoms that require intervention, and so on?"

"Yes. He's well qualified."

"But Captain Straker can't fly for the time being?"

"No."

"And that's because he needs to be monitored…?"

"Ah," said the doctor. "Not exactly. There are two other reasons – the air pressure in a passenger cabin is much lower than the ten millibars at sea level, making a stroke more likely; and the difficulties of dealing with a medical complication during the flight."

"So would keeping him at ten millibars of pressure throughout the flight prevent that?"

"It would reduce the risk."

"So if that was to be guaranteed, how soon could you clear him for a flight home?"

The doc sucked his teeth.

"I'd really prefer to keep him here for a full week," he said finally.

"Which is what you're insisting to the hierarchy – who, in spite of everything, still say they want him back in Thiepval Barracks for the Board of Inquiry."

"Yes."

"So you stick with that advice. But how about if Captain Straker was to do his medically supervised rest and recuperation somewhere the same sort of distance from here?"

"Not until tomorrow," said the doctor. "I'd like him here for one more night."

"Then you'd release him to us?"

"Yes."

"Could you actually sign him over to the Medical Officer at Hereford?" added Riley.

The doctor nodded. He and the Hereford MO were friends.

To Arrosa, it seemed like Straker had evaporated. Back at the gatehouse he'd looked dreadful, almost robotic while working on the casualties. He'd known exactly what he was doing, following the huge medic's orders, so she'd stuck with him like an assistant, taking over when he needed it.

She noted the big chief superintendent, Ciarán's boss, looking over at her a couple of times, which made her wonder if Ciarán had said anything to him. She'd guessed Ciarán was inside the gatehouse, and tried to keep her back facing its sloped glass observation portals. All she could do was hope he didn't come out.

The sirens and flashing lights closed in, surrounded them, bringing Army medics carrying stretchers and dark green canvas holdalls as they set up a frontline dressing station. The chief superintendent came over and spoken quietly in her ear.

"Thanks for your help, doctor," he'd said. "You probably don't need to get caught up in all this, so I can get someone here to escort you away through the cordon…?"

That's when she realised Straker was gone – along with his frighteningly efficient white-van men. She'd nodded and walked through the layers of the cordon in a numbed silence. The world was bright and confusing, but deathly silent.

She'd panicked momentarily when an Army sergeant grabbed her arm. But he'd given her a cup of hot sugary coffee, then poured warm water into a green plastic basin so she could wash the blood off her face and hands.

This was when she remembered seeing Duffy throw the bomb; the fury she'd directed at him and Carragher. Surprisingly, that anger was now gone as if it had never existed. She chose not to think about why or how; just that she was lucky it hadn't latched itself on to her. She'd seen too many people here broken by it – poisoning every day of their lives.

She wasn't part of this, and would survive so long as she remained so. But the pressure was always there – "you're either with us or against us", interconnected in such bizarre ways; no secrets; just the dark swirl of hatred, rumour, and betrayal.

She guessed they'd taken Straker to Musgrave Park, then realised that Carragher would draw the exact same conclusion. It was only four miles away; she could run there in twenty-four minutes. But then she thought of the speed at which Straker's white-van men had thrown themselves into action, getting him out of there in less than twenty minutes. They'd keep him safer than she could.

Despite her training and the depth of her involvement here, she was powerless to actually *do* anything. She'd always known this.

She now realised Chapman was the same; although for her, living over here, it was more fundamental. And her ineffectiveness only became apparent when she saw people like Straker's team in action.

Chapman had been right all along. The SAS did look after themselves. So she walked home, took a long shower to warm herself up, then went to bed.

Carragher told O'Donnell by phone the bare bones of what had happened. He'd been very angry.

"I told you to leave it, Séan. But all the time you were putting together this plan – what the fuck?"

Carragher had stayed very calm.

"For once," he said, then paused, "we'd got reliable information of exactly where this guy would be, at a specific time. Intelligence like this is as rare as rocking-horse shit, Breandán. If you don't take chances like this, you might as well give up."

"Did you even stop to think you were being played?"

"Of course I did. But the guy was there on the dot of seven and it wasn't a set-up. What else do you want from an informer?"

O'Donnell backed off, remembering the number of times he'd ordered actions based on this man's tip-offs. The information was always accurate.

"This is the positive statement we needed to make, Breandán," continued Carragher. "Just bombing Castlereagh in itself strikes a blow in return for all the Volunteers who've been interrogated there. It also sends a message to those who're in there now – and those who will get taken there in the future."

O'Donnell thought about it.

"OK," he said. "So that's us attacking a symbol of Brit oppression. But what about the SAS bogeyman?"

"I don't know," replied Carragher. "I couldn't actually see him. Duffy did, though – said the guy shot at him as he was throwing the bomb."

Duffy's bravery could not be questioned. He'd now done far more than just vindicating himself.

"But even so, Duffy threw the bomb accurately – over the vehicles and into the gateway. The vehicles were wrecked, and the gatehouse was so badly damaged I can't see anybody outside it having survived."

Carragher heard this from the dickers. But he wasn't going to tell O'Donnell that he'd run away before Duffy made the attack.

"I don't suppose it matters if the SAS captain was actually killed or not," said O'Donnell thoughtfully. "The precision of this attack is demonstration enough, with no innocent bystanders even injured."

"I can't see him having survived," said Carragher.

"Well, that's splendid," said O'Donnell. "Three birds with the one satchel bomb: total precision, getting us rid of a distraction, and reducing the effect of SAS demonisation on PIRA morale.

"Onwards and ever upwards… We enter the New Age."

Chapman was in the office at his usual time, and had just completed his *café au lait* ritual when his secure phone rang. He'd been expecting to learn what had happened, but not quite so quickly.

"The Sunday Service," said the voice. "Slow news – but your captain's made his point, plus Carragher's also done well. *Nil points* to the security establishment – in my opinion."

Chapman gave the occasional lecture about informers to various of the UK internal security agencies, and even to trusted foreign friends. The Cold War had given him an agent-handling reputation that not even his detractors at MI5 could argue with.

"The credibility of an informer increases with each piece of accurate information they provide," he would tell his audiences. "And if they stay anonymous, once they've earned credibility, they can deal with anybody they want and, with care, play one side off against another."

However with his informers the boot was usually on the other foot. He recruited them early, mostly as paid agents, so he knew who they were, but they didn't know much about him; and rarely cared so long as the money kept coming in.

Chapman's audiences were surprised by his cynicism regarding informers. MI5 too, from which he presumed meant they took most of what they were told at face value.

"The consequences of what informers pass on is irrelevant," he'd say. "In Northern Ireland there are so many factions and overlapping interests as to make prediction impossible. So the successful informants stay completely independent, relying solely on their own judgment, keeping to their own agenda."

Chapman didn't control Cold Hook. No one did. In understanding this, Chapman was unlike Cold Hook's other clients.

But in any case, as Chapman wasn't operating in Northern Ireland, he had no infrastructure to assess Cold Hook's information. And so, like Cold Hook, Chapman trusted his own personal judgment and kept to his *own* private agenda.

Jacko had a long chat with Straker, on their own without either Riley or the doctor present.

"The plan is to drive you out to your godfather's place," he said. "Then after this week of rest that the doc says you need, we'll fly you from there direct to Hereford. I'm still working this on the unofficial net, on a 'mate's favours' basis, because it seems to me that although the headshed are on our side, none of them want to take responsibility.

"We're still in very deep shit. Anything that draws attention to us could release the mudslide. But it's Christmas holidays, so maybe..."

"Are the RAF Special Forces flight guys OK about bringing over a Puma?" interrupted Straker.

"It's medical training," said Jacko. "Low level all the way – three hundred feet above sea level. The aero-med consultant loves the idea, and the resuscitation team can't wait. Plus I'm sending Hooves back to liaise and come across with them. He's good with nurses."

"Won't they have to clear the flight with the Det and HQNI?" said Straker.

"Yep," said Jacko. "But who's going to object to SF Flight practising a medium-range resuscitation run? Plus my mate there owes me big time."

"But what about HQ Northern Ireland?" continued Straker.

"They'll only get to hear once it's done and dusted. And what's it to them where you convalesce?" replied Jacko. "Any case, you being back in Thiepval Barracks again would be embarrassing."

"But what about the Board of Inquiry?" said Straker.

Jacko shrugged his shoulders.

"All fucked up. Captain Riley says it's probably not happening – he thinks because of the RUC. We just have to get you out of province, away from HQNI and RUC jurisdiction."

"Won't HQNI object?"

"Like I said, they're not going to know."

"They will when the week's convalescence is up, and I don't show."

"Captain Riley says that once you're back in Hereford, they'll back off. But he's offered to continue representing you – which, personally, I'd go for as the Hereford DALS guy was only interested in whatever the CO said."

Straker shook his head slowly, looking very tired.

"We're a long ways outside the bubble," he said.

"Bubble?"

"Where they all live."

"We're on our own," replied Jacko. "*We* decide what's right, then we stick with it."

"I can't see them understanding."

"These kinds of ops always end like this," said Jacko. "Even the headshed know that."

But Straker was thinking of his father – hearing the voice of disapproval.

"The man on the ground is always right," continued Jacko. "We don't explain anything. Agreeing the story is for when we're back in Hereford and it's all over."

"OK," said Straker firmly; and his father's voice went silent.

MONDAY 15 DECEMBER

The next day they set off by road for Ardglenna. Straker insisted on walking out of the hospital on his own, wearing theatre greens so he looked like a medic. He'd also asked for a civvie car to replace the white Transit, but Jacko hadn't thought that necessary.

The Range Rover had driven round to the ambulance entrance, which was hidden away behind rocket wire and sandbags, and he'd jumped into the back with Rory Ennis-Boyd and Ian O'Neill. Once they were clear of the hospital, Jacko and the Farmer slotted in behind them in the white van and did the follow.

Straker had insisted they use the personal radios, which Jacko thought a bit over the top but hadn't disagreed. They'd also been armed.

Immediately they left the hospital grounds, Straker did a running commentary on the vehicles behind them from the rear bench seat of the Range Rover. The Farmer listened in and kept a 360-degree watch using his wing mirrors, but saw nothing of concern. Jacko tried to sleep.

They arrived at Ardglenna without incident, Straker's concerns unfounded. The white van was hidden out of sight in the carriage shed.

Straker was ordered to bed by the Farmer. He and Abigail were so ruthlessly uncompromising that Straker had no choice but to go along with it, sleeping solidly for several days.

With Straker in bed, Jacko was left to his own devices. As he'd done outside Castlereagh, he reappraised the situation. He realised – as then – that he'd been wrong to try and over-ride Straker's wishes.

SAS senior NCOs were not thought to practice self-castigation, and Jacko's caution – verging suspicion – of Ruperts generally was the product of hard-won experience. Over-riding Ruperts on operations was invariably justified as lessening exposure to dangers the officer hadn't anticipated. But this very clearly hadn't happened in his dealings with Straker. With a sudden gut-wrenching *actual* pain, Jacko remembered his reluctance to evacuate the observation building.

He next thought about if they'd taken Straker away from Castlereagh without treating the casualties. Stymied by the Farmer siding with Captain Straker, he'd been angry, letting them get on with it while he secured the area. He'd then very nearly crawled through the wire fence to pursue the bomber – which would have led to disastrous complications. The senior police officer had brought him to his senses. But even then, he'd dismissed Captain Straker's fears about them being followed to Ardglenna; and now felt embarrassed that he'd slept while the Farmer followed Captain Straker's radio commentary.

So now Jacko asked Ian O'Neill to show him round the estate grounds, and the woods through which ran the Ardglenna House access road. Then he'd patrolled 24/7, randomly but intensively, refusing to allow O'Neill to allocate others to share the burden.

After three days he was exhausted, which was when Hooves returned. Jacko was furious, as this was in direct disobedience of Jacko's having ordered him to come back over in the Puma.

"There was nothing to do in Hereford, Sergeant Major," said Hooves formally, pre-empting Jacko's rage while standing to attention. "Everything's totally organised with the flight, and I've formally signed over some gear for us which they'll bring."

Jacko swallowed his anger, realising that as with Captain Straker, Hooves' initiative had its own logic – which hadn't let them down. He didn't even ask what this "gear for us" might be. So he briefed Hooves on the patrolling requirement, then rearranged the patrol stags between the two of them.

With Hooves out in the darkness, Jacko took a hot bath, during which he realised that would have been why Hooves had returned.

CHAPTER 46

Straker was walking very slowly from the kitchen up the winding dark stairs using the curved handrail to pull himself along. It was very cold, and his bedroom wouldn't be much warmer despite its huge and beautiful but useless cast-iron Victorian radiator.

He smelled cigarette smoke and stopped.

"I never did show you my new tower room," said Abigail from the darkness.

Another narrower and much tighter spiral staircase led from the end of the first-floor corridor up into curved stone walls with the narrowest of windows at every full circle. The stairs ended after two turns, with an open door into a circular room with a small woodburning stove.

"A roof-light window would be good," said Abigail, "but it'll have to wait until we've got the money to redo the slates. But it's cosy."

She was tense; polite but distracted. She waved the cigarette then sat in a battered leather armchair. Straker followed her, closing the door behind him to sit in the other armchair.

"I'm so sorry about all this," he said.

"What?" she said, looking up, abrupt and unsmiling.

"I should never have involved you," he replied.

"What else might you have done?" she said coldly.

"I should have got on the ferry," he replied.

She laughed without humour.

"And been arrested – or whatever they were going to do to you?"

"I could have worked something out," he said. "This is my problem."

She got up quickly, using the asbestos glove to open the stove door and flicking the cigarette into the flames.

"I know that's what you've been thinking – and it makes me very angry," she said, standing with her back to him, staring at the small arch-topped window as if imagining the view in its small, black-reflected panes.

Straker didn't know what to say, so he sat silent, feeling suddenly nervous.

"You're completely right," he said eventually. "And I don't know what to say."

"For God's sake, Peter," she said. "You're making this much worse. So shut up and listen."

Abigail looked like she was going to light another cigarette. But then didn't.

Finally she turned away from the window and faced him.

"Rory should have told you this years ago."

She sat down slowly, making an obvious attempt to relax.

"I can't have children," she said quietly. "But Rory can."

Straker had the sense to remain quiet.

There was a wind buffeting the turret, which now stopped.

"It was clear to me when I first met Rory that there'd been something between him and your mother. He'd been her lover, then introduced her to your father. But it was more than that."

The turret room seemed to have separated itself from the rest of the house, as if the booster rockets had fallen away to leave it flying silently through space.

"I met Rory as he was about to command the regiment. We married soon after that. He was already your godfather. Your mother's sister was your actual godmother, so I got to be the associate."

She smiled, but then shook her head before he could say anything.

"He won't tell you this, but Rory's been through some very difficult times – after the war, then when the SAS was reformed; and when he finally returned from Borneo. Stuff that's extremely difficult to deal with on your own. I can see the same in you – and I know he can too. We've talked about it…

"When we met, he was being terribly stiff-upper-lip, and it was some time before he levelled with me. But he did, and we've got it mostly under control. It's normal – the price you warriors must pay. But it's not easy.

"Your mother, however, wasn't quite so straightforward..."

Straker was jolted by this abrupt change of direction. He thought he'd understood where this was going. Now he was lost.

Abigail paused.

"I met you on your first birthday – the adults' lunch party when I was allowed to hold you. Your mother had been doing her usual flustering with Rory. But then I noticed she was unable to look me in the eye.

"Which was when I noticed how much you looked like Rory..."

Suddenly this conversation made sense. Straker shifted as if to ask a question, then changed his mind.

"I must have reacted," continued Abigail. "Your mama rushed off and put you in one of those crochet hats – a disguise, I suppose."

She smiled.

"So that night, Rory and I convened what we now refer to as 'Rory's post-nuptial confessionals'..."

She smiled again – absently, to herself, without looking at him. Straker again shifted in his chair, the cracked leather creaking slightly, then waited.

"It's something as old as warfare itself," she said after a long pause. "Shell-shock..."

Another change of direction.

"I did the reading: it's caused by explosions, blows to the head, prolonged stress and fear – physical and psychological. Nothing much by way of new research, but lots of names: combat fatigue, soldier's heart, or whatever it was made Epizelus go blind after the Battle of Marathon... It can take months or years to develop.

"Rory and I think this will apply to you as well. But that's just something for you to know now, and for you and me both to talk about very soon...

"But to continue: Rory didn't meet me until after you were born – and let's just say that a year or so before that, on his own with the demons, your mother helped him... And I'm so glad she did."

Abigail was sitting very straight in the armchair. There was no hint of irony or bitterness in what she was saying.

"She was living in one of those bloody awful officers' quarters at the end of the London Overground – Bushey or somewhere dire – while Roland worked long hours at the MoD. She'd been married over four years, still no children… so she probably needed help too.

"Rory was working in London. So, for a while, it was as you'd expect with two very lonely people who cared for each other."

She picked distractedly at the wool of her fingerless gloves.

"But Rory and your mother were sensible enough to know this wasn't anything permanent. And it was your arrival – or, at least, the first signs of the pregnancy – which gave them both what they needed to break it off."

Straker must have looked puzzled.

"You know how she is, Peter; resilient and loyal, now having the baby she'd wanted from Roland, on which she could lavish all the love that he, poor chap, didn't seem to want from her. And now her life made sense."

Abigail opened the stove door with the glove, quickly flipping a small log onto the flames.

"And thanks to your mama – and to you – Rory's life also made sense; new life, something good from the darkness."

She leaned towards him.

"You were conceived with love, Peter," she said. "You were wanted… Actually, I'd say that you were *needed*."

They sat in silence for what seemed like a long time. Then Straker shifted his weight in the armchair.

"Can I ask you a question?"

Abigail nodded.

"How did you feel when… my father told you?"

She suddenly smiled.

"Very happy."

"What?"

"Six months after we got married, I'd had an illness; then I'd had to tell Rory I couldn't have children. He really wanted a family, and of course he needed a son for the estate."

She paused, then sighed deeply.

"I was ready to give him an annulment."

"What?" repeated Straker. They were both practicing Catholics. He was horrified at what seemed to him an appalling confusion of motives and emotions.

"So when I saw you were Rory's baby, I knew he had a son. I was happy the moment I first saw you."

Straker still couldn't understand this.

"But he kept it from you… I'd have thought you'd be angry."

She shook her head.

"After I told him I couldn't have children, he could hardly have told me about you."

Straker felt stupid. Of course he couldn't.

"Anyway… we did as most people do," she continued. "Maintained the pretence so as not to rock the boat."

She added another log.

"However, the pretence couldn't continue for ever. And after what you've been through now, it *mustn't* continue – as I know from dealing with Rory's experiences.

"But there's one complication," she added.

Straker found himself smiling. Then he laughed out loud.

"Yes," said Abigail, smiling back. "Just the one…"

She lit the cigarette she'd been holding with a match from the firelighter box.

"You can't know this from me. Rory has to tell you himself, in his own time."

They sat looking at each other, listening to this strange little room breathing: the wood burning in the stove, and the wind somewhere above their heads in the darkness.

"Does… Roland know he's not my father?" asked Straker.

"No," replied Abigail. "Roland doesn't know – for your mother's sake."

She finished smoking the cigarette.

"There's one further thing," said Straker, waiting until she'd stubbed it out.

She looked concerned.

"Since I first came here, this has been my home," he said. "Before that I didn't know what home meant. And I didn't know why being here felt so special. So all this makes complete sense. But it's home for me both with *you* as well as with Rory – with Dad…"

"Where are my cigarettes?" demanded Abigail.

She lit one, inhaled, then with a grimace opened the stove, swearing as she burned her fingers, and threw it into the flames.

He stood up, and went over to kneel beside her.

"Thank you for telling me," he said. "But it does create problems…"

Abigail nodded.

"I suggest Roland remains permanently out of the loop," she said.

"Agreed, but that's not what I'm worried about. Tomorrow we're doing what we always do over here – finish the tour with a sigh of relief, then fly home to safety, normality, and family…"

"Ah," said Abigail. "Normality and family – so *now* you can't do that?"

"True, but I couldn't have done that anyway. At Christmas I usually walk across Scotland."

She shivered. "Rather you than me."

"The problem is what I've been worried about all along – getting you involved in this mess that *I'm* in."

"Peter, we're 'involved', as you put it, all the time. And you really don't need to think about this as you leave us behind. Life goes on here despite everything, with all manner of accommodations."

"I suppose it's military siege mentality," reflected Straker. "Soldiers only feeling safe inside security bases.

"When I joined the Army," he continued, "I blanked out a lot of things, particularly Ardglenna, so as to avoid problems like the ones I've inflicted on you now."

Abigail put her hand on Straker's shoulder, patting him gently.

"We understand. And you really mustn't worry. Nothing's changed. You've always been part of all this, even though you hadn't understood quite the extent of it.

"You know several of the Army men in the village – they're still as they were with you back then. Rory's remained in touch with the County Tyrone PIRA commander. They've known each other all their lives. They'll tell us if there's any problems.

"You'll fly out when the medics say it's OK – after Christmas. Everything will calm down, including Máire Carragher's husband, and we'll be over to London in the New Year."

She smiled.

"Situation normal."

They again sat, quietly thinking – companionable and relaxed now, in the crackling warmth of the stove.

"But we've got ourselves very behind," said Abigail suddenly. "Do you know what day it is?"

"Not a clue," said Straker.

"It's Thursday the 18th of December. Ian cut our Christmas tree this afternoon. How about we decorate it?"

Straker laughed. This was indeed normality, exactly as they'd done every Christmas before his joining the Army and renouncing that normality for the warrior ethos.

But as he'd now realised, the real world was anything but binary; ambivalence did not have to be a contradiction.

EPILOGUE

This was easily the best away-from-home, on-operations Christmas any of them had experienced.

Jacko was already reconciled to it, managing to persuade his wife and daughter that he wasn't in any danger and would definitely be home for a hybrid Christmas combined with New Year – as they'd already done several times before.

The Farmer liked it out here in the countryside, and had been happy to leave Straker in Abigail's hands while he shared patrolling duties with Jacko and Hooves in the woods.

Nobody was going anywhere, so Hooves was reconciled to a quiet time in the sure and certain knowledge of a New Year's Eve in the flesh pots of Knightsbridge with his Household Cavalry mates.

Straker tried to feel reassured. It seemed that once again normal life had been restored to Ardglenna which, after Abigail's revelations, he'd thought would now feel even more important to him than before. He was surprised to find this wasn't the case, which made him realise that Ardglenna was just a place, whereas the people he associated with it were what was important to him.

Ardglenna the place did, of course, have an implacable narrative, which was driven by the momentum of history rather than the emotions of the day. This was due to its people – now and previously over the centuries – who cleaved to their shared past as a community. Down the generations, they'd suffered injustice and violence but had weathered it together. They endured. There was stability here, in stark contrast to the desperation of the urban communities.

He hoped this wasn't just what he wanted to believe. And it didn't exactly make him feel better, particularly because it was his leaving that would restore Ardglenna's carefully nuanced "normality" and put the rest of the madness into perspective.

There were massive difficulties over here. Straker knew he'd played a part in their continuance. And it looked like the "if you're not with us, you're against us" mantra had finally tied him down.

He was now unavoidably a part of it; although there'd been no great change, just a new level of clarity, especially regarding knowing where he could make a difference.

That was the lesson. Nobody could save the whole world.

But if you thought about it very carefully, you could make your tiny part of it just a little better than it had been. Everything else would find its own way.

AUTHOR'S NOTE

The year this novel was published – 2023 – is the 25th anniversary of the Good Friday Agreement, signed on 10 April 1998 to end the Northern Ireland Troubles, which themselves lasted for thirty years.

Today in Northern Ireland, the Troubles are a backdrop to life; the mainly positive reminder of what sectarian prejudice does to everyone it infects. But there's also a much darker legacy of still-present paramilitaries looking for opportunities.

My own seventeen years in the British Army began in 1972, the worst year of violence in Northern Ireland, when 479 people were killed and 4,876 injured; the annual median over the thirty years was around 117 deaths. When I left in 1989, the Troubles were still going strong: that year there were 75 deaths: 39 police and Army, 6 paramilitary, and 30 civilians. In most years, more civilians were killed than anyone else, so 1989 was a good year for PIRA.

But 1989 did provide a beginning to the eventual end of the violence; dominant Republican politician Gerry Adams called for the formation of a non-armed Republican political movement, and Secretary of State Peter Brooke said that the IRA could not be defeated militarily, so there should be talks to end the violence. The Troubles continued for another nine years, with 516 further deaths.

The complexity of the Troubles made them so hard to resolve. Having been part of it myself, while commanding an infantry company in Armagh, I tried afterwards to understand. Vehemently held beliefs motivated the various factions. They were intractable and fiercely opposed, including between the different agencies of the security forces: the police, RUC and Special Branch, the British Army, and MI5.

I was then, as I am now, particularly interested in the Irish Republican Army and their highly capable northern offshoot, the Provisional IRA, and in the Republican communities upon which PIRA depended. PIRA had declared war against the British Army, but they mostly fought in their own neighbourhoods. As with the Loyalist paramilitaries, their actions deeply affected the lives of ordinary people, especially in their own community, which is reflected in the statistics of civilian deaths.

And now, even though the violence has pretty much stopped, the trauma lives on down through the generations. Recovery requires forgiveness, which is easier to recommend to others than to find in yourself, and compromise by people who've suffered injustice.

With the battlefield of a civil war being the domestic world of ordinary people, tragedy makes the hatred more extreme by being so personal. A peace settlement can't suddenly take all that away.

Huge amounts of government money have removed the slums of West Belfast and brought in jobs. But some people still resent the compromises their leaders had to make to achieve the Good Friday Agreement. And so that historic agreement was only the start of a process that has now been running as long as the Troubles themselves, and they remain an important part of Northern Ireland heritage. And although most people would never tolerate a return to violence, a small and violent hardcore of dissidence remains.

Ireland's eleven-month Civil War of 1922 had the same basic causes as the Troubles, which will probably come to be seen in time as Ireland's *second* civil war. Although the Troubles were fought primarily in the North, all of Ireland was affected.

Soon enough the people who lived through the Troubles will no longer be here to remind us of the causes. So there's the all-too-common danger of forgetting how fragile stability actually is, of repeating the mistakes and once again declining into turmoil.

And those same causes remain, albeit hedged by an Eire made more cautious by economics as well as security. As was the case for West Germany at German reunification, the cost to Eire of the North's six counties becoming part of the southern twenty-six would be considerable. So it's doubtful (I would hope) that Eire would seek to do more than pay lip service to the idea of uniting Ireland.

But the 2021 UK census showed that Catholics are no longer a minority in the North. Previously there'd been roughly one-third Catholic to two-thirds Protestant. In 2021, the figures were 45.7% Catholic and 43.5% Protestant, following on from the previous 2011 census numbers: 45% Catholic and 48% Protestant. Catholics are a younger demography of larger families, likely to increase still further.

The Republican political party Sinn Féin has increased its influence correspondingly, now the largest in the devolved Northern Ireland Assembly, and is calling for a referendum. In September 2022 Reuters stated: "A vote on Irish unification is at the discretion of the British government, and opinion polls have consistently shown a clear majority favour remaining part of the United Kingdom."

This could easily change, however. The 2016 Brexit referendum was opposed by 56% of voters in Northern Ireland, which included some Protestants. And the 2021 census confirmed a lessening of the number of people identifying themselves by religion. So it's logical to think that some of the Protestant Brexit opposers might prefer EU membership to remaining in the UK, further increasing the numbers that might support Irish unification.

So the future could see a significant swing among the people of Northern Ireland towards unification. But like the overall UK Brexit vote, that majority would be marginal, but far more significantly, it would take no account of the vehemence of the very large number of Protestant Loyalists. They've always been deeply suspicious of Republicans, and of the Eire and British governments. Forcing Northern Ireland Protestants into citizenship of a Catholic country would meet with their implacable opposition.

The path of lesser evil looks to me like a compromise that the majority might not see as a compromise at all; that Northern Ireland remains a part of the United Kingdom irrespective of the numbers. Some would see that as caving in to the men of violence – this time round, to the Protestant Loyalists. But others might prefer to live with that than to have history repeat itself. And so the British government seems to me unlikely to agree to a referendum any time soon.

This is the slipperiest of slopes. As in 1969, Britain could not countenance the violence and chaos, and would again deploy the British Army.

But unlike with the Troubles, a third civil war in Northern Ireland is unlikely to be constrained by the north–south border. It would also be greatly complicated by Eire's membership of the EU, and the intervention of Brussels. There would also be meddling from the USA, whose self-regarding politicians kept the Troubles bubbling along by encouraging NORAID funding of PIRA.

A truly grim scenario, against which this novel aspires to remind.

Hugh McManners
17 March 2023
New Walk, Leicester

ACKNOWLEDGEMENTS

This five-book series is the product of several iterations, each separated by considerable periods of time when other books and projects intervened. *The Sunday Service* emerged from both the Covid "isolations", but then a sudden, life-threatening, ambulance, surgery, intensive care adventure which I was extremely lucky to survive; and gave me the "job of work" that I needed when I began to recover.

Despite having written non-fiction books for Big Five publishers, creating a work of fiction that's how I want it to be – as opposed to conforming to genre, has been extremely challenging.

Throughout all this, I was lucky enough to have a massively supportive, expert and professional consulting editor Jenny Parrot, whose structural assessments, guidance and encouragement over those difficult years were the guiding light I needed.

I'd also like to mention my wife Megan McManners in her capacity as series editor; she's edited countless drafts, plus managing publication and promotion via Nightstrike Publishing. Only rarely do close family members provide anything other than encouragement; when fearless criticism is what's needed. Although English is not Megan's first language, she's read more classic literature than I ever will; and through her relentless reading of my many drafts, showed me what I needed to do to make each of my characters come to life. Sometimes it was enough just for her to highlight one paragraph. Other times we talked at length, especially about my main character Captain Peter Straker, who despite my setting him up to be completely different to me, ended up being similar enough to be very difficult for me to write about.

Serving in Northern Ireland with the British Army didn't give me much first-hand knowledge of the Catholic community over there. When I discovered that my musician friend Paddy

McCullough's biography almost exactly matches that of my protagonist, the PIRA officer Sean Carragher (born just off the Falls Road, then brought up on the Ballymurphy Estate), I asked him to read my manuscript. Any errors that remain are mine; but as the aim of all my books is accurately to portray lives and times, I'm most grateful for Paddy's suggestions and encouragement.

Typesetter Laura Kincaid guided us expertly through the technical difficulties that face books that are longer than is usual for genre; with thanks also to Claire Rushbrook for proofreading the final manuscript.

Patrick Knowles provided us with a cracking cover, and Jessica Read corrected that which was in need of correction (especially the timelines) in her copy-edit of the manuscript.

I'd also like – as with all my previous books, to thank my literary agent since 1983 Barbara Levy, who's been encouraging me to write fiction for decades and commented on several of the early drafts from which this book evolved.

One hesitates to quote British Rail, but "We're getting there."

ABOUT THE AUTHOR

Hugh McManners was born in Oxford in 1952. He served in the British Army for 17 years, leaving as a major in 1989.

His first book *Falklands Commando* (pub 1984), describes his work leading a naval gunfire forward reconnaissance team behind enemy lines, also working with the Special Boat Squadron and the SAS.

He then wrote a definitive book *The Scars of War* (pub 1992) about the psychological effects of combat on modern professional soldiers, which became the basis of the largest ever veterans' group action against the MoD, in the High Court in 2002-3. After the MoD successfully avoiding responsibility, and a dearth of actual clinical evidence, Hugh then founded the "Scars of War Foundation" at the University of Oxford's Queen's College, with neuroscientist Prof Morten Kringelbach. Despite the MoD's refusal to allow neuroimaging of serving soldiers, the Foundation developed radical new brain modelling techniques that are now being used by Israeli psychologists to benefit members of the Israel Defence Force, to determine the neurological development of combat-related trauma and PTSD, by which to mitigate and treat.

Hugh wrote two "Forgotten Voices" history books describing the Falkland War and then the Gulf War, using eye-witness accounts. He's also written "Top Guns" about modern fighter pilots, an account of the British Commando Course that's officially recommended pre-course reading, and a whole series of outdoor activities books ranging from his own trip across China to attempt on an unclimbed Karakorum mountain The Crown, to the best-selling Dorling Kindersley survival, walking and outdoor activities guides.

Hugh's first experience of war was in Cyprus 1974 as a member of 41 Commando Group during the Turkish invasion. He also served in Northern Ireland.

Hugh was brought up in Tasmania and then Sydney where he attended Shore School. Then back to Oxford and Magdalen College School, and Leicester for his teenage years (and the beginnings of his music career with Coalville heavy rock band Medusa).

The Sunday Service is Hugh's first work of fiction.

Printed in Great Britain
by Amazon

67371040-d168-4e04-8c7d-622157107c87R01